A doorbell _____ ___. Birche blinked several times as ___ ___ _____ed to the feeble light. There was smoke in the air, and a sick-sweet odor—incense.

"Well, good morning!" A fat woman waddled out of the rear room. Tapping her mind, Birche could tell that the woman was as shrewd a businesswoman as she was, but driven by an overpowering greed. "What can I do for you two?"

"We're browsing," Julian said. He picked up a hex sign and looked at it. The wooden disc was about six inches across and painted with a dazzling, intricate pattern.

"That there's a genuine Amish hex sign," the woman said. "Handmade in Pennsylvania. It hypnotizes witches. The pattern freezes their brainwaves solid, so they can't think about nothing."

"That sounds good," Birche said. Her Mental Health Bureau bracelet had slid out from under her sleeve, but the woman was so intent on making a sale that she hadn't noticed the eye-catching orange plastic. Birche casually slid her left hand over it; this was no place to attract attention.

SIDESHOW

W. R. THOMPSON

SIDESHOW

A Baen Books Original

Baen Publishing Enterprises
260 Fifth Avenue
New York, N.Y. 10001

First printing, January 1988

ISBN: 0-671-65375-X

Cover art by Alan Gutierrez

Printed in the United States of America

Distributed by
SIMON & SCHUSTER
1230 Avenue of the Americas
New York, N.Y. 10020

Dear Dr. Grant—

I'm sorry I can't say good-bye, but between the Mental Health Bureau and the Redeemers I have to move fast—the MHB has a warrant out for me now, and a couple of Redeemers shot at me a little while ago. I'm all right, though. When my family calls please tell them I'm okay, and I'll call them as soon as I can.

We both knew I'd have to go into hiding like this sooner or later. It was obvious last month, when that crackpot beat me up—and the cops refused to investigate it. It just isn't safe for a telepathic to live in the open these days.

I know what you're thinking: they won. They ran me out of town, and I won't be able to fight them at UC Berkeley any more. Let *them* think that; maybe they'll stop harassing the other espers on campus, at least for a while. Meanwhile, remember that when I get run out of one town, I get run *into* another. I'm going to continue to make a nuisance of myself to the Redeemers and to anyone like them, wherever I am. I'm good at that, which is why they wanted to get rid of me—it's amazing how much trouble I can cause by asking the right questions at the right time (kind of like one of your final exams, Herr Astronomy Professor).

Don't worry about me. There are groups of telepaths all over this country, and even more people who sympathize with us, so I'm not all alone. Money is no problem—I know how to find odd jobs, and law or no law, quite a few people are happy to hire a telepath. If things get too hot for me in one town, I'll move on to another. I always have liked travelling and meeting new people.

I'll be all right. There are plenty of bad people in this world, but they're heavily outnumbered by the good folks, and I'm sure they'll win out in the end. Maybe that's why this witch-hunting business doesn't upset me as much as it does you.

Take care.

—letter, Julian Forrest to Lyman A. Grant, Ph.D., 19 March 1998

1

CHAPTER 1

SUNDAY, 11 JUNE 2000,
to MONDAY, 12 JUNE 2000

First things first: I am not a telepath, but I am telepathic. A telepath is someone who does nothing but tap other people's thoughts. A telepathic person is some-one who can read minds, among many other things. That distinction may seem subtle, but it means a lot to me.

Let's put it this way: there you sit, reading this book and learning what I think. Does that mean you are only a reader? That you don't have any existence beyond reading books? Of course not. Like me, you also have friends, a family, a job. You have your own ideas and beliefs. You do things that fascinate you and avoid things that displease you. You've got strengths and weaknesses. You have things in common with other people, and you have your own unique quirks.

And, sometimes, you make mistakes.
    —from the introduction to Sense and Non-sense, *by Lyn Amanda Clancy (Universal Press, 1993)*

His ears still rang from the sound of gunfire: six quick shots, fired down the length of the alley, the sound waves trapped and focused by the high brick walls. The gunman had felt a surge of joy as he took aim at a living, running target, and that had given Julian the warning he needed. He had dropped to the pavement and rolled to one side, a quick motion that ruined his attacker's aim.

2

The gunman stopped to reload, and Julian grabbed the chance to escape. He scrambled down the alley, stumbling in the late evening shadows. He turned the corner at the end of the alley and found himself on a crowded sidewalk. A few people gave him apprehensive looks—he was wide-eyed and breathing hard—but the others ignored his presence. He looked like one more drifter, a sight most people had learned to overlook. Julian hurried down the sidewalk, hoping to lose himself in the crowd.

It worked. After a long moment he sensed wariness . . . the twin emotions of fear and hate . . . a wordless animal frustration as the gunman tried to spot him. With fear sharpening his senses, Julian found it easy to separate the man's thoughts from the telepathic babble around him. The gunman had lost him.

The killer wouldn't give up, Julian knew. He would keep hunting, and in a little while he would call for help. By that time Julian planned to be on his way out of Oakland . . . although he would have to leave a trail for the hunters to follow. Julian intended to lose them, but if he simply vanished, they would assume he had remained in Oakland. That would endanger every telepath in the city.

Julian glanced around and found a street sign. He hadn't been in Oakland long, but if he remembered things correctly he was near the bus terminal. That determined his next move—unless the gunman could outguess him.

The bus terminal wasn't especially busy, which suited his needs. Julian tapped the thoughts of the ticket agents and gauged their personalities. Average, decent people, bored with their jobs and daydreaming a bit— there, that one. The gnomish man was a cheerful, easygoing gossip; no hiding *that* from an experienced mind reader. Julian looked over the schedule on the wall, then approached the man. "Has the Chicago bus left yet?" Julian asked.

"Let me check." The man consulted his computer

terminal. "Yep, just pulled out. Next one leaves in four hours."

Julian had known that. He fished money out of a coat pocket and pushed it at the man. "Well, give me a one-way ticket to, uh, Los Angeles."

"Not too fussy about where you're going, hm?" He typed an order into the terminal. "Los Angeles isn't Chicago, you know."

"So I hear." Julian took the ticket. "Thanks, Lloyd. Keep the change." Julian hurried toward a stairwell marked *Departures*, while the agent's surprise echoed through his mind.

In a little while, Julian knew, the gunman and his cohorts would search the bus depot for him. They'd quiz the ticket vendors, of course: *Did you see a guy in here, white, maybe twenty-five, five-foot-four, with brown hair? Acted kinda spacey?* When they got around to Lloyd they'd hear, *Yeah, a guy like that bought a ticket to L.A. a while ago. Funny, he knew my name. You suppose he was psychic?* Just let it happen after the bus leaves, Julian hoped.

Julian boarded the Los Angeles bus, gave the driver his ticket, and took a seat. As he sat down his mind strained for any touch of the gunman's thoughts. There were a dozen people around him, potential witnesses, but there was no safety in that. His pursuer didn't care about witnesses . . . and he might not go to trial for killing a witch.

The bus lurched forward and rolled out of the depot. As it headed up a freeway on-ramp Julian told himself he could relax. He saw a day-old newspaper lying on the seat across the aisle, but when he reached for it, his hand shook so badly he couldn't get a grip on it.

One of these days I'm going to get killed, Julian thought suddenly, as he watched his hand tremble. All the skill and luck in the world couldn't change that.

The endless corridor had a floor of ankle-deep tar, and the doors lining the hall were locked shut. A blank wall loomed ahead of him, as bleak as a tombstone and

as menacing as the formless things snapping behind
him—

The nightmare dragged on after Julian woke up. He
looked around the bus, trying to locate its source. Most
of the other passengers were awake, their faces lit by
the early morning sunlight, their minds filled with the
concrete problems of life. The man behind Julian was
still asleep, however, his face twitching with fear. The
hall floor was dragging him under—

Julian reached back and shook his shoulder. "Hey,
are you okay?"

The man's eyes snapped open, and the nightmare's
oppression lifted from Julian's mind. "Yeah . . . yeah."
Confusion replaced the nightmare. "Wha—why'd you
wake me up?"

"Well, uh, you looked like you were having a nightmare." The evasion made Julian uncomfortable. He
wished that he could come out into the open; the
constant need to lie and hide galled him.

The man shifted around in his seat and stared blankly
through the bus window. "Well, I'm fine," he muttered. Except, his thoughts ran on, he had no money,
no job, and no idea of what he'd do in Los Angeles. He
was an unemployed corporate administrator, and he
had a suicidal conviction that the world no longer wanted
him.

"I don't know about Los Angeles," Julian said suddenly. He'd tried to kill himself once. He might be
endangering himself here, but he couldn't walk away
from someone with the same problem. Besides, he told
himself, he could handle this without revealing what he
was. "They're organizing that big clean-up project, but
there must be a million folks trying to get jobs on it." He
waited for the man to respond.

"I know. I'm one of them." The reply took an effort.
"Those jobs are all taken by now, I suppose."

Julian grunted, and hoped he was taking the right
approach. "Yeah, and it'll take those bastards forever to
get things rolling. You know how those piss-ant paper
shufflers are, gumming up people with their red tape—"

The man had just enough energy left to take offense. "You think it's easy to run something as big as that project?"

"Hell, yes," Julian said. "It's only demolition work. All they need is someone to hand out the paychecks."

Contempt stirred in the older man's voice. "Well, that shows how ignorant you are."

"Knocking down buildings is easy—"

"Only when someone arranges everything first." The man sat up in his seat, a chill on his face and in his thoughts. "This show covers a big area, and it's going to employ a hundred thousand people. Without someone to coordinate them, they're just a mob."

"Well, it *looks* easy enough—"

"You don't know how much work it takes to make things look easy." The man frowned as he thought of the jobs he had organized over the years. Some of them made the Los Angeles Renovation project look simple. The operation must have a crying need for men with his skills.

Julian settled back in his seat, suppressing a grin. It had always fascinated him, the way a few well-chosen words could lead a man to reassert his sense of worth and dignity. The stranger had already put Julian from his mind as he considered the best way to get a job on the project.

The newspaper was still there. Julian picked it up and started reading. Penny Katella, child star of *The Beaver's Grandkids,* had been commended by President Delanty for "inspiring the youth of America." The Secretary of State was shuttling between Paraguay and Bolivia in an effort to stop the border war between the two nations. California entrepreneurs expected record crowds at the beaches this year.

A small item caught Julian's eye: NASA ANNOUNCES PLANS FOR LUNAR COLONY. Julian read eagerly for a few lines, then lowered the paper.

I should have been in on that, he thought. Two years ago he had been a postgraduate student in astronomy, just months away from earning his doctoral degree.

Back then his telepathic sense hadn't presented more than a few annoying problems. Now he was a fugitive, judged legally insane, with the Mental Health Bureau waiting to put him in an institution.

Maybe I really am crazy, Julian thought, not for the first time. Sometimes that seemed the only way to explain everything. He wished that were true . . . or that someone would wake him up and tell him it was all a bad dream.

"Hey, buddy." The man behind him tapped his shoulder. "If you aren't going to read that paper, how about letting me have it?"

The Los Angeles earthquake had been the most powerful in California's history, and evidence of its impact lay everywhere. Even around the city's prestigious Civic Center heaps of brick and shattered concrete squatted on empty lots. Temporary power and water lines, laid down almost a decade ago, still ran everywhere. Until recently, the city hadn't had enough money to clean out the wreckage, much less rebuild.

As Julian got off the bus he noticed that some things had changed. The newspaper stands in front of the bus terminal were fully computerized. Stat sheets and flashprinters, connected to central computers, allowed each newsstand to dispense up-to-the-minute editions. Monochrome screens displayed the headlines: **President Delanty To Visit Moscow This September, Arms Pact Hinted. Dollar, Dow Jones Drop As New Unemployment and Inflation Figures Are Released. American Teams Leave for Summer Olympics.** Julian found himself transfixed by one: **Iron Guard Takes Credit for Attack on Notorious Mind Reader, Vows to Make State Safe.**

The Iron Guard? Julian wondered, as the morning crowd surged around him. Since when did a political outfit get involved in witch hunting?

"Julian? Julian Forrest?"

Startled, Julian spun around and saw a young, pretty girl looking at him. She smiled nervously as she addressed him. *"The thea said I'd find you here. Stay with us?"*

"Thank you. I'd like that." He realized this was a stroke of luck for him. There were perhaps ten thousand telepaths in the whole United States; simple arithmetic said there were only five hundred of them in the Los Angeles area. He'd expected to spend hours or days finding one. *"What's your name?"*

"Anita de Villanueva. Our place is an hour's walk from here—less, if we hurry." She was already walking down the sidewalk, taking small, rapid steps.

Julian shared her edginess. They were the only telepaths in this area—and many of the people around them roiled with an ugly anger. *"Has there been much trouble?"* Julian asked.

"Not for us," Anita answered, *"but there's a big Sere rally in Macarthur Park today."*

"Oh." Julian cursed his talent for walking into the middle of trouble. Sere was a radical environmentalist group, one that claimed the Depression was the result of too much industrial growth and scientific progress. Their solution to the Depression was to smash factories and machines—and anyone who disagreed with them. *"Think there'll be any trouble?"*

"What else does one expect?" Anita's black eyes darted around, taking in the people surrounding her. They were the grim, angry unemployed, and they walked with an elusive sense of *purpose*, as if they looked forward to a confrontation with—what?

Moved by curiosity, Julian tapped the mind of one of the men, letting the hard, strong thoughts roll through him. At once he saw how years of unemployment had made this man bitter. His frustration was fueled by the sense that *something* had created his problems, had taken his job and put him on welfare, and he was by God going to smash and pound and kill until he had what was *his* again—

"Estupido! Stop that!" Anita's telepathic outburst shocked him back to reality. He felt something tugging at his arm. Looking down, he saw a slim olive hand

encircling his wrist. It dawned on Julian that he had stopped walking and had let his face go slack as he tapped the stranger's mind. If the people around him hadn't been so engrossed in their own problems, they would have noticed his almost stereotypically psychic behavior.

"*I'm getting careless,*" Julian thought, in apologetic self-analysis. "*Using other people's problems to forget my own. Damn. Thanks for pulling me out of it, Anita.*"

"*De nada. Let's get out of here.*"

Anita led Julian to one of the abandoned neighborhoods that dotted the Los Angeles basin. The ground here had heaved and liquefied during the earthquake, destroying many houses and leaving the rest to stand at random angles. With no way to make repairs, the homeowners had collected their disaster-relief payments and left. Squatters had moved in later, claiming the lessdamaged houses and furnishing them with salvaged odds and ends.

Anita belonged to one such group of squatters: a half-dozen telepaths who occupied a two-bedroom house. Seven telepaths, Julian thought, if you counted their thea—although that was a debatable point. A thea was a form of group mind, a projection of the personalities and emotions of the people who created it.

On the surface, the welcoming process was quick and casual. As Julian stepped through the door he felt other minds press on him, asserting their identities in the telepathic equivalent of handshakes. At the same time they tapped Julian cautiously, probing his sanity. Among psis certain types of madness were as contagious as pneumonic plague, and even more feared. Insanity was a living death, the ultimate destruction of the *self* . . . but these people had just assured themselves that Julian was sane, a thought he found comforting.

The thea guided Julian to a chair. As with all illusions, Julian found that the thea's features changed when he tried to concentrate on them. It looked like a teenage girl, a shy and nervous redhead. "*Welcome to our coven,"* she said formally, clasping her hands in front of her.

"Thanks. Pleased to be here . . . coven?" The word raised an odd mixture of amusement and disapproval. Julian was a thorough rationalist, and he preferred to leave the superstitions to others.

"And the fun, too," Malcolm said patiently. *"It's a game, Julian. The redeemers and other nuts are going to call us witches anyway, so why shouldn't we turn it around?"*

"What, and give them what they want?" Julian stopped and smiled sheepishly. *"Sorry, I'm twitchy today."*

"Getting shot at will do that to you," Malcolm agreed.

"You heard about it?" Julian asked.

"It was on the radio." Betty gestured at a battered portable radio, and laughed nervously. *"They claimed you were dead. I take it that didn't happen?"*

Julian sighed. *"I'm not too sure what* did *happen. I was walking down the street when this fellow recognized me. The next thing I knew, we were playing freaks 'n' sneaks."*

The thea laughed at him. *"Which is worse, Julian, calling yourself a freak or a witch?"*

"Touché," Julian conceded. He frowned, and strained at a memory of something half-sensed. *"He saw a picture of me somewhere . . ."*

"A wanted poster," the thea said, probing his memory. *"He saw a handbill with your picture on it—offering a reward."*

That got the attention of everyone in the house. *"Was it the Redemptive Faith?"* Hazel asked.

"Assassination isn't their style," George said. He was in another part of the house, sewing a patch over a hole in his shirt. The cracked plaster walls were no barrier to mental contact. *"Usually they just beat the daylights out of people. Anyway, can you imagine them giving away any of their money?"*

"The Iron Guard claims they did it," Julian said.

"That's just hot air," Jesse said. *"Why would the IG take an interest in witches? We're nothing."*

"You don't kill 'nothings,'" Julian said sharply, responding to Jesse's forlorn tone—an emotion that echoed in the other minds, and showed in the diffidence of their thea. Life was wearing down their resistance. They needed something to strengthen them, he knew, something to show that they were more than harmless, helpless lunatics.

Jesse came out of the kitchen and gave Julian a sandwich and a glass of water. Surprised by his hunger, Julian wolfed it down. As he ate, he took a good look at his surroundings. Holes gaped in the plaster walls, exposing studs and cross braces. The electrical fixtures had vanished, and stains on the floor showed where carpet had been ripped out. The windows were empty holes.

"Looters did that," Anita explained. *"After the quake, everybody needed wiring and pipes and things to make repairs, so scavengers stripped these places."*

"You wouldn't believe how much an unbroken picture window brought," Betty added.

Julian nodded and sipped the water. It had a rubbery taste, as if it had come out of a garden hose.

"The water main still works," Hazel told him. *"The city keeps turning it off, but there's always someone who can fix that."* She came out of the back bedroom, and Julian saw that she was wearing a bright orange ID bracelet.

"George and I are still on the Mental Health Bureau's rolls," she said. *"I'd like to jump parole . . . but we have to eat. Their payments are enough to keep all of us going."*

"You can jump it," Julian said. *"There're ways to live without the MHB on your back. Tomorrow we'll look for—"*

A loud *thwock-thwock-thwock* made Julian sit upright. He tried to identify the noise and failed.

"Police helicopters," George said. *"That demonstration must have started."*

"It has," the thea said. Her face mirrored the fear

felt by the entire coven. *"It's spreading. The police have started using gas."*

"Already?" Julian heard sirens then, and a low rumble of shouting. *"Is anyone coming this way?"*

"Not yet," the thea told him.

"But they will," George said. *"After last year's demonstration a lot of rioters hid out in this neighborhood. Then the cops cleared everyone out."*

"But you came back," Julian said.

"Where else can we go?" Betty asked. *"God damn the MHB,"* she added without passion.

Julian felt a reflexive anger. *"You can't spend your life letting their legalistic bushwa—"*

There was a sudden roar as a helicopter passed low over the neighborhood, its prop wash kicking up a dust plume as it shot toward the riot. For a brief moment Julian could tap the pilot's hunger for battle, and his resentment that his only weapons were anti-riot devices, mere toys—

"It's all right," Julian said, getting to his feet. Without thought he and the others had dropped to the floor or crouched by walls in a primal effort to stay hidden. *"They aren't looking for us. No one knows we're here."*

"That won't last," the thea said. *"Some of the rioters are running this way. They plan to hide around here—"*

"How long until they get here?" Julian asked.

"Not long. They're running hard. They— You can't do that!"

"Why not?" Julian walked out the door and looked up at the sky. Several helicopters circled over an area a mile or so to the west, dispensing gas canisters. Julian could sense the panic of the rioters and the fear of other squatters in the ruined houses around him. None of them were telepaths, but they were as scared as the coven members.

The thea appeared at his side. *"Julian, get back inside!"*

"Not yet." Julian looked around. He couldn't see anyone yet, but he could feel the minds of the rioters now. Some of them were in the industrial park west of

the houses. A helicopter swooped over that area, dropped some canisters, spun back toward the heart of the riot.

A trio of rioters came out of the factory area. Two of them dragged a man between them—a sight Julian had half-expected. Riots always meant injuries. Julian watched the three approach a house, turn away when a squatter fired a shot over their heads.

"Here! Over here!" Julian shouted. He glanced at the helicopters. "Come on, move it!"

The thea was quaking with terror. *"You're crazy! If the cops find them with us—"*

"They won't. Calm down, will you?"

"What in hell are you planning?"

"I'm not sure," Julian admitted, *"but I know that one of those guys is going to die unless he gets help. I've seen too many people die already."* Julian watched the refugees come to him. The third man was all but unconscious, the result of gas and an electric dart. The other two wore nose filters and goggles. "In here," Julian said, and led them into the house.

"We'll need some water and blankets," Julian said, as they laid the injured man on a sagging couch. After a second's hesitation the other telepaths moved into action. Julian sniffed, and caught the orange-blossom tang of gas on the man's clothes—a clinging scent that would betray him to the police. *"What can we do about that stink?"* he asked.

"We can try washing it out," George said, as he brought a pan of water out of the kitchen. *"But we'd better worry about his eyes and lungs first. Should we give him aspirin? We have some."*

"He won't be able to keep it down," Anita said. She took the water and trickled it over his face, while Julian peeled back his eyelids. *"His eyes look all right, but he'll have trouble breathing for a few days. We'll have to keep him warm and quiet."*

"But he's okay." Julian looked at the other two refugees. *"How about you two . . ."* Silent laughter floated around him, and he remembered that the newcomers

weren't psychic. "Your friend will be all right," Julian said aloud. "You two weren't hurt, were you?"

"No, the pigs didn't touch us," one said. Now that he was out of danger, he displayed a relaxed arrogance. He looked around the decaying room as if to make the house his own. Julian noted how he dismissed his hosts even as he saw them—and the contempt he felt for these weaklings who played at being good samaritans.

The second man showed a different reaction. He hadn't missed the smooth functioning of these people as they took care of the hurt man. Their odd silence grew more and more unsettling. "Granger, these aren't people—they're *witches.*"

"Telepaths!" Julian snapped, offended.

"Stinking *things,*" Granger said angrily, giving Julian a look of hate. His hand crept toward the pistol in his belt. Julian glared back at him, clenching his fists at his side—and Granger's nerve failed in the face of the unknown. "Norton, we're getting out of here."

The other man gaped at him. "We can't leave Whitney with these things!"

"He's done for. The pigs are coming. Move it!" Granger spat on the floor and stomped out of the house. Norton ran after him.

Malcolm looked amazed. *"You scared them off."*

"People like that are always afraid," Julian said. He shook his head at his own naïveté. He'd endangered everyone because he'd assumed that these people from Sere would accept an unspoken truce in exchange for help. I keep forgetting that other people don't always think the way I do, he thought.

"You did the right thing," Anita said, looking at the injured man. *"Come on, let's get this guy patched up."*

CHAPTER 2

For political reporters, rumors and scandals make up our stock-in-trade. Give us a juicy tip on a little corruption and we're in business, producing column after column of rhetoric. It's fun, it's easy, it pays well. That's what makes this particular column so damned annoying to write.

You know about the Owens Valley Aqueduct contracts, don't you? The word is that Governor Quentin took a hefty bribe to give the contract to the Suomi Corporation. Rumor has it that the only bidding was on the size of the bribe. Well, word and rumor have it wrong, dead wrong. The rumors come from the offices of the Hydro-Push Company. I have memos and taped admissions, among other things. The governor is innocent, innocent, innocent.

What's my source? That doesn't matter.

—from Steve Magyar's column, "Pork-barrel People,"
Los Angeles Post, 6 June 2000.

Most of the people who knew her thought of Birche Holstein as a business *wunderkind*. She had taken over Boulevard Books less than a year ago, shortly after her twenty-third birthday, and turned it into one of the most successful bookstores on the West Coast. She had five excellent people on her payroll, plans to open a second store in October, and a secret: she was psychic.

Birche had discovered that when she was eight years old. At times she would hear voices, have odd dreams, or *know* things with an ice-cold certainty. She had heard the voices rarely at first, but now they whispered inside her head much of the time. It took an enormous effort to block them out. She battled to remain normal . . . a battle she knew she would lose some day.

Ordinarily the bookstore kept Birche's mind off the threat of psychic powers, but the parcel post had just spoiled that by delivering a shipment of books from New Day Publishers. New Day specialized in the occult and mystic, and its latest books had such titles as *Protect Your Mind from Espers* and *Confessions of a Witch.* It was exploitative trash and Birche hated having it in her store—but it sold and sold and sold, and that helped keep her business out of the red. With the economy in shambles—inflation and unemployment were both on the wrong side of twenty percent—that was nothing to sneer at.

Just the same, she thought, she liked the old days better. A decade ago, only crackpots and tabloid papers had taken ESP seriously. No one had taken it for granted, and certainly no one had accused telepaths of undermining the country.

Birche put the last of the New Day books on the shelves and stood up. As she straightened she saw her short, chunky figure reflected in the store window. Her father had been a professional football player, and she had inherited his wide frame and muscles. At least I haven't turned to fat like he did, she thought. Birche had been an athlete in high school and college, and she still kept herself in condition.

She walked over to the counter and picked up the phone. "Hello, Steve."

Steve Magyar answered after a shocked pause. "Kid, you ought to let it ring before you answer."

"Damn," Birche muttered, and looked around the store. None of the browsers had noticed anything odd. The two clerks had guessed her secret, but neither of them would tell anyone. They would lose their jobs if anything happened to their employer, and this was not a time to be thrown out of work. "I'm sorry."

"Don't worry," Steve said airily. "Are you busy tonight?"

"I don't have anything planned."

"How would you like to go out to dinner? Your choice, my treat."

"Hm." Birche knew Steve wanted something. She could feel her psi sense quivering to learn details. She forced it down. "Anywhere?"

"Just name the place, kid."

"I don't know," Birche said, stalling. Steve's generosity always had a price, although he wouldn't mention what he wanted until after dinner. His technique was to pay the bribe first, and spring the trap after it was accepted.

"I don't feel like going out tonight," Birche said, realizing that he wanted a *lot* this time. She kept her voice light as she tried to negotiate an advantage. "Why don't you come over to my place for potluck?"

"The idea was to give you a treat. Suppose you come over to my place?"

"Okay," Birche said reluctantly. "Is seven o'clock all right?"

"It's precisely what I was thinking. See you then." Steve hung up.

I wish I had the nerve to break it off, Birche thought, although she knew it would never come to that. She didn't know if she still loved Steve, or if he had ever loved her—but they hadn't come together through love.

Six months ago a member of the Redemptive Faith had learned Birche's secret. Outraged at finding yet another witch on the loose, and unable to take any real action, the Redeemer had reported Birche to the Mental Health Bureau. The MHB had sent a pair of polite men to investigate her, although that was merely a formality required by the Compton Act. There had never been any question that she was psychic.

The agents would have taken her into custody for further testing and certification, but they hadn't come alone. Steve Magyar, a political columnist for the Los Angeles *Post*, had been investigating reports of abuses within the MHB. He had watched in silence while the short, husky brunette had answered a variety of questions, including some the men hadn't asked out loud.

That had suggested possibilities to the reporter. Steve had taken the MHB agents aside and spoken with them. All of them, he had said, knew that their bureau suffered from a lot of unfair and distorted reporting. As a professional journalist he hated such sensationalism, and he would enjoy fighting it with a story about the MHB's efforts to protect an innocent citizen and her rights. Certainly the MHB would appreciate such a story—along with the men who had made it possible. The agents had taken the hint, cleared Birche, and left.

Steve's move had defined their relationship, Birche thought, as she retreated to the safety of her office. Whatever she was to Steve, *he* was her shield against the MHB and the Compton Act. That made an effective leash.

She didn't know how much longer she would have her shield. Steve had hoped to use her ESP to collect secrets, but he had soon learned about the talent's disappointing limits. An esper could not see into the future, or look through walls, or control the mind of another person. Birche couldn't see mental images, or rummage through a politician's memory as though it were a file cabinet. Normally she had to be fairly close to her subject, and then she could only sense his emotions and immediate thoughts.

Steve had tried to work within those limitations. He had taken Birche to a number of dinners, parties, and other functions. There Steve would ask questions of various politicians and businessmen, and Birche would tap their thoughts as they accepted or dodged the questions. To Steve's dissatisfaction she had uncovered no major scandals, nothing that could catapult him into Pulitzer Prize territory.

Shaking her head, Birche sat down at her business computer. With a little luck she would manage to forget about her problems . . . at least until seven o'clock.

Steve's apartment was in a good section of town, although before the earthquake, the neighborhood had been on the skids. Most of the buildings had survived the quake in good condition—they were built on bedrock—and that had made them valuable. A sharp development company had purchased most of the area, spruced up the buildings, and rented them out at a tidy profit. After the quake, housing had been in short supply, and new construction had been slow and expensive. Tenants were happy to get what they could at any price.

Even so, Steve Magyar had a good home. The apartment was large and comfortable, and a good deal more luxurious than Birche's single unit. With the lights turned down, as they now were, Steve's apartment felt safe and cozy. Only Birche's vague awareness of the other people in the building, a cloudy telepathic sensation, spoiled her illusion of normality.

As she finished eating her dinner, Birche stared out the window. A city maintenance crew was at work, sandblasting graffiti from the side of a building. Some resident must have pulled strings to get that done, she mused. The city crews usually quit at five o'clock, and graffiti wasn't one of their high-priority items.

"A bunch of punk kids messed up that wall last month," Steve explained, when Birche commented on it. "But the city wouldn't do anything, and nobody wanted to pay a private company to do the work. So Jake Brill went out this morning, painted 'Anarchy Now' on the wall, and reported it to the cops." Steve laughed. "You just have to know which nerve to hit, kid."

"I wish I'd thought of that," Birche said. "My neighborhood is lousy with wall-art." She picked at her dessert, wishing she could enjoy it. If only Steve would tell her what he wanted! But he wouldn't do that yet, and she wouldn't ask. It would spoil the illusion of a warm, romantic evening.

A thought intruded on her: she could read his mind. Birche thrust that idea away.

"Brill took a stupid chance," Steve said. "The cops have shot people for that. They don't mind the mess, but radical politics makes them nervous." He paused,

then went on thoughtfully. "At least left-wing radical-
ism does. The cops don't show much interest in groups
like the neo-nazis or the Iron Guard."

"I'm not surprised." The MHB agents hadn't been
policemen, but Birche's encounter with them had shaken
her trust in the government. She had always thought of
herself as a respectable citizen, and it had shocked her
to learn how easily she could lose her rights. "The
radical right keeps prattling about 'law and order.' Who
could suspect such nice people of anything nasty?"

Steve grunted. "You'd still think the cops would keep
an eye on them." He pushed his plate aside, a signal
that dinner had ended. "Take the Iron Guard. They've
killed over two hundred people in the past five years,
but they've gotten away with it because they keep a low
profile."

Birche raised her eyebrows. "Steve, how can you call
lynchings and torchlight rallies 'low profile'?"

Steve waved a hand in dismissal. "They don't start
riots or blow up public buildings—well, they don't take
credit for it. And they're selective about who they kill
and how they do it. They're cunning, and that makes
them more dangerous than any pack of bomb-throwers."

"I suppose so," Birche said uneasily. She wondered if
he would ask her to spy on them. The thought made
her shiver. It was clear that whatever he wanted would
involve the IG.

"Right now they're up to something big," Steve went
on. "Their propaganda has changed lately. They've
stopped condemning Transpac—"

"Who?"

Steve gave her the smile of a knowledgeable insider.
"Transpac. It doesn't exist, not officially. It's a political
action committee of sorts. Its members are industrialists, financiers, politicians, publishers, brokers, bankers—"

"The people who run America."

Steve shook his head. "No one group runs America.
Transpac is an unofficial group that's trying to get the
economy on the move again—on terms that would help

its members, naturally. Well, until a few weeks ago, the IG painted Transpac as a den of thieves."

"And now they've stopped?" Birche asked. "Why? Are they forming an alliance?"

"I think so," Steve said. Birche sensed his irritation, and realized that he thought she had read that idea in his mind. "Anyway, the IG has stopped damning the Redeemers, too, and established some ties with the Redemptive Faith." Steve smiled wryly. "Some of the bastards have even gotten Perry Fountain to baptize them with olive oil. If you ask me, this all means the IG is trying to move into mainstream politics, kid."

I wish he'd use my name, Birche thought. She couldn't recall the last time Steve had called her by name. She shook off that thought. "Fountain could deliver a lot of votes. There are millions of Redeemers, aren't there?"

"Fountain says so, but the votes aren't the big thing. What counts is the RF's ability to raise money—enormous piles of tax-free, deductible, easy-to-launder *money*.

"But all that is easy to understand. It's the other things that make no sense. What do Transpac and the Redeemers stand to gain? And dealing with them goes against all of the Iron Guard's doctrines. For some reason, the rank-and-file members have accepted this without protest—and your typical IG trooper isn't the sort that takes anything quietly. A policy change this big ought to have shattered the Guard."

"Then there hasn't been a change," Birche said. She leaned forward and rested her elbows on the table. "Steve, the leaders *must* have told their followers that it's a ruse—that they're conning Transpac and Fountain."

Steve looked at his empty plate and scowled. "I wish you wouldn't do that."

"Do what? Read your mind?" Birche felt offended. "Steve, why is it that every time I have an idea, you think I got it from you?" She pushed her chair back and stood up. "Why don't you tell me what you want?"

"All right," he said. "The Guard has always claimed that a group of conspirators started the Depression, and has profited from it. They've stopped claiming that

Transpac is part of the conspiracy." He paused and smiled at her. "Guess which group just joined their list."

"Telepaths." She felt her throat tighten.

"Right." Steve got up from the table and led her into the living room. He turned up the lights, then picked up some papers from an end table and handed them to Birche as they sat on the sofa. "The Guard has distributed these to its members all over the country."

"Wanted posters?" Birche shuffled through the photostats. Each sheet carried a photograph and sketch of a different face, along with a description, a name, and a reward. "Twenty thousand dollars isn't a big bounty," she commented, feeling puzzled. Would anyone actually commit murder for the price of a beat-up used car?

"Organized crime charges twenty or thirty times as much for a killing," Steve agreed. "It's especially cheap when you consider the quarry—Maggie Reese, Lyn Clancy, Julian Forrest, and a few others whose posters I don't have."

Birche knew the names. "Reese was on the cover of *Time* once, wasn't she? With that team of parapsychologists."

"Yes, back in '91, when they discovered telepathy. The Redeemers have always held that against her—as if *she* created ESP. Clancy wrote *Sense and Non-sense*, so you can imagine how the religious nuts feel about her."

"I never read the book."

"What?" That surprised Steve. "I thought it was required reading for telepaths. It's practically a handbook on how to develop your powers."

Birche laughed, a nervous rumble. "That's why I never read it." She sensed Steve's impatience to get on with business. He wanted to interview one of the witches—yes. She picked up one of the posters. "Julian Forrest. What do you want with him?"

"Information. Do you know what happened in Oakland last night?"

"I caught the morning news—hey! Wasn't he killed?"

"No. He's in Los Angeles. He hopped a bus in Oakland. The driver saw him get off in downtown L.A. this morning."

"Maybe it was someone who looked like him." Forrest didn't have a memorable face, Birche thought, not by any stretch of the imagination. She could have mistaken him for a dozen other people. "Even if it *was* him, why would you want to meet him?"

"I'm playing a hunch. Why is the Iron Guard hunting witches?" Steve held up a hand before she could speak. "If they wanted to please the Redeemers, they could kill a few freaks at random. Instead, they're going out of their way to get certain people—and the IG has put some of its top killers on the job."

"Maybe they need the practice," Birche suggested.

"They already get enough of *that*, kid. The IG is making a big effort here. They *must* have a logical reason for it. Did these witches learn some IG secrets? Have they done something to damage the Guard? Or has the Guard's leadership gone crazy? I want to pump Forrest for information."

For a moment Birche wished that she could tap his thoughts clearly. "But you're not interested in Forrest himself?"

"No," Steve said. "What happened to him may be dramatic, in a way, but anti-witch violence isn't news any more. No one cares about it except other witches, and that doesn't sell papers. Anyway, I'm a *political* reporter. I'm hoping that he can tell something politically useful."

"So you want me to set up a meeting with him." Birche dropped the poster onto the coffee table. "How?"

"I don't know. Get in contact with him—" Impatience showed on his narrow, angular face. "Look, you're the witch, not me."

"Steve, telepathy isn't magic. I can't find one specific mind in this whole city."

"You do it with me all the time—like today, when you answered the phone."

"That's different. We were only a few miles apart,

and we're—attuned, I guess . . ." Birche shook her head in confusion. "I don't know."

"Look, you can try, can't you? Sit down and concentrate on his picture, or something—whatever it is you people do," he said vaguely. "Forrest is fully telepathic. Let *him* read *your* mind. Then you can swap thoughts with him."

"No. It's too dangerous."

"Don't get paranoid," he said in annoyance. "You know I've protected you so far."

So far, she thought in apprehension. The implied threat was more than clear. Birche stood up, started pacing back and forth in front of the couch. "Steve, you can't protect me from telepathy. Every time I use it it gets stronger, like a set of muscles. If it gets too strong—"

"—you won't be able to hide what you are."

"That's only part of the problem—but it's bad enough." Birche stopped pacing and looked at him. "Steve, once the MHB declares you insane, you don't have *any* rights. The government appoints itself as your guardian. It holds all your money and property in trust, and you have to live on welfare. If you behave yourself, they keep you on parole. If they feel like it, they can commit you to a mental institution—"

"I know," he said impatiently. "The Compton Act was never meant to cover telepaths. People are abusing some loopholes in it—but that can't go on forever."

"Why not?" Birche shook her head. "Steve, even if there wasn't a Compton Act I'd still feel afraid. You don't understand what telepathy can do to me." She looked around the apartment as if she could see the people beyond its walls. "There are all those other minds, pressing on me. Sometimes I can't tell which thoughts are mine and which aren't—and when somebody dies, it feels like it happens to *me*." She squeezed her eyes shut. "And people wonder why so many telepaths go insane."

Steve got up, stood in front of her, and put his hands on her shoulders. "This is a lot bigger than your problems. I have to do *something* to fight the Iron Guard.

They're big and powerful, they're getting more dangerous every day, and I don't have anything to fight them with."

"The posters—"

"I can't *prove* that the IG drew them up." Steve grimaced. "The man who gave them to me has vanished—permanently, it seems. My other contacts in the IG won't talk. Forrest may be my only opening."

"I can't do it. Steve, it's too big a risk—" She stopped speaking as his hands slid from her shoulders to cup her breasts, an opening move he hadn't made in months.

Birche turned away from him, upset by the cool calculation in his mind. Ambition was driving him now, and her reluctance was just another obstacle for him to overcome. He hadn't been this detached when they had first met, she remembered—

"I'll do it," she said suddenly, hoping that the promise would break the spell ambition had cast on him. "At least, I'll try."

"Fine," Steve said. He took a small step back from her. He seemed almost embarrassed, although he said nothing.

The silence stretched for an awkward moment. "Look," Birche said finally, "I ought to leave. I brought a lot of paperwork home—"

"So did I," Steve said. "If you need a ride, I can call a cab."

"My car's outside." Birche turned for the door quickly, hiding her disappointment.

It shouldn't be like this, Birche thought, as she walked out of the apartment building. Steve should have tried to keep her from leaving. Instead, she noticed, he had already put her from his mind. By the time she reached her car he was on the phone, trying to arrange a late date with another woman.

"Good news, sister!" The coarse, booming voice took her by surprise. Birche looked and saw a trio of men approaching her. Redeemers! she thought in alarm. Did they know about her? She fumbled with her keys, trying to unlock the car door. Then they were around her.

"Good news," the leader repeated. He carried a sheaf of handbills, and he pushed one at Birche. "Reverend Fountain is bringing the American Life Crusade to town. Be there and be saved."

"Oh." Birche looked at the paper. She couldn't read it in the dim twilight. All she could make out was the curving rood-symbol of the Redemptive Faith.

"The Reverend is doing the good work, sister," another one of them said—or had he thought that? Birche looked at his lips, which were obscured by a bushy beard and the waning light. They seemed to be moving; she wasn't reading his mind. "He's going to free America from evil and bring us all together in his flock. It's a great task and he needs money to finish it."

"I see." She found her wallet and pulled out a hundred dollar bill. "Here."

"Skinflint," the leader said—no, he had thought that; his lips hadn't moved. "I'm sure you have more appreciation for the Lord's work," he said out loud.

"That's all I have," Birche said. She looked from face to face, trying to decide if they were thinking or mumbling. If she slipped up, they might turn her in—or turn on her.

"It's a paltry amount to give," the leader said.

"Now, Royce," one of his companions said. "If the Lord wanted more from her, he'd move her to give it. We thank you, sister."

Birche watched in relief as they walked away. At least I was on guard this time, she thought. Lately she had become—not careless, but more prone to make mistakes, as if she had some inner urge to reveal what she was. *That* thought was as disturbing as the things that would happen when she was exposed.

CHAPTER 3

From: Attorney General Whipple
To: Director Randall, FBI
Date: 11 April 1995 1:54 P.M.
Subject: Political violence

*Tony, the President is working on plans to create a
'Counter-Terrorism Bureau,' which will mean taking
counter-terror activities out of the FBI's hands. I think
you can beat him to the punch by submitting a plan of
your own, now. This will allow you to keep some control
over the area, if Clark likes your ideas—so make 'em
good. One suggestion: offer Hutchins as a potential director of counter-terror activities. He's second rate, but
Clark likes him, and Hutchins would arrest himself, if
we gave him a warrant. We can control him.*

*I know, I promised you I'd change his mind. I couldn't.
The situation is impossible, and Clark thinks domestic
terrorism is getting out of hand. If decisive action isn't
taken soon, there's a distinct possibility that we'll lose
the election next year. The country can't afford that, so
we'd better look decisive fast.*

—coded memo, hand-delivered.

The clean air still surprised Montague Hutchins. Every time he came to Los Angeles, the CTO Director
braced himself for the dingy, eye-stinging smog . . . smog
that had almost vanished. Factories and refineries had
shut down in the wake of the Depression, and there
were fewer cars on the road now. There was still some
haze in the air, but it no longer obscured the mountains that ringed the Los Angeles basin.

I never thought I'd miss smog, Hutchins thought, as the helicopter rose from the airport. He knew people who talked about smog nostalgically, remembering it as a sign of better, more prosperous times.

The helicopter made a turn, giving Hutchins a look at the new Federal Building. Even from a distance it was an imposing sight, a massive brick edifice the size of the Pentagon. It had been built in the years immediately following the quake, and the architects swore that it could withstand any conceivable shaking. Its high, flat walls and thick support towers gave the building the appearance of a medieval fortress.

The helicopter settled onto one of the landing pads atop the building, amid well-manicured gardens and displays of *art-lumiere* sculpture. The decorations concealed both the armored concrete of the roof and a variety of security devices—including automated weapons that saw action every few weeks. As Hutchins stepped out of the helicopter, some of the equipment tracked him, identified him, and permitted him to enter the building.

The Director of the Counter-Terrorism Office took an elevator to the residence level, signed in, and got a suite. Hutchins went straight to his room and flopped down on the bed. The flight from Washington hadn't tired him, but he felt an urge to delay, to escape this assignment.

Yesterday's phone call from the attorney general had struck him as a bad joke: an order to capture several telepaths. "A witch hunt?" Hutchins had asked in disbelief. He couldn't tell if Schulze had been serious; the scrambler circuits had leached all emotion from his voice. "Mr. Schulze, this is June. Halloween is in October."

"And the election is in November," Schulze had said—angrily, Hutchins thought. "This is serious, Monty. Some radical groups are turning fugitive telepaths into a political football. You know the drill—if the Administration can't handle a few escaped loonies, how can it cope with the economy, et cetera. The President expects you

to take the ball from them and run with it. Score all the
points you can."

God save me from politicians who play football, Hutchins thought, as he stared at the suite's acoustic-tile
ceiling. He was certain that President Delanty had some
other reason for this sudden interest in psychic freaks,
but it eluded him.

The doorbell chimed insistently. Hutchins rose to his
feet, sluggishly, and answered the call. Louis Farrier,
the CTO's Western District Director, stood outside the
door with an armload of computer printouts.

"I hope you had a good flight," Farrier said, as he
pushed into the suite. He was a large, burly man, and
he cultivated the image of a no-nonsense cop. As part of
that image he carried a brainwave sensor in his vest
pocket. Hutchins knew that the miniature lie detectors
were unreliable, but they unsettled many people, and
Farrier wasn't above a little intimidation.

"The flight was tolerable," Hutchins said. "What have
you got for me, Bear?"

"Damned little." Farrier put the sheets on a table
and spread them out. "These are the MHB files on the
names you gave me. We should get more info later on.
By the way, I've confirmed that rumor. One of the
freaks on your list is in L.A."

"You mean Clancy?"

"No, Forrest. We questioned the driver of a Grey-
hound bus; he recognized Forrest as a passenger. Ditto
a ticket agent in Oakland. Forrest's behavior was odd
enough to stick in his mind."

"Uh-huh." It must be hard to miss a lunatic's antics,
Hutchins thought. "Have you asked the local authorities to help us?"

Farrier nodded, a ponderous movement. "So far, the
L.A. County Sheriff has ignored my request. I haven't
asked the LAPD Chief yet, but he'll be here in—" He
glanced at the ornate wall clock "—another half-hour.
I'll broach the subject then."

Hutchins raised an eyebrow. "Why's he coming here?"

"Sere instigated a small riot yesterday. Chief Shelburn expects more trouble from them."

Sere, Hutchins thought, reviewing his mental files. It was near the top of the attorney general's watchlist. It combined environmentalism with Marxist ideology and fanatic discipline. It maintained that industrial civilization was in a crisis, which would resolve itself either in the destruction of the world or in the creation of an ecological paradise.

Apocalyptic predictions are popular these days, Hutchins thought. The Redeemers, Communists, survivalists, fascists, economists—everyone forecasted disaster. The interminable Depression encouraged such thinking . . . and this was the year 2000, the end of the millennium. For the past decade, every mystic and crackbrained preacher in the country had prophesied chaos. "*Will* there be more trouble?"

"My field agents think so. Sere has been active among the local squatters." Farrier paused, a thoughtful look on his face. "We ought to deal with Shelburn's situation first. That should make it easier to get his help."

"Yes." Hutchins' mouth puckered sourly. Compared with an organization such as Sere, a few psychic oddballs meant nothing. Hutchins looked at the stat sheets and frowned. "Lou, how would you describe our chances of catching any of them?"

"Slim," Farrier conceded. "These people do their best to avoid attracting attention. Forrest surfaced only because some crank tried to kill him. Aside from violating the Compton Act they don't break any laws, so most police forces ignore 'em. They're insane, which makes them unpredictable, and I suppose their ESP would help them avoid entrapment."

"That's not what I want to hear." Hutchins rubbed his chin thoughtfully. "How do these fugitives survive? They can't take regular jobs without risking exposure, and they can't collect welfare on the run. So who supports them?"

"I couldn't say."

"Have somebody look into it. That angle could help."

Hutchins sighed. "Our orders are to catch as many of these mind readers as we can, quickly. This is priority work."

"I see. Is there any *particular* reason for this?"

"Presidential orders," Hutchins said. "I'm not sure, but I'd imagine Delanty is under pressure. He's too shrewd to order this without good reason." Hutchins paused and thought for a moment. "I don't know what's up, but if we catch one or two of these freaks fast enough, Delanty might declare a victory and let us get back to our *real* work."

"Yes, sir." Farrier's face showed scornful amusement. An adroit politician himself, he despised anyone who tried to use him as a tool. "In that case, sir, I suggest we concentrate on Forrest, and let the others go hang."

"I concur." Hutchins picked up Forrest's record, sat down on an overstuffed chair, and began reading.

The facts were scant. Julian Forrest: five-foot-four, one-thirty-eight pounds, born 27 November 1974 in Des Moines, Iowa. Educated at the University of California, Berkeley: bachelor's degree in astronomy earned in 1994, master's degree in 1996; work on doctoral degree interrupted when he went underground in March 1998. Winner of assorted scholastic awards. Hardly the CTO's typical quarry, Hutchins mused, but these days you never knew.

Forrest had been certified legally insane in 1993, on a diagnosis of idiopathic dysfunction. Aside from a failed suicide attempt, he had kept out of trouble for five years, reporting to his observation officer once every week. He had been taken into custody in 1998 for unspecified asocial acts; he had escaped custody while being transferred to a public mental ward. After his escape the MHB had classified him as violent and unpredictable.

Damned sloppy work, Hutchins thought, setting the folder aside. He would never have permitted anyone in the CTO to file such a vague, slipshod report. Nothing in the file told Hutchins what he might expect Forrest to do, or even much about what he had already done. It didn't even mention the fact that Forrest could read minds. How could he hope to catch the man when he knew so little about him?

The intercom chimed. "Mr. Farrier, Chief Shelburn is here to see you," an anonymous voice said.

"Send him in," Farrier said.

Jim Shelburn was a craggy, silver-haired man who carried himself as though he remained in the prime of life. "I'm very glad to see you," he said warmly, shaking Hutchins' hand. "Although I never expected the top man to come out here. I appreciate the attention."

Hutchins smiled. "The truth is I'm in town on another matter—and I'll need your help on it. Of course, I'm interested in your problem with Sere. I'd like to hear it first."

Shelburn smiled quirkily as he sat down. "I hope your problem is smaller than mine. Sere instigated a small riot yesterday, and it's threatened us with bigger and deadlier demonstrations."

"Unless you meet their demands, no doubt," Farrier said.

"They've only made one," Shelburn said, "not that anyone understands it. You know about our reconstruction project?" Shelburn watched the two men nod. "Well, they've demanded that we cancel it."

"Naturally," Hutchins said. "Sere's a revolutionary group. Your project would stimulate the local economy, reduce poverty, and cut into unemployment. That would make people content. People don't join revolutions when they're content."

"I suppose not," Shelburn said. He drummed his fingers on the edge of his chair. "Well, I'm a policeman, not a politician. I need to know what to expect from Sere, and what steps to take. My intelligence branch can't tell me anything; their budget is so minuscule that they're almost out of business."

"That's why *we're* here," Farrier said. "I have some spies inside Sere. They tell me that Sere has been working among the squatters, organizing some of them into a paramilitary force. You can't start the project until you relocate the squatters, and Sere won't let you do that without a fight." Farrier looked sardonic. "There're over eighty thousand squatters in Southern California. Take them away and you remove a large part of Sere's power base."

"If we can." Shelburn put a hand over his eyes. "You're telling me to expect a bloodbath."

"Not necessarily," Hutchins said. "We've defused similar situations in other cities—Chicago, Memphis, and the Bronx in New York. Places with lots of poor and unemployed on the loose, and radicals agitating them."

Shelburn looked disconcerted. "I've heard rumors, but I had no idea—the *scope* of the problem—"

"It's not the sort of thing that gets much publicity," Hutchins said. "Even the liberal media is reluctant to talk about the scale of the crisis. The truth is that this depression is much worse than the one of the 1930s— *much* worse."

"That's neither here nor there," Farrier said. Hutchins noted that he sounded perfectly at ease. "The immediate problem is Sere. If we can get a handle on its leadership, we can break Sere in less than a week."

"One week?" Shelburn asked. "Are you sure?"

"We have a good deal of experience," Farrier said. "Once we remove the leaders, the rest of the outfit will be too disorganized and demoralized to fight much. Now, did you arrest any Sere members during the riot?"

"We have a couple of agitators in custody—"

"Good!" Farrier smiled. Hutchins found it a disagreeable sight. "We'll arrange to transfer them into CTO custody. Our questioning techniques—"

"I've heard about them." Shelburn didn't quite shudder.

"Medically augmented interrogation is well within the law," Farrier said. "Congress authorized its use in terrorist cases. It's safe and reliable—and we can't piss away time with half-measures."

"No . . . no, of course not. All right. We'll transfer the detainees this afternoon."

Farrier smiled. "And we'll have results in a few days."

"Yes." Shelburn took a deep breath, let it out slowly. "So much for my problem. What can I do to help you, Mr. Hutchins?"

Bite the bullet, Hutchins told himself. "The President has ordered us to detain several telepaths. We know that one of them, a man named Forrest, is currently in Los Angeles. We'd appreciate your help in apprehending him."

Shelburn looked puzzled, as if he didn't know how to react. "A telepath? What's he done?"

"I'm not at liberty to discuss that." The evasion came easily to Hutchins. "It'll have to be enough to say that he's violated the Compton Act."

"Well, that's the MHB's problem," Shelburn said.

"The MHB has already requested your help," Farrier said. "They *have* tagged Forrest as dangerous. The law requires that you—"

Shelburn's face darkened. " 'Dangerous.' The MHB says *that* every time it screws up. Haven't you ever dealt with those clowns before?" The police chief looked at Hutchins. "What has Forrest *done?* Espionage? Blackmail? I *want* to help you, but I can't spare the manpower for another one of the MHB's circus acts . . . and doing their dirty work for them always causes morale problems in my department. I can't afford that now, not with this Sere powder keg under us."

"We can't discuss the reasons," Farrier said coldly. "The fact is that the President has requested this, and you are in no position to refuse him—or us."

No wonder people call him "Bear," Hutchins thought. "We're not asking for a special effort," he said quickly. "Just ask your people to keep their eyes open. Bring Forrest in if they happen to see him."

"I can do that much," Shelburn said.

"That's terribly generous of you," Farrier murmured.

Shelburn gave him an icy look as he got out of his chair, but he addressed his words to Hutchins. "There's some paperwork involved in transferring the detainees;

I'll have my secretary expedite things. Good day." He left the suite.

"I never thought I'd see the day," Farrier said, after the door closed behind Shelburn. "A small-time cop, bucking orders from the President—"

"I heard," Hutchins said curtly. He marveled at the quiet anger in Farrier's voice. It was as though he didn't realize he had provoked Shelburn. "He's no small-time cop—and unfortunately for us, he's in the right. Helping us find Forrest is a judgment call on his part."

Farrier shrugged off the criticism in Hutchins' voice. "What this means is that we'll have to turn to the MHB. They don't have the LAPD's manpower, but they have experience chasing witches."

"I can't say that their experience impresses me," Hutchins said, "but we'll have to bring them in anyway. Meanwhile, I want *you* to concentrate on Sere. Give Shelburn all the help he needs. Cater to him."

Farrier's eyes narrowed to slits. "After the way he talked—"

"Let's not mention the way you talked. You let me down, Lou. We might have coaxed more help from him." Hutchins shook his head angrily. "Let's remember that our first duty is to fight groups like Sere—not to run off on wild goose chases. Or witch hunts. I expect your first report on Sere by noon tomorrow."

"You'll have it," Farrier promised sullenly. He rose from his seat and left, moving with the implacable force of a glacier.

Sometimes he's more trouble than he's worth, Hutchins thought—but despite his bulldozer personality, Farrier remained an asset to the CTO. He got things done. He was no hack, avoiding risks in a desperate effort to protect his career.

Shaking his head, Hutchins went to the suite's computer terminal, seated himself, and accessed his office in Washington. He had left a considerable pile of work there, and the backlog had mushroomed in his absence.

Hutchins ground his way through the work, delegating some things to his staff while attending to items that demanded his attention. One such matter was the CTO news summary, a specialized service which gave its users an overview of terrorist and subversive activities around the nation. As director of the Counter-Terrorism Office, Hutchins made a point of learning which way the political and social winds blew. Sometimes he could catch a gust before it swirled into a full storm.

Hutchins skimmed the material as it rolled across the screen. Several letters in the New York *Times* demanded clemency for some condemned anarchists . . . an editorial in the Des Moines *Register* deplored bombings, assassinations and riots, but praised "the healthy broadening of the American political spectrum represented by new and diverse political parties" . . . a consumer group had demanded nationalization of all medical services, while denying that this was a socialistic idea. None of the developments startled Hutchins, but sympathy for extremists and their causes paved the way for even more radical things.

He continued reading. The Golden Circle had used a broad-band transmitter to jam every TV and radio station in the Cincinnati area . . . the shock-rock group Bloodbath had just released an album that praised Nazi ideals, and two cuts from the album were already in the youth Top Forty . . . the Iron Guard had claimed responsibility for attacks on witches in several cities, and had promised to keep the country safe from "psychic terrorism."

Hutchins froze the screen and went over the entire report. One IG communiqué identified one of the dead witches as Julian Forrest. A second message admitted that Julian Forrest had survived an attack, but swore that the next attempt would succeed—while a third message from a different branch of the Iron Guard labeled the other notes as hoaxes.

Perplexed, Hutchins shut off the terminal. Most of the Iron Guard's members came from the middle class, and their interest lay in protecting themselves from the Depression. Lunatic theology didn't interest them. The militant wing of the Guard was hardheadedly atheistic and even less likely to take an interest in witches . . . but they had.

At least that explained why Delanty wanted those witches dragged in, Hutchins reflected. In 1996, small spoiler parties such as the Iron Guard had bled away a fifth of the votes, and that had allowed Delanty to unseat President Clark. Now that Delanty was up for re-election, he wouldn't care for another such upset; he'd had enough trouble winning the recent bout of primary elections. If arresting a few freaks could neutralize one spoiler party and gain him a few votes, he'd do it.

Hutchins forced down a yawn and glanced at his watch. It was well after midnight—no, he was in California, not Washington. He reset his watch to half past nine . . . but his body still said midnight. I'm getting old, he thought. Jet lag and long hours had never bothered him before.

He went into the bedroom and sagged onto the bed, suddenly too tired even to undress. Hutchins wanted to drop off to sleep, but his mind refused to cooperate. His thoughts kept returning to Shelburn, and his refusal to obey the President's orders.

Maybe we worry too much about anarchists and radicals, Hutchins thought. Perhaps the real threat to the country's stability lay in something as simple as a policeman's indifference to an order from Washington. If the government could lose the support of men like Shelburn—

That was hardly a thought to sleep on.

CHAPTER 4

TUESDAY, 13 JUNE 2000

People always say there's a split between logic and emotion, which isn't true. They weave together in the human mind, and we're at our best when both are present. A mind that is ruled solely by emotion is a weak mind, a sad mind, the sort of mind that will lie and cheat, or march behind a Hitler because it feels good. Sometimes we have to run against our emotions.

I've never tapped a mind that runs by pure logic, and I never will. It's impossible for such a thing to exist—no? Can you name one logical reason to stay alive—one reason that doesn't involve some emotion, such as fear of death or enjoyment of life?

Neither can I. A purely logical mind has no reason to wake up in the morning. That makes emotion as much a strength as a weakness.

—from Sense and Non-sense, *by Lyn Amanda Clancy*

"Her name is Birche Holstein," the thea told Julian, as he breakfasted on cold cereal and instant orange juice. He ate slowly, unconsciously trying to make the meal last longer. Nobody starved in this coven, but life was a tentative thing at best. "A friend of hers is a reporter and wants to interview you."

"Me?" He almost choked on the juice. "What for?"

"I couldn't say." The thea appeared to sit at the table with him. One of her fingers traced a pattern on the bare wood. "The friend's name is Steve Magyar. He works for the L.A. Post."

38

"Is he telepathic, too?"

"No. In fact, Birche isn't a full telepath herself." The thea paused as though trying to recall something. *"She has enormous potential, but she's holding back because she's frightened."*

"I have the picture," Julian said wearily. Birche Holstein was a lone telepath in a hostile world, with everything to fear and no one to help her. *"Where can I find her?"*

"She works in the Prospect Park shopping mall. It's a two-hour walk from here. Go south to Wilshire Boulevard, then turn west." The entity hesitated. *"Julian, are you sure you ought to get wrapped up in this?"*

He nodded. *"I don't want to leave this woman by herself. It's wrong."*

The thea seemed to stare at him as she gauged his emotions. *"It's also dangerous. There are police patrols everywhere, not to mention vigilantes and Sere troopers. Charging out into the middle of that could be suicidal—"*

"One of my strong points." Unconsciously he fingered the scars on his wrist. *"None of them are looking for me."*

"They wouldn't mind catching you by accident." The thea held up her hands in a gesture of impatience. *"Julian, would it hurt to wait a few days to find her?"*

"Would it help?"

"No . . . but it's still dangerous—and it won't help anyone if you get killed." Shaking her head, the thea got up and left the table. She faded away as she walked toward the door.

Julian finished eating, then pulled a creased, scuffed snapshot from a coat pocket. It's been a long time, he thought, looking at the picture of his family. He hadn't seen them in over two years, and as long as he was a fugitive he didn't dare visit them. At least neither his sister nor his two brothers were telepathic; the gene that produced the sense had skipped them, sparing them from the interests of the MHB and assorted fanatics.

Julian was about to leave the house when Malcolm

called him. *"Cliff wants to tell you something—out loud."*

"How gauche," Julian smiled. He entered the bedroom.

The ex-rioter lay on a mattress, an assortment of blankets piled over him. "Malcolm says you're going downtown," he said, in a voice still hoarse from the gas. "You shouldn't."

"I have to find someone."

"You'll find trouble." He coughed harshly. "You know I was in Sere."

"Uh-huh." Past tense, Julian noted. Cliff Whitney had quit Sere when his friends had abandoned him.

"There're supposed to be more riots this week. The plan is to keep the cops off balance." He stopped and drew a long, grating breath. "Have mini-riots all over town, instead of one big brawl."

"That'd make it hard to avoid trouble," Malcolm told Julian.

"I'll stay out of its way," Julian said. "I know when to run."

"Hah!" Cliff coughed again. "Can't outrun riots. Spread like wildfire—and the cops are careless about stamping them out." He shook his head. "And if Sere catches you, Forrest, you're dead. They have it in for witches."

"Lots of people do," Malcolm said.

"Not like Sere," Cliff rasped. "They say the government used genetic engineering . . . to make witches. Needed you for their secret police. So killing you helps the Revolution." Cliff couldn't read minds, but he could see the set look on Julian's face. "Idiot. You always this stubborn?"

"He was worse on Monday," Malcolm said. "Now shut up and rest, or I'll sick Hazel on you."

"Promises, promises." Cliff rolled over and dropped off to sleep.

"I'm glad he got that off his mind," Malcolm said, as he and Julian left the room. *"Are you still going?"*

"I'll step lightly," Julian promised.

"Famous last words." Malcolm pulled a thin paper-

back book from his hip pocket. *"If you stay alive that long, give this to that woman, okay? Maybe it'll help her."*

Julian glanced at the book. It was a coverless, well-thumbed copy of Clancy's *Sense and Non-sense*, its spine held together with masking tape. It was a rare and valuable book; only one edition had ever gone to press, seven years earlier, and most of the copies had been burned by the Redeemers.

"She'll appreciate this," Julian said, sliding the book into a coat pocket. *"Thank you."*

I wonder where they all come from, Julian thought, as he entered the shopping mall. It was a clean, airy place, filled with shoppers and browsers who looked untouched by the massive inflation and unemployment of the Depression. They had a complacent solidity about them, and in the face of their thoughts Julian began to doubt his own memories . . . until he noticed the near-desperation with which they avoided looking at him. He was a visible reminder of the Depression, a ghost at their banquet.

Given the number of people in the area, Julian expected to spend several hours looking for Birche Holstein; telepathy was not an efficient way of locating someone. She might not even be here today, he thought. Even if she was, he might overlook her.

Telepathy isn't the only way to use your brain, he reflected. Julian looked around for an information booth. "I'm looking for Birche Holstein," he told the woman in the booth. "She works somewhere in the mall. Could you tell me where to find her?"

"The woman at Boulevard Books?" The woman smiled professionally as she looked at Julian. He was clean and freshly shaven, she saw, but his clothes had seen better days. "I'm sorry, sir, but I can't give out that information."

"Well, thanks anyway." Julian walked away, brushing at the sleeve of his coat. He'd always been fastidious, and the necessity of wearing old clothes bothered him, but what money he had always went for more immediate needs.

Boulevard Books was a roomy shop, brightly lit and painted in warm earth tones. Julian meandered into the shop and searched the minds around him for Birche Holstein's thoughts, in the same way that one of the customers might shop for just the right book. He picked them up after a moment. She was in her office, going over an order list with one of her clerks. So she's the boss, Julian thought. Interesting.

Julian stood idly at a table of discount books, charmed by the touch of her mind. There was fear in her, but it was only one undercurrent in a mind that bubbled with humor and vitality. Birche had a vague awareness of the minds around her, and a sudden, uneasy feeling that someone was watching her. Julian knew it wouldn't take her long to get to the bottom of *that*, and he smiled at the thought of meeting her.

Out of curiosity, he picked up a book on magic and leafed through it. The coffee table book gave him instructions on how to defeat mind readers. They were easily hypnotized; the intricate patterns of a hex sign could put them into a trance. They showed psychotically compulsive behavior: scatter sesame seeds in front of them, and they would be overwhelmed by an urge to count each one. Because they were ashamed of the way they destroyed the privacy of real people, they couldn't bear to see themselves in mirrors.

Julian put the book down. The mixture of superstition and psychology might have been funny if so many people hadn't taken such things seriously.

He saw a book of astronomical photographs. *Much* better, he thought, looking at the lush color plates. Julian had been in love with astronomy ever since he had received a toy telescope for his seventh birthday. Clusters of stars and wispy nebulae had an insubstantial beauty that never tired him. The beauty had remained alive when he studied astronomy in school. Uncovering the secrets of the spectrum and learning the equations that governed the stars in their orbits had added the dimensions of understanding and recognition to that beauty.

Motion caught his eye, and he saw Birche emerge from her office. She was as pretty as her thoughts, he decided. She had an engaging smile, and large brown eyes that suited her full-moon face. She said something to the cashier in a soft voice, then approached Julian. "Can I help you?" she asked.

"Yes, you can," Julian said, enjoying her innocent friendliness. She seemed to see him without noting his frayed appearance. "You were calling me last night, weren't you?"

"Christ on a crutch," Birche muttered, recognizing him. She was suddenly frightened, and her reaction was strong enough to leave Julian physically shaken.

"I didn't mean to scare you," he said in a hushed voice. Her reaction made him feel like a boor, as if he had just smashed some masterpiece of art. "I only came here to talk with you."

Birche nodded dumbly, her face ashen. She turned to the cashier. "Jenny, I'm going out for a while—no, don't call security. Everything's fine."

Julian walked out of the shop with her, while the cashier gaped at them. "You don't have to be afraid of me," he said. He kept his voice low and confidential, a response to her tension. "I won't make any trouble."

"No?" Birche looked at the other people strolling the plaza. "What if you're recognized? Forrest, why did you have to come *here?*"

"In the second place, you asked to see me—something about an interview."

Birche glanced at him as they walked along. "What's the first place?" she asked suspiciously.

"To see you."

Birche grimaced, and decided to get this over as fast as possible. "Steve's the one who wants to see you. He thinks you know something about the Iron Guard."

"Such as?"

"Such as why they tried to kill you in Oakland."

"It really was the IG?" Julian shook his head. "I

wasn't sure. I couldn't tell much from what the hit man was thinking, except that he'd seen a wanted poster with my picture on it."

"The IG printed that poster," Birche said, "although Steve can't prove it yet. For some reason, the IG is hunting . . ." She let her voice trail off as a couple of window-shoppers passed within earshot.

Julian smiled at her reticence. "You don't need to *talk* to me."

"*Oh, that's right. It would be safer that way.*" Even so, her lower lip trembled.

"And if you'd relax, *I* wouldn't need to talk, either. You can tap thoughts as well as I can—"

"No, I *can't*," she said, with a vehemence that surprised both of them. After a moment she continued: "Forrest, I know what I am—but I have it under control. I am *normal*."

"So am I. I'm a perfectly normal telepath." Julian saw a nook between two blocks of stores. He steered Birche into it. The nook was packed with outsized potted ferns, and it concealed a bench that was too decorative to be comfortable. Now I *know* I'm in Los Angeles, he thought, seating himself on the wrought-iron monstrosity.

Birche stayed on her feet. She had regained her composure, enough to put some color back in her face. "I'll call Steve now," she said, pulling her phone from her coat pocket.

"Okay," he said, and sensed her relief at his agreement. Birche wanted to get rid of him . . . and perhaps Steve would return to normal once he had finished with Forrest. His ambition was the only obstacle to their romance; on those occasions when he could put it aside he was a thoughtful, almost tender lover, even if he never showed much passion—

—and in a cascade of embarrassment she realized that Forrest had overheard everything she had thought. Birche fumbled with her phone, punched in the wrong number twice, and cursed.

"Here." Julian took the phone from her and tapped

in the number she had thought. A querulous voice
answered. "Magyar here."

"Steve? Julian. Birche tells me that—"

"Julian *Forrest?* Goddamn! Where are you? No, don't
answer that, not over an open line! There's no telling
who's listening."

"Uh-huh." And they say *I'm* paranoid, Julian thought
wryly. "What do you want to talk about?"

"Well, first—no, wait. Can you read minds over the
phone?"

"Are you kidding? Telepathy isn't magic."

"No?" The excited voice calmed down. "Forrest, I
can't talk now—I *can't*. I've got to see you but I can't
manage it today. Look, our mutual acquaintance can
arrange something for tomorrow. You know you can
trust her. All right?" He hung up.

"All right," Julian said dubiously. He returned the
pocket phone to Birche. "He said—"

"I heard." Birche shivered and sat down on the iron
bench. "He's up to something stupid, I know it." She
shook her head. "And you. Damn you, Forrest, you
didn't need to come here. Why did you do it?"

Julian fumbled for words. "To see you. You need
help."

"What help? To turn me into a full telepath? I don't
want to be one."

"Like it or not, you *are* a telepath. I can help you
adapt to it."

She snorted in disbelief. "Why would you want to do
that?"

"Why not?" Julian felt bewildered. He hadn't expected an easy time—novice telepaths always had
problems—but he hadn't come prepared for an argument over philosophy.

Or had he? He reached into his pocket and pulled
out Malcolm's book. He offered it to her. "You don't
have a copy of *Sense and Non-sense*, do you?"

Birche drew back from it. "No, and I don't want it.
It's too dangerous."

"Since when is a book dangerous?" Julian asked.

"It has guidelines on how to develop the power—"

"It's an *ability*, not a power," Julian said. "And there's a lot more to it than reading some instructions. Look, most of the book is just Lyn Clancy's autobiography. It tells what she went through when her ESP developed, and what she thought about it."

"What makes you think that'd interest me?"

"It helps to know you aren't the only one going through this," Julian said. "And it's beautifully rational. Lyn tells how she learned to think and reason—to keep her own mind in order as a way of coping with telepathy. Nothing makes telepathy easy, but that makes it a bit easier."

"You think so?" Birche hesitated, then took the book, telling herself that she didn't have to read it . . . although she would have done that just to get rid of this scruffy oddball—"Sorry," Birche mumbled. She blushed and looked away from him.

"It's okay," Julian said, smiling. When she hid the book inside her coat, he noticed that she had had a tailor add extra pockets to the garment. He found that practicality oddly appealing. "You should tap me; I *always* think embarrassing things around beautiful women."

Birche stood up and turned away from him. "I'm not beautiful."

"No?" Julian eyed her, watching the sinuous movement of her compact, rounded figure as she turned. That was as pleasant as tapping her mind, he decided. "You were an athlete in college, weren't you? I'll bet you were on a swimming team."

Birche looked at him and shrugged. "So you read my mind."

"I didn't need to. You *look* like a swimmer. I can picture you climbing out of a pool after winning a race. I'm right, aren't I?"

"Yes." Birche hesitated, then said, "I almost made the '96 Olympics, but I wasn't fast enough in the qualification trials. I would have made it if my legs weren't so damned short."

"Your legs look fine," Julian said. "You still work out, don't you?"

"I have to keep in shape, unless I want to turn into a butterball. I already look—why am I telling you this?" she asked gruffly. Julian sensed her suspicion that he was conning her, using flattery to chivvy something out of her . . . or to set her up for a pratfall. *Nobody* said she was beautiful and meant it.

"Then it's time for a change." Julian stood up. "You're beautiful. I could look at you all day, and talk with you, and love every minute of it. You've got a mind like none I've ever tapped, and it comes with the loveliest shape and face I've seen in years."

Devastated by a need to *know*, Birche felt her defenses slip. She tapped his thoughts . . . and Julian sensed her astonishment—at his sincerity, and at the notion that anyone could find her attractive. Shaken, she took a step back from Julian. "Look, you still have to meet Steve," she said.

"Who? Oh, him. Right. What do you have in mind?"

Birche made a quick decision. "Do you know where I live?"

"I do now."

"Can you come there tomorrow night, around nine? I—it's safer than coming *here* again. The people in my apartment building never notice anything."

"I'll be there," Julian promised. He stepped in front of her and cupped his hand under her chin. I thought I had more self-control than this, he thought, and kissed her. Birche returned the kiss, then pulled away in confusion. She bustled off to the sanctuary of her store.

Julian began the long walk home, wondering if he should have accepted her invitation. He wanted to see her again—but not if it would endanger her. He was a target for too many people; she deserved better than to be placed at risk. He should have made different arrangements. The knowledge that he hadn't thought everything through annoyed Julian; he had always prided himself on his rationality.

Yet he knew he would keep the appointment. Birche

needed help, and he could give it to her—and Julian felt that he'd been hit by a thunderbolt. He kept reliving their encounter as he walked along, enjoying the memory while fretting that he had come on too strong. *I haven't acted this oafishly since high school,* he thought. The girls he'd known then had found a certain klutzy charm in him, but Birche would expect more from a man.

Immersed in his own thoughts, Julian didn't notice the marchers until they were almost upon him. They came streaming down the sidewalk, over a hundred strong, boisterously cheering and shouting. A tall woman waved her arm over her head like a baton, and led the mob in a Sere battle chant:

"The revolution has begun.
"So I'll go home and get my gun,
"And shoot that man in Washington."

Julian ducked into the doorway of a shop as the riot erupted around him. He clung to the doorjamb, anchoring himself against the mental storm that roared around him. The marchers wanted chaos . . . anarchy . . . the complete destruction of the society around them. Julian felt his mind withdrawing into itself, retreating in fear from the sudden madness boiling around him.

He became aware of an alarm clanging somewhere nearby. Julian fought to concentrate on the sound, using it to steady himself. Realizing that he had squeezed his eyes shut, he forced them open, released his grip on the doorjamb, and looked around. The rioters were at work, smashing windows and overturning cars, while merchants and shoppers and passers-by fled. His attention drawn by a spike of sadistic glee, Julian watched one of the rioters level a stun gun at a knot of runners. The man fired an electrodart into the crowd, and a man in a business suit collapsed in convulsions.

Why am I standing here? Julian wondered. The rioters wouldn't ignore him much longer—and the police would come soon, in an inevitable counterattack.

A car erupted in flames with a loud *whump*. Rioters

dashed away from it as flaming gas poured from its
tank. One of the rioters swerved to avoid tripping over
the fallen businessman.

Crouching, Julian hurried into the street. He bent
over the man, pulled the dart from his back, and hooked
his hands under the man's shoulders. Julian flinched as
the rioters put the torch to another car, a dozen yards
away. He started pulling the man as hot black smoke
blew over him.

I'd better get him inside, Julian thought, as he dragged
the man to the sidewalk. The mob was breaking windows and looting a few displays, but beyond that, Julian
noted, they were ignoring the buildings.

Almost by reflex Julian ducked as someone fired a
dart at him. The needle snicked into the wall behind
him, and he heard a quick hiss as the stun charge
vaporized the wire that connected the dart to the gun.
Julian pulled the man to a shopfront, kicked the door
open, and hauled him inside. Strained and out of breath,
Julian slumped down against a counter.

He looked through the smashed window and watched
the riot, which was still going at full force—although
the rage of the rioters had transmuted into a carnival
sense of abandon. Tapping their minds, Julian discovered that most of them were new to Sere. They didn't
care about Sere's doctrines now; they were looking for
excitement.

That'll change fast when the cops get here, Julian
thought. Some of the rioters would die in the fighting,
and many of the others would come to see the police as
their enemy. For Sere's purposes, that was a more
effective recruiting device than any amount of propaganda.

Julian got up and bent over the unconscious man. He
was breathing without difficulty, and his thoughts were
those of a man in deep sleep. The stunner had hit him
hard, Julian decided, but he had escaped real injury.

I ought to get back to the mall, Julian thought. It
wasn't too far from here, and Birche was there. If the
riot spread she might need his protection—

Something harsh and determined caught his attention. The police? Julian wondered. No, the thoughts he tapped lacked the disciplined edge of a cop's mind . . . and he heard no sirens, no helicopters. Intrigued, he studied that mind.

The woman was searching for an electrical substation she knew to be in this area. She carried a pair of small bombs, and she had orders to destroy the substation. There was no mistaking the contempt she felt for the rioters around her. They were merely a diversion, something to keep the cops busy while she and other saboteurs cut the power to critical parts of the city. That made the rioters useful, but they were fools for allowing themselves to be used—

Julian shook his head, as if to break the contact. The woman's attitude was so *alien* as to be incomprehensible—yet it seemed typical of Sere. Human lives meant nothing to them . . . not even the lives of their own people.

Protect Birche? he asked himself suddenly. He would try, but now the idea struck him as sheer vanity. Julian had no illusions about possessing magical powers.

CHAPTER 5

The humblest moment in my life came when my Lord appeared to me and told me to dedicate my life to His holy work. Scientists had led our children astray into a night of uncertainty and doubt; secular humanists had seduced the people into forsaking Divine revelation for so-called logic and rationalism. I was to lead our flock of humanity back unto Him.

The beauty of our Lord's word is that it cannot be

doubted; it is perfect and need not be questioned. This knowledge has been my inspiration and my strength, and my assurance of my ultimate triumph. Science can offer only doubt and uncertainty and questions. The Lord and I offer absolute truth and certainty. People want that above all.

—*from* My Lord, My Self: The Inspiring Autobiography of the Most Reverend Percival Fountain. *(Fountain of Eternal Life Publishing House 1998.*

Steve Magyar found himself facing an embarrassment of riches. He needed to see Forrest, and his phone call should have come as a welcome surprise—but he already had another meeting lined up, and it could prove far more informative.

A half hour before Forrest had contacted him, Steve had taken a call from a man who claimed to represent the Redemptive Faith's inner circle. The anonymous caller had said that Perry Fountain wished to discuss the RF's goals with the *Post*'s senior political reporter—and that there were other, bigger things in store. If Steve was interested, he would be given a ride to a secret meeting place.

Steve had consulted the phone's voice-analyzer while the man spoke. The machine had found the voice logged in its memory crystal; the man was an Iron Guard organizer. There it was, Steve thought, one more bit of proof of a link between the IG and the Redeemers. It was also a chance to get some answers. They might not be honest answers, but Steve had learned that even lies can contain a bit of the truth. He had accepted the offer and jotted down instructions on how to catch the ride.

Then Forrest had called. It was a hell of a dilemma, he thought. He couldn't pass up the chance to investigate the IG—but he might not get a second chance to see Forrest, either. The next news item on the freak was likely to be his obituary.

There was a sharp rap at the door, and Claire Daniels entered Steve's cubicle. "You look like a man with a problem," the editor said, sitting down in front of his desk. "Talk."

"I've got an interview with Perry Fountain in a while."

"*That's* nothing." The tall, thin woman looked amused. "The old fraud's always after publicity."

"It may be more than that," Steve said. "The fellow who called belongs to the Iron Guard's upper echelons."

"Curious."

"There's a definite link between the two groups—and it involves Transpac, somehow. Anyway, this character offered to give me a ride to a secret meeting place. That's a typical IG move."

"And you accepted?" Daniels looked as if her teeth hurt. "Steve, a lot of people don't come back from rides with them."

"I'm in no danger," Steve said. "They must have something they want reported. I can't deliver if something happens to me. That's my insurance."

"I hope you won't need to collect on it."

"I won't have any trouble—this time." Steve smiled, baring his teeth. "Mrs. D., if I can collect just a little more info, and verify a few things—"

"You'll be on your way to winning a Pulitzer Prize." Daniels looked him over carefully. "How absolutely wonderful. So why is it that when I walked in here you looked as if the IRS had created a new tax bracket just for you?"

"I also have a chance to interview Julian Forrest."

"Who?"

"He's a telepath. The MHB has been trying to net him—"

"He's not newsworthy," Daniels said. "Only cranks are interested in witches—and we don't publish the *Post* for cranks. Don't waste any time on him."

Steve did his best to sound patient. "Mrs. D., the IG has put several telepaths on its death list. They *always* have a goal when they murder someone. If Forrest can help me learn their goals—well, *that's* newsworthy."

"No." Daniels tapped a bony finger on the desktop. "Steve, you cannot use anything a mind-reader tells you. They're insane, and that makes them unreliable—ask any psychologist. Using one as a source could damage the *Post*'s credibility, and yours as well. If you hand me a column that relies on what some mystic says, I'll spike it. Any editor in this country would do that."

"But if I can verify what he says—"

"That doesn't matter." She stood up. "Concentrate on Fountain and this Iron Guard matter. Anything else is a sideshow."

Steve sighed. "All right."

"And be careful," she added. "The courts may not have convicted anyone, but we both know the IG has killed hostile reporters. You're an asset to the *Post*, and I don't want some trigger-happy maniac to remove you from our staff."

"Same here," Steve said, after she left.

Steve opened a desk drawer and took out a pair of recorders. One was a standard unit, and he slipped the card into his shirt pocket, letting its microphone wire poke into the open. The second one, which he had camouflaged as a bank debit card, went into his wallet. It wouldn't give a clear, crisp playback, but he wouldn't risk losing it.

As Steve walked out of the Post Building, he wondered if he ought to call Birche and give her some questions to ask Forrest. It was a way to cover his bets; she might hear from him again, and Forrest might tell her things he wouldn't reveal to a normal person. Mrs. Daniels wouldn't have approved, but there was no need to trouble her with details, not if Forrest put him on the trail of something he *could* use.

I ought to stop seeing Birche after this, Steve thought as he strolled down the sidewalk. Birche had seemed innocent and vulnerable when they had first met, and she had a rawboned sort of prettiness, but that had worn thin long ago—and her insecurity gave her a maddening tendency to cling. Birche's telepathy had come in handy, but Mrs. Daniels' attitude made it clear that any connection with her could jeopardize his career—

The roar of an unmuffled car engine broke his concentration. Steve glanced at the road and saw a cherry-red sportster tearing down the street. The sleek machine had wide tires and a hood that swelled with airscoops. I always wanted a car like that when I was in high school, Steve thought in warm nostalgia.

The car slowed and came to the curb. "Yo, Magyar! C'mon!" The passenger door popped open.

This must be my ride, Steve thought. The dramatics were in character for the Iron Guard. He climbed in, and as he settled into the low-slung bucket seat the car took off. "Where are we going?" Steve asked.

"You'll see," the driver said. The man wore wrap-around sunglasses and a bristling mustache—a false mustache, Steve decided. The bend in his hawk nose looked familiar, but Steve couldn't place the man.

The driving fell just short of reckless. The driver made several turns down side streets, in an unabashed effort to lose any tails. He didn't realize, then, that one of the credit cards in Steve's wallet was a homing beacon, monitored by the *Post*'s security computer. Steve took some comfort from that.

The car skidded into the parking lot of a two-story office building. The driver left the car without a word, as though he expected Steve to follow him without question. Steve did that, and climbed upstairs to a thoroughly anonymous office, a place of pastel-colored walls and bright fluorescent lights. The only decorations were a small American flag on the desk and a garish picture of Jesus Christ on one wall. This Jesus carried a fiery sword, which clashed with the uplifted, long-suffering eyes.

Steve and the driver sat down on folding chairs and waited. After a moment the door opened, admitting two more men to the office. Steve tagged the first as a bodyguard; he was a burly man whose ill-fitting suit did nothing to conceal the pistol bulging at his shoulder. The man who followed him was Perry Fountain.

"God bless you, my child," Fountain said, shaking

Steve's hand. Fountain sat down behind the desk, while the bodyguard took a stance alongside him.

As he sat down again, Steve sensed that the driver was watching him through his sunglasses. The man slouched in his chair, but there was an undeniable tension in the set of his jaw and shoulders. He's running this show, Steve decided. He felt a wordless conviction that this man held a high place in the Iron Guard—and that he was here to observe Steve. It was a disturbing notion, and Steve found it difficult to return his attention to Fountain.

"I can't tell you how happy I am to see you," Fountain said. He spoke in a cultured Southern accent. "Reporters are God's holy messengers, helping to spread the good word throughout America."

"We're not ministers." Steve shifted around in his chair. The new position wasn't more comfortable, but it let him see the driver from the corner of his eye. "Our job is to report the facts."

"A difficult job, that," Fountain said with a smile. "We all know how the Devil plays tricks with the facts—and his tricks have become legion. The Old One caused the Depression, my child, by deceiving the moneychangers with dreams of false profits. He has undermined the nation with witchcraft, perversion, and communism. Blasphemous books like *Sense and Nonsense* spread Satan's immorality and humanist, 'rationalist' lies. It grieves both myself and the Lord to know that these truths are kept from the American people."

I can't let him turn this into another one of his damned sermons, Steve thought. He decided to launch a frontal attack—and see what response it drew from the driver. "You mentioned witchcraft. I suppose you mean telepathy."

"An old wine in a new bottle, my child," Fountain said. "The scientists may have dressed it in antiseptic words, but this 'telepathy' is still magic of the blackest kind. It is evil."

"So is murder," Steve said. "Do you know how many mind readers have been murdered lately?"

"None, my child. It's not murder to enforce God's laws." Steve saw that his smile never wavered. "It is written, 'thou shall not suffer a witch to live.' "

"The courts call it murder."

"The *secular* courts do, but their days are numbered. We are in the End Times. The Lord will return soon." Fountain nodded to himself. "These witches, with their strange powers, are the false prophets described in the Gospel of Saint Matthew. You see, my child, this is the last full year of the world. Next year will see signs and wonders in the heavens. After that, the Lord has told me to await the Apocalypse."

Steve saw the driver smile tartly. If I had any doubts about him, Steve thought, that smile would settle them. No genuine Redeemer would have smiled that way, or risked letting Fountain see that mocking smirk. Fountain had already prophesied the end of the world twice, but his followers were content to forget that those Doomsdays had come and gone without incident.

First things first, Steve thought. "I imagine that the Apocalypse will change a lot of things," he said, straining to keep the irony out of his voice. "There won't be any politics or elections in heaven, will there?"

"Of course not, my child." Fountain beamed. "Heaven is the *kingdom* of God. There's no place in it for mob rule."

"And with the end of the world coming, this year's elections won't matter, will they?"

"Well, that's far from the truth," Fountain said gravely. "God commands us to show our faith in all matters. That includes voting for those who support God's works. We are to give them whatever they need—and that includes fair and unbiased reporting, my child."

My child, my child, Steve thought in irritation. The mannerism grated on him. "You seem to display your faith through a very few politicians."

"These are evil times. Few men have the faith that transcends party politics."

"Does anyone in the Iron Guard have that faith?" Steve asked. The driver frowned and sat upright at the question, while the bodyguard took a half-step forward. Steve tensed, glanced at the door, wondered just how sensitive a nerve he'd struck.

Fountain remained oblivious to the upset around him. "I've led my children of the Iron Guard to our Redeemer. They've repented their sins and come to my aid in the Lord's work—although, for a time, they must conceal this from the eyes of the wicked."

"When will they reveal themselves?" Steve asked.

"Within a few months, my child. Certainly by November."

In time for the election, Steve noted. "Will you support their candidate for the Presidency?"

"I think that goes without saying, my child."

"Will you donate campaign funds?"

"As much as they need. This election is a skirmish in the battle of Armageddon. The Lord and I want our forces to win."

The driver looked to the bodyguard and nodded curtly. The guard bent over and hissed something in Fountain's ear. "My child," he said, standing, "my time grows short. I know you are of the unrighteous, but I will ask God to open your eyes." He departed at once, accompanied by the guard.

The driver chuckled after the door clicked shut. "And what did you think of our pet holy man?"

"Not much," Steve said, trying to match the cynicism in his voice. "Look, we're both adults. I know you didn't bring me here to listen to that pious dribble."

The driver smiled, showing perfect capped teeth. "Why do you suppose I brought you here?"

"Good question." Steve gestured at Fountain's chair. "It wasn't for him, although it's interesting to learn that the IG has Fountain under its thumb—"

The man frowned sharply. "What makes you say that?"

"Come off it!" Steve snapped. "Fountain may not realize he's being manipulated, but we both know *you* called the shots here."

"You're sharper than I thought." The man got out of

his seat, walked across the office, leaned against the door. "Much sharper. I wonder just how wrong I've been about you." His lips compressed into a thin line.

He's testing me, Steve thought, and I hope to God I pass. He was acutely aware of Mrs. Daniels' warning. "It depends on what you think. If you think I'm impressed by threats, or charades, guess again."

"I see." All at once he smiled at Steve. "Magyar, I like a man who speaks his mind. You're tough and you've got guts. I can do business with you."

Steve felt relief, and he knew it showed. "The question is, who am *I* doing business with?"

The glasses and mustache came off. "Savoy."

"I see." Steve's memory focused on the name. Savoy. Gerald Grofaz Savoy, failed businessman, suspected drug dealer, known murderer. He had gone bankrupt in 1992, along with many other people. Unlike others, he had killed a bank official when a loan company had tried to collect a debt. He had escaped conviction on a technicality—aided, according to one account, by a midnight assault on a juror's daughter. He had joined the militant wing of the Iron Guard in 1995, and risen swiftly. "You're one of the IG's leaders," Steve said.

"*One* of them." He tucked the sunglasses into a pocket. "You know a lot about us." He made the statement sound like an accusation.

Steve wondered how much to risk telling. "I know you have something going with Transpac."

"That's possible," he said vaguely.

"Even with the way the IG has condemned Transpac?"

"Well . . ." He smiled warmly. "We've cleared up our misunderstandings. We may not see eye to eye on some details, but we can get along now."

"Really? Just a few weeks ago you wanted to hang everyone in Transpac—"

"Not me!" Savoy flared. "*I* never wanted to do that, and neither has the Guard. Sure, we've had a few irresponsible men shoot their mouths off, but what group doesn't have members like that? The news media?" He shook his head in anger. "I'll tell you something, Magyar, men like me have a hard time keeping the fire-eaters in line. Each time you reporters publicize them you feed their egos, and that makes my work harder."

Steve bridled. "You can't expect us to ignore—"

Savoy held up his hands in a placating gesture. "Oh, I know, it's your job to report what happens. But you can understand how I feel about being between a rock and a hard place."

Steve scratched his chin. Savoy's rapid mood swings unsettled him—a calculated effect, he felt certain. "I know you belong to the militant wing of the Guard—"

"Not anymore." Savoy chewed his lip. "You know my record, I suppose. I *was* pretty far out, but after a while I saw the futility of extremism. I'd have to say I'm a moderate now. Maybe I've mellowed in my old age— hell, I'm almost fifty."

"Can a moderate man support the Iron Guard's doctrines? They don't strike me as moderate."

"They're more *moderate* than letting this Depression grind on," Savoy countered. "Take our plan to nationalize the energy industries. That sounds radical, right? Even communistic?"

"You said it," Steve commented dryly.

"Well, it's not," Savoy insisted. "Nationalization would take the excess profits away from the greedy few. The revenues would go to pay off the national debt. That would reduce inflation and stimulate the economy. We could slash energy prices in half. With cheap energy, industry and employment would pick up. America would be on her feet again at once. At once!"

Steve looked dubious. "How do the energy magnates in Transpac feel about having their property confiscated?"

"Unhappy. Very unhappy." Savoy smiled like a cherub, then sobered. "But they realize that the resources belong to the nation. They know that the taxpayers and consumers paid for the reactors and refineries. They'll cooperate if they want to keep anything."

That's the sort of talk people want to hear these days, Steve thought. It sounded practical, and reasonable

. . . but there was more than that to the Iron Guard. "Why are you hunting witches?"

"We don't do that," Savoy said. "All we do is offer a reward to anyone who helps apprehend a rogue witch. That's the best way to get people after them—and it's more than the MHB does."

"That doesn't answer my question," Steve said. "What's so important about harmless lunatics?"

" '*Harmless*'? They're anything but harmless!" A dark sincerity spread into his voice. "They've joined the conspiracy to destroy freedom. They've made secret deals with the bankers and the bigots to increase their power. They want the Depression to continue because they thrive on pain and misery, like some sort of emotional vampires. Most of all, they want to control the way we think."

"Have you got *proof*?" Steve asked.

"Can't you see it for yourself?" Savoy said. "There's Lyn Clancy and her witch's Bible. That Reese bitch tries to convince everyone that ESP is 'only' a scientific curiosity, instead of something worse. Julian Forrest has been running all over the country, subverting good people to *his* way of thinking and making them doubt what they're told is true. I don't know what sort of power he has over people, but that bastard of a freak has even corrupted some Iron Guard members—"

"Who?" Steve asked. When Savoy shook his head negligently, Steve realized that the men in question were dead and the subject was best dropped quickly. "What normal people are in the conspiracy?" he asked. "Let's hear you name names."

"I could, but it's not safe. We're preparing to expose them—but they have their telepathic spies everywhere. You'd put yourself in danger if you learned too much."

"I can take care of myself."

"I don't doubt it—but you don't know the score yet." Savoy patted his pocket. "I don't wear disguises because I enjoy dressing up. People have tried to kill me—and Fountain, too."

"Him? You're kidding. Who'd bother?"

"The conspirators." Savoy grimaced. "Neither of us thinks much of the old fool, but millions of people believe in him. He's the leader of an enormous bloc, and that makes him a target for the conspirators. They can't succeed until they destroy all of society's leaders, my child—"

"When you call me that, *smile*."

Savoy chuckled. "You should try talking with him for hours at a stretch. Oh, he's sincere, I'll give him that, and he wants what he thinks is best for America—but we're not here to talk about him. You guessed right on that score." Savoy crossed over to the desk and sat on its edge. As he clasped his hands on his knees, Steve noticed that his nails had been carefully manicured. "I've heard a lot of good things about you, and you write a good column—even when you're attacking the Guard. So when I heard you were investigating us, I decided to take a closer look at you."

"Oh? Why?"

"For one thing, I'd like to see you do a fair and accurate report on us."

"I planned to do that anyway—on my own terms."

"I was counting on that. *I* know that an honest report would be favorable to us, by and large. Aside from that, though, there's the matter of your future. Your talents are wasted on reporting local elections and political breakfasts."

"I'm not certain I understand you." Steve kept his voice carefully neutral.

"I'm not asking you to compromise your ethics," Savoy said. "I'm just asking you to do a full job, and inform the people about us. If you can show us some fair and accurate reporting in the next few months— well, we won't forget our friends after November."

"Do you seriously think the Iron Guard can win the Presidency?" Steve asked. "How?"

"The country is ready for us," he said. "It's that simple. Once we're in, we'll have a big job on our hands. You could find yourself with a lot of power."

"I'm not interested in power."

"Even better! Ambitious men are dangerous. I'd rather trust a man like you with the responsibility of managing the news."

"I see." It dawned on him that Savoy was offering him a position as the party's official speaker—or perhaps something more. The offer left him with mixed feelings. It was unlikely that the Iron Guard could win an election—but if it *did*—

"I'd say it's time to take you back." Savoy got off the desk. He went to the door, opened it, and stood there. As Steve stepped into the doorway, Savoy stopped him with a hand on his shoulder and plucked the recorder from his pocket. "You don't need this."

"The interview—"

"I can't risk letting this fall into the wrong hands." He snapped the card in half and dropped it. Memory colloids oozed onto the carpet. "I know your memory will be accurate."

"You're sure of that?" Steve asked sourly.

"I trust people who are on my side." He smiled. "You'll be glad you've joined the winning team, Magyar. Armageddon *is* coming. It's not the end of the world that Fountain expects—but it's coming a lot sooner than he ever imagined."

CHAPTER 6

Two members of the Investigatory Panel disagreed with our conclusions, stating their unsubstantiated beliefs that ESP and mental illness are not inextricably linked. When the rest of the Panel declined to consider this erroneous proposal, Doctors Howe and Li resigned in protest. As a result, our report is now backed unani-

*mously by the Panel, a fact which we hope will dispel
any lingering questions.*

*Our findings are that psi is a mental illness, specific-
ally, an idiopathic dysfunction, and thus 'psis' (the
accepted label for the patients in question) are legitimate subjects of MHB concern. We find that telepathy is
clearly related to a detrimental change in the structure
of the human brain. Diagnosis of a psi-positive patient
is easily made; treatment is not. Fortuitously, psis are
not violent, so there is no need for confinement, in most
cases. Registration, followed by regular observation as
outpatients, is considered an adequate means of con-
trolling psis.*

*This will mean extra work for the Mental Health
Bureau. The panel strongly recommends that we take on
this work. Appendix C of the report outlines the new
budgetary and personnel demands this expansion will
make. In certain areas, the MHB may need to double or
even triple its size.*

*—excerpt from an internal MHB report, dated 27
                                      January 1992.*

Farrier walked into Hutchins' office precisely at noon,
his face looking worn but confident. He must have
worked all night, Hutchins thought, as he looked up
from his desk. "What have you got on Sere?"

"Quite a bit." Farrier took a seat. "We performed a
medical examination on the LAPD's two detainees. They
didn't know much, but they gave us enough to fill in
the picture." He stopped.

Medical examination, indeed, Hutchins thought. The
euphemism bothered him as much as Farrier's dramatic
pause. "What's the picture?"

"It's about what I expected. Sere plans an insurrec-
tion, to coincide with the start of the renewal project."
Farrier looked oddly satisfied. "Sere has mobilized at
least three dozen platoon-sized units, and armed them
with automatic weapons, grenades, mortars, even
shoulder-fired anti-aircraft rockets."

Hutchins whistled. "Where did they get all that?"

"On the black market. Most of the funds came through

drug deals, so Sere would have plenty of contacts there. I estimate that they have enough ammo to supply an infantry brigade for a full-scale battle against regular forces. In an urban-guerrilla conflict—" Farrier shook his head. "They have enough Stinger missiles to shoot down every helicopter the LAPD has."

"Any leads on where they cached the weapons?"

"No. Our prisoners only know that they have several arsenals in different locations."

"Anything else?" Hutchins asked.

"Just one thing. Our detainees had contacts with the Sere Directorate, but those contacts vanished the other day."

"They've gone under deep cover, then. Ominous."

"Yes. They won't surface until the war begins—unless we upset their plans. Which we will." Farrier permitted himself a tight smile, and consulted his watch. "I understand that you have an appointment with the MHB's regional coordinator. Mind if I tag along?"

So he *does* monitor me, Hutchins thought. "Shouldn't you work on finding those arsenals?"

"I've already put things in motion," Farrier said, as they got up. "I had to kick a few butts, but I'll get results."

"Lou, I wish you'd lay off the high-pressure tactics."

"I wish I could. Chief, I don't know about the other CTO districts, but out here we have a morale problem. Too many of my people are complacent. They don't understand what you and I know—that the American government is in danger of collapsing."

"And it just might," Hutchins conceded, as they walked out of the office. "But there are better ways of breaking people out of their ruts."

"Those ways take time. Sere won't wait for us." He shrugged. "To hell with that. Have you decided what you want from the MHB?"

"I'm going to get them to take over this witch-hunting crap," he said. "Then I'm going to convince the President that the matter is in more appropriate hands. Failing that, Chennault may have some suggestions that could help us."

"You may have trouble getting the MHB to play along. I had the devil's own time getting those files from them." He held up a hand before Hutchins could speak. "I was on my best behavior. The trouble is that Dr. Chennault won't work with outsiders. It's her policy. I had to go to her assistant for some unofficial help."

Interesting that he's telling me this now, Hutchins mused. He wondered if Farrier was covering an error he'd made, or if he had something new planned.

An elevator took them to the MHB's office complex, where a receptionist ushered them into the Coordinator's office. As Hutchins entered Evangeline Chennault's office he was struck by its austerity: the harsh white walls, the metal desk, the worn tiles on the floor. Hutchins had a sudden intuition that this prim, severe-looking woman would prove as intractable as Farrier had warned.

"I understand you're interested in telepaths, Mr. Hutchins," Chennault began, after they had exchanged greetings.

"We need to detain a few of them." Hutchins reached into his pocket, drew out a list of names, and handed them to her. "It's a matter of national security; we're working on Presidential orders. We're here because we need help."

Chennault frowned at the list. "Catching psis is a difficult proposition at best—especially these people."

Farrier grunted. "We didn't come here for you to tell us it's impossible."

"I didn't say it's impossible," Chennault said, putting the list aside. "But it might as well be. Last year we tried to detain over two hundred fugitive psis. We caught five. They're quite good at eluding capture."

"Is that a psychic power?" Hutchins asked.

"Is intelligence a psychic power?" she countered. "The *average* psi has an IQ of 130. The lowest figure on record is 114. Telepathy may let them spot our traps, but it takes intelligence to get out of them—and they have a strong incentive to escape."

"What's that?" Farrier asked.

"Psis have an almost supernatural terror of confinement in mental hospitals."

There's a weakness we might exploit, Hutchins thought. "Can you explain that?"

"I'm afraid not." Chennault sighed. "There's a lot that we don't know about psis. We know that their powers drive them insane, and that at best they're only metastable. But beyond that . . ." She spread her hands. "There are so many unknowns that we're helpless."

"People have been studying ESP for years," Hutchins said. "Some things *must* be known by now."

"Well, they're not." Chennault sounded grimly amused. "Parapsychology is a dead field. Research funds are scarce these days, and the money doesn't go into controversial areas."

"The Redeemers," Farrier said knowingly.

"They're not the only problem. The environmentalists, the radicals, liberals—even some scientists oppose psi research. The subject frightens too many people."

"That's understandable," Hutchins said. "Telepathy is an automatic invasion of privacy. I don't see how you could fit witches into our society without causing a lot of trouble—but that's not a problem, is it?"

"Not when they always go insane." Chennault paused, a meditative look on her face. "There are some people who don't mind the loss of privacy. Sometimes we find them keeping company with psis."

"Exhibitionists?" Farrier asked.

"Not always," Chennault said. "Some of them think that ESP forms a link with the supernatural, or that they can develop their own ESP. It's hard to describe their motives, but they do make trouble. They help psis flaunt our regulations and escape capture."

"Interesting," Farrier murmured, in a tone which surprised Hutchins. "How many people are involved in this?"

"I couldn't say," Chennault admitted. "We've never looked into it too deeply. Psis aren't our real business."

"They fall under your jurisdiction," Farrier said.

"Only through a technicality."

"That *technicality* has been upheld by the Supreme Court," Farrier said. "Legally, and by your own admission, witches are *non compos mentis*. The Compton Act requires you to look after *all* individuals who have been certified as mentally incompetent, not just the ones who've committed crimes."

"I know how the Act is phrased," Chennault said in annoyance. "As a matter of reality, the MHB is here to protect the public from the criminally insane. If it were up to me, that would be our *only* task."

"It isn't up to you," Farrier said curtly.

"I know." Chennault looked at him, fixing her eyes on the brainwave scanner in his pocket. She seemed to verge on making a comment before shaking her head. "It isn't up to you, either. I know where our priorities lie, and I do my best to keep them in mind."

"That's not always easy," Hutchins said, half to himself.

"No, it's not. The MHB is under a lot of pressure. There are people who want us to suppress psis, or remove mentally ill street people from their cities, or shut down halfway houses in their neighborhoods—" Chennault grimaced. "And we have to respond, because the law requires it."

"I can sympathize," Hutchins said, "but I still have my orders. Doctor, this is an official request for help."

"The only help I can give you is advice. I can't spare anyone from my work force. We're stretched thin already."

"Is that your last word?" Farrier asked.

"It is." She nodded at the door, a curt gesture of dismissal. "Good day."

"I'll have to go over her head," Hutchins said, after he and Farrier had left the office.

"That won't help," Farrier said. "Even if she gets a direct order from the President, she'll find a way to circumvent it."

"Yes," Hutchins said. "I wish I could hold it against her, but she's right. The MHB exists to handle felons, not freaks."

"Bull! The MHB is a government agency. It exists to take orders."

"But not from us. We're back to square one."

Farrier smiled slightly. "Maybe not. If you can spare a few minutes, I know someone who can help us."

Hutchins felt sour. "The assistant you mentioned?"

"He's eager to help. This way, Chief."

Farrier led Hutchins to another office in the complex. *Alan Blaine*, the door nameplate read, *Assistant Regional Coordinator*. "Is Al busy?" Hutchins asked the secretary outside the door.

"I'll check, sir." The woman smiled as she consulted her terminal. Hutchins noted how Farrier seemed to warm up, a transition that puzzled him. Certainly the secretary, a parched woman with grizzled hair, wasn't enough to provoke such a change.

Hutchins found himself in an office slightly smaller than Chennault's, shaking hands with a man who seemed on excellent terms with Farrier. "You were right on the mark about Chennault," Farrier told Blaine. "We just had a run-in with her."

Blaine nodded. "I told you she has a one-track mind. What happened, Bear?"

"Just what you predicted. She turned us down cold, and implied that catching witches was close to impossible."

Blaine chuckled. "I'm not surprised."

"Yesterday you suggested it can be done."

"Not with our present techniques. We could do it if we innovated."

As thick as thieves, Hutchins thought suddenly. The saying had been a favorite of his father's, and the obvious harmony between Farrier and Blaine brought it to mind. "I take it you have something in mind," Hutchins said.

"I do," Blaine said, "but I can't act on my ideas. Dr. Chennault insists that we concentrate on the CDs—the criminally dysfunctional. I'm afraid it's a blind spot with her," he added apologetically.

"One that you don't share," Hutchins said.

Blaine pursed his lips. "I don't have Dr. Chennault's interest in the matter. She's a good psychologist, a good administrator, but she's emotionally involved."

"How so? Is one of her relatives a telepath?"

"No, nothing like *that*," Blaine said. He leaned back in his chair, a distracted look on his face. "Back in '85, her daughter was murdered—brutally. The killer was caught at once. There was no question about his guilt. He went on trial, and was acquitted. Not guilty by reason of temporary insanity."

"I thought it was something like that," Farrier mused.

"Yes. The killer was institutionalized for observation and therapy. A year later he convinced a psychiatrist that he was cured. Sane. He was released. He was hardly out the door before he killed somebody else's daughter. That sort of thing happened all the time, you remember."

Hutchins rubbed his chin. "You're suggesting that Dr. Chennault uses her post to pursue a vendetta."

"No, not at all," Blaine said hastily. "She's not vindictive. Her experience makes her dedicated to our main task; it's why she joined the MHB. The trouble is that her dedication gives her a narrow view of our duties."

Hearing the sympathetic tone in Blaine's voice, Hutchins felt a sharp distaste for him. Despite that, he saw how the man could prove useful. "What can you tell me about Julian Forrest?"

"Forrest." Blaine scowled. "Forrest has a real attitude problem. He makes a habit of confronting members of the Redemptive Faith, among other groups, and arguing with them. He also persuades other psis to drop out of sight, and he talks normal people into aiding them. We have plenty of reports on his activities. Dr. Chennault has let him embarrass us for too long."

"How would you go about catching him?" Farrier asked. "Or any other witch, for that matter?"

"I'd give our field agents some police training and non-lethal weapons. It's a small change, but it would have enormous results. Unfortunately, some of our top administrators feel that a medical organization should limit itself to passive tools and techniques."

He's pushing his dislike of Chennault hard, Hutchins thought. "Would it work? If they're as elusive as Dr. Chennault claims—"

"The crackpots have no trouble finding and shooting them, you know. We'd get results if we started using stunners and gasses."

"It's a lot of trouble just to bag some witches."

"Psis aren't our only troublemakers," Blaine said. "A lot of our field workers get injured making pick-ups. Sometimes one of the criminally insane gets loose. It's an enormous problem."

"But you *could* catch witches," Farrier prompted.

"Easily. We get reports on their locations all the time, from law-abiding citizens, so finding them is easy. If you like, I could relay these reports to your office when they come in."

"That would help," Hutchins said. "It would also help if we had some way to predict what these witches will do."

"Impossible," Blaine said. "Telepathy is an idiopathic dysfunction. In layman's terms, that means it doesn't follow any set pattern. Some psis behave almost normally for long times. Some don't. There's no way to tell what they'll do as their condition gets worse. They're almost as unpredictable as normal people."

"I see," Hutchins said, getting up. "Thank you for your time."

"My pleasure."

Hutchins waited until he and Farrier were in the elevator before he spoke. "It's obvious what he wants."

"Chennault's job," Farrier agreed. "And it's to our advantage if he gets it. He's eager to start hunting witches."

"What makes you think so?"

"Simple. The Compton Act has been a success. Criminals have stopped using the insanity defense; it doesn't pay."

"Which was the whole idea in the first place."

"True," Farrier said, "but this success is working against the MHB. They're running out of customers. Unless they branch out, Congress will cut their work force and budget down to a more reasonable size. Blaine doesn't want that."

The bureaucratic imperative, Hutchins thought. Expand or die. He faced the elevator door as he spoke. "You want me to pull strings and replace Chennault with your friend."

"He's not my friend," Farrier said. "He's a means to an end. Pull strings, and let him get to work. One of the first things he'll do is protest our infringement on his duties. That'll give us the chance to get out of this mess."

"I don't know," Hutchins said. He disliked Chennault, but he had to respect her position. She wanted to do her job, not feather her nest.

He listened to the slow creakings of the elevator while he thought over the plan. It was clever, and if it failed it would cost Farrier nothing. If anyone resented what happened to Chennault, Hutchins would take the blame. Clever, indeed. He wondered if this was some part of Farrier's own plans.

"It's our best option," Farrier said, as if sensing his misgivings.

"I'm aware of that." Hutchins reminded himself that it was his duty to defend the country, not to waste time on crack-brained witch hunts. It was unfortunate that Chennault would have to pay the price of that duty . . . along with the witches.

CHAPTER 7

WEDNESDAY, 14 JUNE 2000

Some crystalline structures resonate to radio waves, which is why the first radio receivers used galena crystals as detectors. They were tuned by touching a slender wire—known as a cat-whisker—to the surface of the crystal. An operator would tweak the cat-whisker over the surface of the crystal until he picked up an adequate signal. In the 1920s, radio operators in the U.S. Navy found that they could make their radios much more sensitive by using two cat-whiskers. This fact became something of a trade secret.

The pineal body, buried deep in the brain, is sensitive to light—and to other forms of electromagnetic radiation. The pineal controls our biological clock by responding to the length of the day and the phases of the moon. Exposure to certain forms of E-M radiation, such as the fields which surround high-voltage Power lines, can stimulate the pineal, leading to health problems— which is how this was discovered. It is evident that the pineal can also detect the so-called 'bio-electric' fields which all human beings generate, much like a remote EEG sensor.

In the normal human brain, the pineal is connected to the rest of the brain by a single set of neurons. Mutation has caused this set to double itself in a few brains. This turns the pineal into a sensory organ. People with this mutation—telepathics—are able to sense the thoughts of other people. The energy levels are on the microwatt and picowatt level, and even less, which is comparable to the strength of the sound waves detected

72

*by the ear. The analogy with those crystal radios is
obvious. The double set of neurons act as an amplifier.*

*The analogy is also tragic. Those early radio opera-
tors unwittingly invented the transistor. If contempo-
rary scientists had investigated their discovery, there
could have been profound changes in the course of
science—and history. How much are we losing now by
ignoring telepathy?*

*—seminar speech made by Lyman A. Grant, Ph.D.,
16 October 1997*

Birche woke to the sound of knocking at her door.
Before she could get up, the door popped open and two
MHB agents entered her apartment. "Birche Holstein?"
the tall one asked.

Birche nodded dumbly, sitting up on the edge of her
bed. It was happening at last, and she was surprised at
the *relief* she felt. No more hiding, no more lying. "Can
I get dressed before you take me in?"

"We're not taking you in," the short one said. "We
already know about you. We're here to discuss your
duties, ma'am."

" 'Duties'? What duties?"

The tall one smiled politely. "You're a telepath—the
next stage of human evolution. As such you have grave
responsibilities, Ms. Holstein."

"But—the MHB, the Compton Act—"

"Window dressing, ma'am. Most of us normal people
resent our superiors. People don't like to think they're
going the way of the dinosaur and the dodo."

"I'm no damned superbeing." Birche shook her head
at the idiocy—shook it again, more violently—

She woke up in bed, soaked in sweat and her hair
tangled over her face from her thrashing. Damned nightmares, she thought. She always had them when she was
under stress.

She sat up, shaking. Delusions of grandeur, Birche
thought. It was easy to see the signs of madness in the
nightmare. It was the sort of dream only a Napoleon
could have enjoyed.

The nightmare seemed to have sharpened her psi sense, much as a hangover seems to make every noise painfully loud. The people in apartment 8-A were practicing an unimaginative variation on something they'd found in the *Kama Sutra*. Down the hall, the party in 30-B was revolving around a role-playing game called *Crossed Channels*. They had just drawn their character cards, and now Captain Kirk and Gidget were preparing to cross wits with J.R. Ewing and Gilligan. The insomniac in the room above her was staring at the Late Show: a movie about an inevitably evil telepath who was destroying a family by revealing its darkest secrets. Having seen a dozen movies with the same plot, Birche knew that the witch would meet her end in a flaming auto wreck.

After brushing out her hair, Birche pulled on her sweatsuit and went to the exercise machine in the corner of her shoebox apartment. She adjusted the springs to maximum tension and went to work. A good workout made it impossible for her to worry about matters she couldn't control. Birche had discovered that trick in high school, when she had been forced to cope with a growing sense of isolation from her friends and family. The temporary escape of exercise helped her put things into perspective.

It wasn't working this time. As she finished a set of shoulder-shrugs, Birche found her eyes going to the bookshelves. When she had come home she had placed Julian's gift there, hiding it among the motley collection of college texts, classics, and health books. The Purloined Letter technique, she thought—but the book's taped-over spine seemed to stand out like a beacon, signaling what she was.

Am I really that afraid? she wondered.

Julian hadn't seemed afraid, and Birche found that she resented that. He had adapted to what he was, and even enjoyed it. The glimpse she had taken into his mind had proven that beyond argument—as well as the fact that he thought she was beautiful. He confused her, yes, but he was not afraid, and not crazy.

Birche tapped Steve's thoughts as he came up the stairs. She got up from the flexibar and went to the door, opening it as Steve was about to knock. "Steve, are you all right?" she asked, as she let him in.

"Yes, I'm fine." He sat down on her sofa. "Why do you ask?"

"Well . . . you seem—I don't know." Outwardly, he looked as perfect and leanly handsome as ever, but she could sense some inner tension, something that escaped understanding. "What did you do today?"

"Well, I met Perry Fountain."

"Fountain? Why?" She sat down next to him.

"It wasn't my idea. The meeting was arranged to impress me—arranged by the Iron Guard. They've got Fountain under their control, and they've done it so well that the idiot doesn't know it. I was right; this alliance with the Redeemers is a sham. The IG is milking them for campaign funds."

"What about Transpac?"

"I still don't know what the connection is—but that's not important. I met one of the Iron Guard's leaders. He was there to examine *me*."

That's what upset him, she decided. She found herself probing for details, clumsily and hesitantly, in the hope of finding something that would help him. "What did he want?"

"A sympathetic voice in the press."

"And Savoy threatened you if he didn't get it."

"Not directly. He was menacing, but that was just a game, to see if I'd chicken out."

"He took your recorder."

"Yes, but that happens all the time," Steve said. "He didn't get the one in my wallet. The trouble is, it's a low-quality recording. The computer gave only a seventy-six percent probability that those were actually Fountain's and Savoy's voices, so I can't prove anything."

"That's not what's bothering you. Savoy offered you something." Birche watched his jerk of surprise. "What was it?"

"Damn it, kid, do you have to do that?"

"Read your mind? Steve, I'm just trying to help you. What he offered bothers you. What was it?"

"Well—it's silly. If Savoy likes what I report about the IG, he'll offer me a job as the party's press secretary."

"Steve, it was a lot more than that." Part of the problem became clear. "That's it. Savoy expects to be elected president. You think he has a chance—"

"*He* thinks he has a chance. I don't know what I think." He seemed at a loss for words. "Savoy has an attitude, a confidence. He takes it for granted he'll win. There's something . . . infectious, I guess, about a man like that."

"It takes more than that to win an election," Birche said. "The IG is too radical—"

"No, they're not. Their doctrines . . ." He shook his head and settled back on the sofa cushions.

"How much do you really know about them?" she asked.

"I read about them a few months ago."

He's lying, she realized, as she tapped incoherent bits of memory and fitted them together. After his meeting with Savoy, Steve had returned to his office . . . used the computer library to find the Iron Guard's party platform . . . convinced himself that it was plausible, perhaps even workable. As he had read it, Steve found himself willing to overlook the Iron Guard's past.

Steve was still speaking. Birche concentrated on his voice, fighting against the disorientation of psychic contact. ". . . plans to reduce inflation, unemployment, taxes, and the deficit. They'll fight crime, strengthen defense, and suppress the radicals—right-wing and left-wing. Some of their maneuvers look unorthodox, but when you see them laid out step by step, they're amazingly rational and ingenious."

Birche peered at the man. "Does that include witch hunting?"

"That's just something they're doing to please Fountain, and to distract their radicals while the moderates ease them out of power. It'll end in a few months."

"That's not what Savoy said. He—"

"I know what he said! But it's obvious what's going on. Savoy and the other moderates need Fountain for his money. They need to get rid of the radicals because they're a liability to anyone in mainstream politics. Savoy talked about a conspiracy, but that was just hyperbole. He *is* pretty flamboyant."

"What's gotten into you?" Birche demanded. "I thought—"

"That I hated the Guard?" He nodded without looking at her. "I did. I still hate a lot of the things they've done—but parties are like people, kid. They change. Times change."

"Like you," Birche said. "What happened to the dedicated, objective reporter I knew? You sound like you've joined them!"

"I haven't," he said coldly. "I'm just facing reality. Savoy is moving the Guard closer to the political center. That will give them a better chance of winning in November. It's a longshot, but it wouldn't be such a bad thing if they won."

"Especially if you worked for them. Yes." Birche nodded absently. "Right now Savoy needs a good propagandist, but he'll also need someone to 'manage' the news after he takes over. You'd like to—"

"Stop that!" he barked.

"Take it easy." Birche reached out, put her hands on his shoulders and began massaging them. The tautness in his muscles startled her. "I'm just trying to help."

He shrugged off her hands and stood. "I don't need that sort of help."

"You needed it when you asked me to find Julian for you."

"That was different."

"Because it didn't involve reading your mind?"

"No, because it was something between two witches," Steve said, looking down at her. "It's different when you use telepathy on normal people."

"Except when *you* ask me to use it," she said, her face flushing.

"That's different."

"Everything's different with you."

He shot her a cold look. "I mean that it has to be done to get the news. Sometimes you have to make compromises."

"You can tell that to Julian tomorrow night." She glanced at the clock. It was one-fifteen. "Make that tonight. He'll be here at nine."

"I don't need to see him now." He turned his back on her.

Birche felt anger as her hands clenched on her lap. "Steve, he took a big chance when he saw me this morning. He'll take another chance coming here—"

"Then tell him not to come," Steve said. "I already know why the IG is hunting freaks."

"But why won't you at least see Julian?" Birche demanded. "You're always looking for a good story. Don't underdogs make good copy?"

"Not this time. My editor said she'd kill anything I filed on him. It's her judgment that freaks aren't newsworthy." He looked over his shoulder at her. "And—I think she knows about you. She made a passing comment about credibility and reliance on ESP."

"I thought you said no one knows what I am."

"I could be wrong. I've taken you to public functions, like the Governor's Ball and the city council brunches, and you keep screwing up at them."

Birche stood up and glared at his back. "And I've given you a lot of leads."

"You haven't given me all that many, kid, and I've always had to double-check them before I could use them."

"That isn't my name," she heard herself say.

"I know your name," he said in annoyance.

"Do you? How's it spelled? No, you left out the 'E.' But then, you never use my name, so what's the difference?"

He turned around and looked at her. "I use your name—"

"When?" she demanded. "Have you ever told anyone about me? If one of your friends asked, could you tell them I have an MBA and a minor in English literature? Or that I almost made the '96 Olympics?" She jerked a thumb at a small shelf of swimming trophies. "You're proud of your journalism awards. You never asked how I earned *those*—"

"Calm down!"

"Why? So I can go back to being your tame witch?"

"All you're doing, *Birche,* is making a scene."

"Damn straight," she said, "and you're scared to death that *you* might get in trouble. Well, you're already *in* more trouble than you can handle!"

Steve took a step toward her. "If you think you can threaten *me*—"

"Threaten, hell. I'm going to do something worse." She stopped, realizing how close he had come to threatening to turn her in to the MHB. It shocked her to discover that he was so *shallow.* "I'm going to do you a *favor.* I'm going to tell you why Savoy's offer scared you. You're scared because you want to accept it."

"That's a lie!"

"Really? You're ambitious. You think the IG has a fair chance of winning the election. Just in case they do, you want to keep your options open."

"And you read that in my mind?"

"No." Birche tried to clamp down on her indignation. "Have you listened to yourself, Steve? Yesterday you were all that stood between the IG and civilization. Remember? Now you sound like some smarmy political hack. The only thing that keeps you from making a complete flip-flop is your conscience. If you—"

"That's enough!" He clutched at his head. "Get out of my mind, you fat freak!"

"I'm not in it." Birche felt her nerve giving way, fought to hold on to it. There'd been a sharp note of panic in his voice; Steve might do anything now.

She saw that she was standing between him and the door. She stepped aside. "Think of this as a going-away present, Steve. If you talk with anyone about Savoy's offer, they'll know how close you are to accepting. It's that obvious."

He left, with a door-slam that made her wince.

Birche walked into the kitchenette. In the moonlight she could see the carport roof under her window and the blank concrete wall across the alley. The glass mirrored her: a short, rounded woman in a loose gray sweatsuit.

"Jackass," she told her reflection. She'd meant to help Steve, but she had probably thrust him into the arms of the Iron Guard. More to the point, she had just lost what protection she'd had from the MHB. That would scare me if I had any sense, she thought.

Birche wondered how she could have been so wrong about Steve. She had never known that anyone could turn on her so quickly, so thoroughly. She wanted to tell herself that he'd reacted without thought, but she knew better. He'd already decided that she was a liability, and had made plans to free himself of her. His only concern had been that she would tell someone about their arrangement.

And—*fat freak*. He'd known how much that would hurt when he said it. He'd chosen those words with deliberate care.

She turned away from the window and went back into the main room. It was only a matter of time before somebody reported her to the MHB again. Whether it happened tomorrow or next year, it *would* happen, and she ought to prepare for it. She had a good lawyer; he might know a way to outfox the MHB. Birche made a mental note to call him, first thing in the morning.

Birche took the copy of *Sense and Non-sense* from the bookshelf and sat down with it. The notion of developing her talent filled her with apprehension, but there was no point in holding back.

On an impulse she flipped to the back of the book, and found an appendix on self-hypnosis. As a key to making the change, that was disappointingly simple, but the explanation made sense as she read it. Fear and misunderstanding kept most novice telepaths from using the talent; the only trick to learning was lowering those barriers. The inability to make full use of the talent was a psychosomatic condition, very much like hysterical paralysis. The easiest solution was to relax through autohypnosis.

There must be more to it, Birche thought. The instructions were short and clear, but *nothing* was ever that simple. She reread the appendix several times, slowly, looking for a catch. She couldn't find one, and yet—

The pounding at her door startled her. "Birche Holstein?" The deep, powerful voice matched the pounding. "Birche Holstein, are you in there?"

"Just a minute," Birche said loudly. Who would want to see her at this time of night? she wondered. "Who are you?"

"Open the door!" The pounding got louder. "We're from the MHB. Open the door or we'll break it down!"

They really are from the MHB, she thought—and this time it was no dream. She pulled the door open and saw two men in the blue uniforms of MHB field orderlies. "What do you want?"

"We have orders to detain you for observation."

Birche hesitated, caught in a moment of surprise. His lips hadn't moved; he'd *thought* to her. The pounding and the doomsday voice had been *thoughts*, a simple trick to prove that she was a telepath.

Birche rallied quickly. "Let me see those 'orders,' " she demanded.

"We don't have to do that," the man said. "Come with us."

Birche got ready to slam the door. *"Prove* you're from the MHB. For all I know, you—"

"Okay," the second man said tiredly. Without hesitation they pushed into her apartment, grabbed her by the arms, and spun her face-first against the wall. Birche grunted with pain as they twisted her arms against her back. She heard a quick clicking as cuffs were snapped around her wrists.

Strong hands clamped onto her elbows, pulled her into the corridor. Birche stumbled along between the two men, struggling to keep her balance as they led her down the stairs. As they marched her through the apartment building's courtyard, Birche sensed some of her neighbors watching the action. They knew what this meant, and it scared them.

Afraid of me? Birche wondered, feeling an inexplicable sense of detachment. The answer came to her slowly, as if forcing its way through some mental resistance: no, not her. The MHB. They had no reason to fear arrest by the MHB . . . but its power scared them.

The orderlies had arrived in a van that they had parked in front of the building. The light bar on its roof flashed methodically as the MHB agents opened the side door and guided her onto a seat. One of them pushed her head down with his hand, to keep her from striking it on the edge of the door. The gesture was meant to protect her, but it was carried out with an indifference that made it humiliating. A stray thought told Birche that if she was injured the man would face the *annoyance* of filling out a report.

A seat belt was drawn across her lap. A moment later the van pulled away from the curb, and the acceleration pushed her into the seat cushions. With her hands locked behind her back that was uncomfortable, and she had trouble remaining upright as the van turned corners and stopped for traffic lights.

The orderlies chatted quietly, oblivious to her presence. "I thought the graveyard shift was supposed to be quiet," one said.

"It usually is," the driver said, "but Fountain's in town this week. We always get more Halloween calls when some bible-thumper makes the rounds."

"Well, why can't they call the day shift or the swing shift?" the other man asked querulously. "With the way we're understaffed at night—"

"Yeah, it's a pain in the butt," the driver agreed, "but these calls usually come in at night. Maybe the Halloweeners get scared when the sun goes down."

"Maybe they're ashamed to do it during the day," Birche said. She recalled a bit of advice she had read about kidnappings: when abducted, strike up a dialogue with the kidnappers. Force them to deal with you, to see you as a person. It made them more likely to slip up, which might give her a chance to escape.

It didn't work. The men ignored her words as if they'd been the babblings of a lunatic. "Fountain's leaving town in a few days," the driver said. "Things will get back to normal then."

Normal, Birche thought bitterly, clenching her fists behind her back. She tried to move her arms, feeling a growing numbness in them as her position cut off her circulation. Things would never get back to normal for her.

No, that was wrong, she thought. From now on, *this* was normal.

CHAPTER 8

What does Sere want? We want to live close to Nature, like we were meant. We don't want chemicals in our bodies, giving us cancer and mutating our babies into freaks. We don't want capitalists to make us work for them and starve.

Most of all, we don't want intellectuals telling us stuff. We can all feel the truth, when they don't baffle our brains with bullshit. That's why we hate them more than polluters or capitalists or anything. They use big words to turn you away from what you feel is true.

—from The Sere Manifesto, *by John Dexter Granger. Photocopy publication, 1999(?)*

It was after midnight when Julian returned to the neighborhood. The riot had kept him pinned down for hours, and the side trip back to the mall had taken even more time. He had been forced to run a double gauntlet of rioters and police. That had been a tedious process, but not a dangerous one. Neither side had paid much attention to noncombatants, and Julian had dodged from hiding spot to hiding spot whenever he had sensed that no one was looking his way.

The neighborhood was brightly moonlit. Julian walked the sidewalks here slowly, mindful of cracks and holes in the concrete. Absently he noted that other people were watching him—other squatters, worried that he might be a cop or a rioter.

"*Julian!*" Malcolm came out of the shadows. "*Welcome back. How'd it go?*"

"*Fantastic. Birche is really something.*" A faint gleam caught his eye: something yellow on Malcolm's shoulder. An emblem? He was wearing a new, dark coat—

"*I got a job,*" Malcolm said proudly. "*There's a little shopping mall a mile from here. After you left this morning I got an idea and went there.*"

"*And got a job as a security guard?*"

"*Well, as a spotter.*" Malcolm made a wry face. "*They wouldn't trust me with a stun gun. Anyway, I walked through the place for a while. Then I went into the manager's office, and told him I'd spotted three shoplifters his rent-a-cops had missed—and that the foreman on his loading dock was ripping him off.*"

"*And you parlayed that into a job,*" Julian said.

"*I damned near parlayed myself into the psycho ward. The manager almost called the MHB; telepaths give him the creeps. Or we did, I mean. His secretary was there, and she reminded him how much money the mall lost to theft and pilferage every week. All of a sudden I was his main man.*"

Julian smiled in the darkness. "*Not bad. Not bad at all.*"

"*It could be better. I'm only getting paid two-thirds of minimum wage, and it's all under the table.*"

"*Yeah.*" Julian could sense how that rankled. "*Well, it's a way around the Compton Act—and the IRS will never touch that money.*"

"*No, they won't.*" That brightened Malcolm's thoughts. The MHB, after all, was financed by taxes. "*Speaking of *good thoughts, what happened with you and the Holstein woman? The thea couldn't tell us much; you were too far away.*"

"Well . . . " They walked up the sidewalk to the coven's house. Julian pushed aside the thick blanket that covered the doorway and entered the candlelit living room. He found himself groping for words. "*Well . . . well—she's really something.*"

The thea laughed lightly. "*I hope you managed better than that when you saw her.*"

Julian shook his head. "*I don't think I did. It's hard to talk when you're tripping over your own tongue,*" he added.

"*You really fell for her,*" Jesse said.

"*And I made a fool of myself in the process.*"

"*Not to worry,*" Anita said. "*That's one of the things that makes men so charming.*"

The thea stood facing Julian. He noted how she seemed more mature, more self-assured. Things are going better here, he mused.

"*Don't change the subject,*" the thea ordered. "*You're concerned about the way you acted with her? Why? And don't tell me it's because 'she's really something.'*"

"Well, she is." Julian shook his head forcefully, as if trying to clear it. "*I've been in love before, but I've never fallen for anyone so hard or so fast.*"

"*Describe her,*" the thea said.

"*She's incredibly charming, and intelligent, and my God is she beautiful—*"

The thea looked impatient. "*You're not describing her. Start over. Use small words; I don't think you can handle anything else just now.*"

"*Free association?*" Julian suggested. "*Okay. Strong. Soft. Dynamic. Warm. Inviting, bright, cuddly, firm, vulnerable—I'm contradicting myself, aren't I?*"

"*Everyone's a contradiction, to some degree. Keep going.*"

"*She's like a diamond,*" Julian said. "*Bright and beautiful. Hard and sharp, but fragile along the cleavage planes. Cleavage—she's not stacked like Hazel, but they're perfect on her—"*

"You would think of that," Hazel said in amusement.

Julian blushed. "*I appreciate beauty.*"

"*She's pretty, too,*" the thea observed, tapping his memory. "*And I can see why you're having trouble describing her. She's exactly what you need.*"

That startled him. "*You don't make that sound like good news, lady. What's it mean?*"

"*She's the sort of woman who'd attract you no matter what, Julian, but the reason you've fallen so hard is because you're on the verge of a nervous breakdown. She's a way to help you keep your sanity.*"

"*I—*" Julian checked an urge to argue. It would have been pointless. After all, the thea was a part of him—but with an outsider's ability to analyze his thoughts.

He heard an indistinct whispering from the bedroom: Hazel, explaining things to Cliff. The man wasn't entirely at ease among telepaths, but to his surprise he had begun to fit in. The only thing that hampered him was an odd, confused sense of guilt.

Julian told himself to stick to the topic. "*You said Birche is what I need.*"

The thea nodded. "*You've been on the run for two years. You're strong, but no one can keep going forever. More than that, you find it harder and harder to cope with reality. Crazy people want to kill us all, and the people who should stop them say we're crazy. You can't accept a world that doesn't make sense—*" The thea stopped, looked first puzzled, then alarmed. "*Three men are coming here. They belong to Sere.*"

"*What do they want?*" Julian asked, as Cliff and Hazel came out of the bedroom. Julian strained at the thoughts around him, trying to pick out what he needed.

"What's going on?" Cliff asked.

"We've got company," Malcolm said. "Three people from Sere. They must be running away from—"

"*Three* people?" Cliff said. "And they're together?"

Julian nodded. He could tap one of their minds now. "They're not running. They're coming here—"

"Assassins," Cliff said. "An execution squad. Sere always sends its killers out in groups of three."

"You're sure?" Hazel asked.

"It's so they can watch one another," Cliff said. "Keep one another from chickening out or defecting to the cops. The Sere leaders don't trust anyone on their own." He looked to Julian. "They must be after you."

"Probably," Julian said absently, concentrating on the assassin's mind. "They'll be here in a minute."

"They won't split up," Cliff said quickly. "Only one of them has a gun—the leader. The others just have stunners. That's doctrine."

Julian nodded, and tapped a thought that puzzled him: *"The traitor. Find him and kill him. Kill the traitor."*

"Let's make it harder for them," Julian said. "Split up. Cliff, I'll stay with you."

"I'll slow you down," he said, as the others hurried out through doors and windows.

"No problem."

"You think Sere's after him," Hazel said.

"I don't know. It's crazy, but—"

"I'm staying with you."

"Okay." Julian pointed and spoke to Cliff. "They're out that way, two streets over. Let's go."

They went out the back door and stumbled through a yard choked with knee-high weeds. Julian realized that they were trampling a path in the weeds, a squiggle that stood out blackly in the moonlight. The hit team could follow it—if they could tell it from a dozen similar trails.

Cliff stumbled, and Julian heard a growing rasp in his breath. He's still in no shape to run, Julian thought. He looked around at the houses and tumbled cinder-block fences, searching for the best place to hide Cliff.

"Over there," Hazel suggested. They took Cliff by the arms—

Silver-blue light exploded around them. "There he is!" a voice shrieked. Julian heard him think Cliff's name.

"Scram," Cliff husked, as the xenon light flicked off.

"They're after *you*," Julian said. He blinked hard. The brilliant light had left him night-blind.

"*I can see*," Hazel told him. "*Get moving—to your left.*"

Julian's sight cleared slowly. He saw a roofless house ahead, helped Cliff through the doorway. As Cliff slumped against the inside wall, Hazel started pulling off his jacket. Seeing what she planned, Julian helped her.

"*It might work*," he said. "*Keep low and keep moving.*"

Cliff looked up. "Using her . . . for bait?" he wheezed.

"A diversion," Hazel said, putting on the coat.

"*If they don't follow you, circle back here*," Julian said. "*Stay outside.*"

"*Right.*" She crouched and scuttled out the door.

"If they see her—" Cliff began.

"They should mistake her for you."

"They've got guns!"

"Electrodarts and a silenced pistol. Short-range weapons." Julian peeked out the door, saw Hazel running, saw the brilliant lights play on her. One of the hunters recognized Cliff's jacket and shouted something obscene.

"They'll kill her if they catch her," Cliff husked.

"They can't catch her. She's safer doing this." Julian tapped Hazel's thoughts as she led the killers astray. Yesterday he had spent several hours telling the coven about his adventures. The stories had entertained them—and educated them. Now Hazel was applying the lessons she'd learned.

Julian looked around the smashed room, a small rectangle packed with plaster chunks and snapped wooden beams. It took him a moment to recognize it as a kitchen. "We need to hide you. They'll go away if they can't find you."

"Don't count on it. Why are they after *me*?"

"I don't know. Something about you being a traitor."

"That's crazy! Far as Granger knows, I'm still with Sere."

"Well, it's you they want," Julian said. "They don't even know we're telepathic—damn!"

Cliff started. "Hazel—"

"She's fine. They figured out she's a decoy. They're coming back." Julian gestured. "The hallway. Get behind that board."

"But you—"

"Don't worry. I've done this before."

To Julian's relief, Cliff hid. Julian sat down against the wall, wrapped his arms around himself, and tried to look asleep. Through the doorway he could see the glare of lights. He heard the men's footsteps and tapped their thoughts as they drew closer. One of them spotted the tracks leading into the house and realized they were brand-new. "In here!"

Light burst into the kitchen and a beam shone in his face. Blinded by the glare, Julian shaded his eyes with a hand and raised his head. "Who're you?" he mumbled, in a convincing imitation of grogginess.

"We are Sere!" the man with the pistol declared.

"Sere?" Julian whispered. The man expected him to sound afraid. Julian found that easy. "Why—what do you want?"

"We're looking for someone who double-crossed us." The man walked into the kitchen, followed by the other two hunters. "If you know what's good for you, you'll talk."

"About what?" Julian asked. They don't know Cliff's in here, he thought. He started to stand up.

"Don't move," one of them snapped, and Julian froze. "You'd better tell us what you saw, ugly."

"I didn't see anything." Uh, oh, Julian thought, tapping the man's surprise. He hadn't *spoken.*

The man stepped forward, flashlight in one hand, stunner in the other. Julian felt pinned by the light. "Jackson, this here is one of those mind-readin' mutants."

"You sure?" the leader asked.

"When it answers questions you don't ask, it's a witch." He waved the business end of the stunner in Julian's face. "I'll bet it knows *Sense and Non-sense* by heart."

"Just checking," the leader said. Julian sensed his

predatory happiness as he hefted his pistol. "I'd hate to kill a real person by mistake, but—"

With a wordless roar Cliff exploded out of the shadows. Julian twisted aside and heard the dart zip past his ear, heard a second dart snick into a wall. Out of darts now, he thought tightly.

Julian got to his feet. Cliff was grappling with the leader, trying to get the revolver from Jackson. One of the hit men jumped at Julian and swung a fist. Julian parried the blow with his forearm, dodged out of the way of a second blow. He saw Cliff go down on the floor, tangled up with the other two attackers.

I've got to fight, Julian thought, dancing away from another blow. He made a fist, looked at the man's face, and pulled his arm back.

Julian turned his head and looked at his fist. Why am I holding my hand like this? he thought in confusion. Then something caught him in the chest and he went sprawling backward. His head hit the floor and he saw a pattern of zigzag lines.

Something heavy pressed down on him as he tried to get up. In the moonlight he saw a foot planted on his chest. His assailant was heavy enough to pin him to the ground.

Cliff was caught. The attackers had lost their flashlights, but Jackson still had the gun. The third man stood behind Cliff, holding his arms. Cliff's breath was a strained, exhausted rattle.

"*Julian?*"

Birche? No, Hazel. "*Where are you?*"

"*Outside. I'm coming in—*"

"*Stay there!*" Julian fought down the hysterical edge in his thoughts. He had slipped up when he tried to hit his attacker: he'd throw away any second chance if he lost control again. "*Stay there. I'll need another diversion.*"

Jackson was flushed with elation. "Which one should we take care of first?"

Julian turned his head. His captor didn't like the activity, and put more weight on his chest. Julian's breath groaned out of him. He forced himself to look around and assess the situation.

One of the flashlights had landed near his hand. It was off.

"Julian?"

"Hazel, get some rocks or bricks. When I say so, throw them at this house."

He looked away from the light, but remembered where it was. He'd have to grab blindly—and hope it hadn't broken.

The man atop him grinned in the inky moonlight. "Shoot the freak first, Jackson. My shoe's gettin' dirty."

"So're my hands," the man holding Cliff said. "Do the freak later. It's harmless."

"Right," Jackson said. "We're here for the traitor. Step aside, Earl. This'll get messy." Earl released Cliff and got out of the line of fire.

So that's what it is, Julian thought. It was time to move. He forced a weak laugh. "He's no traitor."

"Shut up, freak." Jackson pointed the gun square at Cliff's heart. "Whitney, Granger told us how you ran out on him."

"Granger left him with us," Julian rasped out. He laughed despite the weight squeezing his chest. "Do you want . . . to hear . . . Granger's secret?"

Jackson spoke without looking from Cliff. "You don't know jack shit, witch." There was no conviction in his voice.

He wants to hear, Julian thought. None of the trio could resist the chance to hear their leader's secrets. It might prove useful. "Cliff got gassed and stunned. Granger and Norton brought him here. Then Granger got scared . . . ran away."

"You lying, shitty mutant—"

"Ask Norton," Cliff said. Julian noted that he had his breath back, might sustain another burst of action—but he was shaking badly, either with nerves or exhaustion.

"Norton's dead," Julian said. "Killed by the cops, right, Jackson? Granger saw it happen. Funny how no one else saw . . ." Julian got ready to grab the light as anger twisted Jackson's mind. "*Hazel—now!*"

Rocks clattered against an outside wall. The killers looked around, expecting an attack. In one smooth motion Julian grabbed the flashlight, pointed it at Jackson's face and thumbed the switch. Jackson squeezed his eyes shut against the actinic glare and tried to shield his eyes. He twisted away, out of the light.

Cliff hurled himself forward and the man atop Julian turned toward him. Julian grabbed his lower legs and the man toppled. He kicked at Julian as he fell, struggling to break his grip. Julian twisted on the dirty floor and held on as the man kicked.

Suddenly Cliff was on his feet, the gun in his hands. "Freeze!" he grated hoarsely, and Jackson's fear was a chilling wave through Julian's mind. "All of you, hold it!"

"Hey, look, Whitney—" Jackson started.

"Don't whine." Cliff stared at Jackson, and Julian sensed how his mind churned. Even with a gun in his hand, he wasn't sure what to do about his erstwhile killers. They were a menace, but Cliff had never killed before.

This is no time for him to start, Julian thought, and cleared his throat. "Jackson you and your friends are going back to Granger," he said, getting to his feet. "You'll tell him you found Cliff with a bunch of witches and killed him, and that the witches ran away. You had to throw away your weapons to sneak through a police checkpoint."

Cliff nodded and deflected his gun. "Get going."

"Wait," Julian said. "When you tell Granger your story tonight, he'll call you heroes. But tomorrow, he'll ask you to tell everything again—and again. He'll want details, and eventually he'll sound suspicious. He'll always wonder if you found out he's a coward."

Jackson's face writhed in a snarl. "You scummy freak—"

"Shut up!" Cliff said.

"Don't wait for Granger to ask too many times," Julian said. "You'll get what Norton got."

"Now get out." Cliff motioned with the gun. Numbed by their defeat, the trio shuffled out.

I'm still alive, Julian thought. He felt a trembling in his knees, a wateriness of muscles that forced him to sit down.

"You all right?" Cliff asked. He put the gun down.

"I'm fine," Julian said, sensing Cliff's confusion. Is that because of the way I froze up? he wondered. "You want to know what happened to me."

"Yeah," Cliff said. "You're not chicken, and I never saw anyone freeze up like *that*. Was there some screwy witch reason for it?"

"I wanted to knock that guy's head off," Julian said. "I tried, too, but I forgot about the feedback problem. A psychic contact gets pretty intense sometimes. You can get mixed up about who you are—"

Cliff made an intuitive leap. "It was like you tried to punch yourself out?"

"Yes. That's impossible—try it sometime. The subconscious keeps you from hurting yourself that way." But that isn't the problem, Julian thought. Cliff understood, but the comprehension only added to his confusion . . . and guilt, shame—

"Julian!" Hazel thought. She was still outside, and so engrossed in tapping Cliff's thoughts that she hadn't moved from her hiding place. *"The problem has to do with Sere, not us."*

"Yes, but how?" Julian asked.

"I can't say. I've tried to help Cliff, but there's a lot he doesn't know about himself. That's been slowing us down."

"Then let's start with the basics."

Cliff was looking at him. "You're talking to someone, aren't you?"

"To Hazel. She's worried about you." Julian staggered to his feet, wincing at the pain in his ribs. Nothing was broken, but he expected to have a good set of bruises tomorrow. "Cliff, why did you join Sere?"

"It's a long story." He looked up at the moon. " 'bout a year ago I had a job with the *Post*. I drove around and put newspapers in the racks, and collected coins from the cash boxes. Then they put in those new flashprinter things, and I was out on my ass. I couldn't find another job and I couldn't get no damned unemployment, and I was starving.

"Then I walked into the middle of a Sere rally. They gave sandwiches to anyone what'd listen to this speech Granger made. After that I talked to some people there, and—" He coughed, and clutched at the wall behind him to steady himself. "I thought it'd be something great. We were gonna change the world, make everything right for everyone. But all it's been is lying and fighting."

"And they betrayed your ideals."

"What ideals?" Cliff shook his head, and thought of all the times he'd casually agreed that witches ought to be exterminated. If he hadn't been half-dead when these witches had taken him in—he couldn't complete that thought.

"You're no killer," Julian said. He gestured at the gun, lying in the moonlight. "When you took that gun you never thought about using it, not seriously. The first thing you thought about was saving me, and Hazel, not yourself."

"But, I—"

"Give yourself some credit, Cliff. If you were evil, would Hazel like you?" This would be simpler if he was a telepath, Julian thought. Then the thea could have helped him to see his own strengths, giving him a new perspective on himself.

"*He has me for that,*" Hazel said, slipping into the kitchen. "*I can take it from here.*"

"*Right,*" Julian agreed. Cliff was still in turmoil, but his anguish had lost some of its edge. "Something tells me I should go," he said to Cliff. He left, propelled by a blast of mock indignation from Hazel.

They're good for one another, Julian thought idly, as he walked back to the coven house. Cliff needed help, and the act of giving that help let Hazel see herself as something more than a freak. Julian found it hard to tell who benefited more.

"*If that matters,*" the thea said, appearing at his side. "*Have you decided what to say when you see Birche again?*"

"*I'm not sure I ought to see her again,*" Julian said glumly. He stopped walking and looked at her. "*I don't want to endanger her.*"

"*Name one witch who isn't in danger.*"

Julian scowled at the apparition. "*I'm different. I'm on a goddamned wanted poster! And if you're going to say I need her help—*"

"*You do.*" The thea scowled back at him. "*You're going to say that I've already identified your problem. I have, but that doesn't mean I can help.*"

"*But—*"

" '*But*' *nothing, Julian Forrest.*" The thea held up a finger in a gesture for silence. " '*Thea*' *may be the Greek word for* '*goddess,*' *but that doesn't make me one. I'm a cut-rate deity, and I can't work miracles. Birche Holstein is what you need.*"

"*I refuse to exploit her,*" Julian said stiffly.

"*There's a lot of difference between needing her and exploiting her,*" the thea said. "*The truth is that you want to deny you need help. You're terrified to admit that you're close to breaking down.*"

He sighed. "*Maybe you're right.*"

" '*Maybe,*' *nothing! You know I'm right. But do you think that's the only reason you want her? You trotted back to the mall during the riot; what did you find?*"

"*That she'd already cleared out of the area.*"

"*Sensible of her—and you admire that. She's the sort of woman you're most liable to fall in love with; the fact that you need her emphasized the feeling. Your subconscious did that to force you to look for her help—but now that you're aware of what's happening, the infatuation will fade. And you* will *see her again.*" The thea vanished with a smile.

"Hell of a way to get the last word," Julian muttered. Then he grinned at himself. The thea had been right about one thing. He *would* see Birche again—no matter what.

CHAPTER 9

When the Compton Act was passed, these many years ago, a few people called it a step toward dictatorship. The Act would give the government the right to arrest anyone it disliked, on the grounds that they were 'mentally ill.' The MHB would drag people away in the middle of the night, without due process of law. Certification would create a class of unpersons; mistakes and carelessness and overwork would ruin innocent lives, and so on.

It's not so. Case in point: Jane Doe, a successful young businesswoman. Yesterday someone reported her to the MHB, claiming that she was a telepath and that she'd caused trouble. Put that way, the call sounds ludicrous, but the MHB takes all reports seriously. Two MHB orderlies—Amos Wornitz and Dick Ruggles—were sent out to make an investigation. I went along.

Needless to say, I watched them like a hawk. From what I'd heard about the MHB, I'd expected a casual brutality that would shame a KGB colonel; you might even say I had hopes of seeing something like that. I struck out. Wornitz and Ruggles were letter-perfect at all times. They made their investigation, satisfied themselves that the report was false, and left Jane Doe's home. I spoke to her later, and Ms. Doe had no complaints to make about the MHB.

I won't say that the MHB is composed of saints. Its workers are underpaid and overworked, and sometimes their job turns dangerous. One thing is clear, however. They're no threat to anyone's civil rights—unless you are a criminal.

—from Steve Magyar's column, "Pork-barrel People," Los Angeles Post, 7 January 2000.

*   *   *

We must be near the Federal Building, Birche thought, as the van slowed down. That was where the MHB had its offices and clinics—and its holding cells. She craned her head and looked through the windshield. The building was a dark, anonymous bulk ahead.

The van twisted past obstacles designed to slow down attackers, and stopped outside a powered door. There was a brief flash of laser light, and Birche sensed a guard's satisfaction as the van passed a security check. The armored door opened for it.

The van drove through an extensive underground parking lot and pulled into a slot along a wall. The orderlies removed Birche from the van and led her to a locked door. The driver slid his ID card into the lock and spoke. "Team twenty-one reporting with one double-echo." The door slid open, revealing a corridor.

Double-echo, Birche thought, as they marched her down the hall. Understanding came to her slowly, as if she was remembering something learned long ago. Double-echo stood for EE, escorted evaluatee. She wondered why they didn't simply call her a prisoner.

They took her to a small room marked *Registration*. An efficient-looking matron glanced up from her desk terminal as the trio entered. "Is this your five-oh-eight call?" she asked.

"Our second one tonight," the driver said, releasing Birche's elbow. "I'll be damned glad when Fountain gets out of L.A."

"You and me both." The matron got up and inspected Birche. Her mind ran through a checklist: belts, laces, jewelry, glasses, pens—all the objects a psychotic might use to injure herself. The woman removed Birche's earrings and dropped them on the desk. "You can unlock the restraints now."

"Okay." The driver got behind Birche and removed her cuffs. As they came off she saw that they were heavily padded things, designed to make self-inflicted injuries impossible. They're all so damned concerned with my well-being, she thought bitterly. Birche started massaging her wrists, trying to rub away the sensation that she still wore the cuffs.

The matron grabbed one of her wrists. Birche started to resist, then thought better of it. There were too many unknowns here, too many dangers; the matron's whims might keep her here permanently. Birche watched quietly as the woman clamped an orange bracelet around her wrist and then pressed a magnetic pen against it. Then she held Birche's hand against a sensor plate on the desk, letting the computer record her fingerprints. "Put her in waiting lounge sixteen," she told the driver.

The lounge fell just short of being a jail cell. Looking around as the door hissed shut behind her, Birche saw a padded bench bolted to the wall. There was no switch for the single five-hundred-watt bulb in the ceiling, and the door was a smooth rectangle without a knob or latch. Smooth plastifoam padding covered the walls. The green pastel paint looked like a dull afterthought.

They can't keep me here forever, Birche thought, as she crumpled onto the bench. They would test her, certify her, and release her. They were supposed to do it that way. She clung to that idea as though it guaranteed her release.

Birche became aware of the other minds around her. She knew that her telepathic sense was unreliable—but it was *there*, and it was the one thing left to her that the MHB couldn't control.

They have other telepaths in custody, she thought, recalling the things the matron and orderly had said. She decided to contact them, if only to share her misery and relieve the fear that weighed on her.

Birche sat up on the bench. Remembering what she had read in the book, she took three quick breaths, tensed her muscles to rigidity, slowly relaxed them. Picture your fear and tension as fists, the book had suggested, gradually unclenching and losing their hold on you. It was a simple relaxation technique, Birche reflected calmly, and if it worked for other telepaths, it could work for her.

The almost-voices grew firmer and more distinct. It

was like listening to voices in a crowd, she thought, as she inexpertly tapped the outside thoughts. She found that she could separate one mind from another with a little concentration.

Most of the minds here had an elusive sameness to them, and it dawned on Birche that they were government workers, bored with their night-shift routines. There were a lot of them; even at night the Federal Building held enough people to fill a town.

Something caught her attention: a strong, alert mind, awake and intent on—something. A conversation. The man was taking instructions on how to walk around his cell. It was vitally important that he move his feet no more than an inch at a time, and that he make perfect pivots when he turned. The Guilt Lord and the Pain Priestess made certain that he obeyed their commands, despite his frantic pleas that they demanded too much from him no matter how much he deserved punishment. He tried to obey even though he was outside his body, working it by remote control because he was dead, Birche was dead, the Guilt Lord raged inside her head, ordering, demanding, twisting—

Birche opened her eyes to find herself curled on the floor, hands clutched over her head as if to shield her mind from the raging hallucination. Her concentration faltered and it receded, to become a feeble noise in the mental chatter around her.

Once, while still in high school, Birche had gone swimming in the ocean. It had been a unique and heady experience, until an undertow had caught her. The irresistible force had pulled her under as the water itself suddenly betrayed her, and only an eddy in the current had saved her, throwing her out of the riptide. She had popped to the surface like a cork, sputtering and gasping for air.

And then I started swimming again, she thought. Birche climbed back onto the chair and repeated the hypnotic exercises. The work seemed easier this time, and she soon found a mind that thought about telepaths.

This was a non-telepathic mind. It was unaware of

her, and it lacked something she had sensed in Julian. With a little work, she discovered that this man was an MHB clinician, giving an orientation talk to a pair of interns.

The man spoke cryptically as he and the interns watched a video monitor. "*This behavior appears random,*" he said, "*but it is typical of psis. There is no known cause for the seizure, and the patient seems quite undisturbed now that it is over. The listless posture and stupor are also typical, as are the unkempt hair, obesity, and general slovenly appearance. By and large, psis are indifferent to their appearances.*"

He's talking about *me,* Birche realized. She looked around the room and tried to spot the camera.

"*The patient may be aware that we're monitoring her. Note the evident confusion. The obvious diagnosis is idiopathic dysfunction . . . No, Mr. Lovat, I couldn't say. We usually give outpatient status to psis, but most aren't as far gone as this one. A staff psychiatrist will make a full evaluation later.*

"*The preferred term is 'psi,' Mr. Carlisle, not 'witch.' Please remember, this is the MHB, not a Redeemer prayerfest. Now, our next detainee is also a psi . . .*"

The temper of the clinician's thoughts frightened her. If they think everything I do is proof of insanity, Birche thought, how can I ever get out?

"*Hello? Hello? Who's that?*"

"*Birche Holstein.*" She felt a moment of triumph. "*Who are you?*"

"*Tom Watanabe. My God, it's good to tap someone else!*"

"*Yes—it is.*" She could sympathize with the near-frantic tenor of his thoughts. "*How long have you been here, Tom?*"

"*I don't know. They brought me in around noon yesterday.*"

"*I think it's around three in the morning now,*" Birche said. On a hunch she tapped through the minds of some of the Federal workers. She found a confirmed clock-watcher in short order. "*No, it's six-thirty already.*"

"They said they couldn't evaluate me until nine A.M."

"Which means we're stuck here a few more hours—at least. They don't strike me as too efficient around here."

"They were efficient enough to net me." Tom hesitated, then went on, *"When they came I thought about running, but . . ."*

"But there's no place to run." His despair was an almost tangible thing, and Birche thought it was even more dangerous than the whirlpool of madness in the schizophrenic's mind—but she could do something to help this. *"Tom, I know there're other telepaths around here. Have you found them?"*

"No, I—well, I haven't felt like trying."

"I understand. Let's see if we can find them."

"Why bother?"

Birche felt taken aback. *"Why—listen, I can't stand waiting like this. Maybe we can find a way out. Even if we can't, I want to be able to tell myself I didn't give up!"*

"Okay," he said reluctantly. *"Where do we start?"*

Birche looked at the foam-coated walls around her. *"Anywhere. Ignore anyone who sounds like a Federal worker; that'll speed things along. And—avoid any real mental patients—"*

"I know." There was a shudder in his thoughts.

Birche began sifting through the other minds again. She noted the work grew easier with practice. She felt a touch of pride; she had always wanted to excel at everything she did.

As her talent sharpened with use, Birche discovered that none of the minds around her were truly alike. There were obvious, sometimes overwhelming similarities, but each mind was unique, a separate and complex universe. Some of them fascinated her, a few bored her, and some—*"Tom? What do you make of him?"*

"I don't know, Birche." He strained to tap the new mind.

The man was an MHB detainee, a criminal, and guilty beyond any question. He'd committed robbery and rape, and then—because the bitch would've talked, no matter what she promised—he'd blown her brains

out. It had been rotten luck that the cops had shown
up, pulled their guns, and busted him like a common
crook.

"*So what's he doing here?*" Birche asked, intrigued
despite her revulsion. "*He's rotten, but not insane.*"

"*Shush,*" Tom said. "*I think I know—yeah, there.
Listen.*"

Time to do something twitchy, the man thought. He
tore off his clothes and drooled on the floor, then chewed
his bracelet and growled. The act had worked so far, he
thought in self-congratulation. The MHB shrinks all
thought he was nuts, and in another day or two they'd
certify him as wacko. That might mean wasting a few
months on the fool farm, but it would keep him off
Death Row.

"*He's in for a shock!*" Tom said, with a fine sneer.
"*Death Row is better than an asylum.*"

"*Not for him. He's no telepath.*" Birche forced herself
to keep tapping the man as he gloated over his plans.
Once he was declared nuts, the prosecutor would have
to drop the charges. As soon as he was in the nut house
he would let the shrinks "cure" him, and in a few
months he'd be on the streets again. He wondered why
no one had been smart enough to try that before.

"*It's been tried. It doesn't work.*"

"*Who are you?*" Birche asked. The thoughts had a
curious flatness to them, as though the new telepath
was too drained to feel any emotions.

"*I'm Pat Lenihan. I've been listening to Shotgun
Danny, there, ever since they hauled me in last night.
He only has about an 85 IQ, so he can't understand the
situation too well.*"

"*Won't his idea work?*" Tom asked. "*It sounds good.*"

"*Only in theory. Sure, the Compton Act says that the
MHB has to free a man when he's certified sane. The
thing is—look, they're going to tag old Danny as a
homicidal maniac, correct?*"

"*Obviously.*" Birche shivered.

"*Yes. Now, before he, or anyone else, can be decerti-
fied, he has to do more than prove he's sane. He has to*

convince a psychiatrist that he's no longer a threat to society. Psychiatrists hardly ever agree to that anymore."

"What? Why not?" Tom asked. *"I can understand that in Danny's case, but—"*

"But what about us? Simple. Can you prove that someone will never commit a crime? Ever?"

"Well, no, of course not," Birche said. That was simple logic.

"Yes. Now, if someone is released and later commits a crime, the psychiatrist who cleared him could go to jail. The Act calls it felony malpractice. That keeps the doctors from releasing the likes of Shotgun Danny, even if they think he's sane—it's too much of a gamble. They don't gamble, ever."

Birche felt a sick tightness in her belly. *"Does that mean they won't release us?"*

"It depends. If they decide we're harmless, they'll give us outpatient status. They have that option in non-violent cases."

"You sound pretty detached about this," Tom said.

Birche sensed a mental shrug. *"I understand the logic. I'm majoring in psychology at UC San Diego . . . or I was. Now I don't know what to expect."*

"Neither do I," Birche said. Her hand brushed against the padded wall. Even the '92 earthquake hadn't upset her life as much as Julian had.

"You know Julian Forrest?" Pat asked in surprise.

"He showed up at my bookstore and talked to me. Is he a friend of yours?"

"No, but I've heard a lot about him." There was some animation in Pat's voice now. *"The Redeemers have been going bananas, trying to kill him. By now some of them must be ready for the orange bracelet themselves."*

"Well, the Iron Guard is after him now," Birche said.

Tom's admiring chuckle surprised her. *"The man has good taste in enemies, that's a fact—hey. Someone's coming."*

Birche tapped the new thoughts. *"He's coming for me."*

"*Ladies first,*" Tom said sardonically. "*Chivalry lives at the MHB. Good luck, lady.*"

"*Thanks.*" Birche stood up as the door hissed open. "*Keep an eye on me. If I make any mistakes maybe you can avoid them.*"

"Holstein?" The orderly gestured with his clipboard. "Come with me."

Birche stepped into the corridor and followed the man. Calm, she told herself. The man's thoughts told her she was on her way to a psychiatric evaluation. She would need to appear calm and rational.

The orderly escorted her into an interview room. It was a small, windowless cubicle, with two chairs placed on opposite sides of a metal table. A computer terminal and recorder unit were mounted in front of one chair. Before the orderly could say anything, Birche took a seat on the opposite side of the table. The man gave her an annoyed look. "Dr. Reston will see you in a minute." He left.

The minute came and went. "*Tom? Pat?*"

"*—Right here, Birche.*"

"*I'm in an interview room—alone. There's no one in the corridor and the door's unlocked. I'm tempted to—*"

"*Don't!*" Tom warned her. "*Not unless you can get that bracelet off first. It has an electronic ID unit built into it. If you walk through any of the checkpoints in this building you'll set off an alarm. There's bound to be a sensor in your room, too.*"

"Oh." Birche looked at her bracelet, then tugged on it with her left hand. The plastic was smooth and flexible, but not enough to slip over her hand. Birche strained at it until the skin on her wrist bunched up and her hand turned numb. "*It won't come off.*"

"*Good try, though,*" Pat said.

"*Not good enough. If—I've got company.*"

The door opened and a man entered the cubicle. "I'm Dr. Reston," he said, sitting down. He activated the computer terminal.

"*I don't like the sound of this guy,*" Tom said.

"*Same here,*" Birche told him. "*Don't talk to me now. I'd better concentrate on him.*"

" . . . already know your name," Reston was saying. "Let's get your file open." He drew a magnetic pen from the terminal, and made a gesture of impatience. "I need to see your ID unit."

"My—oh." Birche held out her arm and watched as he pressed the pen against the bracelet. Birche tapped his thoughts as he read the information on his screen. He was bored . . . and irritated with something. "Are you a telepath?" he asked.

"Yes, didn't they tell you?"

"I just came on duty." After a rough night, his thoughts continued. The rioters had cut the power to his neighborhood yesterday. By the time the idiots in the power company had fixed things, his refrigerator had defrosted and the tropical fish had died. The last thing he needed was trouble with another smartmouthed psi. "It says here that you resisted detention this morning."

"I didn't resist any—"

"You were brought in under restraint."

"All I did was ask your men to identify themselves!"

"They're not required to do that; they're not policemen, after all." Reston typed a file entry into the terminal: *Patient is moderately argumentative and combative.* "After you were placed in the lounge you had a seizure. How often does this happen?"

" 'Seizure'?" she repeated blankly.

"We have a videodisc of you rolling around on the floor."

"*That?* That wasn't a seizure. I made the mistake of reading a schizophrenic's mind—"

He slapped a palm onto the metal table. "That's an obsolete term."

"I don't know what else to call it," Birche said. "He had these hallucinations . . . they were so powerful, so real—"

"Do you always have trouble telling the difference between reality and illusion?"

"Look, what would happen to you if . . ." Her voice

trailed off as he made another entry: *Patient has trouble differentiating between fact and fantasy.* Birche's voice became heated. "Can you at least wait until I answer before you do that?"

"What did I just do?"

He's goading me, Birche thought. "You just made a note that I can't differentiate between fact and fantasy. That isn't what happened. That man's hallucinations overwhelmed me—"

"—because your ESP is so highly developed," he said flatly. *Patient is highly defensive. In addition, she displays the typical psi superiority complex, flaunting her self-proclaimed powers.* Reston pushed his chair back from the terminal, and decided that he had enough information for a preliminary diagnosis.

Her breath caught. Birche forced herself to speak. "What's going to happen to me?"

"Well . . . I wish we could keep you for treatment, but that's pointless; your type of dysfunction doesn't respond to therapy. You're functional, despite some disorientation, and there's no firm evidence that you're dangerous. I'll recommend you for outpatient status."

"Outpatient—you mean I can go?"

"Not yet. There are some reports to complete, and you'll have to take a few standardized tests. If nothing untoward crops up, and the chief of staff agrees, we'll give you outpatient status. Of course, you'll have to report back here once every fourteen days for observation."

"Observation." That tempered her relief—but they weren't going to keep her.

"We'll also maintain your welfare," Reston said, misreading the look on her face. "You'll get food stamps, clothing and housing coupons, and an annual medical examination."

"I see." Birche fingered the bracelet. "When can I get this taken off?"

"The ID unit?" Reston looked blank. "It isn't meant to come off. It's permanent."

CHAPTER 10

*Witches are murdered at a rate ten times higher than
the national average. It is estimated that over the past
five years eighty-five percent of them have been victims
of at least one assault. Less than three percent of these
cases ever went to court, and four out of five of those
that did were dismissed on technical grounds. In 1999,
no less than two hundred and thirty-nine Federal, state,
and local statutes were enacted which—legal niceties
aside—were designed to restrict the rights and activities of witches.*

*This has ominous implications. Breaking laws and
violating rights is like eating peanuts; few people stop
at one. If it's socially acceptable to terrorize witches
today, who knows what will become acceptable next?*
—internal CTO report, 14 June 2000

"Here's some more material on Forrest," Farrier said,
as he entered Hutchins' office. He pushed a thick folder
onto Hutchins, desk. "The gang in Data Analysis is still
checking it for any patterns."

"Good." Hutchins hefted the file. "Where did this
come from?"

"Almost everywhere—school records, medical records,
police files, newspaper clippings, you name it."

"Fast work," Hutchins said.

"I can't take credit for it," Farrier admitted as he sat
down. "Blaine did it. The MHB doesn't bother with
court orders and warrants when it has to obtain certain
records—"

"You're *kidding*."

"It's the God's honest truth, Chief. The MHB isn't a law enforcement agency; it's a medical organization. It can lay its hands on *anything* that's related to one of its wards."

He sounds so damned wistful, Hutchins thought. "Did Blaine have anything else for us?"

"Not directly," Farrier said. "But you remember his claim that, whenever Forrest pops up, several freaks in that area stop showing up for their observation sessions? Data Analysis is checking the reports for patterns. Blaine has always wanted to do that, but until now he's been in no position to do anything."

Until now, Hutchins thought. That was about as subtle as Farrier ever got. "About his position—"

"You've talked with the President?" Farrier leaned forward in his chair, resting his elbows on Hutchins' desk.

"No, with the attorney general. Schulze said he'd have a word with Delanty about putting our worm in Chennault's place. It'll take a couple of days."

"It'll pay off," Farrier said.

"I hope so," Hutchins said. "I had one hell of a time persuading Schulze to have Chennault booted upstairs—and there's no guarantee that the President will let the MHB take over here." He grimaced. "Schulze re-emphasized the President's orders. This witchcraft silliness takes precedence over everything."

"And you're going to carry through?"

"Until I get different orders, Lou, I'll have to make an effort." He made a chopping gesture with one hand. "Enough for now. What's the latest report on yesterday's riots?"

Farrier sighed, and leaned back in the chair. "Casualties were light, but property damage was heavy. Most of the vandalism centered on power lines, water mains, and telephone circuits."

Hutchins mulled that over. "That'll help them when the battle starts."

"It's already helping the bastards," Farrier said. "Riots are one thing, but blackouts and water shortages hit people where they live. Sere is getting more than the usual amount of publicity now."

"We'll have to live with that. How goes the investigation?"

"Piss poor. The Sere leadership has vanished, and if we don't get a break soon—"

The desk phone rang, and Hutchins hit its button harder than he had intended. "Hutchins here."

"Monty? Hal Adler." As always, Adler sounded as if he had a cigar clamped in his teeth. "How's the witch-hunting trade?"

"Slow, but I'm managing." Hutchins looked at Farrier, who was frowning at the phone speaker. Adler owned a television network and belonged to Transpac, and he never wasted his time on anything he considered trivial.

"The boys in my news bureau are curious, Monty," Adler said. "They want to know why the CTO is playing footsy with these circus freaks, when you've got Sere chewing up a major city."

"We're making every effort to contain Sere," Hutchins said. "Nothing has interfered with that, and you can quote me."

"That doesn't answer my question. What's going on with these witches?"

Hutchins smiled tightly. "It's a routine matter, which is why I'm willing to answer over an open line."

"Now, Monty, it's not 'routine.'" Adler sounded relaxed and jovial, a tone that deepened the scowl on Farrier's face. "My newsboys have the full story. I've kept them quiet so far, but you know how reporters are about the news. Independent. They think they've got a good story here, and they don't care how bad it makes the CTO look."

He must have a reason for making this threat, Hutchins thought. "You know I don't let publicity affect me."

"Of course. I'm trying to do you a favor, Monty. I can't keep a lid on this forever—and if my boys don't break the story, someone else will, because it *isn't* routine. For instance—" Hutchins heard papers rustling over the speaker "—you're going to a certain college today, to visit—"

"That's enough!" Hutchins snapped. He looked at Farrier as if to say *Who in hell talked?* Farrier answered with a surprised look and a shake of his head.

"People are going to wonder," Adler's voice continued.

"I'm not the one to ask about this."

"I didn't really think so, Monty." Adler's voice turned soothing. "I'm calling Delanty later today. I know he's the one who ordered this. I'll make him see the light. Meanwhile, why don't you let this witch hunt slide? It'll save us all a lot of grief. Good day, Monty." A click and a dial tone followed.

"Curious," Farrier mused. "Why would he want us off this witch hunt?"

"I think he's more concerned with Sere," Hutchins said. "His network has its studios in Los Angeles. If the riots disrupt its production schedule it will cost him a fortune."

"Then why did he harp on witches?" Farrier asked. "Chief, I hope he can talk sense into the President— but there's something fishy here."

"It makes me suspicious, too," Hutchins agreed. "And probably without reason. Paranoia is an occupational hazard with us."

"I suppose so," Farrier said grudgingly. "Hell. Are you still planning on visiting Cal Tech?"

"Yes—although I'd like to know how Adler learned my plans. Anyway, there's a man there, Lyman Grant, who knew Forrest at UC Berkeley. He's an astronomer, and he was Forrest's academic advisor."

"Berkeley." The Bear looked disgusted. "He's probably some damned liberal who's too good to talk to us."

"Maybe not, Lou. He was forced to resign from Berkeley—by a liberal academic group. He should be cooperative." Which will be a welcome change, Hutchins decided.

I should never read in a car, Hutchins thought, at least not in Los Angeles. The Santa Monica Freeway

hadn't been crowded, but it had a roughness that no
shock absorbers could dampen. There were ripples and
patched cracks all along the roadway, and the driver
had slowed down for none of them. The shaking had
left Hutchins with a bad case of eye strain, and his
reading had told him little enough about his quarry.

Forrest had an intensive education in an esoteric
branch of astronomy, which Hutchins already knew.
The records made it clear that most of his instructors
regarded him as a brilliant man. The few blots on his
scholastic record hadn't kept him from progressing at a
rapid rate. He had taken a smattering of courses besides astronomy, evidently to satisfy academic breadth
requirements: art, anthropology, and music. That last
choice must have come naturally to him; his parents
taught music. The file contained several letters he'd
written to them, intercepted and copied by the MHB
before the Post Office had delivered them.

Over the past two years Forrest had traveled all over
the country, moving every few weeks—usually when
someone tried to kill him. An assortment of police
reports and news accounts showed that was a common
thing. Forrest seemed to go out of his way to provoke
the crazies. He'd had several close calls; he had spent
December of 1998 in a free clinic recovering from a
gunshot wound.

The file impressed Hutchins in one way. The CTO
would have needed weeks to subpoena much of the
material, even under the lenient anti-terrorism laws,
and some of it would have remained unavailable no
matter what. It was no wonder that Farrier had sounded
so *wistful* . . . but such power disturbed Hutchins. It
would be easy to abuse it, he thought.

The car rolled onto the grounds of the California
Institute of Technology, and the driver parked in a
small side lot. He got out of the car before Hutchins
did, in accordance with standard field practice: the
driver's duty was to make certain that everything was
safe for his passenger. He would remain on guard at the
car, in case somebody tried to plant a bomb in it or

prepare an ambush. Such things had happened before, in places even more peaceful than this staid campus.

Lyman A. Grant's office looked like a typical professor's shoebox, Hutchins thought, with bookshelves taking up most of the available wall space. The desk computer looked as if it had been reworked by an expert cybernetician, although Hutchins couldn't guess what the modifications did. One of them bore a disturbing resemblance to a headset, but with electrodes instead of earphones.

"I can't spare much time," Grant said, as Hutchins took the chair in front of his metal desk. He was a pale, egg-bald man in a three-piece suit. "I have a seminar in thirty minutes."

"I won't take long," Hutchins promised. "I need some information on Julian Forrest."

"Indeed? Why?"

"I have orders to detain him—for his own protection."

"Ah." Grant nodded. "You're right, this didn't take long. Good day."

"Doctor, I'm not asking you to betray Forrest."

"Not directly," Grant said, "but the result is the same."

Looks like Lou had it right, Hutchins thought. He sighed noisily. "Doctor, I didn't drive up here for the trip. Either I leave with some information, or I leave with you. Which shall it be?"

Grant looked unconcerned. "You'll need some sort of legal grounds to arrest me. Do you have any?"

"I can hold you—indefinitely—as a material witness in a criminal investigation."

Grant nodded encouragingly. "And what crime are you investigating?"

"As I said, I need to find Julian Forrest—"

"Who has committed no crime." Grant smiled slyly and held up a finger. "Mr. Forrest is legally *non compos mentis*. In the eyes of the law, he cannot stand trial for anything he might have done. *Legally*, there cannot be a crime for me to have witnessed."

"A technicality," Hutchins said. "You could sit in a

cell while lawyers argued the point. How long do you suppose it would take?"

"I've got the time. If—"

The phone rang. Grant picked up its handset and listened to the voice that buzzed in his ear. He punctuated the buzzing with a few short, vague answers, then hung up.

He rubbed his chin thoughtfully as he looked at Hutchins. "On the other hand," he said slowly, "it might help if you told me what you *really* want with him."

"That's not something I can discuss."

"Why not?" Grant asked. "You can't expect me to believe he's done anything untoward."

"He broke his parole with the MHB."

"A matter of survival." Grant drummed his fingers on his desktop. "The MHB was about to place him in an institution. That can destroy telepathics. The mental pressure of tapping a large number of psychotics is unendurable, you see—it's the equivalent of nonstop brainwashing."

"Didn't the MHB have a reason to detain him?"

"Oh, yes, indeed." Grant's voice dripped bitterness. "He upset the Biblical fundamentalists. They filed some complaints with the local MHB office—false complaints, but that didn't matter. When the MHB gets three complaints about one of its 'patients,' they take him in for observation. Automatically."

Hutchins pursed his lips. Was this why the file hadn't named Forrest's asocial acts or the complainants? he wondered. "Can you identify the people who turned him in? And why they did it?"

"A campus ministry took credit," Grant said uneasily. "As to their motives . . . Fundamentalists believe in the existence of witchcraft and Satanism. If they can prove that magic exists, then it implies that *all* of their beliefs are correct. Persecuting telepaths is a way to affirm their faith. The logic is false, but emotionally satisfying."

Hutchins nodded to himself as a pattern began to emerge. "But why did they bother taking credit?"

"To frighten the other telepathics on campus, I suppose."

"Wrong answer," Hutchins said. "Other telepaths would have known who did it, and why. No, they took credit to impress normal people. Perhaps even to frighten them—but why?"

Grant laughed, a brittle sound. "That sounds like a rhetorical question."

"I think they wanted to keep normal people from dealing with witches," Hutchins suggested. Seeing the dismay on Grant's face, he pressed on. "They wanted to break up some *organization* of telepaths and normal people, didn't they?"

The astronomer snorted contemptuously. "I'd imagine that a man with your job *needs* to find conspiracies."

"Have I found one?" When Grant remained silent, Hutchins said, "Fact: you stonewalled me until you got that phone call. Fact: after the call you started talking— and subtly pumping me for information. Fact: you say things like 'telepathics' and 'tapping,' which are terms witches use—but you aren't psychic."

Grant nodded. "I'm not old enough. The mutation didn't show up until the late Sixties. I think the mutagen was one of those Asiatic flu viruses—"

"Don't change the subject, *Doctor*. I don't care if you get ESP by selling your soul." Hutchins leaned on his chair's armrest as he stared at Grant. "I suspect there's an organization of witches and normal humans on this campus. If I'm right, I'm empowered to investigate it, especially if I suspect criminal activity."

"You've no proof of anything," Grant said.

Hutchins gestured at the phone. "I *know* you spoke with a telepath just now. Was he registered with the MHB?"

Grant barely hesitated. "Yes."

"Really? Well, ask yourself a few things. How many telepaths are on this campus? How many are passing for human? What happens to them if I ask the MHB to investigate—"

Grant started. "That's blackmail!"

"It's the law. Failure to report telepaths to the MHB is a crime, Doctor. Your stubbornness could cost your friends a lot." Hutchins stopped to let that sink in—and to give himself time to think. So there *was* an organization of witches and human sympathizers. Was this why Delanty was so concerned? With the powers at their disposal, an organization of witches would be a dangerous thing. God knew there was no reason to trust them.

It dawned on Hutchins that any number of telepaths might be reading his thoughts. Well, damn it, all they could do was learn that he held the high cards. "Answer my questions," Hutchins told Grant. "Satisfy me that there's nothing to suspect, and I'll consider dropping the whole—"

A loud *queep-queep-queep* interrupted him. Annoyed, Hutchins took his pager from his belt. A number flashed on its display strip: 555-9700. The dummy phone number was a coded signal: *Emergency. Return to the office at once.*

"I have to leave," Hutchins said, standing. "But I *will* come back—and you and your friends will be here to give answers."

"Don't count on that," Grant said, his eyes flashing with anger. "Damn you! Do you expect them to hang around and wait for you to call in the MHB?"

"I hope it won't come to that," Hutchins said. "But if *they* vanish, I'll hold you responsible—and if you think I won't toss your ass in jail, just ask your witches."

Damned arrogant intellectual, Hutchins thought as he left the building. Perhaps he'd been too abrupt with the astronomer, but the man had wanted trouble—and this entire business had put Hutchins' temper on a short fuse. It had been a pleasure to cut him down to size.

Quite probably there was nothing serious going on, Hutchins reasoned. You had to expect witches to band together, and Chennault had said that they attracted unstable people. *That* would be par for the course at any university; instability and abnormally high intelligence seemed to go together. God knew that most of the students here looked pretty odd. Glancing around at the walkways and buildings, Hutchins saw at least a dozen youths who fitted his idea of hard-core science students. Cybernerds, he thought; that was the latest slang—

"Hutchins! Look out!" The voice was young and shrill. Hutchins twisted his head and saw a student running his way. "On your right, duck!"

Hutchins reacted instinctively, drawing his gun as he rolled to the ground. On his right? That was the parking lot. He heard a rapid *thwp-thwp-thwp-thwp*, saw a trio of men standing near a late-model car, weapons in hand and aimed at him. Hutchins snapped off a couple of shots, badly aimed but enough to make his attackers dive for cover. Hutchins jumped behind a concrete bench and peeked over its edge.

Motion caught his eye. His attackers were still in the parking lot, crouching behind an undersized sports car. One of them began a dash to the side in an effort to outflank Hutchins. The man went tumbling as he crossed the gap between two cars. With mild surprise Hutchins realized that he had just shot the man. His pistol still smoked from the shots he'd fired.

"Freeze! Drop them!" Hutchins' driver popped into the open, almost directly behind the two survivors. One of the assassins raised his weapon—a large, clumsy stunner, Hutchins saw—then hesitated at the quick chatter of the driver's Uzi. The two men dropped their guns and sagged to the ground as if surprised by the quickness of their deaths.

Hutchins got up cautiously. The three gunmen were down and dead, no question about that. The driver stood in a half-crouch, scanning the area for more attackers. "You all right?" he called.

"I'm fine." People started coming out of the buildings, and Hutchins heard sirens in the distance.

Hutchins saw a fourth body lying on the ground: the student who had shouted the warning. Two bullets had torn open his chest, but the thing that took Hutchins' attention was the orange MHB bracelet on his wrist.

A witch, Hutchins thought, then: of course, how else could he have known my name? And—despite the fact that he *must* have known the threats Hutchins had made—he'd gotten himself killed in the process of saving the CTO chief's life. Why had he done that?

Hutchins looked away and tried to concentrate on a more immediate problem. Who were the assassins? Not experts, certainly; they'd bungled the job by killing the witch. That had given Hutchins the edge he'd needed to save himself. Even rank amateurs, of whom there were plenty these days, knew enough to ignore bystanders. Why had they killed the freak, then?

"Because he knew."

Hutchins jumped in surprise. He found himself looking at another student, a gawky young woman wearing an MHB bracelet. A corner of his mind noted that this was the first telepath he'd ever met. "What did he know?" Hutchins demanded.

"Th-that they weren't from Sere." The stammer matched the slight glaze in the witch's eye. "They belong, belonged to the Iron Guard."

"Oh?" Hutchins couldn't believe that. The hit had all the earmarks of a Sere operation, and Sere had good reason to kill him. As for the IG, it lacked the subtlety to copycat an assassination technique, and it had no reason to kill him.

"But that's why they killed Oliver," she said. "They wanted you to think they were from Sere—no, they didn't know the reason. They just took orders from someone named Savoy."

"Uh-huh." Hutchins shook his head. He couldn't afford to believe that, not when it came from a source that was certifiably, and certified, insane.

"Then decide for yourself! Those dart guns are fakes—real guns in disguise. One of them had a transmitter. He used it to page you, to draw you out—"

Hutchins walked away from the witch. Too crazy, he thought.

The driver walked up to Hutchins, a dart gun in one hand, pocket phone in the other. "Help is on the way, sir," he said crisply. "But you should see this now." He held out the stunner.

Hutchins took it and looked it over. As the witch had said, it was a disguised pistol. Hutchins cracked open the carved balsawood shell, exposing a .45 pistol. An M1911A1 Colt automatic, he observed, with the subtle modifications favored by gun aficionados. The silencer would have cost it some accuracy and killing power, but even so, it remained one of the most potent handguns in the world . . . and it was the weapon preferred by the Iron Guard's hit teams.

"Check the bodies and their car," Hutchins said absently. "They have some sort of radio transmitter. Bring it to me."

"Yes, sir."

Hutchins felt his doubts build as he stared at the pistol. Could the witch have been right after all? If so, what did the Iron Guard stand to gain by killing him? If the attack had worked, everyone would have thought Sere had done it, but—

"Chief?" The driver returned, holding out a small metal box. It might have been a silver cigarette case, except for the button on its side. Hutchins took it and pressed the button, and nodded glumly as his pager beeped. He checked its readout and saw the same number as before.

Hutchins got out his phone and called Farrier. "I'm at Cal Tech," he said without preamble. "Somebody just tried to extract me."

"I know, Chief. We have a team on the way."

"Our security has been breached. I want—"

"Is this something to discuss over an open line?"

Hutchins laughed without mirth. "Lou, whoever's involved here penetrated our security so thoroughly that they know our radio codes. I want us to act, *fast*, before they can react. Locate everyone who has access to our codes. Find everyone who knew my plans for today. Contact Adler and learn who talked to him. We'll discuss other matters later. Move."

"Understood."

Hutchins broke the connection. He could count on Farrier for the fast action that *might* find answers to this bloody mess. That was chancy, however. Whoever the enemy was, they weren't amateurs. They'd failed through bad luck—but they must have prepared for failure as well as success.

There would be more attacks, and they would come soon.

CHAPTER 11

At first, I had hoped that we telepathics could fit into society without any fuss. I held on to this idea as long as I could, despite evidence to the contrary. Pop psychologists, like Dr. Hacker, made the rounds on the TV talk shows, telling everyone that espers were different-therefore-crazy. On Halloween Night of '92 the police called on me sixteen times, "just checking," they said. The wicked telepath became a TV and movie stereotype, alongside the mad scientist and psychotic Viet Nam veteran.

The turning point came in a faculty lounge at the end of the semester. Everyone had had a rough day, for various reasons. I was no different, and I got as short-tempered as everyone else. Someone tried to hand me an extra assignment, and I had enough. "Give me a break," I said. "I'm only human."

Conversation stopped and everyone stared at me, and I realized some things. Most of these people thought I was something other than human, something dangerous. I scared them. And these were my friends and colleagues, people who knew me well. What could I expect from people who didn't know me at all?

—from Sense and Non-sense, *by Lyn Amanda Clancy*

*   *   *

This place has changed, Birche thought, as she walked into the Prospect Park mall. In some way that escaped definition, the shopping complex had become an unfamiliar and menacing place. Entering it was like crossing a border into another country.

Birche felt the bracelet rubbing her wrist, and that was enough to remind her that she was the one who had changed. She had tried to hide it under her gray sweatshirt sleeve, but the bracelet kept sliding down her arm and into the open. Like the MHB papers she carried in one hand—the exercise suit had no pockets— the orange plastic caught the eyes of everyone around her. People avoided her, leaving a dead space around her as she walked.

The door to her bookshop stood open, despite the CLOSED sign in the window. "Ms. Holstein!" Jenny Broderick said. The clerk looked and sounded distraught. "A man from the MHB is here. He has a court order shutting us down."

"It figures." Birche shook her head. "How long will the inventory take?"

"A few more hours. I called your lawyer right away."

"Good. Slow down the inventory as much as you can. Maybe we can straighten this out."

"Okay," Jenny said in relief. She might not lose her job—and that was followed by embarrassment at her own selfishness. "Ms. Holstein, if there's any way I can help you . . ."

"Thank you," Birche said quietly. After her confinement in the Federal Building, Jenny's offer had a welcome warmth. She forced herself to smile for the clerk's benefit. "I'd better see Mr. Esposito now."

Birche found her lawyer and the MHB agent in her office, going over the records in her computer. Raul Esposito's mouth was set in a hard, thin line; Birche didn't need to tap him to know that he disapproved of what was happening, and that he had no power to stop it.

The agent looked up as she entered the office. "You must be Holstein. I—"

"And you're Evan Pinckney," she said, speaking before he could identify himself. Birche had felt a need to score a small triumph over this man, to put herself one up on the MHB. Demonstrating that she could tap his thoughts seemed the right course. "What are you doing in my office?"

"Preparing the groundwork to put your property in trust." Pinckney swiveled the chair to face her. "We're taking an inventory now, and I'm afraid I'll be here the rest of the day. I should get around to your home address by noon tomorrow."

"Are you going to shut down my store?" Birche asked.

"I haven't determined that yet, but I think not. You've set up a surprisingly efficient business," he added, with a condescension that infuriated her. She felt her cheeks turn red.

"Birche," Esposito said quickly, "there are some matters we should discuss now. Have you had lunch yet?"

"I—" Birche was suddenly aware of the yawning emptiness in her belly. She had tried, and failed, to choke down the greasy meals the MHB had offered her.

"I saw a cafe when I came in," Raul said, standing up. He put a hand on her arm and led her out of the office. "It looked most informal."

"I know the place." Birche glanced up at him as they left the store. "Raul, is there any way to get me out of this mess?"

"I . . . find it hard to say."

"You think it's impossible—sorry."

He smiled bleakly. "You need not apologize for reading my thoughts. To be honest, I do find it unlikely. Your best bet is to undergo a re-evaluation and convince a psychiatrist that you are sane. You are entitled to do this once every six months."

"That won't work," Birche said bitterly. "Don't you know? Telepaths are insane by definition."

"So I am informed. Your next best chance lies in persuading the MHB to change its definitions." Raul fell silent for a long moment, while they walked down the mall's central lane. "That, too, is unlikely."

"I know. Too many people are scared of witch— people like me. It's easier to handle us by sweeping us under the carpet."

"Perhaps that is part of the problem. The MHB's problem is one of bureaucratic inertia. It would take a great deal of effort to change their view on espers."

Birche shook her head as they approached the cafe. "There's no way I'll convince them of anything."

"One must hope." Raul opened the cafe door for her and smiled at the hostess. "A table for two, please."

The smile froze on her face as she saw Birche's bracelet. "Sir, we don't have an open table at the moment."

Raul frowned. "But I see several, my dear lady."

"They're all reserved, sir."

"Indeed? Perhaps I could talk about this with your manager."

"He's not here today, sir."

"A pity." Raul took something from a vest pocket. "My card. Present it to him with my compliments, and inform him that we may meet in court if he wishes."

"*Sir.*" The hostess gestured at a discreet sign above the door: "We *do* reserve the right to decline service."

Birche tugged at Raul's elbow. "I'm not hungry."

"Nonsense, my dear."

"Raul, *please.*" People had taken notice of the scene, and of her eye-catching bracelet. Their mounting hostility was a palpable thing to her. "I want to get out of here."

"Very well," he said, disappointed. He turned and walked out with her.

His disappointment told her something of the gap that had opened between herself and non-telepaths. To Raul, the encounter had consisted of nothing more than disguised unpleasantries and sharp looks. That raw, voiceless *hostility* hadn't registered on the lawyer. "You think I ran away," she said.

"Not at all," he said, then reminded himself that she knew what he thought. "Do you wish to tell me what happened?"

"I didn't want to go—but the things they thought about me in there—"

"You felt pressured?"

"No, I—it was . . ." Birche groped for words that didn't exist. "I had all of their thoughts going through my mind. It was as if *I* was thinking everything they thought—and they hated me."

"So you felt a self-hatred?" Raul shook his head. Her power smacked of black magic, but now he could see it as a two-edged sword. "My apologies."

"You don't have to apologize for anything," Birche said. "Raul, right now I need help. Can I take the MHB to court?"

"No. Your status is that of a legal ward. Only they can initiate legal action for you—if they decide it is necessary."

"It sounds like I'm their property," she said, and the strength of her bitterness surprised her.

"You—that is not far from the truth," he admitted.

Birche looked up at him as they walked through the mall. She could sense his reluctance to discuss her situation. Part of that came from a desire to shield her from reality, she thought, but only part of it. "Can you take *any* sort of action for me?"

"I am afraid not. An outside lawyer such as myself cannot act on your behalf—and before you ask, the Compton Act does not permit the MHB to transfer custody of its wards to an outsider."

"Can you raise a challenge on your own?" Birche asked.

"Other people have tried that," he said. "Most of these motions are dismissed out of hand on technical grounds; one must show that actual harm has been done. Others—in a legalistic sense, the Compton Act is an elegant, flawless work. It resists assault well."

"I guess I expected that." Birche felt as frustrated and powerless as she had in her cell. "This isn't *fair!*

The Compton Act was meant for criminals—why can't people use their common sense?"

"One cannot legislate common sense," Raul said. "We tried that with the Compton Act. To our shame we failed."

"What do you mean?"

"Common sense is a matter of wisdom, experience, knowledge—but not of legal definition. It is like a butterfly; to pin it down and display it is to kill it."

"I didn't mean that," Birche said. "You said you'd failed with the Compton Act—" She bit off her words at his sudden rush of shame and guilt. Birche realized he had *thought* that. "Sorry."

"No, you deserve to know." His thoughts were as bleak as an overcast sky. "I worked for Senator Compton. I helped him to draft the Act and to lobby for its passage."

"I never knew that." Birche was gripped by a sudden fear of herself. Like a careless child breaking a family heirloom, she had stumbled across a secret that pained this man. Her mind focused on the fact that telepathy was a *power* with a terrifying potential for evil.

"I never knew that you were psychic," Raul said. "No matter. The first draft of the Act would have kept felons from misusing the insanity defense, mainly by placing restrictions on its use."

"What went wrong?" Birche asked. She didn't want to press him, yet she could sense his need to explain himself.

"Politics. Our first version of the Act could not pass because a number of liberal senators opposed it. They felt it was unjust and unfair to defendants. Senator Compton would have dropped the matter, but he was up for re-election, and running scared. He needed the Act to give himself the image of a law-and-order man. Thus we worked out a compromise—with Senator Fitzhugh. His philosophy was that the state should take an active role in social matters."

Birche felt confused. "I don't understand, Raul."

Raul looked around the mall, unconsciously seeking a

way to escape from his memories. "He saw an opportunity to create a national mental health system, and he made the most of it. He composed the sections of the Act that defined the legal status of the *non compos mentis,* set up guidelines for their treatment and founded the MHB. His voting bloc wanted that—and they *did* improve an archaic system. Many abuses *were* corrected.

"As for Senator Compton, he saw to it that the Act would keep the criminally insane incarcerated until they were no longer dangerous—and that the laws were tough enough to deter misuse. Thus, he and his bloc could say that they had stopped the courts from coddling criminals." Raul paused, wryness on his face and in his thoughts. "But Senator Compton lost the election, and I came back here to my law practice."

Birche hesitated . . . and sensed that her silence made him uneasy, as though it condemned him. "Can't you think of a way to change that?"

"A minor bit of legislation might do it, such as a bill declaring that espers are not dysfunctional—"

"You don't believe that."

"I have learned that good laws and good intentions can be perverted by bad or careless men."

"That's not your fault. You couldn't have known that any of *this*—" she touched the bracelet "—would happen."

"No, and now I cannot undo things. All I can do is offer you a ride home."

It was late in the evening when Birche returned to her apartment building. Outside the gate she reached for her key, then remembered that she had left it in her apartment. She pressed the call button for the manager, and waited.

The trip home had been a miserable experience. Raul had bought a take-out dinner for her at a Chinese restaurant, and had taken her to a secluded spot in a park. Under other circumstances it would have made a pleasant picnic, but now it was the only way to avoid the embarrassment of getting thrown out of another restaurant. Raul's sense of guilt had made things worse, and Birche could appreciate his relief when he had finally dropped her off at the apartments.

"Oh, it's *you*," Hobart Purvis grumped. The manager glowered at Birche through the gate grille, then opened it. "You made a hell of a scene this morning."

"It wasn't my idea," Birche said.

"Half the tenants bitched about you," the old man said. "You have twenty-four hours to get out."

Birche felt shocked. "But—my lease isn't up until—"

"Your lease is worthless," Purvis said. "The law doesn't let your kind sign contracts."

"You have no right—"

"I asked my lawyer. The only reason I'm giving you an extra day is to let you move your trash out of my building. Twenty-four hours, that's all. If you're still sniffing around here after that I'll call the cops." Purvis turned and stomped away.

What's gotten into him? Birche wondered, as she walked upstairs. Despite his bluster, Purvis had felt no hatred or disgust for her, yet he seemed eager to evict her—oh. Of course. After he threw her out, he could rent her apartment to a new tenant at a higher rate.

I'd have to leave anyway, Birche thought. The MHB was going to supply her with two housing certificates per month, and that wouldn't cover the rent here.

The door to her apartment still stood open, exactly as she had left it. As she stepped through the door she heard something rasp under her sneakers. Puzzled, she stopped, bent down, fingered the grains on the floor.

Sesame seeds. Her neighbors knew about her, she thought, and one of them knew the superstitions. The seeds had been scattered to form an unwelcoming mat; Purvis wasn't the only one who wanted her out.

Birche shut the door, crossed the room, and dropped onto the couch. She felt defeated and alone. The neighbors knew she was back, and she was conscious of them phoning one another, peering out half-opened doors and wondering what the freak would do next.

Birche wondered herself. She might have to take up

Jenny's offer and stay with the clerk for a few days—although Jenny would face hard times herself. Birche felt certain that any trustee the MHB appointed would run her store into the ground.

"Remember, you idiots, we need her alive."

Birche was halfway to her feet when the door burst open. Three men came striding into the apartment, their eyes as hard as their thoughts, pistols in their hands. By the time Birche had stood up one of them had covered her with his gun. "Where's Forrest?" he demanded.

Birche felt herself trembling. They belonged to the Iron Guard, and a casual attitude toward killing marked their souls. "H-he isn't here!"

"I'll just bet," he said angrily. "Leon, Red, look around."

The two men started to search the apartment—and the search turned into demolition. They overturned the bed, kicked in the closet doors, pulled over the book-shelves and scattered books everywhere. The venetian blinds came down with a crash.

Birche saw it all through the corners of her eyes. She couldn't look away from the gun. The muzzle gaped at her, exposing the inner darkness of the weapon.

"Forrest ain't here," one of the men told his leader. "But look what we have here, Jim."

"Cover the bitch, Leon." Jim lowered his gun, and Birche watched him take a book from the red-haired man. Jim smiled and stuffed his pistol into his waist-band. *"Sense and Non-sense.* I suppose your freak buddy gave this to you?" He started tearing the book apart, twisting and shredding the paper. Even through her raw fear Birche could tap the man's overriding hatred of this particular book. Destroying it was an oddly sensual experience for him, as though he had put his hands on a living, malevolent force.

He tossed aside the last of the shreds and stepped up to Birche. "Where's Forrest?" he demanded loudly, spraying her with hot breath that stank of onions and cheap mouthwash.

"I don't know—"

A fist slammed into her solar plexus and she doubled over, losing her breath in a rush. A second blow caught her across the shoulders, knocking her to the floor. She struggled against the pain in her middle to get breath. Her eyes had squeezed shut, but she sensed the leader kneeling over her.

Something grabbed and twisted her hair, turning her face to the side. Birche stared into the muzzle of a pistol. She was so close she could see the metal baffles inside the silencer, and smell the gun oil and burned powder of earlier shots. She heard a loud, harsh *clack* as the man cocked the hammer—and the rough, basic thought that she could talk now or die.

Birche gathered enough breath for one word. "No."

The gun turned away and she heard contemptuous laughter. "It doesn't matter, douchebag. We know Forrest is coming." The hand shoved her head away, releasing her hair. "Let him know, witch. The Iron Guard is waiting for him. If he doesn't show up on time, we'll kill you." The man stood. "Finish up, boys."

The men completed the destruction of her apartment. They smashed lights, destroyed the phones, and slashed the clothes in the closet with hunting knives. They tossed food and utensils onto the kitchenette floor. One man opened the window, climbed out onto the carport roof, and closed the window behind him.

The other two left then. They shut the door behind them, and a moment later Birche heard hammering. They were sealing the door, making certain that the *bait* didn't leave the trap.

Birche sat up as the pain in her belly eased. No bones had broken. She would have some bruises, but she decided that she had been hurt worse in gym classes.

She heard the leader giving orders to Purvis. They wouldn't stay here long. There was no need to call the police. Just hang tight and watch the show, *okay?* Purvis blustered something about the mess, then retreated to his rooms, wishing he'd had enough sense to kick the witch out earlier. The damned things were nothing but trouble, just like Reverend Fountain said.

Birche stood and took a few tentative steps to the window. She looked across the alleyway, sensing rather than seeing the man who watched her window. He lay on a rooftop, sixty feet away, and he hoped that Forrest would try to sneak in this way. He wanted to be the one who killed the witch.

Birche turned away from the window. How had they known about Julian? Steve wouldn't have told them, she was sure of that. Whatever his faults, treachery wasn't one of them. No, the Iron Guard had learned about Julian without using Steve . . . somehow.

Perhaps that didn't matter. They wanted to kill Julian—and they planned to kill her, no matter what. There was nothing for her to do but warn Julian to stay away.

CHAPTER 12

The MHB certified me as insane three months ago, and I'm still learning all the implications of that. Every day I discover something I'm not allowed to do.

That never-to-be-sufficiently-damned orange bracelet has an interesting effect on non-psi people. Everything I do or say is interpreted in the light of my "madness." When they see it, they know I'm crazy, so most of them honestly do not care if I tap their thoughts. After all, I'm only a harmless nut, not a person. I am inferior, incapable of thinking, et cetera.

It's offensive as the dickens, but it has taught me something. When you think of a person as only one thing—a telepath, a woman, a lunatic—you automati-

*cally underestimate her. It's always a mistake to under-
estimate anyone.*

—*from* Sense and Non-sense, *by Lyn Amanda Clancy*

Julian fought an urge to hurry as he walked to Birche's
apartment that evening. There weren't many people on
the streets and sidewalks, and the ones who were out
acted suspicious of everyone they saw. The riots had set
their nerves on edge, and this was no time to do anything that might attract attention.

Julian was still a mile from the apartment when the
sun set. Suddenly the town looked abandoned, and he
wondered if there was a curfew in force. Perhaps so . . .
but when he tapped a few minds he learned there
was no curfew. People had run inside because they
feared more trouble. The city had the tense air of a
battlefield.

At least no one's going to worry about witches tonight, he thought. He could visit Birche in peace.

Julian started tapping for Birche's thoughts, hoping
to find her in the psychic clamor around him. He had
no luck, a fact that filled him with a detached sense of
annoyance. Telepathic communications were filled with
unknowns and wild variables. There had to be explanations for them, of course; all natural phenomena had
explanations. He would have to look for them when this
witch-hunting idiocy ended.

If it ever did—

Julian shook his head forcefully. It *had* to end sometime; people were basically decent, and someday they
would see how wrong it all was. Until then, though, he
would have to keep running, avoid the maniacs, stay
away from them—stay away— stay *away*—

"*Birche?*"

"*Julian!*" Relief and fear in a torrent. "*Stay away! It's
a trap!*"

"*Trap?*" He felt a moment of shock and fear . . . and
in that moment he lost the thread of her thoughts.
Julian stopped walking, took a deep breath, released it
slowly. He tried to find Birche again, but couldn't.

He resumed walking, warily alert. This was nothing new to him. He'd escaped more than one MHB trap—but they'd never used another telepathic as bait. The Redeemers might have done that, but quick lynchings and beatings were more their style. A trap was a calculated thing, done for reasons they lacked.

I'm probably walking right into it, Julian thought, as he went around a corner. He could see Birche's apartment building from here, across the street and a hundred yards away. There were several cars and vans parked along the curbs, and a dozen people on the sidewalks, and any of them could be part of the trap. Julian went down the street, tapping minds all the way.

He was halfway down the block when he found what he wanted. The man watched the front of Birche's apartment building, and thought about the orders he'd received. Julian shuddered, then turned into the door of the nearest shop—an all-night convenience store.

The clerk wore radio earphones that pumped the latest Fiery Cross hit into his ears. I wish they'd tune their instruments, Julian thought, as the shock-rock sounds echoed in his head. It was bad enough that they were perverting music to spread evil, but the discord made it hard to think. Struggling to ignore it, Julian stepped in front of the magazine rack and pretended to browse. His eyes traveled blankly over the rack while he tapped the watcher's mind.

The watcher sat in the front seat of a van, parked right in front of the apartments. His night-sight glasses gave him a good view of the entrance, and the cannon mike let him hear every sound the freak made in her cage. At least she wasn't howling like last night, when she'd mouthed off to that dimwitted reporter. So far there hadn't been any action, but when Forrest showed there'd be hell to pay.

Julian caught himself nodding in agreement. Two heavily armed men waited in the back of the van, and like the watcher, each wanted to become known as *the* man who'd killed this particular witch. The need for

glory was a twisting hunger in them—a way to become
more than powerless faces in the crowd.

Julian forced himself to keep tapping, to find more
information on the trap . . . but what he heard sickened
him. The watcher had been "gentle" with Birche, but if
there'd been the need, he could have made her talk.
He took pride in his ability to extract information with
his fists.

Noticing that the clerk's eyes were on him, Julian
went to the register and traded money for chocolate
bars. He dropped the candy into a coat pocket and
sauntered out. There *had* to be more men around here—
but where?

"*Never mind that, idiot! Get the hell out of here!*"

"Oh, hi, beautiful." Julian gave the link with Birche
all the attention he could spare. "*Where are they?*"

"*One's across the alley, watching my rear window.
There's another parked around the corner in a sports
car. Now will you clear out before they see you? You're
the one they want to kill.*"

"*I know.*" Julian walked back up the street and crossed
at the intersection. "*Details: where's this guy in the
alley?*"

"*On a rooftop, three stories up. He has a walkie-
talkie, infrared glasses and a .44 magnum revolver.*"

"*Okay.*" Julian stopped at the entrance to the alley.
The lane ran the length of the block and was fairly
wide. The sun was down now, and if he stayed in the
shadows on the alley's north side, the man on the
rooftop might not see him.

"*And he might!*" Birche said. "*Julian, listen. I've been
tapping their thoughts. Their leader, a guy named Savoy, told them you're a threat to the Iron Guard—that
you could destroy them. That's why they want to kill
you.*"

"Bushwa. He was giving them a pep talk. Even men
like them need a good reason to commit murder." He
entered the alley, sticking close to the north wall. "*Now
let's make plans. Does the man on the roof move for
anything?*"

He tapped her exasperation with him—and her fear. *"No. This guy is some sort of killing machine. He waits."*

"What does he do when a police copter flies over? Wave?"

"He's under a blanket, and it's the same color as the roof. They can't see him."

Julian nodded. Perhaps they were too well-prepared, too confident. Perhaps they had no plans for upsets— *"If we run, they'll chase us."* Birche told him, *"Then they'll kill us."*

"If they catch us." Halfway down the alley he found himself behind her apartment. *"Birche, I don't see any openings between any of these buildings. No walkways or side alleys—"*

"Land's too expensive here for that. You'd never believe what a curb-foot costs here."

"Probably not. The only exits I see are the openings to the alley." He looked around. *"Most of these buildings have rear doors. One of them must be unlocked. I'll check."*

"Don't bother. One of them already checked. Julian, they want us to run. For the sport."

"But they don't think we will." He looked at the carport. *"You have a car here, don't you?"*

"The brown Toyota. The MHB is confiscating it tomorrow."

Julian fought down a chuckle; the watcher might have heard it. *"Maybe not. Do you have the keys?"*

"Yes . . . somewhere. This place is a mess."

"Find them." He saw her car, and it gave him a bleak feeling. It didn't look like the sort of car a successful businesswoman would own. The suspension was bad, and the dim light in the carport made the faded brown paint look like rust. *"Are you sure that thing runs?"*

"Like new. Almost. Hey, I have the keys now."

"Good. When I give the word, open your window, climb down, and get into your car—fast. I'll keep your admirer busy—"

"Julian, I won't run while you get yourself killed."

"Hear me out," he said coldly. *"I know how to divert*

him without getting hurt. I'll run down the alley; you pick me up. Then we'll see about outrunning them."

"And what will his buddies do while this is happening?"

"Nothing." Julian smiled up at her window. *"Nothing at all, beautiful. He won't call them because he wants to kill me one on one. We'll have a good head start by the time he does call for help."* He tapped her sudden feeling of hope . . . the near-frantic realization that she might live after all. *"Get ready to move."*

Julian felt a moment of hesitation. He'd done similar things before: run away from a gunman, then dodge and twist in the instant he pulled the trigger. So far that had always destroyed a killer's aim—but it had always been a move of desperation. Julian had never stepped in front of a gun on purpose, and he was surprised to find that he was already out in the open, looking up into the surprised face of the gunman. *"Now!"*

The gunman had his own instant of uncertainty. This might not be Forrest; the IR glasses made it hard to tell—yes. He raised his gun. Julian turned, took several steps, then threw himself at the wall as the man started to squeeze the trigger.

There was no shot. It took Julian the barest instant to understand that this man was a full professional. His reflexes were so *fast* that he could tell when a shot was ruined, and ease up on the trigger before the hammer fell. He was everything Birche had said: a killing machine.

And Birche was out the window.

Julian ran across the alley. He dropped, jumped up, hopped sideways, and all the time sensed the man working to line up a good shot. There was no heat in the killer's thoughts, not even when he realized that the woman was on the ground and getting into her car. He decided there was no way to get a decent shot now; he elected to climb down the fire escape and go after Forrest on foot.

Julian heard Birche swear lustily before her car coughed to life. The gunman ignored her as he sped down the ladder—until he saw that she was driving *toward* his quarry, not fleeing in panic after all. He stopped climbing, and clung to the ladder with one hand as he pulled out his walkie-talkie.

Can't shoot now! Julian thought. He ran toward the car and grabbed the passenger door handle as the car slowed. It was still rolling as he pulled himself in, accelerating as he slammed the door. The car sped toward the exit, then slowed. "*What's wrong?*" Julian asked, sitting upright on the seat.

"*Traffic!*" She *had* to slow at a blind corner. A wreck could kill them as quickly as—

There was a gunshot, followed by the sound of metal punching through metal and insulation. Birche hit the gas and fishtailed around the corner. There was a second shot as she turned, and glass slivers sprayed through the car, glittering like diamond dust in the moonlight. Julian looked over his shoulder and swallowed hard when he saw the size of the hole in the rear side window. The opposite window had vanished as the slug exited through it.

The van appeared behind them, skidding around the corner in a turn that almost lifted its wheels from the pavement. Julian watched it gain speed as it rocked on its suspension. "*Uh-oh.*"

"*I see them,*" Birche said, glancing at a mirror. She mashed her foot into the accelerator.

"*The man in the sports car just picked up the other fellow,*" Julian told her. Car and van were in radio contact, exchanging terse code words, and Julian felt the van driver's tense assurance that they'd soon bag these freaks. One of his passengers had rolled down the side window—

"*Try to stay on the driver's side,*" Julian told Birche, as the passenger poked a shotgun out his window. "*Get as far to the left as you can.*" He clung to the dashboard as the car slammed over a pothole. "*That'll make it harder for him to aim.*"

"*I'll try—oh shit!*" The car shot through a red light.

"*Take it easy. Drive. I'll watch for cross-traffic.*"

"Never mind that!" The thought was more emphatic than any shout. *"What about that van?"*

"Just don't let that passenger get a bead on us." Julian took another look. The van was fifty yards behind them and closing in—and the sports car was back there, guided by the van and nearing rapidly. Both vehicles rocked wildly. The road had twisted and buckled in the earthquake; even the repaired sections were too rough for high-speed chases.

And the van had a high center of gravity—

"At the next intersection, brake hard and turn left, as tight as you can." Julian tapped the passenger's thoughts as he leaned out the window. The van swerved then and the man snapped off a shot. Julian saw the silver-blue muzzle flash just before the rear window shattered into a spiderweb of cracks.

"Sawed-off shotgun," he told Birche. *"Low muzzle velocity, limited range and accuracy. Let him get closer before you turn."*

"Okay." She licked her lips, eyed the next intersection, nodded. *"Any traffic?"*

"Yes—don't turn! Slow down!"

Birche slammed on the brakes as they entered the intersection, and a car raced in front of them with feet to spare. Birche hit the gas again and swallowed hard. *"What about the next intersection?"*

Julian checked. *"Turn left there. Left!"*

"Hang on!" Birche hit the brakes and spun the wheel. The car lurched around the corner. Momentum shoved Julian hard against the door, and he heard it creak under the force.

The van followed them into the turn.

Julian tapped it all. The driver hit the brakes—too late. The van skidded, and the driver *felt* the wheels lose traction, *felt* the right side rise up as the van began to roll over, *saw* the world turn sideways and rush at him in the shape of a parked truck—

"I didn't think they'd try it," Julian said, shaken. How could anyone be so *stupid?* He turned his head,

saw the van catch fire, the yellow flames spreading rapidly as they lit up the night.

The other car negotiated the turn at high speed, shot past the wreck, and came after them. Julian noted the pleasure of the two men in it. The others had just blown it, probably dying as they did so, but *they* had what it took to do the job.

"What now?" Birche asked. *"I can't outrun them."*

"We still have to—hey!" He saw a silvery tube on the floor: a xenon flashlight. If he could shine it in the driver's eyes and blind him, they'd *have* to quit. Julian picked it up and flicked the switch.

The batteries were dead.

"I was going to get new ones next week. Honest!"

"Okay." Julian dropped it and saw something. *"Hey! The freeway!"*

"Got it." Birche eyed the on-ramp, a half-block away. *"Let's see how fast I can take it."*

Birche stomped the brake pedal as she turned onto the ramp. The car slowed through the turn, then picked up speed sluggishly as it climbed the ramp. Julian saw twin headlights through the cracked safety glass behind him. Lighter and faster, the night-black sportster pulled up right behind them, jockeyed to pass them.

"Get us into the far left lane," Julian told Birche. *"Don't let that passenger get a clear shot at us."*

"I'll try." She looked over her shoulder, saw the traffic on the freeway. It was light and fast at this time of night. *"We can't lose them in this."*

"No. Buy time. If—duck!"

At once they bent as low as they could, and bullets punched through the rear window. Julian heard several slugs bounce off the car roof, a metallic hammering with an oddly musical tone. He saw the wide-eyed look on Birche's face, wondered if he looked just as scared, realized he did. When he sat up he saw bullet holes in the windshield—on his side only. Wind whistled through the holes. Most of the rear window had vanished.

"He's reloading," Julian said, as Birche worked the wheel. They had stayed down for seconds, but the car

had drifted across several lanes. *"He's a damned good shot. He'll try for the rear tires next, to make us stop."*

Birche nodded and put the car into the fast lane. The sports car stayed with them, weaving back and forth, maneuvering for a good killing position.

Julian looked past Birche and saw the freeway's center divider flash by. On this stretch of the highway it was a simple chain-link fence, mounted in a strip of dirt between the two sides of the freeway—

Dirt? *"Get us as far to the left as you can."*

"Done." The ride got rougher as dirt and pebbles gritted under the tires—and a plume of dust rolled behind the car. A pebble flew back, smashing one of the sports car's headlights. It flared in the darkness and went out. Anger raged in the car as the rooster-tail of dirt engulfed it, blocking the view.

"We should be okay for a moment," Julian said. *"They can't see us, and they won't risk pulling next to us—we might sideswipe them—"*

Then there was light behind them, lightning flashes in the dust cloud—shots fired blindly. One bullet smacked into the trunk with a harsh crunching roar, and Birche decided that *enough was enough*. Julian had just enough time to brace himself as she tensed her muscles and tramped on the brakes.

There was the howl of grinding metal and glass as the cars hit. The force of the impact shoved Julian forward, a sensation even stronger than the *surprise* the men behind him felt. Then Birche hit the gas again and her car staggered forward.

Through the gaping hole of the rear window Julian saw the sportscar, billowing steam like a live volcano. Its hood popped open suddenly while the car swayed and skidded to a halt. Then it was lost in the night behind them.

"Still alive," Julian thought, letting his breath out. His nerves were on the ragged edge of adrenalin exhaustion. *"Are you all right Birche?"*

"Fine." She frowned thoughtfully, listening to the noises her car made, feeling the new roughness of the

ride. The smell of burning insulation filled the car. *"We'd better get off the road. This crate won't run much longer, and if a cop stops us—hell. What should we do?"*

"First we hide and make sure they've lost us." Julian looked at her, absently admiring her round, beautiful face. She smiled shyly in response, and steered the car across several empty freeway lanes. Julian clung to the seat as the car rolled down an unreasonably steep off-ramp. The motor coughed and stalled, then caught when Birche keyed the ignition.

They had entered an old industrial zone. All of the buildings sagged with age and neglect, and many of them looked abandoned. *"Park over there,"* Julian suggested, pointing.

The car lurched into a lot behind a brick building, and Birche parked next to the wall. Julian got out, glanced at the car, then stared at it. The rear end looked like crumpled aluminum foil, the paint scoured away by shotgun pellets. Bullet holes peppered it. One taillight assembly dangled by a set of wires, and the muffler drooped on the ground.

Shaking his head, Julian surveyed the area. The car couldn't be seen from the street, so no one would spot it any time soon. That would give him and Birche time to vanish.

"Vanish," Birche echoed bleakly. She still sat behind the wheel. For the first time Julian saw the orange bracelet clamped to her wrist, glittering in the moonlight.

The implications hit him at once. *"I really wrecked your life, didn't I?"*

"You?" She shook her head and got out of the car. *"The MHB did it . . . and the Iron Guard. Did you know they turned me in? The things I heard them think . . ."* Her thoughts trailed off as a numbing fatigue washed over her.

Julian put an arm around her shoulder and led her away from the car. Exhausted, he thought—and no doubt with good reason. He shied away from wondering what she had been through this day.

"*I'm okay,*" she told him. "*I only need some sleep.*"

"*Same here. There should be a good place around here—nothing fancy, but the price should be right.*"

"*Price, hell. What about the neighbors?*" She touched the bracelet half-consciously. "*I'm not ready to be the life of another party.*"

"*I think we can find a quiet room with a nice view.*" This area was deserted, aside from a few night watchmen and vagrants in different buildings. All they needed—there. An old gas station stood on a corner, its windows broken and its pumps torn out. Julian checked and found that it was empty. "*That'll do.*"

"*Charming,*" Birche said, as Julian helped her through a window. Enough moonlight came through to show that the interior had been stripped. "*What's that smell?*" she asked, sniffing the air. "*Orange blossoms?*"

"*Riot gas. There must've been a fight here today.*"

"*More trouble? Please, no—*"

"*No, not at night, especially not with so few people around.*" He smiled at her, wanting to reassure her. "*Right now you couldn't even start a heated argument around here, much less a riot.*" Julian sat down against a wall. When Birche sat down next to him he slid an arm around her, cushioning her back against the metal sheeting. Holding her was a wonderful sensation, and he pulled her closer. Her hair had an intoxicating scent.

Tired as she was, Birche could still feel an abstract sense of surprise. "*I really turn you on?*"

"*Absolutely,*" he said. "*I wish I knew a better way to say it, but—*"

"*I'm not complaining.*" She snuggled against his shoulder, smiled, and fell asleep.

Julian felt a moment of frustration . . . yet it was oddly flattering. As she had dropped off to sleep she had felt *secure*. Deep down, she believed that he could protect her from anything.

He wished that he could.

CHAPTER 13

THURSDAY, 15 JUNE 2000

You had better understand that everyone wants to be used. Just make sure you're using people the way they want to be used, and you'll own their souls. You find a man's talents, you see, and praise him when he puts them to work for you. For instance, if a guy likes blood and violence, give him a chance to fight for you, and pat him on the head when he obeys.

There's always the smug fool who thinks he can't be used, or that he can use you. A guy like that is pathetic. It's so easy to handle that kind that I won't bother to describe any techniques.

—excerpt, letter from Gerald G. Savoy to the cadre leaders of the Iron Guard, date ca. March 2000

Damned inconsiderate, Steve thought, as he groped around for the phone. His nightstand clock said it was just after midnight. The caller was probably Reade, the *Post*'s night editor, looking for another update on Steve's column. The curse of electronic publishing, Steve thought. The current edition was never current enough. His hand groped the phonepad. "Gargh."

"Magyar, this is Savoy. We need to talk. I'll meet you at your apartment in ten minutes." The speaker clicked off.

Steve sat up, grumbling. He doubted that Savoy had a good reason to haul him out of bed—but Savoy was news . . . and his offer interested Steve. He told himself that he didn't take it as seriously as Birche had suggested . . . but it was always a good idea to keep your options open.

Ten minutes later, dressed and reasonably awake, Steve climbed into the cherry-red sportster. "What's up?" he asked Savoy.

"Plenty, and not a damned bit of it's good." Savoy gunned the engine and pulled away from the apartment complex. "We're both in grave danger. Damn it, Magyar, why didn't you let me know you've been doing business with witches?"

"I—what?" Steve found it impossible to read the man's expression. That might have been concern or anger or anything on his hard, sharp features.

"You've used a witch named Holstein as a spy," Savoy said, "and you planned to meet Julian Forrest. I wouldn't mind—I know you reporters have your own rules—but some of our hotheads found out a while ago."

"What? How?"

"Who knows? They learned that Forrest was going to the slut's apartment tonight. They tried to ambush him." Savoy's hands convulsed on the steering wheel. "They botched it. The freaks got away without a scratch—"

"Is Birche all right?"

"I just said so, didn't I?" Savoy looked pained. "And what's a witch to you, anyway? You've put me in a hell of a mess, Magyar. I was forced to report her to the MHB this morning—"

"You—"

"Shut up and listen," he said brusquely. "I'm just barely in charge of *one* faction of the Guard. Bringing you into it is a major move on my part—and a risky one. I'm trying to strengthen my position, so I can rein in our loonies, but my enemies think I'm weakening the Guard. They used your connection with the witches to move against me."

"They didn't attack *you*," Steve said.

"Not directly. Not yet. But there was a confrontation this morning. I had to do something to prove I'm not soft on witches—and what I did wasn't enough. Our radicals decided to take matters into their own hands."

Steve tasted something bitter in his mouth. "So you turned Birche in to save your skin."

"And yours, Magyar. Our hotheads play *rough*. Everyone does. A lot of people could get killed in a power struggle." His face darkened as though he was brooding over some ancient wrong. "And before you get maudlin over that freak, hear this: she thinks *you* turned her in to the MHB."

Steve felt shocked. "Birche knows I wouldn't do that!"

"What, you think the fat slob trusts you?"

He hesitated. She knew he had thought about it, but—"Yes."

"Then you know nothng about witches. They don't *need* to trust people. If they have any doubts, they settle 'em by reading your mind."

"Birche never did that."

"Come off it!" He made a sharp, fast turn down a side street. "Reading minds is automatic with the freaks, like seeing or hearing is with us normal folks. If she said she didn't read your mind, she lied."

Steve couldn't find an answer. True, Birche had often responded to his thoughts and moods, even though she'd claimed she tried not to—

Orange light flared outside the car. "Hang on." Savoy's voice was tight with control as he gunned the engine. The acceleration shoved Steve back in his seat. He looked out the tiny rear window and saw a fire burning on the street. A jeep rolled behind them, weaving back and forth as though the driver was drunk.

As he watched, the man in the passenger seat stood up. One hand clutched the jeep's roll-bar as he braced himself against speed and wind. The other hand threw something that glittered in the moonlight. Steve saw it tumble through the air, then hit the ground to the left and rear of the sports car. Flames burst out as it broke open.

Savoy pushed the sportster through a bootlegger's turn. The road spun dizzily, and Steve watched flames loom ahead of the car, surround it, then fall behind.

"I wonder how in hell they found me," Savoy muttered angrily. 'You see what happens when you get careless, Magyar? I should have seen that jeep coming."

"What in hell were they throwing? Grenades?"

"Some sort of Molotov cocktails. You notice how they didn't catch fire until they hit? That's a damned clever touch."

"It didn't work," Steve said. "Why didn't they use guns?"

Savoy snorted. "The police can't run a ballistics check on a firebomb, or lift fingerprints from it. It almost *did* work. If I hadn't spotted them when I did, they'd have cooked us alive."

"Who did it?" Steve demanded. He felt an outraged sense of violation; someone had just tried to kill *him*.

"I don't know. I have beaucoups of enemies. Here." Savoy opened the glove compartment and took out a silver flask. He opened it one-handed, took a swallow, and gave it to Steve. "Nerve medicine. Buck up, Magyar; they didn't want to kill you."

Steve's ears buzzed as he swallowed whisky. Shaken as he was, he took note of its smoothness as it slid down his throat. Savoy had excellent taste in liquor, he thought. The drink calmed his nerves. "You said I'm in danger. If *that* wasn't it—"

"Our bad-boys screwed up their ambush. They'll have to make up for that somehow. That means killing you."

I'm dreaming this, Steve thought. The intensity of Savoy's voice only heightened the surrealistic undertones of the conversation—but after the firebomb attack he could believe anything. "What good would that do?"

"It would embarrass me, by showing that I don't control them and that I can't protect my friends. It would also scare off anyone who might side with me; you don't work with weaklings and losers." Savoy glared at the empty street ahead of his car. "Power, Magyar. Force. That's what politics and life are all about. If you aren't strong, if you can't make people do what you want, you're finished."

"So I'm a pawn in a power struggle."

"My enemies think so," Savoy said. "They attacked your witch buddies first, to scare you off—they wanted to see you run. That would have made *me* look bad—as if I'd chosen a coward." He watched the streetlights slip past his car, then smiled savagely. "But you're only a pawn if you let people use you. How do you feel about turning the tables on our bad-boys?"

Steve grunted. "I'm no fighter."

"You are—where it counts."

"And when there's a reason," Steve said. "I'm not part of the IG. Why should I help you fight your battles?"

"Aside from saving your own hide?" His mouth twitched, and Steve got the impression that Savoy was negotiating with himself. "Magyar, if you went to Hell you'd spit in the devil's eye."

"No, I'd ask him for an interview—an exclusive, too."

Savoy laughed, a shrill sound that jarred with his resonant voice. "By God, you *are* something! Magyar, whether or not we win in November, the Guard is going to start its own news agency—no, not a propaganda service. We'll have our own reporters, and we'll expect them to report the *news*, by God—not pap that sells newspapers and offends no one. It's going to be a major operation—especially after we win; it'll become *the* model agency for the rest of the media, showing everyone how to report responsibly, accurately."

He does love the sound of his own voice, Steve thought. "I'd rather have something more immediate."

"Name it and we'll see."

Okay, Steve thought. "How do you expect to win the election?"

"By winning half the votes. I told you before: America is behind us. They see the national will in our party."

"Along with twenty other parties," Steve said. "How does Transpac figure in all this?"

"They've promised not to obstruct us, nothing more." Savoy frowned. "I expect they'll take a more cooperative approach."

Okay, so he doesn't trust me, Steve thought. Savoy was concealing something; the key to the man was to find a subject he *would* discuss freely, and see what slipped out. "What do you plan to do about witches?"

Savoy shrugged. "We haven't defined our policy yet. A few of our people favor annihilation, but they're the ones who always reach for the gun. I favor vigorous enforcement of the Compton Act. I hope that's enough; I'd hate to see stronger measures forced on the country."

"What 'stronger measures'?" Steve asked. When Savoy remained silent, he continued, "The Compton Act practically revokes their rights; about the only thing left to do is kill them."

"That might prove necessary," Savoy said, "but not through these damned witch hunts! Magyar, I've learned—the hard way, I admit; you must know my record—I've learned the importance of law and order. America cannot tolerate anarchy."

"But what would you *do?*"

"Well . . ." Savoy studied the road as the sports car cruised along. "Strengthen the MHB, give it more power to incarcerate the freaks. We can't have order with them running loose—especially not with this conspiracy they've joined."

"Savoy, is this conspiracy just talk, or have you got proof?"

Savoy turned his head and glowered at Steve. "Don't overestimate your importance to me. How can I trust a man who balls a witch?"

"We've broken up," Steve growled.

"Good. Well—we know they plan some sort of demonstration of their power, some coordinated action that will demoralize the country. Something that depends on psychic powers—"

"What, black magic?" Steve scoffed.

"No. Witches are only one part of the conspiracy. They'll use their powers the same way you used that fat slut: to get information. We're all helpless against that sort of spying." Savoy grimaced. "But right now we have an *immediate* threat on our hands. We can work together or die separately; it's up to you."

"If some of your people are trying to kill me—"

"They are," Savoy nodded. He glanced at the street around the car. "That's why I'm taking you to the Post Building. It has good security. Better yet, only *I* know you're going there, and *I* won't talk." His grin would frighten children, Steve decided. "And this is a good deal for you, Magyar."

Steve's laugh sounded anything but amused. "A bunch of maniacs want to kill me, and *that's* a good deal?"

"For a reporter. You know what *really* happened with those freaks tonight. More than that, you have my official statement that all this was the act of an outlaw faction of the Iron Guard." Savoy pursed his lips. "Frankly, I'd rather hush up this whole mess—but dragging it into the open has its good points. It will show everyone, including our fire-eaters, that our street-brawling days are over."

"Meanwhile, what do I do about your outlaws?"

Savoy waved a hand in dismissal. "I'll have *them* under control in a hurry. In fact, things will go faster if you're back on the job at your paper. Write an article that shows you're not scared of them; they'll respect that."

"You're certain?" Steve asked.

"I deal with them all the time. They're not too subtle, Magyar. A few raps on the knuckles will bring them into line."

"I see." Steve found it hard to accept that he was in much danger—and the assurance in the man's voice was catching.

Looking out the windows, Steve saw that the car was within a block of the Post Building. Savoy pulled up to it and braked to a halt as if he had practiced the maneuver for years. "I'll call you the moment everything's fixed," he said as Steve got out. "You'll be laughing at this before breakfast."

I hope so, Steve thought, as he walked up to the building. He pressed his hand against the security plate, and waited for the computer to recognize his finger-prints and body-electric fields. Inside, he nodded to the receptionist and took the elevator to his office. After he locked the door behind him, Steve sat down at the computer and checked the crime reports.

The list was long. Many of the reports dealt with Sere activities; they'd spent much of the day in patternless hit-and-run strikes. There was a good deal of vigilante activity as well, directed against Sere and Sere members. Steve wondered how much of that violence was actually directed against Sere. With this sort of chaos, a lot of grudges could get settled without drawing too much suspicion. He made a note to investigate that notion.

"Magyar here," he said, answering the phone.

"There's a Lieutenant Heyerdahl from the LAPD on line two," the switchboard operator said.

The secure line? Steve asked himself. The *Post* had one, but it was a status symbol, rarely used. "Magyar here, Lieutenant."

"Mr. Magyar, your apartment was bombed a half-hour ago," a brisk voice said.

"Bombed!" Steve glanced at his watch. A half-hour ago—it must have happened right after Savoy picked him up. "What went down?"

"We're not sure yet, Mr. Magyar. A witness saw you drive off in a red BTK. A minute later another car came along. Its driver shot out your window and threw a bomb. As near as we can tell it was a crude bomb—chain wrapped around dynamite. I'd say five or six sticks, judging by the damage."

"Was anyone hurt?"

"Three people are in the hospital. There were a bunch of superficial injuries, band-aid stuff. The fire was under control in ten minutes, but your place is a total loss."

"I see." Steve stared blankly at the phone unit. "Any—do you have any suspects yet?"

"No. We'll try to send someone to your office for your statement later. Will you be there much longer?"

"Several hours, at least. When will—"

"As soon as possible, Mr. Magyar." The man's voice was testy. "We're stretched tonight." Heyerdahl hung up.

Shaken, Steve leaned back in his chair and squeezed his eyes shut. Bombed! He was used to threats, and once Security had grabbed some crank with a gun— he'd even taken the attack on Savoy's car in stride. But a bombing in his home, his *own home*—that was different. If Savoy hadn't come for him when he had—

With a shiver, Steve forced his attention back to the computer. He fed in a search program and hunted for anything involving witches. Nothing on Birche or Forrest—nothing about Birche's neighborhood—no mention of the Iron Guard anywhere.

Steve cleared the screen and rubbed his eyes. Yesterday had been a real meat grinder; he'd spent his time checking out a report that the governor would declare a state of emergency in Los Angeles. The report had proven false, as Steve had expected. The governor hadn't wanted to take responsibility for that move; he was waiting for the mayor of Los Angeles to make a formal request. The mayor, who was running for governor, wouldn't do that; she had maintained that the LAPD was in control of the situation. Chief Shelburn had refused to comment on that.

Turtles, Steve thought angrily—turtles cowering in their shells. Sometimes it seemed that the entire government was composed of men and women like that, afraid to make decisions, unwilling to risk losing anyone's vote or support. With leadership like that, it was no wonder the country was paralyzed.

The governor and mayor made a feeble contrast with Savoy, he thought. For all his crudity and street-tough manners, he was willing to admit mistakes and correct them. Most politicians looked for ways to blame others for their mistakes.

Steve answered the phone and heard Savoy's voice. "I was just thinking of you," Steve said. "Maybe I'm psychic."

"Let's hope not, Magyar. Anyway, you'll be pleased to hear that everything is under my control now."

"We're out of danger?"

"Yes, our troublemakers are back in line. I wish I could take full credit, but the truth is that they've got egg on their faces." Savoy laughed. "Their ambush boomeranged. Three of our mighty warriors are in the hospital, and two are in jail. They got into separate car crashes while they were running away! They're very eager to live it down."

"I suppose they are." Steve regarded the blank computer screen. "Do you know their names?"

"Just two of them—Leon Kyle and Ted Springbock, Springbach, something like that. They're petty hoods, and we're better off without them." Savoy paused, and Steve heard him drumming his fingers. "Do you plan to put this in your column?"

"Absolutely," Steve said, feeding the names into the terminal.

"Good! Everything I said before goes. The Iron Guard does *not* condone any form of criminal activity, and we do *not* fight, except when attacked." Savoy spoke with a vehemence that made the speaker buzz. "It galls me to air our dirty laundry in public, but this is a time for candor."

"Good," Steve said. "Maybe you can tell me who bombed my apartment?"

"What! When did this happen?"

"Right after you picked me up."

"Close! Very close. Well, none of our people would have done it; our fighters prefer guns to bombs." There was a pause, and Steve heard static on the line. "Magyar, you know who I think threw the bomb?"

"Your conspiracy again."

"It's a natural suspicion. I could be wrong this time. Sere has been up to a lot today, and I'm sure you've got your own set of enemies." He paused. "It might be a good idea if I sent a couple of my men to guard you. We can't afford to lose you."

"Hell, *I* can't afford to lose me," Steve said. "But I can't do my job with a bodyguard."

"No, I guess not." Savoy sounded disappointed. "Well, you've got guts. I'll call you later."

A complex man, that one, Steve reflected. He was coarse and unrefined, but that highlighted his strengths. He had a dynamic confidence that made him a natural leader. Objectively, Steve knew he had little chance to take the White House . . . and yet—

"First things first," he told himself. An attack on a couple of witches by some nuts wasn't especially newsworthy; even the bombing of a reporter's apartment meant nothing when compared to the Sere mayhem. On the other hand, Savoy's statements would give him some good material for his next column. The public always demanded "good" news, and a report that a radical group had changed its ways would help satisfy that demand.

With a smug string of beeps the computer finished its search and presented the reports on the men Savoy had named. Kyle and two other men were in the prison wing of a hospital. The highway patrol had picked up Springbock and another man on the Hollywood Freeway. They were being held on assorted weapons charges, including a running gunfight.

Steve looked at the reports, and felt something unraveling in his head as he double-checked the times. All the arrests had been made shortly after nine o'clock, right after the ambush . . . yet Savoy must have talked to the men afterwards, because he claimed that Birche blamed Steve for turning her in to the MHB—

—and how had he known about Forrest—and Birche, for that matter?

· He'd said that the bomb had been *thrown*. How could he know that? And the firebomb attack, which had so conveniently failed—how *had* they found Savoy?

He stared blankly at the computer screen, and tried to accept two stark facts. Savoy had lied through his teeth—and Steve had believed him.

The facts humiliated him, and he tried to rationalize them away. One of the men could have phoned Savoy. He could have guessed the bomb was thrown. Witches *were* crazy; Birche or Forrest might have talked. The men in the jeep might have had a telepath to help them, or they might have been skilled trackers.

The rationalizations fell apart. Steve forced himself to admit that Savoy had manipulated him . . . and he was afraid to learn why.

CHAPTER 14

It's funny, but people get upset when I tell them that telepathy isn't magic. It isn't because they want to believe in a quaint, romantic universe that's filled with enchantment. What they're looking for is something for nothing—the power to do things without cost. They want spells and incantations that can move mountains and give them control of great nations.

It's time for me to come clean and confess that there truly is magic afoot. If you wish to have unlimited power, the proper spell is writ "$E = mc^2$." For the ability to shape the destiny of the world with words, read the speeches of Winston Churchill. This is white magic. It takes both talent and years of study to master it, as any scientist or statesman can tell you, but if you persevere you will develop the ability to do everything a wizard might do, and then some.

If you are lazy, there is always black magic. Greed, fear, stupidity, lust—it takes very little to exploit them. If you are the sort of person who wishes to take this route, you will have to sell your soul. You won't need to look far for a devil, though. You'll find one staring out of the nearest mirror.

—from Sense and Non-sense, *by Lyn Amanda Clancy*

*   *   *

Birche couldn't imagine where they had come from, or how they had found her. The Redeemers swarmed around the gas station, waiting for her to come out. They had guns, of course, and wet ropes, but the main attraction was the wooden stake and unlit fire.

"*There is an escape,*" the demon hissed in her mind. "*Destroy them with your powers.*"

"*No.*" Birche looked away from the demon, looked toward the head Redeemer. His gun had a muzzle the size of a house, and it was pointed at her.

"*You have done this before, sorceress.*" The demon wrapped its talons around her wrist in an unbreakable grip. The abomination pulled her arm and aimed it, and lightning flashed from her fingertips. When the smoke cleared away she saw a pillar of charcoal, sculpted in the shape of a badly surprised Redeemer. The others had fled in mortal terror.

This is a *dream,* Birche thought, quaking in horror. Knowing that, she *willed* the demon to vanish. It shrank away, but somehow kept its death grip on her wrist. Birche shook her arm savagely, slamming the orange monster against the wall in a desperate effort to free herself—

"*Take it easy!*" She woke up, saw Julian, felt the MHB bracelet on her wrist. "*You were having a nightmare, Birche.*"

"*I know,*" she said crankily. The dreams had ruined her sleep, with their mixture of dark images and recent events . . . although this time, the nightmares had been impossibly brief. "*You had something to do with that,*" she stated.

"*Yes.*" Julian stood up and stretched like a cat. Spending the night with a beautiful woman in your arms was as romantic as all hell, he reflected, but it was even more uncomfortable, especially on top of the bruises he'd collected the other night.

Birche started to nod at that, then winced and massaged the crick in her neck. "*How did you control my dreams?*"

"*I didn't control them. I influenced them . . . made*

suggestions that your subconscious picked up. It's a fairly simple mental interaction."

"It sounds like hypnosis."

"The effect is similar," Julian agreed. "The subconscious is highly responsive to telepathic messages—that's something to keep in mind, by the way. It makes us all vulnerable to outside influences."

"I see." That had unpleasant implications—but there were more pressing matters. "What do we do now?"

"Take a walk," Julian said. "We're ten, maybe twelve miles from where I've been staying. I want to get back."

"Ten or twelve miles," Birche repeated. That struck her as a long way to walk before breakfast. Her stomach was deplorably empty.

"We can do something about that." Julian dipped into his pocket and pulled out the chocolate bars he'd bought last night.

Birche hesitated before taking one. She was hungry, but—candy. She remembered jokes and warnings about fat, and the hoglike snufflings her father had made whenever she'd gone for a snack or second helpings.

"—Hey," Julian said, putting his hands on her hips. "You look magnificent."

"You really mean that." It was so strange to feel that hot male desire directed at her—but Julian meant it, she thought, looping her arms around him. Well, he was strange himself, which would explain—"Oh, damn," she muttered.

"It's all right," he said in resignation. Her attitude had hit him like an ice-water shower: the self-poisoning belief that she had no worth as a person, that there must be something wrong with anyone who liked her. "I know what it's like."

"You? Impossible." He couldn't know what it meant to be ugly—

"Looks don't have anything to do with it," Julian said. "I decided I was worthless once, too. So I tried to kill myself. But I learned better and so will—"

Out on the street a truck backfired. They both jumped, and Julian shook his head. Her appetite was gone now, killed by embarrassment. He put the chocolate back in his pocket. *"Let's get going."*

There were few people in the area to see them slip out of the gas station, and none paid any attention to them. No one had found the wreck of her car yet, Birche learned, and no one gave any thought to fugitive witches or the Iron Guard. Their thoughts came to her easily, without the vagueness she had grown used to over the years.

"That surprises you," Julian said. He looked at a street sign and decided they should head north.

"It does. I figured it would take me months or years to get this good at reading minds—that I'd have a lot to learn."

"Tapping thoughts is easy," Julian said. *"It's a sense, just like hearing and seeing. But learning how to use it, how to keep from making mistakes with it—that's the hard part."*

She remembered the mistakes she'd made with Steve and Raul, and others, and nodded dumbly. *"I knew it was too easy."*

" 'Easy'?" Walking alongside her, Julian wrapped an arm around her waist. *"You did it by yourself, in an MHB cage. That wasn't an easy way to learn the basics."*

"I didn't mean that. Steve was right; I always screw up. Why couldn't I have been born normal?"

"You were."

She stopped walking and glared at him. "I know what I am!" she said out loud.

"Do you? Are you really a fat freak who always screws up?" He had a thought that caused him a twinge of jealousy. *"Birche, maybe you should talk with Steve again."*

"What for?"

"For your own good. You still care about him, but he really hurt you when he said those things."

"Yes." The idea of talking with Steve filled her with reluctance, but now that Julian had made the suggestion, the need was undeniable. *"Is there a phone around here?"*

Julian looked down the street and pointed to an open phone stand. *"Let's see if it still works."*

Birche clasped his hand as they approached the booth. Tapping his thoughts told her how much he enjoyed her touch—and—and— *"What's this about a nervous breakdown?"*

"There's a lot to explain—"

"Wait . . . wait . . ." Information came to her in a dizzying surge—memories of fear and madness; the way he'd felt when he first met her, conversations with a strange woman . . . *"So I'm not the only one with problems."*

"No, you're not. I need help." The admission came with an ease that caught him by surprise. Until this moment, Julian had not taken the matter seriously. But now—yes. He'd tried to escape from his problems once before, through suicide, and what was insanity but another form of escape? It was worse than death, though; the mind turned into a crippled parody of itself, unable to die and unable to live in the real world—and it *was* happening to him—

"It's all right," Birche said. His sudden fragility shocked her. She touched his cheek as if to assure herself that he was still solid. Her fingers felt the cold sweat beading his face now. *"You're going to be all right."*

"I . . . yes." Julian regained his composure. Something about her convinced him that everything *would* be all right. He had the sudden, unfamiliar conviction that he would be alive tomorrow. After the past two years that was an almost painful sensation. *"You see why I need you?"* he asked.

The knowledge that there were other problems returned to him. *"There's the phone."* He dropped his last two dollars into it, dialed, and gave Birche the handset.

Cold feet beset her. *"What should I say?"*

"Tell him about last night." Julian leaned against the telephone stand's plexiglas bubble and watched her.

"Magyar here," Steve's voice said.

"He sounds so strange." "Steve, this is Birche. Are you all right?"

There was a long pause, long enough to make her wonder if he would answer. "I'm the one who should ask that."

"You heard about last night?" she asked.

"I . . . talked to Savoy around midnight. He told me he set the MHB on you. Birche, you've got to believe me, I didn't do it!"

"I know. I never thought you did. Steve, the Iron Guard tried to kill Julian and me last night—"

"Savoy told me. He claimed his enemies were trying to scare me off—"

"No," Birche said sharply, surprising herself. She'd never interrupted him before, never forced him to listen to her. "They were there to kill Julian. They sent in five of their best to do that one thing. Are you recording this?"

"Yes."

"Good. One was a man named Theodore Springbock. They call him 'Red.' He killed two FBI agents in Eugene, Oregon last month. He used a .44 magnum pistol. Two others were Leon Kyle and James Carmichael. They've killed a dozen people in the Denver area this year. The drivers—well, they've never killed anyone. One was named Greg Xavier. The other one was an electronics wizard named Cotter Wendell. He used a cannon mike to eavesdrop on us the other night."

"So that's how they knew." Steve's voice sounded distant in the earpiece. "You're sure about all this?"

Birche nodded absently. It was a reasonable question. "I spent over an hour tapping everything they thought. Savoy had Wendell follow you after you met him. Savoy ordered everything else. Can you use any of this?"

"Yes, but . . ." She heard him swallow. "Birche, I'm sorry, but there's nothing I can do about the MHB now. I can't pay you back."

"I didn't call for that." Birche rested her hand against the phone. Without needing to ask or tap, she knew that Steve was glad that she had used the phone, instead of coming to see him. The phone saved him from the need to look her in the face. "Steve, for some reason, killing Julian is very important to the Iron Guard. Find out why."

"If I can." He hesitated. "Is there any way I can help you?"

"No. I'm going to go underground, or something—"

" 'Playing freaks 'n' sneaks,' " Julian said. "That's what we call it when someone goes on the run."

"Julian calls it 'playing freaks and sneaks.' I'll call you again when I can."

"Wait! There's something I have to say. I—want to thank you. For that favor you did me. Goodbye, Birche." He hung up then.

"Favor?" Julian asked, as they walked away from the phone.

"The last time we met, I tried to warn him against joining the Iron Guard. He must have listened." The idea gave her a feeling of relief—and joy. She had saved him from that, after all.

Julian felt a faint amusement at his own jealousy. "You want to see him again, don't you?"

"I'd like to be his friend . . . or become his friend. But that's all. Anything else—" She had an unpleasant moment of self-discovery. "I've been using him as part of a fantasy—telling myself that he loved me, that he wanted me for more than my ESP . . . that even our problems were normal ones. But I was stupid to think he was something he isn't."

"Don't be so hard on yourself," Julian said.

"Don't tell me that," she said in anger. "I know better, but I worked hard to fool myself. Steve must think I'm an idiot."

"After that call? He knows you're a brave woman who keeps her head in an emergency—and that he lost a lot when he didn't hang on to you."

"You really mean that, don't you?" she asked, looking at him. It occurred to Birche that Julian stood only two or three inches taller than she; she could look him in the eyes without craning her head and getting a stiff neck . . . and she liked his cool green eyes.

She smiled slyly. *"Do you still have that chocolate?"*

Julian felt an urge to know all about Birche, and as they walked along holding hands he tried to satisfy his curiosity. It was an enjoyable process, but a slow one; Birche described herself in terms of the people in her life, so that Julian ended up learning as much about her friends and relatives as he did about her.

"I gave everyone a hard time," she said regretfully, as they strolled into a run-down shopping district. *"Like the family reunion we had when I was nine. I could tell my aunt and uncle were miserable over something, and I wanted to help, so I tried to talk with them. I asked some questions—and they started shouting at one another. It turned out he was hooked on cocaine, and she was sleeping around, and they had a big fight in front of the whole family. They got divorced after that."*

"That wasn't your fault," Julian said. *"You were trying to help—"*

"I know. Nobody blamed me for what happened, but some of my relatives started avoiding me . . . or I started avoiding them. It was the easiest way to keep from causing more problems." Birche felt his hand squeezing hers, just firmly enough to reassure her. *"You never had trouble like that, did you?"*

"I was lucky. My folks were the original peacemakers, and—they knew I was different, *but they always tried to help me fit in. They did their best to think everything through, and that was a lot harder for them than for me."*

"But they managed," Birche said. *"What were they? Psychologists? Therapists?"*

"No, musicians. And good parents. I really was lucky."

"Musicians?" She giggled. *"And you went off and became a scientist."*

He laughed lightly. *"It's not that odd. The best science and the best music have a lot in common. Bach is almost as mathematical as Maxwell's equations, and making a discovery can be as uplifting as hearing Lennon for the first time. The only difference is that musicians create beauty and scientists look for it.*" Julian smiled and put an arm around her. "*And find it.*"

"*I may believe that if you keep it up.*"

"*I will,*" he promised. He wanted to make her happy—and safe. Julian looked around at the neighborhood, assessing it. The few people out in the open seemed furtively alert, as if they expected a cop to stop and question them at any moment.

"*They do,*" Birche said. Information came to her easily, straight from the thoughts of the people working in the buildings. "*Everything here is more than it seems. That thrift shop—the owner doubles as a fence for stolen goods. The print shop specializes in forged documents.*"

"*What about that magic store?*" Julian smiled, taken with an idea. "*Let's go and have a look.*"

A doorbell tinkled as they entered the shop. Birche blinked several times as her eyes adapted to the feeble light. There was smoke in the air, and a sick-sweet odor she couldn't place. Birche could sense someone asleep in the back room, someone whose mind felt ancient and cynical.

"*Incense,*" Julian told her, his nose wrinkling. It was the strongest odor in the air, but not the worst. "*It drives out evil spirits, along with covering up smells like—*"

"Well, good morning!" A fat woman waddled out of the shop's rear room. For Birche, looking at her was like staring at a funhouse mirror. The woman was roughly her height and weight, but she sagged with blubber. Thick mascara partly covered pockmarked cheeks. Tapping her mind, Birche could tell that the woman was as shrewd a businesswoman as she was, but driven by overpowering greed. "And what can I do for you two?"

"*Julian?*"

"*Take notes, beautiful. Learn something about the people who push the superstitions.*"

"*I've learned enough already.*" The similarities between herself and the shop owner disturbed her as much as the woman's selfishness. Could I have ended up like her? she wondered.

"We're sort of browsing," Julian said to the woman. He looked at the junk crammed into the long, narrow room, and showed the woman an encouraging smile. "You know."

"That I do," she agreed earnestly, resting a chubby hand on a glass countertop. "You got to look around before you find exactly what you need."

"Right." Julian picked up a hex sign and looked at it. The wooden disc was about six inches across, and painted with a dazzling, intricate pattern.

"That there's a genuine Amish hex sign," the woman said. "Hand-made in Pennsylvania. It's got four hundred years of tradition behind it, and you know those old Amish never get any grief from witches."

"It's *really neat*," Julian murmured, gazing at it. "*And the tag on the back says 'Made in South Korea.' Watch this; she'll never notice what I'm doing.*" He smiled idiotically at the hex sign.

"It hypnotizes witches," the woman said. She looked at Birche and decided she was the one to convince; she looked a bit rumpled, but that elegant gray sweatsuit suggested lots of money. "The pattern freezes their brainwaves solid, so they can't think about nothing."

"That sounds good." Birche said, bemused by the woman's greed. It showed as much in her rolls of fat as it did in her mind. She had an enormous, uncontrollable appetite—for food, for money, for everything.

"Oh, it's real good, honey, 'cause witches are just startin' to make trouble." Her voice took on a confiding tone. "You know what year *this* is."

"The last time I checked, it was two thousand—"

"You see!" she crowed. "This is one of them bad times, like Friday the thirteenth, when all the evil things can happen."

"That sounds like what Perry Fountain says," Birche said idly. Her MHB bracelet had slid out from under her sleeve, but the woman was so intent on making a sale that she hadn't noticed the eye-catching orange plastic. Birche casually slid her left hand over it; this was no place to attract attention.

"*Don't worry, beautiful,*" Julian said. He let his jaw go slack as he stared at the hex sign. "*You see? She's too interested in money to notice anything else.*"

"*I just wish you wouldn't clown around here. It scares me.*"

The fat woman chuckled. "Ol' Fountain doesn't know *everything*, honey. It isn't just the Devil making trouble this year, it's everything evil. The Bermuda Triangle is acting up and the Saucer People are makin' ready to invade. All them old-time wizards are coming back from the astral plane—Simon Magus, Giles Corey, Nostradamus, Julian the Apostate—"

"*Who?*" Birche asked in shock.

"*My God, a classical allusion!*" Julian thought. He felt smugly amused. The woman hadn't noticed that he continued to stare at the hex sign, and he doubted she would, not with the dollar signs in her eyes.

"There's this one freak what calls himself Julian," the woman said to Birche. "He's *really* an old Roman Emperor, one who turned away from Jesus and tried to make everyone worship pagan gods."

"*Actually,*" Julian told Birche, "*my parents named me after Julian Lennon—you know, the son of the old Beatle.*"

"*You're kidding.*"

"*I told you they were musicians, didn't I? They thought John Lennon was God with a guitar. So they named my brothers 'John' and 'Sean,' my sister 'Cynthia,' and me 'Julian.' If I'd been a girl they would have called me 'Yoko.' *"

"*When you said they were musicians, I thought you meant classical music.*"

"*That's their favorite, but Mom and Dad like all . . . huh?*"

The sleeper in the back room awoke. He was young and small and ill, Birche realized, and—

Julian threw the hex sign and it shattered a glass display case. Birche saw his face twist into a glare of animal anger as he turned on the shopkeeper. "You . . ."

The woman gaped at Julian, and then saw Birche's bracelet. The impossible sight of witches in her store filled her with terror—they might take her money—if they ran away with the child—she should call the MHB, the Iron Guard, *somebody* who could handle witches—

"You won't," Birche said quickly. Julian was helpless with rage, caught between the urge to punish this creature and the inability to harm her. The woman's mounting terror pushed on Birche like a powerful current, and she had to fight to put menace in her voice. "You wouldn't *like* what I'd do to you."

The woman's mouth worked silently. Her fascination with her money broke long enough to let her imagine the horrors these monsters could inflict on her. She turned away from Birche and ran blindly out the door.

Birche looked at Julian, saw him quivering, sensed that he was on the verge of withdrawing into himself. His outrage had ended, and now he wanted to escape what lay ahead . . . and the only way out lay in catatonia.

"Julian, help me," Birche said. *"I frightened her. It was fun. I'm scared that I could get to like doing that."*

Julian pulled back from the edge. *"You're all right,"* he said weakly, and gestured toward the back room. *"We'd better hurry. That woman will come back soon."*

"Not the way I scared her."

"She'll get over it." Julian hesitated, then walked into the rear room, with Birche on his heels.

Birche put a hand over her mouth and nose. The smell of incense was stronger here, but not strong enough to mask the stench. Light came from some candles on the floor, and when her other hand found the light switch she saw a child sitting on the floor, ringed in by candles and a chalk circle. The boy—Birche decided it was a boy—had stringy black hair and wore ragged yellow shorts. He was the size of a three-year-old, but Birche guessed he was several years older.

He looked at them and sniffed in disdain. *"You aren't real witches."*

"Neither are you," Julian said.

" 'course not, you ugly puke-freak. I'm the demon Asmodeus."

Birche sat down heavily on a stool, feeling dizzy. This *child* believed he was a devil, and the shopkeeper had been exploiting his telepathic sense, using him as the centerpiece of fake seances. A hell of a racket, she thought idiotically, numbed by shock. She felt grateful for her numbness; like an anesthetic, it allowed her to keep functioning. *"Julian, we have to hurry. Someone will come in soon—"*

"I can't rush this, Birche. He has to show himself that there's no magic holding him. If he can do that—" He squatted down outside the chalk pentacle. *"We're leaving here, son. Come to me."*

"I can't, stupid. If I cross the Power Circle I'll go back to Hell." He spat on Julian. *"Is your pecker as short as the rest of you?"*

Birche lurched to her feet. *"Just grab him! We have to run!"*

"No. He has to walk out of the pentacle himself. Birche, look around, I know there's a cash box in this room."

"But—"

"Find it, damn it!"

Birche started digging through the junk and litter in the room. There was a portable stove in one corner, next to a sagging cot. Old clothes and rubbish were heaped under the cot. That woman must live here, she thought, pulling out a bag full of empty food cartons and rotten fruit. Birche's hand found a metal box and she pulled it out into the open.

Money. The box was filled with bluebacks, thousand dollar bills neatly clipped together. Birche's business experience told her what had happened here. The woman ran the shop as a front; she would obey every business regulation, and her records would satisfy the toughest IRS auditor. The real profits would come from what she charged her clients for a session with her 'captive demon,' and none of *that* money would show on her books.

"*I can't touch it, you dumbshit,*" the child said to Julian. The notion of trying to escape terrified him, and he lashed out in fear. "*Hey, genius, how many exams did you cheat on? Got all the right answers by reading other minds, didn't you?*"

Birche stared at Julian, sensing the anguish those words caused. "*You can't scare me, son,*" he said steadily. He pointed to the ground. "*Those are just chalk marks. The candles don't have any power.*"

Birche cleared her throat. "*They're too weak to hold the real Asmodeus—*"

"*HE ISN'T ASMODEUS!*" Julian clutched his head. "*I'm sorry.*"

"*No, I'm sorry.*" Anything that suggested the child was anything but a child was wrong; she saw that now. She needed to take another tack—and a more effective one than Julian used. People in the neighborhood had seen the shopkeeper fleeing, and they knew she had a lot of money stashed away. In a few minutes they would come looking for the cashbox. One of them already had his gun but; *nothing* would stand between him and that money.

Birche made herself look at the child. He looked starved; the sores on his skin looked like the symptoms of a vitamin deficiency. She hoped they were nothing else. "*Is that woman a magician?*"

"*She has lots of magic,*" the child said. "*She knows things.*"

"*I don't have any magic, do I?*" Birche asked him. "*But she thought I did. I made her run away with some words. So she doesn't have any magic, does she?*"

"*But—but—*" His thoughts wavered. "*She keeps me here—*"

"*By lying. You know she'd believe anything for money—*"

The child kicked one of the candles with a bare toe, hard enough to send it flying into the wall. He stared at it for a moment, then took a tottering step out of the circle. "*Let's get the hell out of here,*" Birche said, scooping him up.

"*One minute.*" Julian reached for the cashbox, began stuffing wads of money into his coat pockets.

"*Julian, that's robbery!*"

"*Yes—but we need this money.*" He shook a fistful of bluebacks at her. "*That child earned this money. He's going to need food and medicine in a hurry—and I will be damned if I'll let that gross pig get rich off him. If it makes you happy we'll burn what we don't spend on the kid.*"

His brusque anger shocked her. Birche stood, and went to the shop's rear door. She stopped and switched off the burglar alarm. "*What do we do now?*"

"*Here.*" Julian removed his jacket, took the child from her and wrapped him in it. He held the child while she unlatched the rear door, and they stepped out into the narrow alley. "*We have to get away from here as fast as we can.*"

"*That won't be easy,*" Birche said. The child was in no shape to travel, physically or mentally. He had wrapped his arms around his head, to protect himself from the raw blue sky and brilliant noonday sun.

"'*Easy.' Nothing's easy. It just gets worse all the time.*" Julian began slowing down. The strength went out of his legs and he sat down against a building wall, still clutching the child. "*There's always something worse. Always.*"

"*No. There has to be an end.*" She knelt down facing him, and wondered what right she had to say anything optimistic. She hadn't been through half the things he'd experienced in the past few years—no. "*Julian, we have to take care of this child now.*"

"*How?*" he demanded. "*What are we supposed to say when some cop spots us carrying him? 'It's all right, officer, we're a couple of telepathics and we just rescued this kid'?*"

"*No one's going to stop us.*" Birche smiled, took some of the money and kissed him quickly. "*Keep an eye on Junior, handsome. I have an idea.*"

CHAPTER 15

Technology has increased the dangers of terrorism, and I think this shows very plainly in the United States. There are over five hundred organizations on the Attorney-General's "watchlist" of outlawed groups. Some of them, such as Sere, lay claim to thousands of members, perhaps even tens of thousands. Others, such as the Golden Circle, may have less than ten members.

The American authorities are concerned about all of them, with excellent reason. As an example, the very few members of the Golden Circle have used a variety of electronic and cybernetic techniques to disrupt life in the Cincinatti area. The damage is out of all proportion to their numbers due to their technological sophistication.

The great fear is that some group will manage to combine large numbers with state-of-the-art weapons and techniques. Given the power available to all would-be revolutionaries, some experts candidly admit there is no way to stem the rise of terrorism. If American society is to survive, a fundamental change is needed in the behavior of people, a new sense of responsibility.

Sadly, there is no evidence that such a change is forthcoming.

—correspondent's report, BBC World Service, 22 May 2000

"We've had a break," Farrier told Hutchins that afternoon. "We caught a Sere executioner. He's told us where to find their main arsenal—and the Sere directorate."

"He did?" Hutchins looked up from the printouts draped over his desk. So much paper, he thought, and

so little information. He had to ask himself if the
CTO's operatives in the Iron Guard were double agents;
the picture they gave was too reassuring. It didn't jibe
with events, *that* was a fact. "When did this happen?"

"The man turned himself in a couple of hours ago and
applied for protected witness status. We've granted
it—"

" 'A couple of hours ago'?" Hutchins repeated. "Why
wasn't I informed?"

"We thought it was a ruse, Chief." Hutchins took a
seat. "It was just too good to be true—a Sere assassin
comes in and offers to spill his guts? But we gave him a
quick medical exam, and he's telling the truth."

"So our luck has turned. What's the word from
Tactical?"

"Our first assault lifts in—" Farrier checked his watch
"—thirty-two minutes. We have six other teams on
standby alert. If we locate more arsenals, we can take
them out in a hurry. I'm in the first wave."

"So am I," Hutchins said, getting up.

"Chief, is it a good idea for both of us to go? We're
the top two levels of command here, and if something
happens to us—"

"You can stay if you like." Hutchins opened a desk
drawer, got out his service revolver and spare ammunition. "But I have to be there in case something goes
wrong. Remember Topeka? The press had a field day
when that 'paramilitary camp' we raided turned out to
be a Sunday school."

"That was due to poor intelligence and sloppy
navigation."

"It was a mistake," Hutchins said, striding out of his
office. "Mistakes *happen*, Lou. If one happens here—
where's this arsenal located?"

"Alhambra. Right off the Santa Monica Freeway."

"Damn!" He'd driven that road yesterday, on the
way to Cal Tech. "Well, Lou, there are ten million
people within an hour's drive of the place. Imagine how
Delanty will react if the CTO screws up in front of ten
million voters."

Farrier looked unmoved. "If the CTO Chief gets killed in front of ten million voters, it won't look much better."

"No, but at least it'll get me away from my desk."

They're too cocky, Hutchins thought, as he hunkered in the helicopter's passenger bay. The assault troops had bundled themselves in the latest combat gear, and they carried an impressive array of weapons, but they talked and joked as if they were going on a duck hunt. They didn't believe there was any danger, and that was bad.

"Chief?" Farrier, sitting in the copilot's seat, raised his voice over the whine of the turbines. "Priority signal for you."

Hutchins crept forward to the cockpit, hampered by his bulletproof suit. The bubble canopy gave a better view than the bay windows, and Hutchins could see the other helicopters flying in formation. He could also see the cityscape a mile below. "Take us lower," he told the pilot. "We're supposed to be sneaking up on them."

The man looked over his shoulder. "We're already at the minimum FAA altitude."

"Don't argue, Pell," Farrier said. He handed a radio headset to Hutchins. "Six minutes to contact, Chief."

"Good." Hutchins clutched a handgrip as the helicopter entered a gentle descent, and put the headset on with his free hand. "Hutchins here."

"Agent Carruthers. Sir, we've just had another report in connection with yesterday's incident. Mr. Adler has left the country. He took a plane to Nicaragua last night."

And we have no extradition treaty with them, Hutchins noted. "Any details available?"

"His secretary says he's on an extended business trip. He took a corporate jet out of LAX yesterday at four-oh-five. That's all we have now, sir."

"Okay. Out." Hutchins returned the headset to Farrier. "Adler flew the coop yesterday. He hopped a company plane a bit after four o'clock, almost three hours after the attack. Odd."

"Maybe not," Farrier said. "We announced the attack to the media at three yesterday. It would take him an hour to get from his office to his plane."

Hutchins mulled that over. "The implication is that he didn't know an attack was planned—but once he heard about it, he realized he was in hot water."

"Boiling oil is more like it—but why would Adler have anything to do with the Iron Guard? He's a respectable executive, for Christ's sake!"

"We'll have to worry about it later," Hutchins said. "Lou, I need to know something about that defector before we land. Why did he change sides?"

"Granger—one of the Sere honchos—tried to kill him this morning." He paused and listened to a voice in his headset, then continued, "It's strange. The man claims a witch prophesized that Granger would turn on him."

"A witch?" Hutchins laughed nervously. Every time he turned around he ran into the freaks. "What happened?"

"Our turncoat went out to kill a man the night before last. A witch stopped the hit—we didn't have time to get full details, Chief. There was something about Granger, and— *Jesus! Look out!*"

The helicopter flying ahead of their machine erupted in a ball of greasy smoke. After a second, chunks of burning, blackened metal tumbled out of the fireball, and debris hit Hutchins' copter with a series of solid *clunks*.

"My God!" the pilot screamed. Hutchins had time to see an orange fireball corkscrewing up from the ground, a black dot in its center. The pilot yanked the control yoke and the helicopter plunged into a steep dive, turning away from the rising missile. Hutchins fell against the side of the cockpit, and got a glimpse of the horizon, tilted at a crazy angle. The Stinger missile flashed past the canopy, missing the helicopter by yards.

The turbines whined loudly as the copter dived toward the ground. Holding onto a conduit, Hutchins saw the horizon straighten out. The helicopter pulled out of its dive a hundred feet up and sped on. Hutchins got back on his feet.

"Form up!" Farrier snapped into the radio. Hutchins looked out the canopy and saw that the helicopter formation had scattered across the sky. "Form up, we are going in now."

Farrier turned to the pilot. "Turn this thing around. We're going in first."

Pop-eyed, the pilot shook his head. Smelling something foul, Hutchins knew that the pilot had soiled his pants. He couldn't blame the man. If the thickness of the stench meant anything, several of the troops had done the same thing.

Farrier drew his pistol and put it to the man's neck. "You can run later, but right now you fly or you die. Get us back on course." After a few long seconds the helicopter heeled around.

Hutchins looked out the canopy and counted machines. "We've lost four," he said to Farrier.

"One was shot down. The other three are returning to base." Farrier keyed in his radio. "All units, descend to fiver-zero feet altitude. Those missiles are ineffective that low. Spotter one, prepare to lay gas and flashers on the target site."

Hutchins returned to the passenger bay. "Any injuries?" he asked loudly. "Okay, load your weapons and seal your helmets." Hutchins picked up a helmet and fitted it over his head. Radio noises hissed in his ears, and the IR goggles turned the world into shades of red and black. Like staring at a poker hand, he thought, and wondered what sort of a hand he held this day.

The helicopter thumped down and the the door slid open. Hutchins hopped out, looked around, and gestured with his rifle: that way. The helicopter had grounded a block away from the target site, a three-story cold storage building with concrete walls. Going to be a bitch to take it, he thought as he jogged along.

"The cordon is in place." Farrier's voice sounded in his ears. "Power and phone lines have been cut in this area. We're jamming all the freqencies they're likely to use."

"Okay. Have we—" His goggles turned black for a second, cleared, then went through another second of blackness. He heard thumps through his helmet insulation, felt them in his bones. Flash bombs and stunners; anyone inside the building might be too blinded and shaken to fight for the next few minutes. A red light inside his mask told him that there was gas in the air. Hutchins kept moving forward, balancing his pace between speed and wariness.

Something kicked him forward onto his face. He got up, shaken, and saw a hole in the street a dozen yards behind him. One of his men was down, clutching his leg. Another hooked an arm under his armpit and helped him limp out of the street. Bullets stitched the pavement but missed the assault force.

"Bazooka," Farrier's voice said crisply. "Take cover; watch the building. We have them pinned now."

And vice versa, Hutchins thought. He got behind the corner of a building and looked at the storage facility. Its tiny windows and thick walls made it a natural pillbox. There could have been a battalion inside there, and unless those people were complete idiots, they would have all the approaches covered.

A spear of white smoke lanced out of a top-floor window. The rocket exploded against the front of a building. "How many of those things have they got?" a radio voice asked.

"They're rotten shots with them," Farrier answered ambiguously. "Group three, put some rounds into that window."

Hutchins looked at the blank masks of the two men with him. Thank God for those masks, he thought; we can't see how scared we all are. One of them had a sniper's rifle. "Murphy, hand me that weapon—here, hang on to mine."

A wire dangled from the rifle. Hutchins plugged it into his helmet jack, and listened to an electronic rasp. The rifle's "sight" was a brainwave sensor, similar to

Farrier's pocket model, but designed to pinpoint the electric fields generated by a human brain. It wasn't as accurate as an optical gunsight, but it could detect a man at five hundred yards—and no camouflage could fool it.

Hutchins leaned around the corner and aimed the rifle at the building. Nothing. The next window gave no response, or the next— There, an electronic whine. Hutchins wiggled the rifle slightly, trying to decide when the whine was at its highest pitch. He squeezed off three rounds, then got back under cover, wondering if he had killed someone.

"Hold your fire!" Farrier's voice ordered. "You're wasting ammo. I don't want anyone to shoot unless they have a target."

Good point, Hutchins thought. Each man had carried a hundred rounds with him, but the lurkers in the building had an effectively unlimited supply—and no reason to hold back. With what they had, they might even try to break through the CTO encirclement and escape. A distinct possibility, that, especially if the CTO group ran out of bullets. "Farrier, Hutchins. How are we fixed for ammo?"

"Our reserve supply was in helicopter four."

The one that had gone down in flames. "I see. We'll need more."

"It should be here in a few minutes—*get that copter out of here! Unidentified helicopter, clear out—*"

Hutchins looked to the sky. A bright yellow helicopter wheeled over the area. A TV camera pod hung underneath it, and the CTO director could see the telephoto lens swivel around. Then a Stinger missile speared into the machine. The copter staggered sideways in the air, then corkscrewed toward the ground, shedding chunks of metal as it burned. The machine hit the side of a building and disintegrated.

"There goes our secrecy," Farrier said. "All units, cease fire! Spiers, get me the loudspeaker."

"Negotiations?" Hutchins asked. The fighters in the

building wouldn't negotiate; they knew they were winning.

"Psychology. Hurry up, Spiers. Get me plugged into the friggin' thing. Chief, if what that defector said is right, Granger won't be in there now. He'll have run away."

"And if he is—"

"Maybe he'll panic. Our defector said he's a coward. Let's check that. All units, no firing except on my order."

Hutchins saw motion across the street. A suited, masked figure stepped into the open. The colored band around his bulky overalls told Hutchins it was Farrier. He's taking a hell of a risk, Hutchins thought. His suit could stop shrapnel and small-arms fire, but it wasn't invulnerable, especially not against the weapons Sere possessed.

"You in the building!" Farrier's voice came to Hutchins in an odd echo, over the radio and through his helmet insulation. "This is the CTO. I want to talk to John Dexter Granger."

"Whaddya want?" a woman's voice screamed back.

"I want to talk to your leader. Where is Granger?"

"You can't talk to him!"

"Isn't he in there?" Farrier taunted. "We have reinforcements on the way. The only way to save your lives is for Granger to talk to me now."

"He can't talk! He ain't here!"

Farrier waved with the loudspeaker. "We know he was there a while ago. Where did he go? Why won't he face us? He started this, he's got to finish it."

Oh, you beautiful, crazy son of a bitch, Hutchins thought. With any luck the men and women in the building would start doubting themselves and their leader. Farrier walked across the street slowly, presenting himself as a target. He drew no fire, and he unplugged his loudspeaker as he stepped into cover with Hutchins. "Let's give them some time to sweat," Farrier said.

Hutchins rocked back and forth in his suit, an exaggerated nodding motion. "Just how reliable is that bit about Granger?"

"I wish I knew, Chief. That crazy damn witch could have babbled anything . . . but our defector believed it. So does Granger, I'd say. Granger may have killed one man who thought he was yellow, and I doubt he shoots his own people for sport." He slapped his gloved hands together in impatience. "I hope they don't take too long to crack. If we can get in there, get some info about their other arsenals, we can still salvage the situation."

"We'll have to move fast," Hutchins said. He looked into the street and saw the still-burning wreck of the TV copter. No survivors there, he told himself, not in those flames. "The news must be everywhere by now—but if the leadership is here, the rest of Sere may not know what to do. We'll get them."

"I'm not worried about them anymore," Farrier said. "It's their weapons. If they vanish, they'll turn up all over the country. How in hell can the Secret Service protect the President when any idiot can stand outside an airport with a shoulder-fired Stinger missile—"

A dull *whump* cut off his words. Suddenly oblivious to danger, Hutchins went into the open and looked at the cold-storage building. Smoke churned out of a corner window. As he watched, a string of explosions hopscotched across the top-level windows. With a roar a corner of the roof peeled back, then dropped down into the building amid more smoke and flame. The sound of gunfire inside the building sounded faint in contrast to the other explosions. They're shooting one another! Hutchins thought in excitement.

The firing died away after a moment. Another moment, and a door cracked open. "Don't shoot!"

Farrier reconnected his bullhorn. "Come out slowly with your hands up, one at a time."

A dozen people filed out of the building, in suits and masks almost identical to the CTO armor, aside from camouflage mottling. While they were searched and handcuffed, Hutchins followed a dozen of the troops into the building. They tossed flash- and stun bombs left and right, wary of any die-hards making a last stand, until Hutchins grew numb from all the concussions. Several times he stumbled over abandoned weapons: grenade launchers, heavy machine guns, even a flamethrower. There was a cache of food in one room. If the radicals hadn't elected to surrender, Hutchins realized, they might have held out for days.

He found a room that had been remade into a crude command center: radios, telephones, papers—and the jackpot, a large detail map pinned to a table. A corner of the map bore scorch marks, but the plasticized paper had refused to burn. Hutchins called in a radio team and had them relay information from the map to the Federal Building.

Hutchins stepped outside and peeled off his mask. The outside air felt pleasantly cool on his skin. After seeing the world through the goggles, even the gray tones of concrete and old asphalt looked vivid.

"Granger ran," Farrier said in satisfaction. "He sneaked out the minute he heard our choppers—he decided he was too important to Sere's 'Cause' to die here. Most of his cohorts decided they were too alive to die covering his retreat."

"But not all of them," Hutchins said, and sighed. "I hope the media doesn't turn them into martyrs."

"After they shot down a news helicopter?" Farrier laughed heartily. "Journalists all think their lives are sacred. They won't get any sympathy from the press now. Speaking of helicopters—Chief, we're due for a housecleaning. We can't tolerate out-and-out cowardice like we had today. Heads are going to roll tonight."

"No, they won't. There'll be changes, but—"

"Damn it!" Farrier threw his mask to the ground. "We almost died when our pilot turned—"

"Shut up, Farrier," Hutchins snapped. He jabbed a finger into his chest. "When I'm giving orders I'm 'Mister Director,' is that clear? And don't interrupt me when I'm giving orders.

"I know damned well what happened. Our men are

cops. I'd match them against any cop—or hood—on God's green Earth. But they're not soldiers; they weren't prepared for what they ran into today. Rifles and pistols against machine guns and rockets—they behaved better than we had any right to expect."

Farrier glared at him. "Were you pleased, *Mister Director?*"

"I'm pleased that we paid such a cheap price for *my* mistakes. We'll do better next time; I won't send my men into a fix like this again. One other thing: I'm giving you a commendation and the Service Medal for your actions."

Hutchins turned away from Farrier. Chewing him out in public had been a mistake; several of the men had heard the shouting match. Bad for morale, that— but the Bear's accusations of cowardice would have done even more damage.

Changes, Hutchins thought, cataloging the things he wanted. Give each man more ammunition. Training, too; prepare them for surprises, like being outgunned by ragtag radicals. Teach the pilots how to fly low and avoid goddamned surface-to-air missiles. The ideas piled up quickly. Hutchins unbuckled the top of his overalls and got out his pen and notepad. With a growl he threw the pad away; his sweat had destroyed it. Antiquated, he thought suddenly. A notepad was as outdated as the tactics the CTO had used to fight terrorism. If Sere had known how to exploit all the weapons it had possessed—if its nerve hadn't cracked—this would have been a bloody disaster.

Hutchins walked over to where the prisoners were being held. Out of their camouflage overalls now, they looked shrunken, harmless. Their faces said that they expected a medical interrogation; somebody would drip a drug into their veins, and they would spill their secrets . . . eventually. Some of them would end up under MHB supervision, but that was the price of fighting terrorism. Ask any pollster or politician, Hutchins thought.

One of the prisoners was led into a helicopter. Hutchins climbed in after the man and gestured to the guards. "I want to talk to him alone."

"Yessir." They left the passenger bay and shut the hatch.

Hutchins peeled out of his heavy overalls. "We both know about Granger," he said to the man. "He ran out on you."

"And you want to know where he ran? Piss off."

"I don't care about that. I don't even know if Granger's worth bothering with now." Hutchins watched that sink in: Sere was no longer important. "I'm curious, though. How did you hear about Granger's yellow streak?"

The prisoner looked sullen. "Jackson. He and two other guys went out to hit a defector. They told Granger they wasted the bastard. Then last night, well, we all stoked up and got free as hell. Halfway through his third joint, Jackson told us what happened—Granger ran out during a fight, then killed Norton and sent Jackson out to off Whitney—"

"Who are Norton and Whitney?"

"Granger's bodyguards." The prisoner's gaze drifted down to the cabin deck. "Granger was valuable, you know? The Revolution needed him, so he couldn't take chances. Said he really hated that." He shook his head. "Jackson explained how Granger had left Whitney with a bunch of witches, and how this one freak told him everything. That's when Granger come in on us. He called Jackson a traitor and a liar, and said anyone who listened to a witch oughtta have his brains blown out."

"What happened next?"

The man shrugged, a gesture hampered by the cuffs on his hands. "They shouted at one another a lot. That's when I started to think maybe Granger *was* chicken. I mean, why else would he carry on the way he did? And then he heard the helicopters a while ago, and he told us how heroic we were, and he was gone."

"So you decided not to fight."

The man closed his eyes. "Nothin' left to fight for. Sere's dead, man."

That it is. Hutchins thought. A few splinter groups

might stay alive, but Sere was no longer a force in the world. That's one down and a thousand to go, the CTO chief thought wearily.

The helicopter pilot stuck his head into the cabin. "Mr. Director? Agent Carruthers is on the horn."

Hutchins walked forward and held the headset to his ear. "Go ahead, Carruthers."

"Sir, we have something new on the IG affair. Are you near a newsstand?"

Did I hear that right? he wondered. There was static on the radio, but not a lot. "Say again, Carruthers. A *newsstand*?"

"Affirmative. This is in Magyar's column in the *Post*. He had a meeting with one Gerald Grofaz Savoy."

"The IG's head militant." Hutchins looked out the cockpit canopy and saw a newsstand—no, the power was out. The autovendor wouldn't work. "Carruthers, read the article to me. Now."

"The whole article?" He sounded taken aback.

"And nothing but the article. I have time."

"Okay, sir." Electrostat paper rustled over the radio. " 'I always wanted a car like this when I was in high school . . .' "

Hutchins listened silently for many minutes. Outside the helicopter, he saw the fire department arrive and attack the cold-storage building—cautiously. The top floor burned furiously and plenty of ammunition had survived the initial explosions. CTO, police, and news copters competed for airspace around the fire.

"I've heard enough," Hutchins told Carruthers.

"I'm only halfway through, Chief."

"I'll read the rest later." He thought quickly. If a tenth of what Magyar's column said was true, then the damned fool had put himself in danger by publishing it. "I'll see Magyar later. Right now I want him quietly under surveillance, with an eye toward keeping him alive. I expect he's a marked man."

"Understood." Carruthers' voice sounded cheerful. "Everything is under control."

Like hell it is, Hutchins thought.

CHAPTER 16

The essence of telepathy is communication—whether you want to communicate or not. Everything else is a side issue.
—from Sense and Non-sense, *by Lyn Amanda Clancy*

"I'm spoiled," Birche said. She sat down on the curb and massaged her calves. "I'm used to driving everywhere. Twelve miles! I've never walked this far in my life."

"It's your own fault," Julian said, helping her to her feet. "If you weren't so clever, we would have gotten caught before we could walk anywhere. Hang on, we're just a few blocks from home." He started pushing the baby carriage again.

It had surprised Julian when Birche had shown up with the carriage: he had been that far gone with despair. She'd had to *tell* him that she had gone to the secondhand store to buy it— and that no one in the area had connected her, or her money, with the ruckus in the magic shop. That, and her stroke of genius, had lifted his spirits. They had bundled the child into the pram and started walking, obviously a young married couple out for a stroll. The child had whimpered and burrowed under his blanket, hiding from unfamiliar sights and sounds and smells.

"He's been outside before," Birche said, "but not much, and not often. I don't know how he's going to adapt."

"He'll adapt," Julian said. "I'm more concerned with his physical state. Anita—one of my friends here—may

180

*be able to help, but we should get him to a doctor
soon."*

"But you think his mind will be okay." Birche found
some comfort in his—not optimism, she decided, but
resolution. He expected to find a way to help the child,
or to make a way—

"Sarge, does that look like Forrest?"

"Maybe."

Birche tightened her grip on Julian's arm. She saw
the black-and-white police growler driving toward them,
and sensed Julian's sudden decision to run, to draw
them away from Birche and the child. *"Keep cool,"*
Birche said. She leaned her head against his shoulder.
"We're the happy new family, remember? Look like it."

The police car slowed a bit. *"You're right, kid. He
looks like the sketches, more or less."*

"So let's stop and check—"

"What for?"

"Well, the lieutenant said—"

*"The lieutenant isn't out on the streets. Kid, never
mess with a psycho if you can avoid it. Sometimes they
go ape."*

"Forrest is supposed to be harmless—"

*"Don't argue with me. Think. If it's him, so what? If
it isn't, that could be some nut from Sere, or a vigilante. Or anything, in this neighborhood. I'm not taking any stupid chances."* The police car sped up.

Julian relaxed. *"Let's hope they don't make a report."*

*"What, and admit they were too chicken to stop
you?"* Birche felt pleased—and then apprehensive. The
police were scared of this neighborhood. What in hell
was she walking into?

*"It's not too bad, actually. There's some violent crime,
but if you're alert, you can get out of its way. Besides,
most criminals don't like to mess with crazy people—
there's no telling what could happen."* He looked down
the sidewalk and waved. *"Hey, Malcolm!"*

Birche started, seeing a big black man in a blue
uniform. A cop? No, another telepath, wearing a secu-

rity guard's jacket. He walked toward them. *"Welcome home, Julian. Is this your lady?"*

"Birche Holstein . . ." She had a moment of near-dizziness—followed by the awareness that Malcolm Gaudry had just greeted her, that he was an intelligent man and she could trust him, and that she had made an equally good impression on him. It was a unique experience, and she wondered how many more surprises were in store.

"Wait until you meet the thea," Malcolm said. He started to look in the carriage, then checked himself. *"What happened?"*

"Something new," Julian said. He started pushing the carriage while Malcolm tapped his memories and frowned. *"Well, I wish it was new. We'll have to start checking magic shops, gilly carnivals—you name it. I don't think this 'seance' bushwa is unique—but right now we have to take care of this child—"*

"I'm not a child, you stupid freak! I'm Asmodeus."

"—and it's going to be a problem," Birche finished. *"Is this the place, Julian? It looks awfully low-rent."*

"It is," Julian agreed. *"Malcolm, we may have to move. Some cops recognized me."*

"I know. Let's plan later." He helped Julian and Birche guide the baby buggy into the house.

This time Birche was prepared for the greetings. Anita, Jesse, George, Hazel, Betty . . . Birche knew their last names, but the intimacy of mental contact made first names more suitable. There had been a brief hesitation while they decided she was sane; after her night at the MHB, she could understand *that* concern.

And Julian was chattering like a maniac, while Anita lifted the child out of the carriage. *"We've been feeding him all along,"* he told Anita. *"Vitamins, canned juices, fruits—you name it. I think we've gone to every store between that shop and here. Hey, George, you took the bracelet off!"*

"So did Hazel," George said. *"Malcolm's bringing in more money than the MHB payments amount to, so we decided to chuck it—"*

"*Good move. Say, where is Hazel? I need to ask her and Cliff some things. Anita, how does the kid look?*"

"*It's hard to say, Julian. I never studied pediatrics.*"

"*Why ask her?*" The child looked disdainful. "*She don't know crap about us demons, freak-face.*"

Julian laughed. "*His manners are improving already. You want the rest of that juice, kid?*"

"*Gimme!*"

Julian dug into the carriage and tossed aside odds and ends—clothing Birche had picked up at a thrift shop, empty food wrappers, bundles of money, sample-bottles of vitamins. He found a small juice can and popped its top. The child jumped out, grabbed the can, and gulped the juice.

Betty picked up a wad of bluebacks. "*Julian, there must be fifty K-notes here! And there's more—*"

"*Right-o. You know what Robin Hood said—'steal from the rich, that's where the money is.' It's the kid's money, though—he earned it by answering questions at fake seances. Malcolm, on the way home I saw some places that looked good. We might think about moving right now—*"

"*Julian?*" He seemed unaware of the growing wildness in his thoughts. Birche sensed the others trying to withdraw, to shield themselves from his incipient madness. After her stay in the MHB cell she could share their fear—but there *might* be a way to pull him out of it. "*Julian, I want to get rid of this damned bracelet.*"

Julian smacked his forehead. "*Of course! George—*"

"*There's a hacksaw in that gray house on the corner. Hazel and Cliff left it in the bedroom.*"

Perfect, Birche decided. She and Julian had some unfinished business that required a bedroom. She took Julian by the arm and led him out of the house, leaving the other telepaths like wreckage in the wake of a storm.

"*We should have taken this off before we came here,*" Birche said as they crossed the empty street. Weeds and grass grew in the cracks in the asphalt. "*If it has some kind of radio tracer in it—*"

"It doesn't," Julian assured her. *"It has a magnetic memory strip in it, like they use in stores and libraries. It can set off a proximity detector, and carry a few codes and registration numbers, but that's it."*

Birche tapped her wrist. *"Unless this is the new and improved version. But even if it isn't, I want it off, and I want it off now. Wearing it makes me feel like—like—"*

"Like a child," Julian said, *"instead of an adult."*

"Yeah. A couple of days ago I was a responsible businesswoman. But with this thing on . . ."

"You don't have any rights," Julian said. *"The MHB makes all your decisions for you, and you can't do a thing without their permission. I know; I wore one of those bracelets for five years."* Julian looked at the gray house before they entered it, and decided it wasn't likely to collapse in the next few minutes. It had jumped off its foundation block during the earthquake, but the walls hadn't cracked too badly. *"When I took it off, that was one of the best days of my life."*

" 'One?' What was the best day?"

"The very best?" Julian thought about it while they looked for the bedroom. *"It was in 1991. The day the MIT team announced they'd 'discovered' telepathy. I remember reading about it in the morning paper. They explained how they had verified everything—the reporter mangled all the technical details, but I still got the essentials—and they said they were going to have a detailed report in Science. I read that and I started crying and I couldn't stop."*

"And that was the best day of your life?"

"It really was." They found the bedroom. A bare mattress lay on the floor, and a hacksaw waited on a splintered nightstand. Birche rested her forearm on the stand and Julian began sawing. *"Listen, all the evidence said I was crazy. ESP was supposed to be impossible, unless you believed in magic. I didn't have any control over the talent then, and I couldn't handle what was happening to me. Then these people at MIT came out and said it was real, a natural phenomenon you could study in the lab."*

"And that's what mattered the most?" Birche listened to the carbide blade rasp through the metal in the bracelet. The bracelet was tough, but every stroke produced more plastic and metal flakes.

"It took me a while to understand why that meant so much. It was—"

"Rational."

"Yes. It didn't simply mean that there was a scientific explanation for psi. It also meant that it wasn't madness, or magic—that it made sense: that I might find a way to live with it. It was like being on Death Row and getting a reprieve—there!" The bracelet popped open. Julian removed it and studied its frayed ends with a clinical eye. *"Well, they don't make them like they used to. This baby uses memory colloids instead of a magnetic code—strip."*

"Interesting." Birche took the bracelet, tossed it out the window, and hugged Julian. With the bracelet gone she felt suddenly free . . . a sensation accompanied by a wanton horniness. She smiled and toyed with a button on his shirt.

Julian responded with a cheerful male brashness. *"This is more like it! I've always wanted to have a beautiful woman throw herself at me!"*

"Better hope I don't throw myself too hard. I could flatten you." She started unbuttoning his shirt. *"Tell me something. How did you know I'm a swimmer?"*

"I dated one for a while, in college. Viki Saunders—

"What? The same Viki Saunders who got two silver medals at the '96 Olympics? Who did the hundred-meter freestyle in forty-nine seconds flat?"

"That was after we broke up. Anyway, swimmers have a certain look. I don't know how to describe it, but I can recognize it."

"Thick, heavy, muscles like—" Birche cut that off as Julian slipped out of his shirt. *"Why'd you break up?"*

"Living with a telepath was too hard for her. It wasn't just the loss of privacy. The religious nuts got on her back sometimes, and her friends kept bugging her about making time with a certified lunatic. So she just

walked out on me, back in '95." He laughed before any more memories could surface. *"Anyway, she was seven or eight inches taller than me. Every time I'd see her, I'd always end up looking her straight in the nipple—er, navel—"*

It was her turn to laugh. They helped one another undress then, and Birche pulled Julian onto the bed with her. When she touched a hand to his chest she could feel his heart pounding, as much through fear as excitement. Not afraid of *me*, she thought, wrapping herself around him.

Telepathy, to her disappointment, did not transform lovemaking into an act of transcendental joy and communication. Julian was an enthusiastic lover, and he saw her body as a work of art, but his turbulent thoughts offered no revelations, no great insights into his soul. After a moment Birche stopped searching for such things; Julian's manic energy dispelled such thoughts.

Communication came afterwards, while he lay next to her, stroking her brown bangs. *"I was acting crazy a while ago, wasn't I?"*

"You got over it," she said.

"Did I?" Julian shifted into a more comfortable position. *"I feel like a gyroscope. Did you ever watch what happens to one when its flywheel slows down? It wobbles in a lot of directions, then it falls over. Right now I feel like I'm wobbling through calmness."*

"You're not a gyroscope." She ran her fingers up and down his chest. His flesh was bruised and scarred. *"How did you get these?"*

"I got shot once."

Birche looked at the scars. Some of them were fairly tidy holes, while the others were more ragged. *"Six times?"*

"No, just three shots. You've got to figure that a bullet will make a hole coming out, too. I was sitting right next to the guy who did it. I was lucky; he was half-sloshed, and he only had a small-bore pistol. The bullets came in at an odd angle and deflected off my ribs."

"*Oh. And these?*" She stroked his forearm, feeling the parallel ridges of scar tissue at his wrist. "*This must have happened a long time ago.*"

"*No, I did that in late '97.*"

"*Why?*" Birche recalled something. "*The boy said something about cheating in school. If you slipped once—*"

"*Never.*" The broken-down mattress creaked as Julian sat up. "*Funny. A lot of my teachers gave me special exams with different questions, to make sure I couldn't cheat. I always took that as a sign of respect, even if it meant they didn't trust me. They knew I wasn't a fake, or an idiot. They had to accept the fact that I was a good student. Not having an opportunity to cheat helped prove that to me, too.*"

Birche rested on an elbow and looked at his back. There were scars there as well—no, this wasn't the time to go into that. "*But what happened?*"

"*I was working on my doctoral thesis in the fall of '97. Ever since I'd entered college, I'd spent almost all of my time studying and doing research. I felt insulated from the Redeemers and other crazies.*"

Birche sat up next to him. "*That sounds like a good way to avoid trouble—*"

The harsh cackle of his laugh startled her. "*Avoid it! Have you got any idea how scientists feel about psi?*"

Birche was taken aback. "*Why—the MIT study proved it's real, and there've been other studies, haven't there?*"

"*Not everyone accepts their results. There've been plenty of frauds in parapsychology. Spoonbenders. Auras. Dowsers, psionic machines, levitation, channeling—with that track record, why shouldn't this be one more hoax?*"

"*But we know it isn't . . .*" Her thoughts trailed off as she saw what had trapped him. "*So the wrong people decided you were a fake?*"

"*It was more complicated than that. Some scientists think it's all flim-flam. Others try to ignore it, because psi doesn't seem to fit all the known rules of the universe. Even the ones who can face the facts have trouble accepting the existence of psi.*

"*I didn't worry about that too much when I got to college. I kept as low a profile as I could, and things went all right. I never talked about psi with anyone in the astronomy department. I wore sweaters and shirts with long sleeves to hide that damned bracelet. I was careful not to 'act' psychic. Reward: most people treated me like I was normal.*"

"*Until something went wrong,*" Birche prompted. She put an arm around his shoulders. Even if she hadn't been able to tap his thoughts, the tautness of his muscles would have told her of his strain. She pulled him closer and felt him relax slowly. "*You know you don't have to tell me.*"

"*I can tell you. We had a conference in my specialty, stellar evolution—a week-long seminar. We looked at the latest data, compared theories, discussed plans, and kicked around ideas—until the last day. That was when I talked to one group about my theories on the dynamics of the Orion Nebula.*

"*I was halfway through when Dr. Noyes jumped up and started shouting. Thundering. He'd already had that idea, he said. I had stolen it from him by reading his mind. That was when the conference disintegrated.*"

"*Because of one stupid accusation?*" Birche asked.

She felt his head move against her breast as he nodded. "*Birche, Noyes had said that I could read minds. Some of the people there started arguing that he was wrong, because ESP was impossible. They said I was just a clever con artist. Others sided with Noyes, and said that I used ESP to swipe their ideas, that I didn't have any intelligence of my own.*" Julian looked up at her. "*You've gone through that.*"

A feeling of empathy washed over her. "*With Steve, yes. But this was different. These people were your peers, and they'd just turned against you.*"

"*No—not all of them. Dr. Grant and some others stood up for me, but . . .*" Indifferent to his nudity, Julian got up and looked out the glassless window. "*Explanations of suicide always sound so inadequate. Astronomy was the one thing I was good at. The MHB*

*said I was crazy, the Redeemers said I was damned, but
I was still a scientist and no one could take that away
from me. Then some of the best minds in my field said I
was a disgrace, that I didn't belong—"*

"So you took a razor blade to your wrists."

"Not right away." Julian rested against the window-
sill and gazed at her. "I started wondering if Noyes was
right. Maybe, unconsciously, I had stolen ideas from
other people. Maybe I was a moron, ripping off smarter
people. How could I prove anything different? I felt
like I'd been pounded into the ground . . . and that I
was going crazy from it. Dying hurt a lot less."

Birche sat up on the edge of the bed and regarded
him. "You wouldn't do that again. It isn't in you."

"No, I won't let myself give up again. But . . .
sometimes, when I'm alone, I tell myself I'm already
crazy, that everything I remember is a delusion. The
world makes more sense then."

"Because it's easier to explain one lunatic than millions of them?" The redheaded woman looking in through
the window startled Birche. She reached for her clothes—
then checked herself. She knew this woman, somehow.
It was as if they'd met many times before.

The woman looked at Julian reproachfully. "You might
have told her about me, Julian."

"I've had a lot on my mind," he said feebly. "Why
are you here, thea?"

"You're needed back at the house. Cliff says it's
urgent." The woman gave Birche a polite smile and
faded like a Cheshire cat.

Birche looked to Julian. "You know the oddest people."

"Yeah. Anyone else would've told me what Cliff wants."
Julian picked up his clothes and started dressing. "That
was a thea, a telepathic construct."

"A group mind?" Birche felt intimidated by that idea.
To lose her individuality, diluting herself in a sea of
otherness—

"You don't have to worry about that," Julian said.
"It's impossible for two minds to merge into one unit.
The telepathic sense can only handle a fixed amount of

data, and only in the form of emotions and vocalized thoughts. A human personality involves a lot more than that; the data channel is too narrow to pass everything."

"Then what was that?" Birche waved a hand at the window.

"I told you: a thea, It's something that forms when enough telepathics get together. Our minds interact and we influence one another. A thea reflects all of our personalities, our strengths and weaknesses. It's a consensus, a self-image that a group has of itself—"

"A hallucination?"

Julian shook his head. "An illusion, but one with a certain amount of reality. Your mind constructs the image by turning the emotional background into a mental picture, so you can visualize emotions. It's part of your own mind, too—"

Birche snapped her fingers. "That's why she seemed so familiar. Is talking to her the same thing as talking to yourself?"

"Partly, but she's also generated by the rest of the group. That makes her pretty much an outsider in your own skull, which can be useful." He smiled wryly. "And because it's an illusion, a construct, it can appear separately to each member of a group. The damned thing can pop up everywhere."

"I see."

"Which is more than I can say. There's a lot we still don't know about theas—why they always appear female, for instance."

"Maybe it's cultural," Birche said. "Most people learn to think of displaying emotions as a feminine thing."

"Along with intuition," Julian agreed. He watched her move as she picked up her clothes, enjoying the lovely, alluring sight of her. "But a thea is also a creature of rationality, of intellect. It's embarrassing to know that it never appears as a man."

Birche giggled. "Poor Neanderthal. Say, didn't the ancient Greeks think of wisdom as a woman?"

"Athena was their goddess of wisdom. That's why we call our entity a thea."

"*Interesting. Do you suppose there were telepaths back then?*"

"*There's no good evidence. I can explain all the legends about wizards and sybils without invoking psi.*"

"*Oh.*" Too much strangeness, Birche thought. Her mind felt overloaded. She looked at her sweatpants before slipping them on. They were prosaic things, easy to understand. Their only fault was the simple lack of pockets. I should have changed clothes the minute I got home, she thought. Now everything was lost.

"*You can pick up more clothes later,*" Julian said. He felt a moment of regret as she finished covering up. "*Oh, well. You look good in what you have now, Birche.*"

Birche laughed throatily as they left the bedroom. "*Lecher. Julian, should I know who Cliff is? I really don't need any more surprises today.*"

"*I'm not sure what's surprising anymore,*" Julian admitted. "*Cliff used to be a Sere henchman—*"

Her mouth dropped open.

"*He quit, beautiful. He's with us now.*"

"*Are you sure?*"

"*Yes. Cliff is sure, to. He saved my life the other night.*" He held on to her as they walked down the block. "*Birche? Thank you.*"

"*For a roll in the hay?*" She laughed again. "*I had as good a time as you did, sailor.*"

"*I meant for listening. Helping. You saved me.*"

Birche gripped his hand as something stirred in her, a sense of worth and self-confidence that was wholly unfamiliar. In a corner of her mind she wondered when something would happen to upset it.

"*Why should anything happen?*" Julian asked.

"*Something always does. Like—*" She sighed. "*A month after I opened my bookshop, my parents came up from San Diego to see it. I started bubbling about how well everything was going, and then Mom said, 'You know, dear, most new businesses don't make it through their first year, so don't set your hopes too high yet.' She meant well, but . . .*"

"*But it killed everything,*" Julian concluded.

"It sounds stupid, doesn't it?"

"No. She was telling you to expect to fail." Julian fell silent, understanding that she needed to drop the topic for now. It would take time for her to adapt to the openness demanded by telepathy.

They walked into the house, and joined the people gathered in the living room. The child sat alone in a corner, where he stared disdainfully at the thea. Birche noticed two new people, a man and a woman, sitting by a small radio. The radio buzzed weakly, its batteries failing, while the man concentrated on the news. This was Cliff, Birche noted, and he wasn't a telepath. One more oddity, that.

"Not really," the woman at his side—Hazel—told her. *"He can give you the story later. You found the hacksaw all right?"*

"Yes." Birche blushed furiously.

"Now you know why we left it in a bedroom," Hazel said, trying to put her at ease.

Julian cleared his throat. "What's the problem. Cliff?"

Cliff looked up from the radio. "The CTO made its move against Sere today. They nailed the main arsenal, the one in Alhambra. That was headquarters. Sounds like they found most of the smaller arsenals, too."

"So Sere is out of business?" Malcolm asked.

"It looks that way, although I doubt Hutchins' Horrors got everyone." Cliff turned off the radio. "And that's our problem. The riots and guerrilla war were planned to stop the reconstruction project. I doubt the Planning Commission would have done anything soon, but now there's nothing to stop them from clearing out all the squatters."

"When will they start?" Birche asked. Her voice sounded strange in her ears.

"They just announced plans to start next week, ahead of their old schedule," Cliff said. "I guess they want to show everyone they're back in control. Anyway, I heard Granger talk about their plans once. The cops will sweep through the abandoned zones, and work teams will bulldoze any place where they find squatters. That'll put pressure on all the squatters to move out."

"So we'll need new quarters soon," Malcolm said. "Someplace safe. Any suggestions, Julian?"

"Possibilities." He ran a hand through his brown hair. "One thing we should do is to contact the other telepathics in this area. There are organizations at some of the local colleges—USC, UCLA and Cal Tech are ones I've heard of. They'll know more about the local situation than I do. We may have to leave the area—"

"W-w-wait," Anita said. "We c-can't move the child. We shou-should get him t-to a doctor. A sp-specialist."

"How bad is he?" Birche asked. Anita's hammering stutter surprised her. It hadn't shown in her thoughts. Speaking out loud clearly inconvenienced her—but it let Cliff join in the discussion. Everyone was speaking for his benefit, although he seemed unaware of that.

"It's b-bad," Anita said. "Malnutrition. Vitamin d-deficiencies. He was beaten several t-times recently. I never s-saw anything this bad in m-med school. Right now he n-n-needs immunizations most of all. M-mumps or measles could kill him."

The child looked away from the thea. *"You gotta use magic to kill me, jackass."*

"We'll have to find a doctor who won't report this to the authorities," Julian said. "I think the law here requires them to report obvious child-abuse cases. We can't let this kid get lost in the legal system."

"I'll ch-check the f-free clinics tomorrow," Anita said.

"And the rest of us can go to different campuses," Hazel said. "It's about time we got in touch with other telepathics."

"There's something else," Birche said. She looked at the boy, who was glaring at the thea. "What's his name?"

"He doesn't have one," the thea said. *"That is, he doesn't recall one. His parents must have gotten rid of him as soon as they realized he was psychic."* Birche heard Hazel repeat that in a low voice to Cliff.

"So he needs a name," Birche said. "Something appropriate. How does 'Giles' sound?" she asked the child.

"My name is Asmodeus, butterball!"

"No," Julian said to Birche, echoing the shock the others felt. "No witch-names! No superstitions. There's been too much of that already."

("Giles Corey," Hazel whispered to Cliff. "He was one of the Salem witches. He was executed in 1691.")

"That's right," Betty said. "After *this*, how can anyone even joke about witchcraft and magic?"

"You and Julian took over a million dollars from that shop," Jesse said, with an intensity that bordered on hatred. "That woman charged the suckers a thousand bucks for each question. You know what *that* means?"

"I do." Birche felt her nerve slipping. Her suggestion had unleashed the helpless anger they all felt at the way the child had been abused. "It means that hundreds of people came to that shop. It means they saw something evil, and they ignored it—"

"They *joined in*," George said angrily. "Check the things that kid remembers. They'd see a half-dead kid, they'd know he was just tapping their minds—but the bastards *wanted* to believe he was a devil. They gave money to that fat bitch because they wanted magic. That's what all this mumbo-jumbo gets the world—"

"Wait!" Cliff snapped. "Hear her out."

There was a shocked silence, and Birche swallowed hard. "Giles Corey," she said. "He was not a witch. There were no witches at Salem; the whole thing was a mixture of ignorance, superstition, and panic. Just the same he was tortured, pressed to death under a pile of stones, because the witch-hunters wanted to make him confess. He fought back the only way he could—by refusing to confess."

"Birche," Julian said quietly, "he sounds like a good man, but that name has such a strong connection with superstition—"

"Precisely like us," she said. "People call us witches, too, but we're not."

"That isn't the p-point," Anita said. "It's tradition. Th-that name is part of a t-tradition, a cultural heritage, b-but it isn't *ours*."

"It is," Birche insisted. "Giles Corey stood up to the witch-hunters. He didn't cooperate with them, and they couldn't make him say he was something he wasn't."

The child looked interested. *"He gave them the big finger?"*

"He was his own man," Birche said. She looked at the people in the room. "Don't we name children for people we respect? And doesn't a name represent the things we put into it? Julian?" She turned to the child. "Would you like to be called Giles?"

"My name is Asmodeus!"

"Who said so? That stupid woman? The suckers? How do you know that's your real name?"

"I . . . it . . ." He struggled with his memory, sliding past things best not remembered. *"Someone musta said it to me when they called me out from Hell."*

"Do you remember being summoned? Or what Hell was like?"

The boy started to curl up on the floor. *"Don't make me remember! She made me remember all the time."*

The thea had vanished, and Birche shared the group's urge to retreat, to deny the reality of the child's memories. The woman had punished him by *imagining* Hell, and then threatening to send him there—of course. "You know she was afraid we'd take you away," Birche said. "Why was she afraid?"

" 'cause I made money for her. She lose me, she lose her meal ticket, she always thinks."

"So why couldn't she bring another devil out of Hell? Wouldn't that be easy if she had magic? And if you were a real devil, how did you get out of that pentacle?"

"I . . . I don't know." His thoughts buzzed with confusion.

" 'Giles' is a good name," Birche said.

"Maybe." He escaped from his turmoil by dropping into sleep with an animal quickness.

"Is he all right?" Cliff asked, while Anita carried Giles into a bedroom.

"I can't tell." Birche crumpled onto a chair. Her mind felt like a squeezed-out sponge.

"He'll need time to get over this back-magic bushwa," Julian said. He sat on the arm of the chair and took her hand. "But he's already making progress. Did you notice? He didn't insult you once."

"Progress," she mumbled, and recalled Cliff's warnings. It might take Giles years to heal—if the world gave him that much time.

CHAPTER 17

Now that it's too late, I wonder at the role we journalists played in terrorism. Did we encourage it? We've covered it steadily ever since the PLO came into action. We showed presidents and prime ministers caving in to terrorists, while we showed the actual terrorists as Robin Hoods with AK-47s. Terrorism has always meant high drama, and drama has always been the key to grabbing audiences. Hence our concentration on terrorism—which made the idea current.

That's only one part of the question. Another is our use of language. When did men like Savoy (or Khadaffi, or Ortega, or any other of their ilk) become 'moderates'? Moderation does not mean that you kill fewer people than you might. It does not mean that you speak politely when you butcher someone. We've stripped words—important words—of their meanings. It got to the point where Savoy could call himself a 'moderate' and a 'statesman' and a 'liberator' without getting the laughs he deserved.

We made the labels into a convenient substitute for thought.

—*from Steve Magyar's notes for his*
"Pork-barrel People" column

*   *   *

It looks like something out of the Big Quake, Steve thought as he surveyed Birche's apartment. The furniture had been overturned and slashed apart. The food dumped on the kitchen floor had that rotting-garbage smell he always connected with slums and landfills. No lights came on when he touched the door switch: all the bulbs had been smashed. Marks on the door told him that someone had hammered it shut from the outside.

"Who the hell are you?" The man who walked up to Steve had a loud, gruff voice.

"Steve Magyar. L.A. *Post*." Steve showed his credential card. "I'm trying to figure out what happened here."

"I don't know anything about this," the old man said. "How did you get in?"

"I did. Are you the manager? Hobart Purvis?"

"All I know is, you're trespassing on private property. I could call the cops."

"You do that," Steve suggested. "I think the cops should see this. I know this hasn't been reported yet."

"There wasn't anything to report," the building manager asserted.

"No?" Steve bent down. Amid a scattering of sesame seeds he found a torn-up book. Someone had shredded it so thoroughly that Steve needed a moment to identify it as Clancy's *Sense and Non-sense*. "What happened to the woman who lived here?"

"I don't know. She went away."

"Is that all?" Steve got up, angered by the man's bald-faced lies. "I'll tell you what happened. The Iron Guard trashed this apartment. Then they tried to kill the woman who lived here. She got away. Shots were fired. Do you expect me to believe you don't know anything?"

"I wasn't here."

"Listen," Steve said quietly. "We both know the IG did this. That means the CTO will investigate, and they'll start by asking you questions in a private room." He paused to let that threat sink in. "On the other hand, if they decide you're cooperative—"

"I didn't have any choice," Purvis said. "These guys

had guns. They said they'd kill anyone who got in the way. Anyway, she was only a damn witch. What was I supposed to do, let them kill me?"

They intimidated him, Steve thought, but they didn't threaten him, not directly. There wasn't the right sound of fright in his voice. "How long were they here?"

"Only a few minutes. The woman got out the window and drove away. They left before I could call the cops."

"When?"

"Nine, I think. I didn't check."

Almost twenty hours ago, Steve thought. "Thanks, you've been a big help."

Steve walked out past the manager and went to the apartment next door. "I'm Steve Magyar, L.A. *Post*," he told the man who answered his knock. "I need to find out what happened in apartment 39-B last night."

"Which unit is that?" he asked.

"The one next door."

"I don't know, man. I was asleep." He shut the door.

Steve got similar answers from most of the other residents. He was on the verge of leaving when he found someone who was willing to talk—anonymously.

Steve fiddled with his column for several hours, struggling to get the *precise* phrases which would supply the maximum impact. He finished shortly after seven o'clock. The results didn't please him, but he told himself they would do. He filed the article, watched the computer process and accept it, then set to work on his next column.

The *Post*'s computer library contained some extensive files on Perry Fountain and the Redeemers. Steve hunched down in his office chair and skimmed the material as it marched across the terminal screen. It was all interesting and all useless, he thought after a while.

There was no question that Fountain was everything he appeared to be: a sincere, incorruptible man. No one had linked him to any scandals. There were no bleached blondes serving him as "social counselors" (a phrase left over from one of last year's forgotten scandals), no million-dollar luxury jets, no mansions stuffed with fine clothes and limousines. The money he raised went to support his American Life Crusade, his Bible Basics Institute, and any politician who would agree that America stood for Fountain's principles.

Supporting the Iron Guard looked to be his first serious blunder. Chalk it up to Savoy's charisma, Steve thought—no. He knew better than that. Just last night Steve had persuaded himself that Savoy was the right man to lead America out of its crisis. Fountain might have made the same mistake, seeing precisely what he wished to see in Savoy.

"Hello, Steve." Mrs. Daniels walked in, carrying a handful of papers. "You're working late."

"So are you," Steve said.

"It's this Sere thing," she said tiredly. "It gets full coverage until everyone gets sick of it. The CTO assault, what a Sere victory might have meant, how the man in the street feels—that sort of thing. But you aren't writing on that."

"That's not my job." He'd barely noticed the destruction of Sere. As Steve saw it now, today's raids were a flashy distraction. Sere, with its radical environmentalism, had never had a chance of overthrowing the government. The Iron Guard was the real threat.

"This isn't your job, either." She put the papers down in front of him. "Steve, this is a brilliant piece of writing, but we can't publish it as it stands."

"What!" Steve took the papers from her. They were a printout of the column he'd just turned in. Blue pencil marks covered large parts of the article.

"I told you that witches aren't a legitimate topic," Mrs. Daniels said. "Even so, I'll clear this if you revise it."

Steve looked at the areas she marked off. "No. Either it runs as it is, or not at all."

"Steve, *please*." She squeezed her eyes shut as she spoke. "I'm not asking you to pull your punches. It's only that a lot of this is irrelevent—"

"It's all relevant," Steve said. "I pieced together most of what happened in that apartment. The break-in, the threats, the escape—"

"I'm not questioning that. But why make such a fuss over the fact that this woman was a witch? And that bit about *Sense and Non-sense* has to go. It's a crackpot book—"

"Have you ever read it?" Steve demanded.

Mrs. Daniels opened her eyes and looked at him. "Have you?"

"I can't find a copy—literally." Steve put a hand on the computer. "I ran a search program. Some libraries removed it from their shelves. Others reported their copies were stolen. Hackers have erased it from electronic libraries. The funny thing is that other books—on black magic, astrology, Satanism, what-have-you—are left alone. Even factual books on parapsychology, written by other telepaths, are ignored. This is censorship, directed against one book in particular."

"You're overstating the case," the editor said. "The lunatic fringe—"

"No! Mrs. D., there is something in this book, this particular book, that frightens people. It frightens them enough to ban it, to burn it, to tear it into shreds with their bare hands. Why? How can I find out when I can't read it?"

She looked pained. "Steve, if it was up to me, I'd run this article as it is. It's like the Kitty Genovese murder, with all of those people refusing to help the victim—"

"That isn't the point!" Steve said. He stood up, took two quick paces across his cubicle, turned around and faced her. "This whole thing was done by a political group, for political motives. This time we can't laugh off killing freaks as simple craziness. And whatever is going on here is important to the Iron Guard's plans—"

"Which you don't know."

"I don't," he admitted. "But I know how violent the IG is. I know how ruthless and clever their leader is. Count on this: they'll do something that'll make Sere look tame."

"And you want to attack them through this?" Mrs. Daniels put a hand to her forehead. "Steve, I know exactly how the publishers feel. Controversy is fine, it does wonders for the *Post*'s circulation. But this? Our advertisers will start getting letters from the Redeemers. As long as you run ads in the *Post*, they'll say, we won't do business with you. That pressure *works*, Steve. The money we make from advertising keeps us in business—and we're in trouble now. Sere smashed a lot of our autovendors, and replacing them will cost a fortune."

Steve sat down and looked at the small plaster bust atop his computer. H.L. Mencken, the upright patron saint of newspaper columnists. Suddenly the plaster icon struck him as affectation, put there to impress visitors. "You're saying that our business is business, not the news."

"I'm saying that we have to stay in business to report the news." Mrs. Daniels sighed noisily. "I know how you feel. In an ideal world, we'd never compromise with accountants, or deadlines, or anything else."

"Or with cantankerous reporters." He handed the papers back to her. "Mrs. D., if that doesn't run, I'll walk."

To his surprise she laughed at him. "You won't walk far, Steve Magyar. Remember the contract you signed?"

He smiled genially. "It allows me to stop writing at will—and the *Post* has to keep paying my salary."

"I know. I inserted that clause myself." She smiled back at him. "I also wrote the exclusivity clause. As long as you're under contract to us, you can't write for anyone else. How will you feel about losing the public eye?"

"How will you feel about explaining my absence?" he asked, faltering. No, he would not enjoy even a temporary dip into obscurity. A strike was a useless gesture, and he would accomplish nothing if he silenced himself—no. He forced himself to stare back into her eyes.

Mrs. Daniels took a chair. "Magyar, someday I hope you find yourself stuck between management and labor.

All right, I'll tell them you're standing on your principles. Give me a few days to work on the folks in the penthouse. Until then, can we say you're doing an extended investigation, or something?"

"Fine," Steve said. Time to make a concession, he thought, something that might serve his purposes. "I'll keep writing. When I come back, I'll be ready to go with a couple of columns on the Iron Guard. That'll mean more to them than my principles."

"Yes," she said, as if she knew it might mean more to him as well.

That was uncomfortably close to the truth, he thought, walking downstairs to the lobby. After his brush with Savoy he felt that his principles made poor ground for any sort of a stand. The First Amendment? If Savoy ever became President, the man would set himself up as a dictator, and freedom of the press would mean nothing. That had been implicit in his offer to appoint Steve as a press manager.

I can't even tell myself that I'm doing this for Birche, he thought. God knew he felt guilty, but the same God probably knew this was a great opportunity for a reporter. At the moment Steve was the sole proprietor of this story, and if he did everything right and had a little luck, he'd find himself with a Pulitzer Prize. Doing the proper thing would cost him nothing.

"Mr. Magyar?" There was an urgent sound in the security guard's voice. He put himself between Steve and two men in the spacious lobby. "They're from the CTO. Their credentials check out on the computer, and I double-checked by calling their office. They say they're here to take you to the Federal Building."

"That's right," one of the men said. He showed a badge. "Field Agent Hartnell. We don't have a warrant or anything, Mr. Magyar. Director Hutchins wants to talk to you. It's purely voluntary."

At the moment, he thought, as they left the building. "Did Hutchins tell you what he wants?" he asked.

"He read your column about the Iron Guard, sir." Hartnell nodded to a man standing by a black car, and they got into it. "You've heard he was attacked at Cal Tech? The IG did it."

"The reports said—"

"The reports said that it *looked* like a Sere attack, sir." As the car started up he reached for the radio, spoke a few code words, and listened to an acknowledgment. "The chief is going to have our hides. We were supposed to find you hours ago."

"I've been on the move a lot." After the visit to Birche's apartment he had rented a hotel room and bought new clothes, to replace some of what he'd lost. The activity had given Steve time to marshal his thoughts—and to wonder why Savoy had staged two false attacks. The bombings had been meant to impress him, certainly, but to what end? No answer had come to him then, and none came to him during the drive to the Federal Building.

As the gates of the Federal Building closed behind the car, Steve felt a sudden sense of safety. Evidently the CTO agents felt the same thing. "Welcome to Fort Apache," Hartnell said, as the car parked by a door. He clipped a tag to Steve's lapel, then checked his pager. "General Custer is in the cafeteria. Have you had dinner yet, Mr. Magyar?"

"Hell, I haven't even had time for lunch." He followed Hartnell into an elevator. "Were you on one of the raids today?"

"Yeah. We took out an arsenal in Long Beach."

"How did it go?"

"Easy, easy. A few shots, a little tear gas, and they surrendered right away."

"Nothing like Alhambra?" Steve asked.

Hartnell shook his head. "I'm glad I missed that. The Sere Directorate was there. Once we had them in the bag—you know how Sere was organized?"

"Vaguely," Steve said. "It has a couple of levels, different ranks of membership, but only the Directorate has any power."

"Right. It sounds funny, but once we finished them, their subordinates couldn't decide what to do. They were trained to keep from making decisions. The Directorate kept all the power it could, I suppose."

"Most radical groups are like that," Steve said. "The Nazis, all the Communist groups, the Iron Guard—their leaders like to control everything they can." He thought of something, and wondered if he could fit the new idea into a column. Perhaps it was a sign of evil if an organization concentrated all its power in a few hands. "The Redeemers are like that, too. Anybody who disagrees with Perry Fountain is a heretic, or a sinner, or something, and gets thrown out of the movement."

The elevator door opened and they walked down a corridor to a cafeteria. It was nothing fancy, Steve observed, but the food heaped onto his tray was first-rate. Glancing around, Steve saw Hutchins eating at a table with several of his agents.

Hutchins looked up at Hartnell as they sat down at the director's table. "How are things out in Indian Country?" Hutchins asked the agent.

"We kept our scalps."

"Good. You and some other men are running down to Camp Pendleton in an hour. Don't pack. Everything you need is already there." Hutchins held out his hand to Steve. "Pleased to meet you, Mr. Magyar. I hope you don't mind talking business over dinner. We're on a tight schedule now."

"I don't mind." Interesting, he reflected. The CTO had just won a great victory, but its leader looked and sounded as if something disastrous had happened— something worse than losing a helicopter to a missile. "What's going on at Pendleton?"

"Special weapons training," Hutchins said. "The next time we have a showdown like the one today, we're going to know exactly what to do." He regarded Steve. "I take it you don't like the Iron Guard."

"I don't."

Hutchins took a bite of steak. "We checked the information in your column. It turns out that three members of Transpac—Hal Adler, John Wycliffe, Arne Richmond—have been dealing with the IG. They want the

President to raise import duties and lower taxes. They've been working to present the IG as a credible party in an effort to pressure Delanty."

One of the agents at the table scowled. "That sounds pretty farfetched, Chief."

"No, it doesn't," Steve said. "All they need to do is show Delanty that a certain percentage of the voters agree with some of the IG's policies."

"What if they do?" the agent asked.

"Some of them might *vote* for the IG's presidential candidate this November," Hutchins said, "instead of Delanty."

Another agent snorted. "So what, Chief? No Iron Guard man could *win*."

"He wouldn't have to," Steve said. "Suppose that, say, ten thousand people in Los Angeles vote IG on election day. That could swing a few key districts away from Delanty, and that could cost him the entire state. That's, what, forty-six electoral votes? I could say the same thing about New York, or Ohio, or Texas—"

"The IG's been active there, too," Hutchins mused. "Just last year they were a strictly Far West operation. Now they're popping up everywhere. Interesting."

"Savoy's an ambitious man," Steve said. "He thinks the sky's the limit."

"Having Transpac take an interest in the Guard must have encouraged him," another agent said.

"This Transpac development is only a few weeks old," Steve said. "I don't think the IG initiated it, although I'm pretty sure Savoy was the one who brought Fountain into the picture."

"Savoy's a busy little boy, isn't he?" Hutchins asked carefully. "I wonder what else he's up to?"

The question made Steve hesitate. So far, he had done nothing but repeat what he'd said in his last column. Now Hutchins was calling on him to cooperate with a police investigation. That was an all-or-nothing proposition, and it might ruin his career. Reporters were supposed to be observers, not participants, and most journalists felt that cooperating with the authorities weakened the press's independence. If he divulged his sources to Hutchins, it would be a long time before anyone trusted him enough to reveal anything to him.

Here's where I pay the price, he thought. At least he could make it worthwhile. "It seems we both want a favor, Mr. Hutchins."

The agents at the table looked scandalized, but Hutchins smiled grimly. "A favor, hm? What would you like?"

"The other night the MHB picked up a friend of mine, a woman named Birche Holstein. I want her record cleared. If possible, I want her to have some sort of immunity against harassment."

"I suppose she's a telepath?" Hutchins asked. The calm in his voice sounded odd to Steve.

"She is."

"I'll see what I can do, but I can't make any promises."

"Do your best," Steve said. "And while you're doing it, send a team out to her apartment. Some Iron Guard goons tried to kill her and Julian Forrest last night."

"Witches?" An agent chuckled—a sound cut off by a sharp look from Hutchins. "Julian Forrest? This woman knows him?"

"I wanted to interview him—never mind. Three of the men who tried to kill them are in the prison wing of County Memorial Hospital. Two others, Theodore Springbock and Greg Xavier, are locked up in L.A. Main."

Hutchins stood up. "Let's go to my office."

Steve followed him at a quick march. "The ones in the hospital aren't going anywhere, but you'd better hurry with Springbock and Xavier. They have a couple of damned fine lawyers trying to bail them out."

"I'd expect that. Red Ted Springbock is—well, either utterly innocent, or a damned fine killer. No one's ever pinned anything solid on him. Ever." Hutchins looked over his shoulder at Steve. "How did you learn about this?"

"Birche Holstein called me this morning—"

"Then I'm glad you didn't tell me!" Hutchins said. "We can't use witches as informants. Their testimony has no legal meaning."

"You'd let that stop you?" Steve asked.

"The Counter-Terrorism Act doesn't give the CTO infinite latitude." They entered his office, followed by a pair of agents. "Fortunately, you have other sources, which you conveniently refuse to name."

Steve chuckled at the subterfuge. "My other source is Gerald Savoy. He told me about Springbock and Leon Kyle early this morning, after my apartment was bombed—no, skip that for now."

Hutchins held his hand poised over his desk phone. "Why did Savoy tell you about *them?*"

"I think he wanted to convince me to ignore the incident. He painted Kyle and Springbock as cheap thugs, bunglers. He's persuasive. I believed him, until I did some checking. For instance, the IG supplied the hit men with lawyers almost as soon as they'd been booked. High-caliber lawyers, too."

"We have some of our own," Hutchins said, and picked up the phone. "Where did this woman live?"

Steve gave him Birche's address, and the two agents left the office. Steve seated himself while Hutchins made some calls. No doubt about it, he'd compromised himself now; Mrs. Daniels would probably be happy to extend his separation from the *Post* indefinitely. At least Savoy, who had forced him into this mess, wouldn't get off scot-free.

Steve felt a unique moment of self-disgust. Savoy hadn't *forced* anything on him. He'd walked into this under his own power, looking for an easier way to get ahead in life. Birche, damn her, had been right. He'd tried to keep his options open, even to the point of convincing himself that Savoy and the Iron Guard were what the country needed.

Hutchins hung up, elation on his face and voice. "All five of them are still locked up! Mr. Magyar, this is the first real break we've ever had with the Guard."

"I'm glad. I hope it amounts to something." Steve rubbed his chin thoughtfully. "Would you mind telling me something?"

"It depends."

"That battle in Alhambra—was it a catastrophe, or just a disaster?"

Hutchins frowned carefully. "I wouldn't say it was either."

"What, then? You don't act like it was a success, and your men talk like they're under siege—'Fort Apache.' 'Indian Country.' 'General Custer.' "

"Okay," Hutchins nodded. "Part of the problem is this Iron Guard thing— Hartnell told you they tried to extract me at Cal Tech? Good. But, yes, we had trouble in Alhambra. I can't fault my men. It's just that they're not trained to fight a guerrilla war, or whatever in hell you call what hit us this morning."

"Bad?" Steve asked.

"Have you ever watched an anti-aircraft missile home in on *your* helicopter? Or have someone fire a bazooka at you? It's quite an experience, but it's not exactly an 'E' ticket attraction at Disneyland."

Something in his tone kept Steve from laughing. "So you want to give your men more than special-weapons training?"

"I want that, too, but I want to prepare my men for this sort of crap. Terrorists have gone high-tech." He paused. "To add to the fun, we didn't capture all of Sere's weapons today. A big fraction of their stockpiles is missing—including a crate of anti-tank mines, three flamethrowers, and a dozen Stinger missiles."

"My God." He had a vision of a Sere die-hard, hiding on the outskirts of a major airport with one of the rockets.

"None of this is for publication, of course—is something funny here, Mr. Magyar?"

Steve broke off his laugh. "I think my journalistic career is shot, now that I'm cooperating with you. Anyway, I'm on strike—" The soft chimes of his pocket phone interrupted him. "Magyar here," he said, answering it.

"Magyar, this is Savoy. It's about time you answered your phone."

"It hasn't rung all day," Steve said "Come on, Savoy, you can tell better fibs than that."

"Magyar, what's gotten into you? I read your column this morning and, frankly, I'm shocked."

"The truth always does that to me, too."

"My lawyers have advised me to take legal action."

"That'll make a nice change for you." Steve looked at Hutchins, who was working frantically with a computer keyboard. Tracing a phone call was finicky work, even though the Federal Building's circuits were relaying the signals. *Keep him talking*, Hutchins' expression said. "Say, are these the same lawyers who tried to bail out Springbock and Kyle?"

"I don't understand your attitude, Magyar, but I'm willing to avoid trouble. I can see you, Monday afternoon at four. I'll even let you pick the place, if it'll soothe your paranoia." The connection broke.

Hutchins studied his screen. "He called from a booth on Olympic Boulevard."

"And he's probably driving away at full throttle," Steve said. "He drives a cherry-red BTK, by the way. No license plates and a supercharged engine."

"That's a help," Hutchins said. "Mr. Magyar, I've got a lot of questions for you."

"I have some of my own."

"I said I'd do what I could for the Holstein woman."

"That isn't it." Steve pocketed the phone. "Savoy offered to meet me anywhere, so long as it's at four o'clock on Monday afternoon. What does he have planned for then?"

CHAPTER 18

MONDAY, 19 JUNE 2000

I've never seen any evidence of life after death. None. I have tapped several people while they were dying; they have simply faded out of existence. They have not left for some bullshit astral plane or paradise. I refuse to mince words here, mainly because I find this fact to be too painful for hypocrisy. Even the most peaceful death is a disturbing experience, because you feel as though you are the one who's dying.

As with every telepathic I know, tapping death has scared me, and changed me. Now I understand why people run into burning buildings to rescue someone, or throw themselves on top of grenades to save their buddies. Life is so valuable that any death, even that of your worst enemy, is a needless tragedy. Any effort to preserve life is worth making. It makes trading your own life seem like a bargain.

This attitude is more or less a necessity for telepathics, and the few times I've heard it praised, it's embarrassed me. I'd save the praise for the non-telepathic people who feel this way. With them it's a matter of choice—and I can understand why it isn't an easy one.

—from Sense and Non-sense, *by Lyn Amanda Clancy*

"*This knowledge was ancient when Atlantis was young,*" Julian said, setting the enormous book on the kitchen table. He opened it and leafed through its pages. "*It brought the Empire of Mu down to ruin. It devastated the Galactic League of the Saucer People. I'm telling you, Birche, this is heavy shit.*"

"Then why are you fooling around with it?" she asked.

He looked at Giles. *"Look at what normal people did to our son. Look at how they've treated us. There's only one way to end this: by developing the psychic powers latent in all men."*

"He means we're gonna turn all the peoples into witches," Giles said. He and the thea started chalking a pentacle on the floor. *"Serve the bastards right."*

"It's the best revenge," the thea agreed. *"Once we cast the spell, everyone on Earth will be exactly like us."*

"I don't think that's a good idea," Birche said. The chaos of such a transformation would destroy too many lives. *"I'd rather let them decide what they want to be."* She picked up the grimoire and looked at its index. There ought to be something useful in here, she thought, like a good love spell. Trying one on Julian could be a lot of fun. He was no Don Juan, but he had a lot of potential.

"And I'm working on it, beautiful," he said as she woke up. He was running a wind-up razor over his face, whisking away the stubble. *"Maybe we can find the time to develop my potential some more."*

"Right." She felt a mild embarrassment, although it wasn't as bad as it would have been a few days ago. Right now she was more concerned with a vague feeling of urgency—oh. This was Monday morning. Time to open the bookshop. The MHB had taken it from her, damn them, but the sense of responsibility lingered.

So did the embarrassment. None of the other people at the house minded their life in a mental fishbowl, but Birche did. They all understood how she felt, but that didn't help her.

Birche got up, dressed, and had a quick breakfast. Giles had stepped outside the house, she noticed. The damned overwhelming openness of the outside world scared him, but he was determined to overcome that. Seen through the kitchen window, he looked like an astronaut taking his first steps on a new planet.

Birche tapped into the mental interchange around her without joining it. The other telepathics were discussing the thea, trying to figure out why the creatures always appeared as women. Some of the ideas had a serious ring, involving psychology and cultural inheritance, while others invoked male and female chauvinism and were taken as jokes. It was the sort of topic that could be kicked around without ever reaching a conclusion, and the others were doing that just for fun.

"Anita says the kid is ready to travel," Cliff said, coming into the kitchen. "And there's a pediatrician who'll see him; she talked with the doc last night. We can go any time."

"Fine. Cliff?" She felt hesitant. Asking for help did not come easily to her. "Can you tell me something?"

"I can try."

"How did you get used to this?" She gestured at the walls and the people beyond them. "There's no privacy here, no secrets."

"It was like this in Sere, too," Cliff said. He sat down on the edge of the counter. "No, that isn't exactly right. In Sere, we had this thing they called 'constructive self-criticism.' You were supposed to let everyone know what you thought about everything, and explain to everyone which of your ideas was wrong. Everyone would argue with you until you toed the line."

"It sounds like brainwashing," Birche said.

"It was, I guess. And it happened all the time." Cliff looked sour. "I got worked over once, after I made a joke about the weather. Granger almost threw me out of Sere over it."

"Because of a joke?" She felt balanced between her need for an answer and his urge to talk, to release a special tension. She set her elbows on the table and rested her chin on her hand. "I wouldn't think they'd care about humor."

"My joke wasn't right—I told Malcolm about this and he said it wasn't 'ideologically correct.' You see, in Sere *everything* is connected to the revolution, the Cause. If you think the wrong thing is funny, maybe you'll start thinking the wrong stuff about what you're doing in Sere. So they make you keep all your thoughts in line."

Birche's forehead wrinkled. She found it hard to think that way—that anyone could want the power to control what other people thought. "They pressured you into telling everything you thought?"

"Sort of—but it still wasn't anything like this place." His face showed animation, as if he had a secret he needed to share. "Here, it's like everyone wants to help you think for yourself. They *want* to hear my ideas, too—that's why everyone talks when I'm around, so I can join in."

Birche nodded silently. That respect plainly meant a lot to him.

"It took me a while to figure out what's going on here," Cliff went on. "Did anyone tell you how I came here?"

"Yes."

"For a while I thought I was here as a bad example," Cliff said. He sat down at the kitchen table with her. "You know. They'd saved my life so they could see what made me tick."

"Julian and I were doing something like that when we found Giles," Birche said.

"Well, this was different. I know they were scared because I was with Sere, but that didn't stop them. They hauled me in and took care of me, and Hazel got interested in me. I didn't understand any of it until a couple of my ex-buddies from Sere turned up to kill me.

"They nearly got me, and Julian too, but we beat 'em. By then I thought I understood him, so I didn't think there was any mystery about him saving my ass. So we had these three guys at gunpoint, and I don't know what to do next, and that screwy sonofabitch starts *talking* to them. He *warned* them that Granger would kill them if they went back to Sere. He wasn't just trying to save their lives. He wanted to help them quit Sere."

"That would hurt Sere, wouldn't it?" Birche asked.

"A scratch. Julian wasn't thinking that, anyway. To him, everyone is important, even these people what tried to kill him. Valuable, just because they're people and they have brains. He wanted them to have a chance to run their own lives." Cliff shook his head. "I'm not saying this right."

"You make him sound like an old-time missionary," Birche said, "going out to save pagan souls." She had tried to speak lightly, but after the first few words, she realized how close she was to the truth.

"Sort of." Birche sensed the way he grappled with the ideas. Cliff was a high-school dropout, and his IQ was only average, but he was trying to make the most of his intellectual tools. "Maybe that's why people admire him. We're surviving, but he's got a *reason* to survive. I think that's what it is."

"I think you're right." That could be what drives Julian, she thought. She knew most of the things he'd been through in the past two years. Without a goal, something to give his life a purpose, he would have stopped fighting long ago.

"Don't bet on that, gorgeous," Julian said, coming into the kitchen. "Are you ready to take a walk?"

"I don't like this neighborhood," Julian told Birche. The look on his face reminded her of pictures she'd seen of men in combat: the too-wary eyes, hunting out the first sign of an ambush. She felt that way herself, as did Giles. This area of downtown Los Angeles was crowded, creating an intense mental babble. They looked out of place, and that drew attention.

"At least we look like a family," Birche told Julian, *"and families don't look suspicious."* Yesterday she had picked up some clothes at a Salvation Army store: old jeans, a flannel shirt, and a Dodgers ball cap. They made her stocky, stubby frame as inconspicuous as an old car; people forgot her the moment they saw her.

"Not everyone, love." Julian looked at the numbers on the buildings. *"Are we anywhere near the doctor's office? I can't figure out this fool numbering system here."*

"*It's right there on the corner.*" She smiled. "*Poor Julian. Los Angeles doesn't impress you, does it?*"

"*I've been run out of better towns. You know what really bugs me? It's all the lights at night. The sky is so bright I can hardly see any stars.*" He shook his head. "*Iowa was never like this.*"

The trio was passing in front of a row of glass-fronted shops, packed with jewelry and lead-crystal ornaments. One shop peddled hex signs and love potions. Julian tapped the thoughts of its clerks, hoping he wouldn't find another child like Giles. Let this be a fluke, he thought, scratching the child's hair.

The store had no captive demon; its clientele bought their charms and expensive books because such things were in vogue this season. Business was good, one clerk mentioned to another, and now that the Iron Guard, or whoever, had killed Lyn Clancy, things would get better. It wouldn't make a big splash in the news, but it would bring in more paying customers than usual.

"*They got Lyn?*" The thought staggered Julian. He stopped walking. "*No. She can't be dead.*"

"*Why not?*" Giles asked indifferently. "*She something special?*"

"*Quiet,*" Birche said, tapping Julian's upset. "*You knew her, didn't you?*"

"*I met her once. Damn, damn.*"

Birche felt a moment of hopelessness; what was she supposed to say? "*What was she like?*"

"*Wonderful. You would have loved her.*"

"*I never got to read her book,*" Birche said awkwardly. "*Those men tore it up.*"

"*Censorship. Her beliefs went against everything the Guard stands for. Now they've censored Lyn too.*" He shook his head and looked down at Giles. He looked exhausted. Julian and Birche had taken turns carrying him, letting him walk only short distances, but the trip had taken its toll on him. "*Come on, we still have to see the doctor. I hope he's as good as Anita claimed.*"

They entered a medical building, and followed Anita's directions to an office on an upper floor. Julian told

the receptionist that they were the Villanueva family.
Birche thought that his Midwest accent did funny things
to the Latin name, but the slim receptionist overlooked
that. "Doctor Gray will see you in a few minutes," she
said, after speaking into her intercom.

Birche sat down, with Giles between herself and
Julian. The boy felt perfectly at ease in the small waiting room, but it bothered Julian. *"You don't like doctors' offices?"* she teased.

"Not when they don't have a good escape route." He
looked at the door. *"Only one exit. No windows, no
attic crawlspace, nothing. If there's trouble, we're sunk."*

"We're safe here." She tapped some minds. The receptionist had no idea of who they were; the doctor was
busy preparing his examining room. *"Why would you
expect trouble here?"*

"Habit." Julian sighed. *"I was in a free clinic in
Philadelphia when some Redeemers found me. They
dragged me out and beat the tar out of me with wet
ropes—the poor man's bullwhip."*

"All those scars—" Birche began.

"Fatso used to hit me with a black thing," Giles told
Julian.

"That must have hurt a lot."

"Of course it did," he said in disdain. *"That's why she
did it."* Giles lapsed into silence.

"Why were you in a clinic?" Birche asked, after deciding Giles wouldn't say anything more.

"That was when I got shot." Julian said. *"I hitched a
ride out of Arlington with a trucker. He was all right.
Then he turned around and shot me with a .22 revolver, just like that."* There was a mental finger snap.

"A werewolf," Giles said. *"You never know when a
people is going to turn into one. They don't even need
a full moon to do it."* He slid off the couch to his feet.
"That Gray dude wants to see us now."

Dr. Gray had a neat Van Dyke beard, and its point
waggled as he spoke. He was quietly delighted to see
them enter his office. "Let's get you up on the table and

look at you," he said to Giles. "What's your name, young man?"

Giles grabbed Birche's leg. *"Keep that ugly bastard away from me!"*

"It's all right, Giles." Birche patted his head and looked at Gray. "His name is Giles. New people scare him. He's been through a lot."

"Giles, eh? Well, you don't have to worry about me, Giles." As Birche picked up Giles and put him on the table, she noticed how the man relished the name. Giles. He found something appropriately *witchy* about it. "What can you tell me about his past?"

"Not much," Julian said. He helped Birche unbutton Giles's shirt. "We found him in a magic shop a few days ago. I'd call it general physical and emotional abuse."

"Can you talk, Giles?"

"I'm not saying anything to a people," Giles told Birche. *"All this one wants to hear he's a good guy. I don't have to make them happy no more."*

"He doesn't like to talk to non-telepaths," Birche said to Gray. "It has too many bad memories for him."

"Such as?" Gray touched his stethoscope to Giles's chest and frowned at the read-outs. He took Giles's emaciation into account, along with sores and mild dermatitis. His blood pressure was too high and his pulse too rapid.

Julian sighed, and Birche tapped something odd in him—a sense that he was giving in to the inevitable. *"Please bear with me, Giles."* "The woman who had him used him as a medium. He'd read the minds of her clients, and tell them exactly what they'd want to hear. That was the only time he ever talked. She'd beat him when he didn't perform right, and she only fed him after a seance."

"The things people do," the doctor said. Satisfaction alloyed his grimness. He *wants* to think people are bad, Birche realized.

Giles gave Julian a look of betrayal. *"You tell this shit any more about me, and I'll give him prophecies what'll curl his hair."*

"Take it easy," Birche told him gently.

"Giles, please, this is how we have to pay the doctor. I'll do it now."

Birche sensed something then. *"By groveling?"*

"You think I want to? We have to let him know how damned noble he is for helping us." Julian cleared his throat as the doctor took more readings. "Doctor, we can pay without any problem, but what about paperwork?" After a pause he continued, "None of us can afford to have the MHB catch up with us; we'll never get out. Giles—I don't know what would happen to him. They'll never find a foster home to take him, the MHB doesn't know how to help him, he'll end up in some institution—"

"Well, we can't have that," Gray said. Despite his neutral voice, Birche could tap his deep satisfaction. The doctor felt that he was like the people who had helped Jews escape from the Nazis, or guided escaped slaves on the Underground Railroad, and knowing that these poor people recognized his goodness gave him a warm glow—

"And if the cops come," Giles said hoarsely, "you turn us in to save your ass."

"Giles, please!" Birche said sharply.

"He just like the people what came to the seances! Always got to tell them stuff what makes them feel good. Fuck him!" The boy glared at the doctor, who looked offended. This was *not* in his personal script. "You read the Clancy book once. Didn't teach you how to tap minds like you always want, did it?"

"Giles!" Couldn't he see how much this was costing Julian? Birche struggled with an urge to turn him over her knee and wallop him—no. He'd had far too much of that already. No matter what it cost now, she wasn't going to control him by hurting him. She regretted that she had even considered that.

Giles looked at her in confusion. The things Birche thought were so far outside his experience that he had no idea of how to react.

"I read *Sense and Non-sense* once," the doctor told

Julian. He picked up a small flashlight and peered down Giles's throat. "I can't say it impressed me."

Julian swallowed hard and looked at Giles. "No."

"Telepathy might be a useful talent, in some ways, but I can't spend a few years developing it." He noted that Giles's teeth were in fairly good shape, considering his obvious chronic malnutrition. The gingivitis and looseness of some of the teeth suggested the early stages of scurvy. "I think Clancy overstated its power. Sensing body-electric fields might let you gauge emotions, but you couldn't detect actual thoughts."

"You can make some good guesses," Julian forced himself to say. *"He didn't understand a word she wrote."*

"That goes without saying." He opened a locker and extracted a number of vials, one by one. "Of course, her whole philosophy was nonsense. It reads a lot like Sunday school Christianity, if you ask me."

"Yes, it does."

"You can't run the world on that simplistic nonsense." Gray gave Giles a injection, spraying broadspectrum immunizers into his system. He prepared a dose of multivitamins and system stimulants. "You just can't trust people to behave themselves; that's why we have a government. You don't get social justice through pious platitudes."

"That's true. Most people are very selfish at heart."

Birche decided to intervene; Julian was at the end of his tether. "Is there anything we should do for Giles? A special diet, or something?"

"You'll want to give him a lot of dietary supplements— vitamins, minerals, and so forth." Gray gave Giles another shot, and put the injector aside. Birche helped Giles slip back into his shirt. "Of course, a good diet and plenty of exercise are important. Mrs. Wesley will give you some detailed literature, but the main thing is to let him lead a normal life. Don't subject him to any mystical nonsense."

"I'll make sure of that," Julian said.

"I hope you do," the doctor said, although he found it unlikely. Persecuted or not, he had to remind himself, their kind did have mental problems. The mutant neural structures that made them abnormally sensitive also scrambled parts of their minds. Any number of studies had proved that.

Birche maintained a mental silence while Julian paid the receptionist and picked up an assortment of pamphlets and fliers. He felt ashamed of himself—for abasing himself, for agreeing with the doctor, for not standing up for Lyn Clancy.

Birche looked at Julian as they left the office. *"That was the finest thing I ever saw, Julian."*

"It was worth it," Julian said. He picked up Giles, feeling a new respect for him. The child had gone through that sort of thing every day for several years; no wonder, then, that his blood pressure was high—but he'd still had the nerve to stand up to the doctor. *"You really are your own man."*

"We should be able to tap them now," Birche said. She shifted her hold on Giles, who clung to her like a small monkey. *"Where is everyone?"*

"We're not close enough," Julian said. He looked at the buildings and made an estimate. *"We're still a mile from home."*

"I've tapped minds from farther than that," Birche said.

"But not reliably. Telepathy relies on electromagnetic radiation, just like radio and TV. That puts it firmly in the grip of Maxwell's equations and the inverse—square law. The normal limit for an individual is around a thousand feet, but there are conditions that allow contact over a longer distance."

Birche thought that over, and recalled things she'd learned in her high school science classes. *"Like the way the ionosphere reflects radio waves at night?"*

"Yes, exactly. Telepathy uses a fairly low frequency, one that penetrates solid objects pretty well—" He grimaced. *"There's another theory that says it uses an extremely high frequency, although I don't hold with that idea. The human brain can generate low-frequency*

radiation—alpha waves, for example—but I don't see how it could emit UHF or EHF frequencies."

"But nobody knows?" Birche looked around as they crossed a street, idly noting that there was less traffic than normal. *"I'd think there would be lots of data by now."*

"Research is slow. Most of it's done by amateurs, hobbyists."

"So it's hard to coordinate work—say!" Birche gave him a suspicious look, as if she suspected him of pulling her leg. *"That night when I first called to you—"*

"—how did I read your mind over all that distance? I didn't; everyone in the group did. The thea coordinated our minds. It's like using a computer to link a lot of small radiotelescopes. The effect is to make an enormously sensitive receiver, one that filters out noise and amplifies signals. The individuals aren't conscious of what's going on, but . . ."

Julian looked at Giles, who had fixed his tiny, ice-blue eyes on him. The boy knew nothing about Maxwell's equations or radio interferometry, but he had grasped something far more important to him in Julian's words. *"It really isn't magic."*

"No," Julian agreed. *"Telepathy is full of unknowns, but we can understand them someday."*

"Not telepathy." The boy squirmed around in Birche's arms. *"Everything. Fatso always tell me ev'rything was magic. Sun, lights, everything. The peoples act like they do because stars and planets control them, or someone hexes them. Always say everything a mystery, never understand, so don't look for answer."*

"She lied to you," Birche said, *"And to herself. There are always answers."* Saying that, Birche glimpsed the thing that had fascinated Giles. There was something consistently rational about Julian's outlook on life, as if he applied a scientist's attitudes to everything.

"It's more than just that," Julian told her, *"and it's really Lyn Clancy's philosophy. She always thought out everything."* He looked at Birche. *"You're a lot like her that way."*

"Thank you . . . say, is that Cliff?" Birche asked. Something was wrong, badly wrong—

"Yes." He tapped the man's panic before he saw him. Julian looked around, motioned for Birche and Giles to get into the nearest alleyway. He saw Cliff running down the sidewalk, his feet pounding. Julian heard a gun popping away at him. He was about to call to him when Cliff saw him. *"That fire escape,"* Julian told Birche. *"Get up there."*

Birche climbed while Giles hung on to her. She reached the roof, three stories above the ground, and slid over the ledge with the child. She hung on to him while she listened to Julian and Cliff. "What happened?"

"Vigilantes, man. Came at us all at once." Cliff panted for breath as he went up the ladder. "Drove in, surrounded the area. Told everyone to get out now. They set some houses on fire. Then they went crazy."

And started shooting, Birche thought. Sere had been crushed, but the vigilantes must have feared a resurgence. Cleaning out nests of squatters would help prevent that. Sere had drawn most of its strength from their numbers, and its arsenals had been placed in abandoned or depressed neighborhoods.

Cliff came over the ledge, trailed by Julian. "What happened to everyone?" Julian asked.

"We tried to get out," Cliff said, sitting down against the ledge. "We were doin' it, too, when one of them found out some telepaths were in the area. They started shooting, and the next thing I knew it was the Fourth of July. I saw Malcolm and Anita get caught in a crossfire. Hazel collapsed on me. Then she—just died." His voice broke suddenly. He pressed his fists against his temples.

"Shock," Julian said. He sat down on the roof, in shock himself. "From too many people dying too close to her. One death is bad, but many—you couldn't have done anything for her, Cliff."

"Where were the cops?" Birche asked. She felt numb, and wondered if that was a blessing. *I hardly knew those people,* she thought suddenly, *and now I'll never know them.*

"A patrol car showed up," Cliff told her. "These two cops tried to stop the attack, so the viggies shot them, too, and took their guns. This was all—" He gave his watch a surprised look. "Five minutes ago? They got everyone."

Julian groaned. "I should have been here. I could have done something."

"Done what?" Birche asked. The numbness was fading, and she wiped at the tears in her eyes. "Julian, you can't work miracles."

"I might have thought of something. I'm the one who knows all the tricks." He looked out over the rooftops. Most of the buildings were higher than this one, but he could see smoke from the burning houses now. Guns still popped away, and there were distant sirens.

Birche looked at Giles, who was unmoved by the tragedy. Despite her growing pain, she felt a sudden pity for him. "Cliff, Julian, we have to think about him now."

Julian nodded mutely.

"Yeah. I'll bet the filthy bastard went up here." The vigilante tucked his gun in his belt and started climbing.

Julian got up. There was a shed on the flat rooftop, an entrance to a stairwell—and the door was locked. There was no other fire escape, no other way off the roof. Trapped, Birche heard him think. He'd blundered again, taking three people with him into a corner—

"Is someone coming?" Cliff whispered hoarsely.

"Yes," Julian said. Another mistake; he'd forgotten to tell Cliff. "One man, with a pistol."

"I can take the son of a bitch," Cliff said. He smacked a fist into an open palm, transmuting his grief into anger. "Get behind that shed, don't let him see you."

Birche was halfway to the shed with Giles when the man slung himself over the ledge. He weighed at least two hundred pounds, but Cliff hurled himself at him without a second thought. The gun went off.

They hung balanced for a second or two. Then Cliff fell back on the roof. Birche shuddered from his realization that he was dying, and felt his fear that he might not have done enough to save his friends.

The vigilante's gun clattered on the roof. He swatted at the ledge frantically, a man suddenly alone with the prospect of his own death. The ledge was slick with Cliff's blood, and he lost his grip on it and fell away.

Birche walked over to Cliff, who lay in a spreading pool of blood. Each step took an eternity of deliberate effort. She shared his fear of the darkness closing in on him, even as he lost consciousness. Birche was left trembling in the wake of his passing, dazed by the finality with which everything that was Cliff faded into oblivion.

"Julian," she said, out loud, her voice hoarse. She felt tears rolling down her face. *"We have to think about Giles. We can't stay here. We have to go."*

"I know." He stood up. *"Bled and fled. Defeat and retreat. You know, I never got a chance to say goodbye to my friends in Oakland? And now I can't do anything for Cliff, or the others."* He bent over the crumpled body and straightened it out, thinking that it was all wrong to leave a friend like this.

"We've got to think about Giles," Birche repeated. The boy was staring at the corpse, and making an effort to tap Cliff's thoughts. Giles seemed oblivious to everything except Cliff's annoying refusal to think to him. *"He doesn't understand what happened. We have to get him to safety."*

"Yes." He picked up Giles, and followed Birche down the fire escape. In the alley, Julian took a couple of steps and sat down on a milk crate.

Birche heard a groan, and saw the vigilante lying on a heap of garbage. It had broken his fall, enough to spell the difference between death and serious injury. If I leave him there, Birche thought, no one will find him anytime soon, and he'll die. She walked over to him, took him by the wrists, and began pulling. His bulk made him awkward to handle, but Birche reminded herself that she'd pressed heavier weights in gymnasiums. She dragged him onto the sidewalk and left him there. Let some passer-by find him and call an ambulance, she decided; Julian and Giles needed her more now. *"Julian?"*

"*Defeat and retreat,*" he thought, holding his head in his hands. "*The rhyme of our time is defeat and retreat.*"

"*Julian?*" Birche walked up to him and shook his shoulder. His mind went blank, withdrawing from everything. "*Julian?*"

"*Something wrong,*" Giles thought coolly. "*He can't tap us.*"

Birche knelt down in front of him and spoke. "Julian? Are you all right?" What a stupid question, she thought, seeing the confusion in his eyes. "Julian? Julian?"

"Oh, hi, beautiful." He looked around the alley. "Why are we here? Did we get lost again?"

He finally broke down, Birche thought in dull horror. The distant sirens got louder.

CHAPTER 19

On This Day in History: June Nineteenth

1799: Russian forces under General Suvorov defeated a French army in the Battle of Trebbia.

1867: Mexico executed the Emperor Maximilian, marking the end of the French intervention in Mexico.

1953: Convicted A-bomb spies Julius and Ethel Rosenberg were executed at Ossining Prison, New York.

1992: An earthquake measuring 8.6 on the Richter scale devastated large sections of southern California and northern Baja California.

2000: The Monday Night Massacre marked the start of the June Days.

Birthdays: Anne Murray (1946), Reverend Chesney Dekalb (1955).

Quotable Quote: "If all else fails, immortality can always be insured by spectacular error."
—John Kenneth Galbraith

Thought for today: The passage of time gives us perspective and appreciation.

—*from the syndicated column "Today in History," copyright 2003, Associated Press.*

"Do you get many misfires?" The CTO agent spoke to the general, but he had his eyes on the narrow lane that crossed the firing range. Most of the shell holes were far down the range, but some of them sat uncomfortably close to the path.

"Not hardly," General Diamond said. The marine turned to Hutchins. "Are you ready, Mr. Director?"

"Any time," Hutchins said. He started walking down the lane. He heard Diamond speak an order into his radio, and in a moment the mortars began thumping on his right. In another moment the shells started bursting on his left. At a distance of one hundred yards, the detonations were close enough to be loud without endangering anyone.

"Fascinating," Hutchins told Diamond, as he looked at the clear blue sky. "I never knew you could see those shells in the air."

"The four-deuce mortar throws a mighty big round," Diamond said, and launched himself into a technical discussion on assorted mortars. While he spoke, Hutchins looked at the dozen agents accompanying them. The men knew that the director was testing their nerve. Because of that knowledge they looked jittery, but not badly so.

I'm looking for more than nerve, Hutchins thought. I want to harden you men as much as possible. I want to know that you can take any orders I give. I want to know which of you are sensibly scared, which freeze up, and which are reckless fools. I want—

Several machine guns opened up without warning, spewing tracers a few yards above their heads. In the few seconds of surprise, Hutchins looked at the men and decided that all of them would do—unlike the last group he'd tested.

I also want you to know that your boss is a real bastard, he thought.

The path ended at a firing pit, where a drill instructor and his assistants waited with a set of anti-tank rockets. Hutchins watched with little interest as the DI demonstrated the use of the weapon to the men.

Diamond took Hutchins aside. "You know," the general said quietly. "I'm still not sure this is necessary."

"I am," Hutchins said. He paused while the DI fired one of the rockets. The missile arrowed into a target a mile away, guided by its fire-and-forget electronics. "Sere had a half-dozen tractors, armored with steel plate and loaded with machine guns—"

"I didn't know."

Hutchins chuckled. "General, that's so secret that *I'm* not supposed to know. But what do we do when other radicals get the same idea? Or something worse?"

"I see your point, but . . ." Diamond looked at the agents. "We can't turn your men into experienced troops in two weeks. If you take them into battle—"

"I know," Hutchins said curtly. "But I'm betting that they'll never have to face a properly trained force."

"God help you if you're wrong." The general looked away from Hutchins, ending the talk.

No, Hutchins thought, God help America if I'm wrong. If a ragtag guerrilla team could defeat his force, it would deal the country a psychological blow as severe as Pearl Harbor or Viet Nam. The public would lose some of its confidence in the government's ability to deal with a crisis. Even worse, it would inspire other radicals to take up arms, and if the fire spread too far, the country would collapse. A victory, on the other hand, might turn everything around.

It *might*.

The general's radio beeped and gabbled something. Diamond acknowledged it and turned back to Hutchins. "Your helicopter is on the way."

"Good." Hutchins checked his watch. It was just after noon. He had plenty of time to keep his four o'clock appointment with Magyar—and Savoy.

The CTO helicopter came out of the north, its orange fuselage shining like a beacon. A flying target, Hutchins thought as he boarded it. That was why he'd ordered all of the CTO's aircraft painted that color. He had the machines crisscrossing the Los Angeles basin and circling the airports, in the hope that someone would take potshots at them with the missing Stinger missiles. It was better to lose one helicopter than an airliner and several hundred passengers, Hutchins had reasoned.

He had made certain that the pilots understood his logic. A few of them had refused to fly such missions, but the others had accepted the necessity. Perhaps some of the fliers regretted their decisions, but they were learning to endure the hazards. None of them would turn tail again, and that was the real point.

"Good news, Chief," the co-pilot told Hutchins, while the copter took off. "Our security has been re-established. No more electronic redskins inside the fort."

"Good," Hutchins said. He reached for a headset and got a link with his office. In a moment he heard the telephone ringing in Lyman Grant's office. "Good afternoon, Grant here."

"This is Director Hutchins. I need to see you tonight."

There was a pause, and Hutchins could hear the muted hum of a scrambler system over the headset. "You've got your nerve," Grant said finally. "I don't need to see *you*, and I won't."

"Doctor, I don't have the time to worry about your feelings. Either you cooperate, or you pay the consequences."

Grant laughed at him. "Hutchins, you used up your only threat last week. Five of my students are playing freaks 'n' sneaks now. A dozen others were picked up by the MHB—"

"What are you talking about?" Hutchins demanded.

"I knew you'd say that." The voice in the earpiece became quietly acid. "Maybe that means I'm psychic.

Maybe you should turn me in, too. You can't be too safe."

"I didn't report anyone to the MHB—" He heard a click as Grant hung up.

"This could be too melodramatic for our own good," Farrier said, as he helped Hutchins into his bulletproof vest. He looked out the window at the restaurant terrace. "You have no idea what Savoy wants."

"That's right, Lou." Hutchins put on his shoulder holster and jacket, then looked in the mirror. The make-up and dye weren't an elaborate disguise, but they made him unrecognizable. "But what he wants isn't relevant. We're here to arrest him. Are the troops deployed?"

"They are. We have snipers on the rooftops and agents in three vans. If Savoy tries anything cute, he's dead."

"No, Lou. We need him alive. I want what's in his head." Hutchins buttoned his jacket and smoothed it out, covering the lumps the vest made. "Speaking of heads, did you talk to Blaine?"

"For a moment. He couldn't say who reported the Cal Tech freaks. The callers—there were several of them—were anonymous." Farrier frowned. "There was one odd thing. The callers identified the witches and complained about them, but Blaine described the complaints as perfunctory. They called, they complained, they hung up."

"To keep anyone from tracing them. That fits the IG's behavior."

Farrier shook his head. "Most of their callers ramble. They either sound guilty or outraged. These were businesslike."

"Maybe they wanted to get revenge on the freaks." Hutchins checked the time, then looked out the window again. Steve Magyar was at a table now, waiting for Savoy. "Lou, have you ever thought that we could make use of telepaths?"

It was hardly a radical suggestion, but Farrier's reaction astonished him. "Absolutely not!" His face turned dark. "Jesus H. Christ, Chief, there is no fucking way we could use those things."

"Why not? It'd be a lot more convenient than medical interrogations, and possibly more effective."

"Because we couldn't control the lice," Farrier grated. "Damn it, how could *we* keep any secrets from the freaks?"

That's not what scares him, Hutchins realized, looking at the brainwave sensor in his pocket. He could see that Farrier knew how he would use that power—and it frightened him. He couldn't imagine anyone making a different use of it. "It was just a thought," Hutchins said, shrugging.

Farrier looked somewhat mollified. "Well, it's out of the question, no matter what. Schulze called this afternoon. He said Delanty wants action on the witches. He sounded pretty antsy."

"I can imagine." Hutchins gave his coat a final adjustment and stepped outside.

Magyar was still at his table, glumly reading a copy of the L.A. *Post.* Sere had finally slipped off the front pages, Hutchins saw; the main headline was a bit of fluff about the baseball season. A man and a woman sat at another table, and like the lone waiter, they were CTO agents.

Hutchins took a table near the reporter. He sat with his back to Magyar, and watched his reflection in the restaurant's picture window. The glass showed his face, including the bags under his eyes. He'd spent much of the past few days at a terminal, doing research and writing articles. "Nervous?" Hutchins asked quietly.

"Only when I think about this," Steve answered. "Are you sure we have to do it this way?"

"Yes." There was no solid evidence against Savoy yet. Interrogating the IG prisoners had proved impossible so far; their lawyers had managed to stall the proceedings. The assassination attempt at Cal Tech, the probe of the security leak, the judicious questioning of Transpac members—one dead end after another. Under the law, the most the CTO could do was to observe the Iron Guard—unless Hutchins could provoke Savoy into doing something rash. "You know the reasons, Mr. Magyar."

"I do," Steve said, while the ersatz waiter brought Hutchins coffee and a newspaper. "But I'm still nervous. I know better than to underestimate Savoy. He has this ability to look less dangerous than he is, to lull you. I've fallen for it myself."

"It's showtime," the waiter said, over the growing roar of an approaching car. As a red BTK rolled down the street, Hutchins unfolded his paper and pretended to read. To his annoyance, he found himself looking at an article on the TV chopper Sere had shot down. The reporter and pilot had been buried yesterday, and their funerals received half a page.

The damned media looks after its own, Hutchins thought bitterly. Hutchins had lost a dozen of his own men to a missile, but there was no mention of their funerals in the paper.

He turned the page and looked at the other articles. The California Chamber of Commerce expected a record number of beachgoers this summer. A spoiler party in San Francisco claimed that the primary election earlier this month had been rigged. Peoria had banned all shock-rock groups from performing after Jackboot had tossed copies of *Mein Kampf* and *Protocols of the Elders of Zion* to its audience.

A car door slammed at the curb. Through the reflection in the window, Hutchins watched a man leave the car and cross the terrace to Magyar. No doubt about it, this was Savoy. Hutchins strained his ears as the man greeted Magyar. Several cannon mikes would capture everything, but if Savoy made a move, Hutchins needed to know it at once.

"I'm not sure where to begin," Savoy told the reporter. "It's strange, but Reverend Fountain is more upset than I am. He thinks you've maligned him."

"I haven't," Magyar said. "Frankly, I don't doubt that he has the best of intentions, or that he's as sincere as all hell about his beliefs. But since when do good intentions and sincerity count for anything? I sat there and listened to him condone mass murder because of his beliefs—or does he deny he said what he did?"

"He denies your interpretation of his words," Savoy said. "In fact, he's thinking of suing you for violating his First Amendment rights."

"Oh?" Hutchins heard the amused disbelief in Magyar's voice.

"The First Amendment gives him the right to worship God as he pleases. Your attacks on the Redemptive Faith are clearly meant to destroy his religion, Magyar. That's unconstitutional."

"The First Amendment doesn't say—"

"The First Amendment is just a scrap of paper, Magyar. What it says depends on how we interpret it." Savoy raised his voice. "Isn't that right, Mr. Hutchins?"

Under his makeup, Hutchins flushed in dismay. Ponderously, he turned his chair to face Savoy and the traffic on the street. "The meaning of the whole Constitution—"

"It means whatever we want it to say, and you know that. Or don't you know how the CTO is able to work the way it does?" Savoy smiled politely. "The voters are scared. That means the politicians are scared enough to pass laws that fight 'crime' and 'terrorism.' The Supreme Court is scared enough to decide that the laws are constitutional. You're scared enough to enforce those laws. Nobody thinks about how they're destroying the Constitution this way."

"This is how he works," Magyar said. He spoke to Hutchins as though Savoy wasn't present. "He takes a complicated issue and puts it in simple terms. Of course, a lot of facts get lost when he does that. You end up seeing things the way he wants you to see them—twisted."

Savoy laughed. "You make me sound like a reporter, Magyar, deciding which news is fit to print and leaving out the facts I don't like." He reached out and tapped the newspaper's front page. "With all the things that happen in the world, how can anyone give the Dodgers a front-page headline? When you decide not to publish something, it's censorship, no matter what your motives are."

"Funny you should mention that," Magyar said. "I've gone on strike over that point. Would you like to know what the *Post* wouldn't publish?"

Savoy ignored him. "You're afraid of me, Hutchins."

Good, Hutchins thought, he's overconfident. He accepted that advantage happily. "I wouldn't say that."

"No?" Savoy studied his surroundings. "That waiter and the love-birds over there are all your people. I saw two snipers on rooftops when I drove up. You and Magyar are both wearing bulletproof vests. That says you're afraid, and I'll bet you don't even know why."

Hutchins smiled, an expression he hoped would irritate Savoy. "Go ahead and talk. Magyar needs more material for his columns."

"I'd say our Mr. Magyar's reporting career is over," Savoy said. "No one's going to trust a reporter who works hand-in-hand with the cops. The liberals in the media will blacklist him."

"For helping to destroy the Iron Guard?" The journalist shook his head and laughed cynically. "This could be the best career move I ever made. Anyway, you were going to tell us why we're afraid of you."

"It's not just *me*, Magyar." He looked to Hutchins. "It's *power*, Hutchins. You and the whole government are afraid of losing power. That's why you've built a Federal Building that's more fortress than office. That's why they made the CTO, and that's why you're turning your agents into soldiers. You're trying as hard as you can to hold on to power. You see, deep inside, you all realize that you've already lost control. The American people no longer believe in the government."

"I don't see that," Hutchins said. "They obey the laws, they pay taxes, they vote—"

"Out of fear and habit, although that's breaking down. Look at the size of the underground economy; the IRS doesn't collect anything on it. The law doesn't scare the terrorists or vigilantes—and wasn't Mickey Mouse the leading write-in candidate in 1996?"

Savoy paused long enough to glance at his watch. "Hutchins, only the people can give you the power to rule them. They won't give it to frightened men like you any more. They're ready to give power to a *leader*—someone with the will to use it. Someone who can lead them out of the Depression and protect them."

"Of course," Magyar remarked, "they have to be informed that you're the anointed leader—and they have to see you in action, so they can appreciate your virtues."

"And you accuse *me* of twisting things!" Savoy said hotly. "Magyar, *no one* can get anywhere these days without media exposure. No one! But I made a mistake when I trusted you."

"No, you made your mistake with those bombings." Magyar nodded to himself. "I'd wondered about them. They were meant to let me see how brave you were under fire, and how you could take decisive action. They also gave you a chance to protect me from danger, didn't they? It was an effective demonstration, Savoy, and you planned it beautifully. It almost worked."

"I could resent your attitude," Savoy said, "but I can't expect anything better from you. You're a weakling, Magyar."

"I am," he agreed soberly. "For a while, I believed that you were *the man*, the one who could stop terrorism and make America strong again, and if you had to do a few *unpleasant* things—well, what if you did? Even when I knew that you'd arranged to have my apartment bombed, and that you'd staged that fire-bomb ambush, part of me still wanted to believe in you. If Birche hadn't talked to me, I would have overlooked all your lies—I might even have convinced myself that there really is a conspiracy."

"Yes?" Savoy's watch chirped, marking the hour. "And what did that fat, gross slob of a witch say?"

"Something devastating. She made me remember my conscience—"

Savoy laughed shrilly. "You played Pinocchio to her Jiminy Cricket? That really impresses me."

"I think it scares you," Hutchins said. "How can you become the great dictator when people refuse to believe in you?"

"Hutchins, wake up." With full arrogance, Savoy turned his chair and faced the restaurant window. He smiled at his reflection. "The people are sheep. The minute they see a strong leader, they want to follow him. The power is mine to take."

"All you have to do is scare people into handing it over," Hutchins suggested. He felt uncertain. For a man who knows he's about to be arrested and medically interrogated, he thought, Savoy is too confident.

"Perhaps," Savoy nodded, "but once I have it, they'll want me to stay on top. You see, I know the secret of keeping power. Convince the people that they control you, my friends, and you control them. They'll see me as the slave of their will, giving them everything they want, and they'll never let me go." He smiled at his reflection. "Never."

Magyar looked at Hutchins. "Something's wrong. He's telling us too much."

"I know." Hutchins stood up, deciding to bluff. "Gerald Savoy, you're under arrest—"

"On what charges?"

"Felony conspiracy to violate the security of a Federal facility," Hutchins said, reaching for his cuffs. "We can prove that you obtained classified data—the CTO's radio codes."

"Proving the impossible is quite a trick."

"We have Mr. Adler's records," Hutchins said. "I'm afraid he didn't shred everything when he left for Nicaragua."

Savoy's reaction caught Hutchins off-balance. He had expected the man to laugh, or to shout a denial. Instead, Savoy looked at something mirrored in the window—then threw himself to the ground. Hutchins heard Savoy curse while Steve Magyar got to his feet. Hutchins kept his eyes on Savoy while he drew his gun.

Savoy looked as if he'd hurt his shoulder, but that might have been a ruse—

The restaurant window shattered as gunfire poured in from the street. His training took over and Hutchins dropped, taking cover behind a chair. He saw a four-door car on the street, with several automatic rifles jutting from its open windows. Their muzzles sparked and shell casings flew like a brass rain. Over the rippling noise the rifles made, he heard the popping of CTO weapons. Motion: something caught the reporter, jerked him off his feet, then spun him onto the pavement.

Red smoke billowed on the street and the car drove into it. Red? Hutchins thought, before realizing that it came from smoke cartridges. The attackers had planned their getaway well. The smoke filled the street quickly, hiding the car from the CTO gunmen. "Cease fire, dammit!" Farrier roared from somewhere. "You're shooting up the whole friggin' town!"

The shooting stopped and Hutchins looked around. Magyar lay on his back, his eyes glassy. He let out a burbling sigh and tried to put a hand over his chest, as if to plug the holes there.

Savoy's BTK roared to life, and Hutchins saw the man wrestle the steering wheel one-handed. The car wobbled down the road as it gained speed. Hutchins raised his pistol, fired once, felt a hot pain slam through his forearm. Confused, he looked at his arm and realized he'd been shot.

"They're already calling it the Monday Night Massacre," Farrier said, while the doctor finished setting Hutchins' arm. Farrier consulted his clipboard. "So far, we have reports on ninety-six assaults. Four hundred and eight people are dead, two hundred and fifty-seven wounded. At least the President is all right—he canceled a dinner appointment at the last minute and missed getting machine-gunned."

"Okay," Hutchins winced as the doctor adjusted the elasticast. "Spotted any patterns yet?"

"Several. Ranking members of three political parties were attacked—the Republicans, the Democrats, and—"

"—and the Iron Guard."

Farrier nodded. "The National Committees of the Democrats and Republicans were decimated. The IG fared better; most of their people survived the attacks."

"Like Savoy. Don't tell me that, Lou. We know this was an IG setup." Hutchins nodded to the doctor as he left—good man, he thought quickly; the doctor knew when to get out of the way. "I'll make a bet. The dead IG men were all Savoy's opponents."

"It's hard to say," Farrier admitted. "Chief, we *had* twenty informants in the IG. Half of them have been arrested in the past month, on various unrelated charges."

"Framed by the IG," Hutchins said. His mind felt impossibly sharp and clear, now that it was too late to do any good.

"I concur, Chief. It's an easy way to remove them from action without making us suspicious. The others are double agents."

"And they fed us false information. That goes without saying." Hutchins adjusted his sling and walked out of the doctor's office. The anonymous corridors of the Federal Building struck him as impossibly peaceful. "What else?"

"Several members of Transpac are dead, along with one senator and a couple of congressmen. Attorney General Schulze caught a load of buckshot in the chest, but he's in stable condition. The Secretary of the Treasury is all right, but—" He smiled puckishly. "—Perry Fountain has gone to meet his maker."

"I wonder why they killed him?" Hutchins asked. They got into an executive elevator and sped toward the CTO office complex.

"Beats the hell out of me, Chief. Assuming that the IG *is* behind this, it looks like they wanted to kill off anyone who might get in Savoy's way. It's too early to say."

"Maybe—but you don't have to *assume* that the IG

staged this show. I know it. Savoy got under cover before the attack began."

"I saw it. Unfortunately, he's been on the news. He claims it was his good luck that he spotted the attackers before they cut loose. Chief, we know he's lying, but we can't *prove* he knew what to expect."

"Do we have a recording of what he said?" Hutchins asked, as the elevator stopped.

"We don't need one." The two men strode out of the elevator. Hutchins felt the pulse throb in his wounded arm. "The networks are running it a lot. They've preempted their regular shows—*Rotsa Ruck, The Beaver's Grandkids*—"

"All the top-rated shows. This must be the first coup scheduled for prime time."

"The first coup *attempt*," Farrier corrected. "We can still beat this. We *will* beat this."

It won't be easy, Hutchins thought later, as he stood in front of a TV monitor and watched an irate Gerald Savoy condemn the CTO and the "spineless government that permitted this outrage." With his arm in a sling he looked like a wounded survivor; no one mentioned that he'd hurt himself while escaping. Savoy denounced the conspiracy, gave names and described plots, while dozens of other people filled the airwaves with rumors, contradictory reports, and admissions that they didn't know what was happening.

The Iron Guard had the script all written, Hutchins thought, turning off the TV. While everyone else floundered in panic, they were presenting themselves as the only ones who understood the situation and knew how to control it. It was an effective presentation and it frightened him. The smile on Savoy's face had been that of a man who knows he will win, no matter what. And he might be right, Hutchins thought.

CHAPTER 20

TUESDAY, 20 JUNE 2000

Every so often I think about that phrase I misused: "Only human." It's something that is said only when someone makes a mistake. It's an excuse for foolishness, bad luck and evil.

It's a silly thing, too, like saying "Some of my best friends are human" (a popular joke among some telepathics.) Everything we do is, by definition, "human." That includes the bad as well as the good, not to mention the indifferent.

One of the best things about being telepathic is that you can find the finest virtues in nearly everyone you meet. It can take very little to bring those qualities to the surface. That makes up for the times when people disappoint you.

—from Sense and Non-sense *by Lyn Amanda Clancy*

You know you're tired, Birche thought, when you sleep through an atomic bombing. She crawled out from under the bridge and looked at the roiling mushroom clouds over Los Angeles.

"It's the genetic imperative," Julian explained to Giles. *"We're the next phase in human evolution. That means the last phase had to clear the stage for us. They did it in the most efficient way possible. The Cold War and the arms race were just manifestations of the imperative, of course."*

Is he crazy? Birche wondered. People were dying at a rate of megadeaths per minute. Her mind felt saturated with the horror, but Julian rambled on with a cold-blooded indifference to it all. When she spoke to him, he became stonily deaf. The thoughts of all the dying people seeped into her mind now, a background noise out of Hell itself—

Julian shook her shoulder, waking her. "Are you all right?"

"*Yes, are you?*" She sat up. Something in him had responded to her distress . . . but he was unaware of her thoughts. "You looked like you were having a nightmare," he said. "Was it bad?"

"It's over now." Birche looked around. They'd spent the night sleeping beneath a freeway overpass. Julian had accepted the need without question. Tapping his thoughts, Birche sensed his odd disconnection from reality, and the fragmentation of his personality. He was settling into a new stability, she saw, in much the same way that the rubble from a collapsed building will land in a solid, stable heap.

"We ought to get breakfast," Birche said, as Giles woke up.

The boy looked at Julian. "*He's still crazy, isn't he?*"

Birche hated the word, but it was the only term Giles knew. "*Yes,*" she admitted.

Giles hesitated, as if uncertain what to say. "*Will he get better?*"

"*I wish I knew.*" She took Julian by the hand. "Come on, let's find somewhere to eat."

It's awfully quiet, Birche thought, as they walked down the road. She guessed that it was around seven in the morning—the rush hour—but there was little traffic on the freeway and even less on the surface streets. The few people in the area seemed tense, as if they were perpetually looking over their shoulders. They weren't afraid of Sere or vigilantes, she decided, but she couldn't pin down exactly what was troubling them.

The answer came to her in a half-deserted diner, while a cook whipped up some orders of bacon and eggs for the threesome. Birche listened to the other people as they discussed or thought about the news. They'd killed a lot of important people, damned near decapitated the country. It was a conspiracy, just like that Savoy dude said. No telling when *they* would hit again. Sure, the witches must've been involved—how else could they have found all those people so easily? To think, for this crapola, they'd pre-empted *The Beaver's Grandkids.*

Somebody must have staged a coup, Birche thought. No wonder everyone seemed scared. Even in countries where such things were common, coups were frightening, bloody catastrophes.

"Never mind that," Giles said. *"What we going to do now?"*

"We have to get some help for Julian," Birche said. *"So we'll have to find some more wi— people like us. Don't eat so fast, Giles. You'll make yourself sick again."*

"But I'm hungry!"

"We can always get more food." Birche tried to think. Julian's friends hadn't managed to contact any other telepaths before they had died. That hadn't dismayed him. Los Angeles contained more people than some countries; the universities were as populous as small cities. Even with the thea to help, he had known it would take time to sift through all those minds.

Right now there was no group, no thea. She was on her own. She would have to look for telepaths elsewhere, someplace where she could count on finding some . . . and there was one such place—

"The Federal Building?" Giles said. He glanced at Julian, who was staring at his plate. He seemed mildly puzzled, as if trying to remember something that eluded him. *"You going crazy, too?"* Tough as he was, that thought scared Giles.

"I'm all right," Birche assured him. *"Telepaths go there all the time, to check in with the MHB's parole officers. We'll catch them coming out, and see what we can find."* She looked at Julian, who had finished eating. "Are you ready to go, honey?"

"Uh-huh." He watched passively while she paid the cashier, then thought: I married a beautiful woman.

Birche covered her surprise by dropping her change and stooping to pick it up.

The walk to the Federal Building took several hours, and that gave Birche time for second thoughts. Going there was a gamble; Julian was in no shape to save himself if anyone recognized him. On the other hand, if she left him alone somewhere, he might get picked up by the police, or—or anything.

"*So leave him somewheres with me,*" Giles suggested. He was riding on Julian's back, saving his strength.

"*What?*" Birche started to protest . . . but the idea might work. She saw possibilities. "*Could you take care of him?*"

"*Sure. I seen crazier peoples than him.*"

"*Yes, you have.*" She tried to think of a safe place to leave them. A theater? They could spend all day in one and go unnoticed—no, the theaters weren't open yet. If they went window-shopping in a mall, sooner or later a security guard would take an interest in them.

The answer appeared in the form of a park, two blocks away from the monolithic Federal Building. It was quiet and all but deserted. Two elderly men sat on a bench, feeding the pigeons and discussing the wave of assassinations. Haven't seen people this scared since that Cuban missile thing, they agreed. Pearl Harbor wasn't half as bad.

"I'm going shopping now," Birche said, trying to ignore the retirees. She gave Julian a quick kiss. "You two have fun."

"We can come with you," Julian said.

"No!" Giles said sharply. "You promised we go to park today."

"We *did* promise him, dear," Birche said quickly.

"Okay," Julian said absently. He had fallen into a timeless *now* in which it was easy for him to think that he'd promised to take Giles to the park. For the present, he accepted any suggestion. Manipulating him this way scared Birche as much as the thought of leaving him and Giles alone. She hugged Julian, then turned and hurried away.

What's gotten into her? she heard Julian think. She acts like she'll never see me again.

Birche went to the plaza at the west end of the Federal Building, and waited near the door where she had been released a week ago. No one will recognize me, she assured herself. Only a few MHB people had seen her for more than a moment. None of them would remember her face or figure. She wished she believed that.

There was an autovendor at the curb. Birche got a copy of the *Post*, sat down on a plaza bench, and opened the paper. While nervous, apprehensive workers hurried in and out of the building, she settled down behind the stat sheets and waited to tap another telepathic mind. That took little effort, and she could spare enough of her attention to read the news.

The reports made the Monday Night Massacre sound thoroughly random, but Birche saw some patterns in it. The attacks on the Republican and Democratic National Committees guaranteed that there would be chaos at the party conventions this August. Some media executives had died. Whatever the attackers had in mind, that assured that the newspapers and TV networks would give events their undivided attention.

And Steve Magyar was one of the dead.

My poor Steve, Birche thought. She put down the paper and blinked with tears. The article claimed he had been conferring with Gerald Savoy and Montague Hutchins when the attack came. Steve must have tried to help the CTO catch Savoy. It was a stupid, stupid loss.

I can't afford to cry now, she thought. Too much depended on her. She dried her eyes, looked around, and saw a young woman leave the Federal Building. She wore an orange bracelet and she was badly frightened. Birche got up and walked toward her. "Hello."

"Who—oh. Hello. Milly Yamato."

"Birche Holstein. I need help. Do you know any other telepaths?"

The woman smiled slightly. "Yes. I'm part of the UCLA group. What sort of help do you need?"

"A friend of mine, another telepath, has had a breakdown. Julian is—"

"Julian Forrest?" She looked even more surprised than she felt. "What sort of a breakdown is it?"

"I don't know how to describe it. It's like he's one step away from catatonia. He takes suggestions, but he doesn't think for himself . . . except for one or two things. He thinks I'm his wife. Can you help him?"

"I . . ." She sensed Birche's impatience with her hesitation. "Of course I'm scared! Don't you know how easy it is to get imprinted?"

" 'Imprinted'?" Birche echoed.

"It's a psychiatric term. For us, it means that our personalities—our values, attitudes, what-have-you—change every time we tap someone's mind. Ordinarily, the changes we pick up are tiny . . . but someone who's dysfunctional can impose his problems on us." Milly stopped and shook her head. "Well, everything's a risk. Where is he?"

"In a park near here." Birche indicated the direction and they started walking—quickly, she realized. "Slow down. We'll attract attention."

"I just want to get away from the Fed," Milly said. "It's bad in there. All the workers are passing around crazy rumors. The executive types can't decide if they should deny them or believe them or what. None of them know what to do, even when they've got orders straight from Washington—"

A police car zipped down the street, going at least twenty miles over the speed limit. Birche had a few seconds in which to discover that there was no emergency, that nerves made the driver speed. The man thought that anything could happen, any moment now, and then his thoughts were lost in the distance.

To Birche's relief, Julian and Giles were still at the park. The child sat on the swing, looking disgruntled, while Julian pushed him mechanically. "Peoples really think this is fun?"

"Oh, hi," Julian said. He took Giles off the swing and sat on the grass with the women. Milly tapped him cautiously, while trying to distance herself from the wrongness she sensed in Giles.

"It reminds me of hysterical blindness," Milly said after a few moments. "A patient sees too many horrible things, so his subconscious decides, 'That's enough, we won't let ourselves see any more.' It slips into a fugue."

"Bats in his belfry," Giles said. "He can't tap no more?"

Milly looked at Julian, who waited patiently for somebody else to say something. "There's no organic damage; he could recover."

"Will he?" Birche asked.

"He should, in time. He needs peace and quiet." Milly shook her head. "Don't we all."

"You had a bad time with the MHB, didn't you?" Birche asked. She felt ashamed. She'd all but press-ganged this woman into helping her, without considering her own problems.

"They almost didn't let me go! My observation officer—she'd heard rumors that telepathics were involved in the Massacre. She was looking for a reason to keep me in custody—"

"She believed the rumors?" Birche asked.

"No, but she was afraid other people would. She wanted to lock me up for my own good, but the regulations don't allow that." Milly sighed. "Thank God. Well, that's not your problem. Have you ever done any camping?"

"Not since grade school. Why?"

Milly gestured toward the horizon. There was some haze in the air, but the mountains ringing the Los Angeles Basin were visible. "There are a dozen places in the mountains—refugee camps, you might say—where some telepathics are hiding out. It's not an easy life, but it's quiet, and that's what he needs."

Giles stood up. "So how we get there?"

"I can have a friend drive you up there," Milly said.

"*We can take the number twenty-seven bus to his office. The bus stops a few blocks from here.*"

"*Your friend drives?*" Birche asked. "*He isn't a telepath?*"

"*No, of course not. Don't worry, you can trust him.*"

"*Okay,*" Birche said. "*Julian, it's time to go now.*"

"Okay, Birche." He stood and hefted Giles onto his shoulders. Have we been married long enough to have a six-year-old son? he wondered. No, that was right, they'd adopted Gil.

"*He's constructing a fantasy world,*" Milly said. "*He's trying to fit everything into a pattern.*"

"*What pattern?*"

"*I can't say yet,*" Milly admitted, "*but it won't include psi.*" She meditated for a while as they walked along. As with so many questions in telepathic psychology, this one had no cut-and-dried answers. "*I don't know. Maybe Dr. Hardy will have some ideas—*"

"*A psychiatrist?*" Birche felt apprehensive.

"*He's not one of those MHB types,*" Milly said in annoyance. "*The MHB doesn't hire the best; that isn't in their budget—and when they do get someone who's good, and dedicated enough to work for their wages, they work them to the nub. So don't judge the rest of us because the government has some bad policies.*"

"*The rest of—*you're *a psychiatrist?*"

"*Dr. Mildred Mae Yamato, at your service. I'm Dr. Hardy's unofficial aide.*" She smiled brightly. "*Legally, he can't hire me or pay me . . . but if I need anything, he makes it available. The MHB can't do anything about that, and the IRS lets him write everything off as business expenses.*"

"*And you work with the mentally ill?*" Birche felt admiration for her. She couldn't imagine more dangerous work for a telepath.

"*None of our patients are as bad off as Julian,*" Milly said. "*They just need a little help to get along. There's some risk, but when you can help someone, it's worth it.*" She looked down the street. "*The bus stop is in front of that supermarket.*"

"Is it safe?" The parking lot in front of the supermarket was filled with cars. Knots of people stood in front of the doors, struggling to get inside. Even at this distance Birche could tap their sense of urgency . . . and she could see a crude hex sign painted on the storefront.

"It's safe," Milly said, studying the crowd. She pulled her sleeve down over her bracelet. *"They're all buying food, hoarding it. Some people act that way in a crisis. They feel more secure."*

"Don't like this," Giles said. *"They're all scared. They could do anything."*

"We'll have to risk it," Milly said, checking her watch. *"The bus will be here soon."*

"If they're running today," Birche said.

"They are," Milly assured her. *"That's how I got to the Fed this morning."*

They sat down on the bench while people with shopping carts and armloads of bags hustled around the lot behind them. A withered, birdlike old woman was already there, resting her hands on an aluminum cane. She looked at them with rheumy eyes. "Are you going far?"

"We're going to Whittier," Milly said.

"Oh, that's quite a ways, isn't it? I'm only resting my feet here. They aren't what they used to be. Besides, I always meet the most interesting people at bus stops."

Giles climbed onto Birche's lap and clung to her. *"She scares me."*

"Why, honey?"

"She has that magic-thing. The cross."

The woman wore a small, ornate silver crucifix on a bead necklace. *"She won't hurt you,"* Birche promised. *"She's just an old woman."* She stroked Giles's hair, soothing him. Birche was more concerned with the people crowding the market. They were emptying the shelves in their blind need to prepare for a suddenly uncertain future. Already there were squabbles over the last of the milk and bread stocks. Things were bound to get worse.

"They're getting close to the flash point," Milly agreed, while she made small talk with the old woman. Yes, the weather was especially good today. No, she hadn't noticed an earthquake last night. Maybe it hadn't been that strong—

"Hey! Watch it!" The crowd by the supermarket's main door surged, knocking over an overloaded shopping cart. Bottles shattered as groceries spilled onto the ground. A woman dropped a double armload of bags, and then half the people in the crowd were down, grabbing what they could before a fight broke out.

Milly was on her feet. "We'd better get away. If—" She stopped, turned, and ran.

"A witch!" a man shouted from behind Birche. She hugged Giles defensively, then realized that the man had seen Milly's orange bracelet and was running after her, bellowing obscenities as she drew him away from the bus stop. She ran a few steps, saw people ahead of her on the sidewalk, ran into the street and danced back from a speeding car. She spun when a man grabbed her arm, pulling her back onto the sidewalk. He punched her in the face, a thing that staggered Birche like a bolt of lightning.

Birche tried to fight her way out of her daze. It was as hard as swimming through thick, ropy mud—but Giles and Julian depended on her, Milly needed help, the old lady was trapped at the core of a riot. Birche shook her head, cringed at the jolting sensation that provoked, and set Giles on Julian's lap. Julian held the stunned boy and remained oblivious to the lynching.

Milly was down on the concrete, with two men and a woman kicking her. The old lady was on her feet, wobbling toward them, an intense, disgusted anger filling her mind. Going to join the fun? Birche wondered, watching her raise the aluminum cane. She brought it down sharply, slashing it into the shin of one of the men. "You young people stop that!" she insisted, while her victim clutched his leg and hopped around on one foot.

The other man glared at her. "This is a witch, you old bat!"

"And that gives you the right to beat up a little girl?"

"Maybe this 'little girl' killed someone last night," the woman said. "*They* used witches to find their victims."

"That's how they found Schulze in that theater," the injured man said. Several people around him murmured in angry agreement. "Everyone knows that."

"*I* don't know that."

"It was on TV!" the man said, as if that settled it.

"The TV!" the old woman said. "Is that the same TV that told me to vote for Delanty?" One of the onlookers laughed suddenly, and the old woman gestured to Birche. "You, dear, give me a hand here."

Birche helped Milly onto the bench, while the old woman took a handkerchief from her purse. "*I think I cracked a rib,*" Milly said, while the old woman dabbed at her bleeding nose.

"*That MHB shrink was right,*" Birche told her. "*It's dangerous now. You ought to get rid of the bracelet and come with us.*"

"*I'd have to stop working with Dr. Hardy. I can't abandon our patients like that. And I haven't put up with all the hassles to run out now.*" She looked up at the old woman. "Thank you."

"You're welcome, dear." She cackled merrily. "My grandson thought I was crazy, putting a steel rod inside my cane. 'You're an old woman,' he said. 'It's too heavy for you.' "

"They might have killed you," Birche said.

"Oh, I thought they'd stop if they knew how foolish they looked," she said. "All that talk about witchcraft. Good Christian people shouldn't say those things."

"I *am* a telepath," Milly said.

"And your friends, of course," she agreed placidly. "But my minister explained that you don't get your power from the devil. He has a friend who reads minds, so he knows what he's saying. There, dear, I think the bleeding has stopped."

"It has." Milly touched her face cautiously, feeling the fresh bruises. "I must look awful."

"Try not to think about it." The old woman reached down and pulled Milly's sleeve over her bracelet. "I think your bus is coming." The woman limped away, while the bus pulled up in a hissing of airbrakes.

I never asked her name, Birche thought, as the bus pulled away from the stop. She felt as if she was caught in the riptide again. Steve and all the others dead, Julian perhaps worse than dead, another friend nearly killed and events whirling around her—

She felt Julian's hand on her arm, giving her a reassuring pat. His mind remained blank, however. It might have been a random movement.

"No, it wasn't," Milly said. *"His conscious mind has cut off his ESP, but his subconscious can't do that. That may be the key to bringing him out of this fugue."* She took a breath, then winced at the sharp pain in her ribs. *"I wish I could say for certain."*

"So do I." She looked down at Giles, who had buried his face against her side. He was confused as well as scared. *"Are you all right, honey?"*

"Don't know. That old woman. Why she do it?"

Birche stroked his hair. He doesn't wonder why a group of people suddenly went mad, she thought, but one act of decency is beyond his comprehension. *"You'll understand someday,"* she promised him. *"Maybe we both will."*

CHAPTER 21

WEDNESDAY, 21 JUNE 2000

History will call these the June Days, the days that shaped the course of human destiny—the triumph of the Iron Guard. And now we must plan for the future.

The Security Unit is to draw up a watchlist of dangerous people for appropriate action. All recruiters must find suitable people to aid us; at this stage, skill and experience are more important than patriotic fervor. For the moment, the Treasury will have to continue to work on a shoestring, but Dekalb is about to deliver big. (A note to Security: once Dekalb coughs up our money, we won't need him anymore. He might prove troublesome, even though I think of him as a candidate for sainthood, just like Fountain.) I want Information to keep spreading the word on the conspiracy, especially about the freaks. Show some subtlety for a change. If you don't, I may have words about you with my boys in Security.

I can't answer every nit-picking question you idiots have; I'm only human. If you can't figure out what to do in a given situation, I suggest you look at the things the MHB and the CTO do. They're setting a good example and a hell of a precedent, and after I'm inaugurated, I'll have uses for them.

Burn this letter; make and keep no copies.

—letter from Gerald Grofaz Savoy to the cadre leaders of the Iron Guard, 20 June 2000

"The IG has fallen into a definite pattern," Hutchins told the conference, "and that's their weakness. They stage an attack, then move in and accomplish their goals while everyone else flounders around. The attacks are designed to cast them in the best possible light, and their reactions are honed to take maximum advantage of the ensuing chaos. That pattern showed in the bombing attacks made on the late Steve Magyar. It showed again in Monday night's operation."

Some of the CTO agents nodded. "But we'll never convince the public that the IG is guilty of anything," Hartnell said. "Our version of events sounds like a paranoid fantasy."

"It is," Agent Pulaski said, drawing shocked looks. "The staff psychologists have drawn up a profile on Savoy. He shows paranoid and megalomaniac tendencies. In hindsight, it's obvious that he'd come up with these Byzantine schemes."

"A wonderful thing, hindsight," Farrier murmured.

The man looked resentful. "It explains some things about Savoy," Pulaski said. "Paranoids have a world-view that places them at the center of events. They usually feel that they have a mission in life, and that they're being obstructed by powerful enemies—"

That produced a sour chuckle. "Sometimes we all feel that way," Agent Manette said.

"And Savoy knows how to strike a chord with that," Pulaski agreed. "If he's persuasive, it's because he believes he's right. Savoy is quite intelligent. He can rationalize anything."

"It might explain his preoccupation with witches," Farrier said thoughtfully. "An enemy with a power he can't control—"

"—*and* the ability to see through him, expose him," Pulaski added. "I'm convinced that terrifies him."

There must be more to it than that! Hutchins thought. Until the IG came along, no one took the freaks seri-ously. Savoy must have realized that; why was he risk-ing so much by drawing attention to the witches? But this was not the time to get sidetracked. "Would it help if we leaked that profile to the media?" he asked.

"I'm afraid not," Hartnell said. "Tuesday's papers—did anyone catch the news yesterday?"

"We've all read the summaries," Farrier said.

"I mean the *news*," Hartnell protested. "The papers and the tube—the things the public sees. The IG has grabbed center stage. They've got a conspiracy theory that seems to explain everything, and they're filling an information—and confidence—vacuum. Savoy is the man of the hour, and the longer this drags on, the more trouble we'll have striking against him."

"I concur," Farrier said. "Right now the IG comes across as a target of the Monday Night Massacre. A dozen dead Guards make a strong argument for that view."

"Even though killing them was an integral part of the plan," another agent said. She handed a sheaf of papers to Hutchins. "You were right, Chief. All of the dead were IG moderates, and Savoy's rivals. Their deaths leave Savoy in full control."

In full control of seven or eight thousand extremists, Hutchins mused, skimming the papers. "The IG was attacked, along with the Republicans and Democrats. In the public eye, that makes all three parties equally important. Overnight, the IG has become a major party. Savoy is a front-runner in the presidential race."

Farrier snorted. "That's still a long way from the presidency, Mr. Director." He placed just the faintest sneering emphasis on the title.

"And he's going to stay a long way from it," Hutchins said, ignoring his tone. "The pattern: right after an attack, the IG exploits events with maximum efficiency. Therefore, we need to observe how people have re-acted to events, and see whose moves serve the Iron Guard's needs. Let's do that." He pointed to an agent. "Carruthers, what's the latest on Adler?"

"He's still in Nicaragua." The man checked his notes. "He's made some campaign contributions to the IG in the past, and there're some irregularities in his finances that may be connected."

"Connect them," Hutchins ordered. "I want to make an example of our Mr. Adler. I want him facing jail and bankruptcy, and I want the rest of Transpac to know about it." He turned to another agent. "What about Transpac, Wigener?"

"It's split," the woman said. "Chief, I don't see a serious connection between the two. It's the way you called it—a few Transpac members tried to use the IG to bludgeon concessions out of Delanty."

"The same way the German industrialists tried to use Hitler, when he rose to power. He ended up using them." Hutchins shook his head. "I want to know what they're doing *now*."

She hesitated. "Sir, Transpac is busy reorganizing. One of its co-chairmen was killed in the massacre, along with its treasurer. When things stabilize—all I can say for sure is that Transpac will come down on the side of profit."

"Agreed. Keep watching them." Hutchins looked to a third agent. "Leonard, isn't it? What have we got on those IG killers?"

"We've established that they belong to the Guard," the man said. "We can't make a good case out of the attack on the witches—no witnesses will come forward, and even if we had the victims, they couldn't testify— *but* we've had some luck tying Red Ted to the killing of an FBI agent in Oregon. In another forty-eight hours we should have sufficient grounds to run our medical interrogations." His smile gave his face a stony look. "Their lawyers won't be able to stop us then—and we're investigating *their* connections to the IG, too."

"Forty-eight hours." Hutchins cursed the crazy-quilt laws that hamstrung him at times like this. He pointed to Pulaski. "What about the Redeemers?"

Pulaski looked pleased. "We may have something. All of the leading RF ministers have been praising Fountain as a martyr—when they haven't been busy trying to take the reins of the ministry. Of the four major contenders, all have been targets of some highly damaging rumors—*except* for Reverend Dekalb."

"Recent rumors?" Hutchins asked.

"They've spread within the past few weeks, sir. There are reports of graft, debauchery, sexual improprieties— the usual."

Farrier nodded. "Someone must have set them as groundwork, to discredit every candidate except the IG's man."

"I concur, sir," Pulaski said.

Hutchins frowned, as much at the respect shown Farrier as at the possibilities. "But Dekalb looks as pure as the driven snow?"

"Outwardly. But on the inside—we've tapped his phones, of course. When Dekalb isn't busy bewailing Fountain's death, he's busy pulling strings to take Fountain's place. And—" he smiled nastily "—this saint-on-Earth has a trace-resistant scrambler phone in his office, which he has used twice in the past day."

"To call Savoy," Hutchins said.

"Or a middleman. Savoy works through them. It keeps his hands clean."

"Wait," Hartnell said. "A few good scandals will destroy the RF. What's the point in taking over the movement if it disintegrates?"

"Money," Hutchins stated. He looked to Pulaski. "What do you have on the RF's financial status?"

"In the past year, they've taken in over one billion dollars." The figure drew a surprised, respectful murmur around the conference table. "In real property—buildings, stocks, bonds, TV stations, aircraft, and so on—the RF is worth twice that."

Hutchins rapped his knuckles on the table. "If anyone still thinks of Fountain as a mountebank or a fool, disabuse yourself of that notion. He was a sharp businessman. It's obvious that the IG didn't kill him to create a martyr. They expect their man, Dekalb, to take control of the RF's money."

"And thereby bankroll a full-scale presidential campaign," Pulaski agreed. "Before he died, Fountain only made token donations to the Guard. He may have had second thoughts about making large contributions, or Savoy may not have trusted him to give enough. But he can count on Dekalb to gut the RF."

"And lose his ministry?" Hartnell protested.

"He won't be the first preacher to sell out," Farrier said.

"That's irrelevant," Hutchins said. "What matters is the money. We must keep it out of the IG's hands. If we can do that, we can beat them."

"It'll sure put the whammy on their presidential campaign," Hartnell said, "but it'll be tricky. The law lets us seize and freeze accounts and possessions, but only if we can establish a clear, direct link to terrorist activities."

"We don't have the evidence for that," Farrier said. "We need proof that this Dekalb is in league with Savoy. What we have now is circumstantial, although I'd go with it if we could."

"That would boomerang," the staff lawyer said. "This isn't a tactical situation, where we're allowed to charge in on probable cause. Any action we take now could only serve to alert Savoy."

"So we have to sit on our hands until Savoy gets the money?" Farrier asked. "Hell, he'll launder it so fast— don't we have any options?"

"We're monitoring the RF's accounts," the lawyer said. "We'll know if anything happens. One thing is on our side. Dekalb can't do anything until and unless the RF's board of directors puts him in charge."

"We'd better not count on that," Hutchins said. "Find every possible way to impede Dekalb, do it fast, and don't tell me it's impossible." Hutchins looked away from the man, whose face said it *was* impossible. Hutchins looked around the table and waited.

"You're overlooking the most important factor," Farrier said.

"No, I'm not," Hutchins said, pleased to be able to take the Bear down a notch. "Savoy and the Guard. If we can get Savoy, nail his ass to the wall, our problems are over. What have we got on him?"

"Nothing yet," Farrier conceded.

"Except for the fact we *know* he's guilty as sin." Hutchins leaned forward, setting his elbows on the table—gingerly. His wounded arm hurt, and he couldn't afford to take painkillers now. "If we dig, we'll find something. Does anyone know where to dig?"

"A minor problem, that," Farrier said, with restrained sarcasm. "He's concealing his whereabouts, as usual."

"We start with Savoy," Hutchins said, ignoring him. "He doesn't exist in a vacuum. He gives orders. Someone either obeys them or delivers them. We have to find out what we can about the people around Savoy, and attack him through his underlings." He looked around the room. "The attorney general hasn't banned the IG, *yet*, because Savoy has been extremely careful with his terrorist activities—at least, enough to avoid conviction in a court of law. But intimidating juries and tax collectors is strictly bush league. We're going to show Savoy how the big boys play." Cripes, Hutchins thought, I'm starting to sound like Delanty. "I want hard evidence on Savoy—evidence that will stand up in court—and I want it yesterday. That's all for now."

Farrier lingered as the meeting broke up. "Mr. Director—"

"You can cut the crap now, Lou."

"With all due respect, sir, your plan sucks." Farrier sat on the edge of the table and looked down at Hutchins. "For one thing, it's a bit late to do anything about Adler."

"I know." Hutchins touched his arm. "Are you asking if I'm out for revenge?"

"The thought hadn't crossed my mind."

He'd make a fair actor, Hutchins thought—but only fair. "I want to make an example out of him. I want everyone in Transpac, and anyone else who may want to back Savoy, to know that they can't play both sides here. Either they give their full and undivided loyalty to the government, or they face the consequences of committing treason."

Farrier pursed his lips. "They may gamble on an IG victory. *President* Savoy could hand out a lot of pardons, or appoint an attorney general who'll turn a blind eye to anything."

"*If* he can win," Hutchins said. "Savoy would have to win a plurality of the popular vote—and a majority of the electoral votes." Which explains why the IG is concentrating its energies in the big cities, Hutchins reflected. Savoy knew that he needed to win over half the electoral votes; if he didn't, Congress would decide the election, and it would certainly never elect Savoy.

Farrier might have been tapping his thoughts. "If the issue winds up in the electoral college's hands, or if he loses big on election day—well, we can count on more violence; Savoy strikes me as a bad loser. He may stir his supporters into some Samson-in-the-temple stunt."

"I agree," Hutchins said. "You've heard the tapes? Savoy thinks he's a man of destiny or something. He's not irrational, but his view of reality is skewed."

"Yes. We can't afford to play games with him, Chief. The sooner he's removed, the better—especially if it's permanent."

Hutchins looked at Farrier for a long, cold moment. "Assassination has never been an American policy."

"Tell that to Castro, or Khadaffi. Look at what Savoy's done to our country, Chief. He's killed hundreds of people, both top leaders and innocent bystanders. He's got people looking for conspirators everywhere, and finding them in every shadow." Farrier leaned forward. "If Savoy wins, he'll use executive powers to turn the presidency into a dictatorship. If he loses, he'll do his best to smash the country."

"Perhaps," Hutchins said icily. "But we are not assassins."

"Not yet," Farrier said. "But look at everything we've done to protect the country. We watch newspapers that run seditious editorials. We damn near torture suspects. We hold some people on pretty vague charges. The Bill of Rights, *habeas corpus*—"

"Those are emergency measures, Lou."

Farrier nodded. "I'm aware of that. The Founding Fathers left us Constitutional loopholes for emergencies—the 'necessary and proper' clause, and clauses about 'cases of rebellion' and 'domestic violence.' The Supreme Court is willing to stretch a few points in the face of 'clear and present dangers.' The people—hell, half of them favor summary execution for *suspected* terrorists."

Hutchins lifted an eyebrow. Savoy had said similar things. "You'd like my job, wouldn't you?"

"I'd like to see your job get done," Farrier said. "The Iron Guard caught you with your pants down—because you've been screwing around with this witchcraft crap."

"I have orders from Delanty." Hutchins forced a mild tone into his voice. "You remember the President? The man we answer to?"

"You could have found ways to get around his orders."

"That's not my job. Right now our job is to break the IG—and you'll stick to that if you want to keep *your* job. Now quit wasting my time."

Maybe he's right, Hutchins thought, as Farrier left the conference room. Savoy was gaining fame and influence with frightening speed, boosted by the intense news coverage of the Monday Night Massacre. Savoy came across as a decisive, powerful leader. People were taking an interest in his plans to end the Depression, and contrasting them with Delanty's ineffective measures. Killing Savoy might be the only way to stop him.

"Chief?" A staffer stood in the doorway. "There's a Mrs. Daniels to see you. She's the editor of the *Post*."

"I know who she is. Send her in."

He offered the woman a seat as she entered the conference room. "I'm sorry about Steve Magyar," he said. "He was a good man."

She nodded. "How did he die? I understand he was wearing a bullet-proof vest."

"He was, but the IG's hit team used teflon-coated bullets—"

"The ones they call 'cop-killers'?"

"Yes. Those bullets can punch through concrete walls. The IG knew—" He stopped for a moment, feeling a cold fury. "They knew that Magyar was working with us; somebody talked. They guessed he'd wear a vest— but they didn't need to guess where to find him. Savoy knew. He tailored the attack to kill Magyar."

"So the man's claim that Steve caught the bullets meant for him—"

"Pure hypocrisy," Hutchins said. "The attack on Savoy was a sham, a publicity stunt."

"Can you prove any of this?"

"Not in court." Frustration has a taste, Hutchins thought. His mouth felt thick, salty. "Yesterday we got an anonymous letter, claiming that one of our clerks leaked the details to a prostitute. There was even an action photo of the two as proof. I'm sure the same 'evidence' would reach Savoy's lawyers at any trial."

"So you've no hope of bringing Steve's killers to justice." She looked sad. "But I didn't come here to ask about that. The last time we spoke, Steve went on strike—but he told me he would keep writing. Do you know if he did?"

Hutchins nodded. "I'll release his files to you. Will you print them?"

"I'd like to," she said ambiguously.

"I've read some of them," Hutchins said, eyeing her. "They're highly damaging to the IG, and there's nothing in them that they can dispute. Magyar could get a Pulitzer Prize for them."

"He always wanted one." She looked at him. "Strictly off the record, what are your chances of defeating Savoy?"

In different words, Hutchins thought, how safe is it to attack the Guard? When it came to dissent, President Savoy would prove as intolerant as any Communist dictator. This woman had the future of her newspaper on her mind—not that Hutchins could bother worrying about that. "We'll beat them," he said, and had an idea. "If I were you, I'd assign several reporters to Savoy, and keep him covered around the clock. That way you won't miss the story when we get him."

"I'd planned on doing that anyway," the editor said. "He's news, so we can't ignore him—although I suppose we'll be accused of encouraging him and other terrorists, once this is safely over."

"Not if you publish Magyar's columns. I'll have them transmitted to your office."

Hutchins relaxed slightly as she left. Let Savoy get press coverage, and the more the better. He wasn't used to operating under public scrutiny, and that pressure might make him blunder. If nothing else, it would make it easier to keep tabs on the man; Hutchins knew that reporters were as persistent as any of his agents.

Hutchins returned to his office and picked up the file he'd gotten from the MHB. *Holstein, B.*, the typed label read—Magyar's friend, the witch the Iron Guard had tried to kill. The woman Forrest had rescued, and with whom he was now (presumably) keeping company. Understanding her might help him locate Forrest.

The witch hunt was no longer a matter of pleasing Delanty. As long as the IG pursued them, the freaks were a potential weapon against Savoy. Hutchins had thought of ways to turn Savoy's witch paranoia against him. When an opportune moment came along, he'd reveal those ideas to the Bear, and take the insubordinate bastard down a few more notches.

The mug shots in the file didn't impress him. They made Holstein look disoriented and dull-witted, the sort of woman who would rob a liquor store and come away with a few dollars in change. The psychiatric report made her sound like a harmless lunatic, and more of a danger to herself than society. With her height and weight, she was either a glutton or a glandular case, which would have added to her psychiatric problems.

The rest of the file, culled from other sources by the MHB, described a different woman. Like Forrest, she was an excellent scholar; unlike the man, she was an athlete, one who'd come within a hair's-breadth of competing in the '96 Olympics. In less than a year, she'd parlayed a small bank loan into a successful business. Holstein was an almost frighteningly successful woman, and she must have put her psychic powers to good use to get that way.

How would she influence Forrest? It was hard to say. Despite the few things Magyar had said about her, she evidently had a strong personality. She wouldn't get along too well with Forrest, who was as independent as a cat—in two years of running, he'd never spent more than two weeks in one spot, and he never traveled with a companion. He'd find it difficult to change, even if he wanted to.

Hutchins had just set the file aside when the desk phone sounded. "Director Hutchins?" an unfamiliar voice said. "The President wants a word with you. One moment, please."

After making Hutchins wait the requisite moment, Delanty came on the line, his voice flattened by the scrambler circuits. "What's the situation out there, Monty?"

"We're holding our own, sir. We've got evidence that the Iron Guard was behind the Monday Night Massacre, and we're building a solid case now."

"Excellent. I'm sure you'll roll up a good score against them, but we've got another matter to finish. I understand that you've unearthed a conspiracy among these mind readers."

"A conspiracy? No, sir. All I've found is a sort of mutual admiration society, a social club thing."

"That's not what I hear. There are normal people working with these mutants, helping them to flaunt the law and thumb their noses at the government. The question is, what are these renegades getting out of the deal? You can't expect me to think they're risking jail for kicks!"

Hutchins felt pained. "It's possible, sir. The evidence makes me think—"

"Let me tell you what I think. These freaks may be crazy, but the people who help them are crazy like foxes. They're all a bunch of university eggheads, the sort who think they have the answer to every question. Combine that arrogance with a new kind of power and they'll try anything."

The CTO director waited impatiently for a break. "Sir, I've investigated the matter very closely, at the expense of my other duties. The freaks are harmless. The Iron Guard is the greatest danger—"

"Leave them to me, Monty," Delanty ordered. "Savoy's a political problem. I'll clean his clock in November, if he's still around. But this ESP business is chock-full of unknowns! I don't want to get out of bed some morning and find them running the world, or—or anything. Now, are you going to carry the ball, or do I have to send in a new quarterback?"

"I'll do my best, sir," Hutchins said, hating himself.

"Good! Go for the top conspirators. Forrest, Clancy—"

"Clancy's dead, sir."

"Well, bring in the live ones. It'll help me whip the IG, too. They're raising a hell of a flap over these freaks."

"Sir, that's just a gimmick!"

"Well, it's a damned effective gimmick. Every political hack in the country is talking about witches. The American people are concerned, and that means their President is concerned. Now get cracking!" Delanty hung up.

Farrier, Hutchins thought. He must have informed Delanty about Hutchins' visit with Grant and the things Grant had admitted. Farrier would have used that to feed Delanty's suspicions. With the country in its present state, that would have been easy.

The Bear had maneuvered brilliantly, Hutchins thought, as he walked back to his suite. If Hutchins kept after the witches instead of the Iron Guard, he would undermine his own authority in the CTO. If he dodged the President's orders, Delanty would replace him, quite probably with Farrier.

In his suite, Hutchins sat down at the terminal and called up the daily news summary. In spite of the Massacre, terrorist activity was actually down. Chalk that up to the destruction of Sere, Hutchins thought. Each time an extremist group took a decisive defeat, the thrashing gave pause to the other radicals.

If I could smash the Iron Guard now, Hutchins told himself, if I could deliver one more major blow, then organized terror in America would grind to a halt. The country would have a chance to get back on its feet, free of the fear created by men like Savoy and Granger. Instead, Delanty had ordered him to chase a phantasm, while the moment for action went spinning off into history, taking the United States and liberty with it.

Realizing that he had just read the same sentence five times without absorbing it, Hutchins clicked off the terminal and went to the suite's easy chair. His brain, logy from too much fatigue and coffee, demanded a rest. He switched on the television and flitted through the channels.

Hutchins found a live cablecast of *Sudden Death Playoff*. The play was the latest rage: a black comedy set in a football locker room, where two washed-up players on the Missouri Mules discussed their upcoming game against the Green Bay Pachyderms. They had an enticing offer to throw the game, and they debated it while people from their pasts drifted in and out, engaging them in witty, telling arguments.

In the final act a referee entered the locker room and

announced that the game had been canceled; the fans had lost interest in their team. The referee, who was Death Incarnate, informed the players that they had also forfeited their lives. It was at this point that Hutchins recognized the play as a subversive little satire of the Delanty administration, and when Death turned to leer out of his screen, it struck Hutchins' fatigue-heavy mind as an especially chilling omen.

Omens, he thought. Black magic and witchery and deals with the Devil. Perhaps magic was the only way to save the country—

Perhaps it was; perhaps he'd thought of something. After a long moment Hutchins picked up the phone, placed a call and waited for an answer.

"Lyman Grant here."

"This is Director Hutchins again."

"What's with you? Can't you take 'drop dead' for an answer?"

"Doctor, please listen." He hesitated. He'd never imagined it could be so hard to say anything. "I need your help."

CHAPTER 22

SATURDAY, 24 JUNE 2000

Becoming fully telepathic was not a surprise; I'd always had psi experiences, so I was prepared, at least to an extent. The first thea was a shock, though because it (she? What's the gender of a paranormal entity?) wasn't anticipated, any more than a Victorian scientist could have anticipated what happens when you put together a lot of uranium.

*One evening I got together with a dozen other tele-
pathics. We were the first gathering of telepathics, which
gave us the thrill of discovering things we now take for
granted—the ability to sense someone's identity, the
ability to tap the semiconscious memories the mind
dredges up while thinking. We were having such a good
time that we almost didn't notice our companion, loung-
ing in a chair in a corner and smiling at us. . . .*

*A thea is something like a bureaucracy. It takes a
number of people to create one, and the more the merrier.
When it works well, it's great; when it doesn't, it's a
nuisance. It always seems like it's completely out of
control, but it can coordinate individuals into a formi-
dable force. And, of course, it takes only one misfit to
gum up the works.*

—from Sense and Non-sense, *by Lyn Amanda Clancy*

Julian reached for the light switch, then smiled at
himself. There was no electricity here; that was one of
the pleasures of roughing it. The entire world consisted
of the campsite and this rugged mountain valley. Everything else might have vanished down a black hole,
including the astronomy research that had kept him
busy the past few years.

Julian got up. Stretching, he left the tent, enjoying
the pine scent in the air. This forest didn't impress him
as much as the redwood stands in northern California, but
it was still a great place to vacation. The camp consisted
of tents and crude huts, dotted around a small clearing.

A fly buzzed around him and he tried to slap it away.
The flies were one of the camp's shortcomings, along
with the dirt and the outhouses and the isolation.

He saw his son sitting on a boulder, reading one of
the newspapers someone had carried in. Julian had to
smile; Gil looked so damned *serious*. Sometimes he
seemed more of an adult than a child . . . but this
vacation was doing him a world of good—and Birche,
too, wherever she was right now.

The boy looked up from the paper. "She's out chopping wood."

"Thanks, Gil." An amazing kid, Julian thought. Sometimes it seemed like Gil could read his mind—although that was silly. He was just bright and observant; not many six-year-old kids could read a newspaper, or would want to. Still, he wished that the boy would get out and play with the few other children at the camp. It would do him good.

"Uh-huh. What's a black hole?"

"Have I been talking to myself again?"

"No." The boy sighed. "Birche wants to talk with you."

He still won't call her "mother," Julian noted—but give him time. The welfare people said Gil had had a rough time. That still showed, although his grammar was improving and his language grew less scorching each day.

Julian took the north path, which was just slightly smoother than the rest of the mountainside. This place gave new dimensions to the word "inaccessible;" the nearest road was three miles away, and the town, a winter ski resort, was two more miles down the road. A long, narrow lake zigzagged the length of the valley. Birche liked that, though. It was a good lake for swimming.

Birche. We ought to be happier, he thought, but there was something wrong between them, something missing. It haunted his dreams. Last night Julian had dreamed that he and Birche stood on opposite sides of the valley, while she tried to speak to him. He'd been unable to hear her; instead of trying, he'd explained to her that there was no such thing as hearing. The strength of sound waves never went above milliwatts per square centimeter—and billionths and trillionths of watts were more typical. There was no damned way that something as small and simple as the human ear could detect sound or speech.

Does all that nonsense mean I don't want to talk with her? he wondered. That idea frightened him more than anything could. At one time he had felt wonderfully close to Birche, as though they knew each other with an impossible intimacy. He couldn't explain what had come between them.

He found Birche Forrest splitting pine logs with wedges and a sledgehammer. It's a strange way for her to spend her vacation, he thought, but it was a pleasure to watch her move.

Birche smiled and put down the sledge. "Glad you think so," she said, peeling off her work gloves. "How are you feeling today?"

"Never better." Damn it, Julian thought, do I vocalize all my thoughts? Over the past few days he'd noticed that Birche and Gil—and the other vacationers, for that matter—seemed to answer his thoughts. He *must* have been vocalizing; overwork could do strange things to a mind.

"It can," his wife agreed. She sat down on a stump and mopped the sweat from her face. "Julian, d'you remember what you were working on before we came here?"

"The structure of the Orion Nebula," he said. "We were looking at the way sectors of the cloud accrete to form protostars."

"Who were you working with?"

He shrugged. "Does it matter, beautiful?"

She hesitated, then smiled at him. "Julian, I hardly know anything about your work. What sort of data did you collect?"

"Nothing spectacular." Julian laughed. "We can talk about it later, honey. This place may not be the Club Med, but we ought to enjoy it while we can."

Birche hesitated again, and Julian had the odd feeling that she was talking with someone else. "You're right," she said. "Why don't we take a swim? We could both use a bath."

"Isn't the lake cold?"

"A little, but I know some fan*tastic* ways to stay warm." She waited, and he watched her intent look fade into disappointment. "I'll be down at the lake if you change your mind," she said.

"Okay," he said, sitting on a log. "I just want to think

a bit first." He watched her walk away. She's got a nice
fanny, he thought, and she was living proof that
everything he'd heard about California girls was the
truth. To be certain, she was in an odd mood just now,
and at times she became distant, unapproachable—no,
it was better to recall her wit and playfulness, or the
way she shifted between coyness and eager aggression
when they were alone.

As hard as he tried, Julian couldn't stay distracted.
There were many things he should have remembered,
he knew. What *had* he learned about the Orion Nebula? More importantly, how had he met Birche, and
when had they adopted Gil? The thought that he'd lost
those memories became a sudden, bitter pain, and he
fought back tears.

"It's all right," Gil said. The boy sat down next to
him. He seemed concerned—and curious. "What are
protostars?"

Julian smiled. This kid really is special, he thought,
as he began answering questions. He always has the
right words.

He's not getting any better, Birche thought. At least
his condition wasn't permanent, as she'd originally feared.
His mind had taken a brief holiday from reality, but
something in him drove him back toward sanity . . .
while something equally powerful held him back.

Birche walked downstream to the small dam that
held the lake. The dam had been built by the Forest
Service to create a holding pond. During forest fires,
helicopters would fly in, dip water drums into the small
lake, and fly off to douse hotspots. The lake was six or
seven feet deep behind the dam, which was more than
deep enough for swimming. It was fairly private here as
well. Although she could still tap the thoughts of the
camp's twenty-plus inhabitants, at least she was out of
their sight.

"And that changes everything?" the thea asked.

"I don't like skinny-dipping in public," Birche said,

sitting down at the water's edge, *"even if everything is public here. Never mind that. How is Julian doing?"*

"You're worried about him."

"Of course!" Birche looked down the valley. Last week she and Giles had led Julian here, jollying him along with talk about a mountain vacation. The people around them had been shocked and frightened by the Massacre, and that upset had allowed the trio to escape notice. Dr. Hardy had given them some camping gear and driven them up here, and since then they'd had peace and quiet.

That respite couldn't last forever. *"Julian can't watch out for himself. What happens if he has to run? If the MHB or the Iron Guard show up—"*

"Would you like me to tell you he's bouncing back?"

Birche muttered one of the words she'd picked up from Giles. *"I know I'm doing something wrong. The thing is, I'm scared of having my mind read."*

"Oh, is that what it is?" The thea sat down next to her and dipped a toe in the water. It seemed to make ripples. Unlike the thea in Los Angeles, Birche thought, this one seemed better defined, more realistic.

"I like my privacy," Birche said. *"I don't want everyone to know when I'm going to the can, or getting laid, or—"*

The thea laughed mockingly. *"Do you think everyone's busy tapping your thoughts? Birche, do you use telepathy to pry into people's lives? Do you even want to do that?"*

"No, but—"

"No 'buts!' " The thea waggled a finger at her. *"This is not about privacy. The problem is that you're afraid to get close to people, including Julian. That's why you're scared to help him."*

Her round face darkened. *"I'd do anything for him!"*

"Has asking him about the past two years helped him?"

"I've been trying to make him see—"

"—that he's living in a fantasy world? That he's a fugitive with lots of fears and problems, instead of a successful astronomer with a loving family? Why should

he give up that fantasy?" The thea leaned forward. *"He'd have to be crazy to stop being crazy."*

"But the way he is—he has nightmares about what happened," Birche said. *"He wakes up and he mourns, and then he slips back into his fugue. He's not coping and he's miserable this way."*

The thea nodded. *"He's isolated; he's lost the ability to communicate with other people the way he'd like. Subconsciously, he's desperate to re-emerge—so why doesn't he?"*

"If I knew why—" She stopped. *"It's because of me, isn't it?"*

"Yes. His psi sense is still working on the subconscious level. It senses that you're scared—"

"And that tells him it isn't safe to return to normal." Birche squeezed her eyes shut. *"But I'm not scared of being close to Julian. I want that."*

"Do you? Have you ever been close to anyone in your life?"

"Of course! My parents—"

"Who told you you were unattractive and a failure."

"Steve—"

"Is this the same Steve who called you a fat freak?"

Birche glared at the thea—a foolish gesture, she knew. The thea was rooted in her own mind. *"So I've been hurt a few times—"*

"Sometimes you've been rebuffed even before you could get close to people. How many friends did you have in school?"

"I never did fit in right." She jabbed a stubby finger at the thea. *"Go ahead, tell me it wasn't my fault. I'd love to hear that."*

"Yes, you would. You'd also love to hear that you can fit in now—but you can't." The thea stood up. *"Those people in Los Angeles—you lived with them for days, and you learned nothing about them. You didn't even ask that old lady her name, right?"*

"No, I didn't—but what's this got to do with Julian?"

"You're afraid to get close to anyone, especially Julian." The thea ticked off points on her fingers. *"One, you*

equate closeness with getting hurt. Two, getting close to Julian has hurt you—even if you don't blame him for what's happened. Three, watching him break down hurt. Four, you know damned well people want to kill him, and his death will hurt you."

"I'll risk that. He's worth it."

"Knowing something isn't the same as feeling it, or accepting it." With that the thea turned and walked away, shuffling across the water.

"Showoff," Birche grumbled.

"Birche? Are you busy?"

She looked up, and saw a woman coming down the valley: Ruth Goldstein, who ran the camp. *"I've got time,"* Birche said, going up to meet her. The swim could wait. *"What's up?"*

"We've got another customer," Ruth said. *"A townie wants to buy a cord of firewood."*

"I'll have another cut by tomorrow night," Birche promised. The camp supported itself by cutting firewood and selling it to the people in the town. A cord of wood brought in enough money to feed everyone for a week. She didn't mind the work; the exercise let her forget her problems for a while.

Birche took one of the sacks Ruth was carrying. The woman had gone into town to buy groceries, a trip that had taken most of the morning. *"How's Julian?"* she asked.

"Pretty much the same." For all their interest in Julian, the other telepaths tended to avoid him now. Birche couldn't resent that. There was nothing violent about his madness, but it still frightened them. *"What's happening in the outside world?"*

"Enough. Blaine replaced Chennault as the local MHB boss."

"Is that bad?"

"From what I hear, he's a real brain-banger. He's increased the reward for turning in fugitive psis to twenty-five grand."

"Should we bug out?" Birche asked.

"I think we're safe," Ruth said. *"Most of the townies*

*like having us around. Some of them are my friends—
the grocer is the one who told me.*"

"*What about the ones who don't like us?*"

"*That's the chance we take,*" Ruth said. "*But there's
good news, too. The Redemptive Faith has broken up. I
guess Fountain was all that really held it together; none
of the other ministers has his charisma, or whatever
you want to call it.*"

"*But they're still preaching against witches,*" Birche
said.

"*That's slacked off. The ministers are too busy fighting over what's left of the RF to worry about witches.*"
They entered the campsite, and put the groceries down
on a termite-eaten picnic table. "*I bought some more
papers for Giles. How's he doing?*"

"*Well enough. He asks Julian questions all the time.*"

"*That's good,*" Ruth said. "*It's hard to believe he
couldn't read a week ago.*"

"*He's a fast learner . . . and he wants to learn.*"
Birche sat down on the table and heard it creak under
her weight. "*He's doing Julian more good than I am.*"

The admission startled Ruth. "*Are you always this
hard on yourself, Birche?*"

"*I am when there's a reason. You tapped that run-in
I had with the thea, didn't you?*"

"*Most of it,*" Ruth admitted. "*It sounds like your
strength is your weakness.*"

Birche grunted. "*You should get a job as a thea.*"

"*I'm not trying to be obscure,*" Ruth protested. "*He
loves you, but your own fear is driving him back,
right?*"

"*I don't know.*" Birche remembered how he'd helped
her escape from the Iron Guard, and the things other
people had told her. "*He's never let fear stop him.*"

"*Not when he's had a reason to overcome it,*" Ruth
agreed. "*If you could convince him that you had some
problem you couldn't handle, it might bring him back.*"

"*Maybe . . . but what? I can't fake something; that
won't fool a telepath. Have you got any suggestions?*"

Ruth shook her head. "*I'll try to think of something.*"

"Thanks." Birche picked up the newspapers and went to her tent, which was on the edge of the camp. Everyone agreed that Julian's mental condition wasn't dangerous—but it made them nervous. The tent's location let the other telepaths feel that they had some space between themselves and Julian, although it did nothing to interfere with mental contact.

Giles was inside the tent now, taking a nap. Outdoor life was a strain on him; he was used to small, dark rooms. Not wanting to disturb him, Birche sat down outside the tent and started reading one of the papers.

Politics dominated the news. In spite of the Massacre, the Republicans and Democrats were returning to normal. The IG swore up and down that witches had been involved, and the sharp increase in anti-psi violence proved that a lot of people took them seriously. Leaving the mountains now would be dangerous.

"Uh-huh." Giles crawled out of the tent, yawning and stretching like a cat. *"Evasive? Elusive?"*

" *'Evasive' means that you won't give honest answers to questions,"* Birche said. *" 'Elusive' means that you try hard to stay out of sight."* Now that Giles could read, he encountered many words he'd never heard while in captivity. He had developed the habit of repeating the words to the nearest adult for an explanation. *"Where did you read them?"*

"In a story about that Savoy asshole." Giles looked thoughtful. *"I guess the writer didn't like him, either."*

" 'Reporter,' Giles. The people who write for newspapers are called 'reporters.' "

"Like that people you knew? He has a thing in the paper."

"Steve? You're sure?"

"Steve Magyar. Hang on." He popped back into the tent and returned with a newspaper. *"Here. Hey, where did Julian go?"*

Birche checked. *"He went upstream, that way—"*

"He promised he'd tell me about numbers today. He said, you understand math, and you can understand how everything in the universe works." Giles rubbed

his nose. *"I don't know what that means yet, but it sounds good. Better than all that bushwa about magic."* He scampered away.

Birche paged through the newspaper and found a boxed article headed by a small photo of Steve. A brief editorial note explained that this was one of several columns written by Magyar before his death, and held for publication.

Steve had attacked the Iron Guard—by attacking himself. He described how he had come close to siding with the Iron Guard, drawn to it through the very best of motives. *For a moment, I believed that this man was exactly what he thought himself: the next President of the United States. In that moment, he was no longer a cynical, power-hungry politico. He was my passport to power—power which I know how to use wisely. Trust me!*

I'm not sure what was going through my mind. What sort of power could Savoy give me? What would I do with it? Probably I'd take judicious control of the news media, and make sure that the news served the national interest—as my mentor and I defined it. Don't worry. We would have made you like our definition.

And there was more power beyond that. Look at Savoy, I thought. He's crude. Clumsy. Ignorant. A smooth operator (such as yours truly) could manipulate him without any trouble. In fact, I would have to do that. I'm a better man than Savoy—take my word for it!—so I would steer him away from his extremism and make him more moderate. It would be a snap to play the power behind the throne.

Birche read on as Steve outlined his drift into extremism. He had written without any self-justification, and Birche found that gave the article a restrained power. He described some of Savoy's plans in brief detail, and then told how he had persuaded himself that there was nothing evil about them. It was dangerous writing, she thought; it skated perilously close to persuading people that the Iron Guard's doctrines *were* right.

What happened next was comical, Steve concluded. *I*

*caught Savoy lying to me. I was outraged. I was sup-
posed to manipulate him. Then I realized that I had
been ready to justify everything he'd done to me, so
what was my problem?*

*When I started this column, I'd wanted to explain
why I was willing to throw away democracy and the
First Amendment. I can't do that. All I can say is that I
don't have a moral anchor, something to keep me from
drifting from whatever may be right. I'm looking for
that anchor, and I wonder if I'll ever find it.*

I think he did, Birche told herself. The words sounded
nothing like the man she remembered. It must have
cost Steve a lot to expose himself in writing.

"Birche, we've got company," the thea said. "*Deputy
Martinez is coming here. You should see him.*"

"Why?" Birche asked. Her first thought was the money
she had given Ruth for food. Thousand-dollar bills weren't
too common. Some bank clerk might have noticed the
bluebacks and decided there was a possible violation of
the Currency Control Act.

"*It's worse than that,*" the thea said. "*The MHB
called him. They've heard about this camp. They're
waiting in town.*"

"My God." Birche located Ruth, got up and hurried
to her. The alarm she felt from the other telepaths
disturbed her as much as her own fear. "You've heard?"

"Naturally. Don't worry. Marty Martinez is a friend.
You want to come along?"

"Hell, no!" Birche said. "But the thea thought I
should."

"Good enough." They walked down the trail toward
the road. Birche felt relief as her contact with the
others in the camp faded out—until it dawned on her
that she was leaving Giles and Julian behind.

"They'll be okay," Ruth said.

"Suppose we have to get out?" Birche said. "Giles is
still in no shape to run. Neither is Julian—and where
can we run to, out here?" She looked at the steep
mountainside and shook her head. "Julian always looked
for good escape routes."

"*Don't we all. Well, there he is.*" Ruth pointed and waved. "*Marty! Good morning!*"

The man at the far end of the trail waved back. "*Morning, Ruthie,*" he thought. "*You've got company in town.*"

"The MHB?"

"*Don't shout. They may have followed.*" The deputy continued to address them as he picked his way along the trail. "*Some damned-fool kids called them for the reward. These two men showed up a while ago. They're waiting in my office, unless they changed their minds.*"

Automatically, Birche looked down the valley. She saw nothing, in the trees or on the trail, and she sensed no other minds. "*We're alone,*" she told Ruth.

"*Unless they're following at a distance.*" She waited until they were face to face with Deputy Martinez before speaking again. "Are there only two of them, Marty?"

"Yes. I told them it wasn't safe to come out here; they might run into marijuana farmers or something, and get shot. I promised I'd check out the report for them. I don't know if they'll believe me when I tell them I didn't find anything."

"You could show them the old campground in East Valley," Ruth suggested. "Tell them whoever was there cleared out recently."

"I'll do that if I have to, but those kids gave them specific directions." The deputy sat down under a tree. "Damned kids. Their folks will skin them alive. Especially Fred Zealand—" Marty grinned suddenly. "I suppose you know he resells your firewood down in the city?"

"And he makes three times what he pays us," Ruth said.

"He'd sure hate to lose that money. It's about all he earns during the off season. Christ, there's not much that's poorer than a ski resort in the summer."

"So you won't turn us in?" Birche asked.

Ruth elbowed her in the ribs. "She's new here."

"Can't blame you for feeling nervous, miss. Don't

worry. Even if your people didn't bring in firewood money, I owe for other things." He looked at Birche, studying her face. "Are you Birche Holstein?"

Birche glanced at Ruth before answering. "Yes."

"The CTO issued a poster with your name and picture on it. They want you for questioning—something about belonging to a psychic underground—" Ruth laughed, and Martinez grinned toothily. "Right. Just the same, the Junior G-Men are looking for you, Miss Holstein. You're supposed to be with Julian Forrest, and they want him, too."

"Julian's here," Ruth said, "but he's got a problem. Sort of a temporary nervous breakdown."

"Will he be all right?" Marty asked.

"He's recovering."

"Good. With all I've heard about him, I'd like to meet him some day."

"Why does the CTO want him?" Birche asked.

"They're charging him with leading a conspiracy. Of course, the Compton Act being what it is, they can't bring any charges against either of you. I figure this is a political thing."

"It must be," Birche said. "I think it has to do with the Iron Guard." The CTO's interest filled her with foreboding. It could only mean that the government took the Iron Guard seriously.

"I see it the same way," Martinez said, frowning. "We don't have any IG members in town, but there're a few sympathizers, what with the Massacre and all." He stood up. "Well, I'd best get back to the station, and tell my guests I didn't find any damned camp. Good day, ladies."

"*Conspiracy*," Birche said, as she and Ruth returned home. "*They have to be kidding! The only thing Julian's ever conspired to do is to get into my pants.*"

"*Uncle Sam must be running scared,*" Ruth said. "*I wish I understood this.*"

"*Me, too.*" Birche looked back down the trail. "*Are you sure he won't turn us in?*"

"*You can count on Marty,*" Ruth said. "*The things he*

said he owes us—well, it won't hurt to tell. He's stuck in a dead-end job in the middle of nowhere. Two years ago he was an alcoholic. We helped him adjust. He's comfortable with himself now."

"I see. I think I see."

"It's more than just that," Ruth said. "We find lost kids and lost skiers. Last year we helped put out a brushfire north of town. And we have a lot of friends in town. There are a lot of good people here, especially Marty."

"Then we can trust him."

"As much as he trusts us, Birche. Didn't you notice? It's his job to turn us in. He's committing a felony by helping us."

"I didn't think of that."

"Neither did he. It came automatically."

"So everything is all right for now—" Birche stopped, sensing trouble, and started running toward the camp. Giles! she thought, her stubby legs pumping furiously. She saw Julian carrying him toward their tent. Is he hurt? she wondered. So far, life here had been merely inconvenient—no baths, cold food, wearing the same clothes every day—but if Giles needed a doctor—

She ran into the tent a moment after Julian. He was sitting on the floor, holding Giles on his lap. The boy had his eyes squeezed shut. He shook in terror. "What happened?" Birche gasped.

"He had one of his attacks," Julian said. "Agoraphobia. We were talking, and it just came over him."

Birche took Giles, and winced as his fingers dug into her shoulders. "Are you all right, honey? What happened?"

"So big. Goes up forever and ever. Felt like I was falling into the sky."

"He's too scared to talk right now," Julian said. "It's okay, son. You're back inside." He settled back while Birche rocked the boy and made soothing noises.

Eventually Giles calmed down. "It almost worked."

"What 'almost worked?' "

"Tapped what Ruth and the thea told you. Figured if

Julian thought something bad happened to me, he might snap out of it."

"It's my fault," Julian said. "We were talking about arithmetic. He wanted to know how big numbers got, so I tried to tell him about infinity. I used the sky and the horizon for examples. I should have realized that might upset him."

"*That's what gave me the idea,*" Giles said. "*Outside is spooky enough, so I cut loose and let it scare me, and—*" He started shaking again. "*Maybe it'll work the next time.*"

"*There won't have to be a 'next time,*'" Birche told him. "*I know what I have to do now.*"

CHAPTER 23

Dear Susan:
I'm glad to hear that your college's administrators have dropped their objections to enrolling telepathic students. Congratulations on your creative arm-twisting.
Since you're going to be their academic advisor, it's time to learn the ropes. MHB regulations force us to go through a lot of ka-ka to enroll telepathics. You will have to fill out insurance waivers (form WW-68), medical waivers (J-5, AA2/13, and 93N), an MHB Compliance Certificate (B-9) and Statement of Supervision (BB-7), along with a contract which states that your college is liable for any misconduct by an MHB outpatient (the dread 389). You must inform the local police, county sheriff, and fire and health departments of the presence of said outpatients on your campus; you'll have to write a separate letter for each telepathic to each of these groups. In addition, you are required to caution each student that they are not allowed to leave the campus

grounds after three P.M. or before eight A.M. "Hiring" them to work for you is even more complicated, believe me, but there are ways.

Like King Charles's saddle sores, these regulations are a royal pain in the ass. Even so, you'll find the trouble worthwhile. It isn't just that they're excellent students. They want to learn, and they have an interesting, stimulating effect on instructors and other students; you can't live and work around people like them without having their attitude rub off on you.

It's impossible to underestimate the importance of this, so I'll put it this way. Given a choice between having a brand-new, state-of-the-art observatory, or having a dozen telepathics as students, I'd take the students any day. People are more important to science and education than hardware.

—letter, Lyman A. Grant, Ph.D., to Susan Cremer, Ph.D, 11 April 2000

For once, the news summary was good, and Hutchins read the hard copy happily over breakfast. First and foremost, terrorist incidents were on the decline. According to the analysts, the rate had fallen by ten percent since the destruction of Sere—a larger and faster drop than he had dared hope.

Better yet, the news coverage of the Iron Guard became more negative every day. Savoy, for all his charm and vigor, didn't know how to handle aggressive reporters. He did his best to dodge the media, claiming that too much exposure would endanger him. The reporters had grown dissatisfied with that; their instinct was to report news, not a lack of it. Magyar's articles had been picked up by a dozen metropolitan papers and both national dailies. The *Post* had launched an in-depth series on Savoy's shady past—aided by a few judicious leaks from the CTO's files.

Problems remained, however. Many newspapers still expressed support for the Iron Guard, either by praising the IG's plans or by neglecting to report on Savoy's flaws. The polls showed that more than a third of the registered voters agreed with at least some of the Guard's doctrines, and half thought there was something in its conspiracy theory. The Guard was gaining ground.

Hutchins looked up as Farrier entered his suite. "Lou, does Savoy have Secret Service protection?"

"No. He hasn't declared his candidacy yet. Why?"

"Just a hunch. Savoy has a habit of staging fake attacks. He may try one again, to keep the press from complaining about his shyness. If we can intercept an attack—"

"It'd make us look good."

"It might give us the link we need between Savoy and the Massacre, something that will convince John Q. Public of the facts." Hutchins got up from the table. "Schulze agrees that the IG was involved; he wants them smashed no matter what."

"I thought the attorney-general was still in the hospital."

"He is, and he wasn't amused by the flowers Savoy sent him. Schulze knows that one goal of the Monday Night Massacre was to paralyze the Justice Department, to keep us from investigating Savoy before the election."

"Or to get us to chase shadows. Speaking of which—"

"I plan to visit Lyman Grant today."

"Really?" Farrier smiled tartly. "I was going to say that what's left of the RF's board of directors will meet today. They're going to appoint a replacement for Fountain, and unless there's a miracle, they'll pick Dekalb."

"I'd hardly call that a shadow, Lou. The RF is still worth a fortune, and we can't touch it—or keep Dekalb from sluicing funds to the IG."

"Speaking of which, we monitored a phone call Dekalb made last night—to Savoy. They used a lot of double-talk, but it's clear that Dekalb *will* finance Savoy's candidacy." Farrier looked puzzled. "And you're going to spend the morning hunting witches?"

"Why, so I am, Lou," Hutchins said amiably. "Curious, isn't it?" The brief disconcerted look on Farrier's face told him that the Bear would move cautiously until he had figured out Hutchins' meaning. That thought eased the ache in his wounded arm.

Hartnell came into the suite. "Chief, we've got something new on the Forrest case," the agent said. "He turned up at a doctor's office last week, with the Holstein woman and a child. They used the name 'Villanueva,' and they didn't try to hide what they are. The doctor's willing to help us locate them, too."

"Good!" Hutchins said. "But can we rely on him?"

"Oh, he's *very* cooperative. We got him on the Currency Control Act. He donated seventy-eight thousand dollars to a legal defense fund for Sere—under the table, in K-notes."

"I see." Hutchins smiled. The Currency Control Act had been passed in 1994 to hinder organized crime, which used thousand-dollar bills for its business transactions. Anyone holding more than fifty K-notes (printed with blue tracer-ink, to further aid the war on crime) was required to explain how they had been earned, or face an IRS audit and a possible jail sentence. "So this Lamborghini liberal has turned state's evidence?"

"He's answered everything we've asked," Hartnell said. "He said that the 'Villanuevas' acted like a family, although the kid was as foul-mouthed as they come."

" 'Villanueva.' " The name rang a bell. Hutchins went to the terminal and began a search program. "Was the kid a witch?"

Hartnell nodded. "They called him 'Giles,' too."

"Cute." The terminal beeped and began flashing data. Bad, Hutchins thought, as facts fitted together. Very bad. The coroner had identified one Anita de Villanueva as a victim of vigilante justice. The viggies had spent several days expelling squatters; evidently they'd wiped out a coven of witches. The MHB listed several of its clients among the dead. Luckily, Forrest was not one of them. Unluckily, he had vanished again.

"But he'll be easier to spot now," Hartnell mused. "Forrest can't run easily."

"Not with a woman and child weighing him down," Farrier agreed. "Interesting, isn't it? These oh-so-elusive witches were caught short by vigilantes. This might help you capture Forrest."

Hutchins raised an eyebrow. "Why would we want to capture him?"

The Bear floundered. "Why—the President's orders—"

"—will be carried out. But first we have other uses for Forrest." He waited, long enough to let Hartnell see that Farrier didn't understand. Let him spread the word, Hutchins thought: the chief still has a few tricks left. "You realize that the Iron Guard still wants him? Once we find him, we'll watch him until they come to him. This could be our first break."

"But why should Forrest hold still for us?" Farrier asked.

"As you said, Lou, he's weighed down."

I hope Grant's neighbors are straighter than he is, Hutchins thought, as his car rolled into the Pasadena suburb. Both the driver and the guard had a sharp look in their eyes. If anything untoward happened while Hutchins visited the astronomer's home, they were liable to come up shooting.

Hutchins had risked eyestrain by reading during the trip. It was worth it; the report on the IG painted a cheery picture. Savoy had a permanent tail of journalists and camera crews now. All of his moves—including his attempts to slip away from the journalists—were reported instantly, which allowed the CTO to track him around the clock. His lieutenants leaked things to the press, hinting at the IG's plans and actions. Savoy had surrounded himself with weak, vain men, Hutchins noted; they couldn't resist the chance to brag.

Grant's suburban neighborhood looked empty. It was Saturday morning, but no one was mowing lawns or washing cars; no children played on the sidewalks. The fear generated by the Monday Night Massacre had not lessened as the days passed. By Hutchins' estimate, about one house in ten had a hex sign hung on a wall or door. The sight unsettled him for reasons he could not name.

"Hang loose," Hutchins told his guard and driver as he got out of the car. With his back turned to them, he switched on the recorder in his watch band. The ace up my sleeve, he thought; if Farrier tried to make trouble over this meeting, Hutchins would have proof of what actually happened.

Grant lived in a small frame house, and he'd left the front door open, almost in defiance of the tension around him. "Come in, Hutchins," Grant called.

Hutchins followed the voice to the den. Grant was there, and as Hutchins had half-expected, he had a telepath with him, a skinny black woman wearing an MHB bracelet. "I want to talk about our mutual problems," Hutchins said, ignoring her.

"Talk away," Grant said expansively.

"It's safe," the witch said, looking at Hutchins. "Your people aren't eavesdropping."

So now they know I'm having trouble with office politics, he thought. Hell. "There's the Iron Guard. It has to be stopped."

"Agreed," Grant said. "What have you got in mind?"

"A bad idea," the witch said. She looked at Grant. "He wants to use Julian Forrest as bait in a trap."

Grant looked pained. "Hutchins, I swear to God, you've got Forrest on the brain."

"I think you'd better hear me out," Hutchins said. "And I mean you, Grant, not your witch. Delanty wants to break up this organization you and your witches have. That includes busting Forrest and anyone else involved. If you cooperate with me, I think I can get Delanty to change his mind."

"And if we don't cooperate?" Grant asked. "You've already set the damned MHB on to our telepathics—"

"He didn't," the witch said in surprise. "Go on, please."

Hutchins paused to show his annoyance. "Delanty expects me to destroy the conspiracy—I know, there isn't one, but he thinks otherwise. You'll see a witch hunt that makes the present state of affairs look tame."

He poked a finger at Grant. "And you won't get away. Delanty knows normal people are mixed up in this."

" 'Normal people,' " the witch muttered. " 'Renegades.' "

"Delanty isn't kidding," Hutchins told her. "The best way to change his mind is to show him that you people are good citizens, that you'll work with us—"

"No." The telepath shook her head decisively. "You don't believe that. Delanty's too afraid of us to be rational."

"I wouldn't put it that way," Hutchins protested.

"He's afraid of a non-existent conspiracy," Grant said. "Is that rational?"

"From what he knows—"

"Wait a minute," the witch said. "Why argue over this? We all want to see the IG out of action. Let's stick to that issue. Now, the IG is operating on peanuts. Before they can start their campaign, they need the RF's money. Correct?"

Reading my mind! Hutchins thought. "Correct."

"That means Dekalb will have to take over the RF and transfer its holdings." She smiled. "And most of the RF's records are on computers. What happens if they get trashed?"

"There are records on paper," Hutchins said.

"And how long would it take to straighten things out? Weeks?"

"I couldn't say. I'm not an accountant. I do know that all the financial corporations have—"

"—extremely sophisticated, multiple redundancy safeguards. So what happens if they're reprogrammed to say there's no problem?"

Hutchins looked to Grant. "Can that be done?"

"Yes," he said. "The trick is to link into the IRS's system; it has direct access to the bank computers. And I'd imagine that if the IRS doesn't know where Perry Fountain stashed everything, the CTO does."

"We do," Hutchins said. It was tempting, he thought. Even a temporary screw-up in the RF's finances would hurt Savoy and delay his campaign, perhaps fatally. On the other hand—

"You'd have to let us into the Federal computer network," the black witch said. "On the other hand, if you don't act now—"

"How do I know—"

"That I won't trash the MHB's systems?" She shrugged. "You don't. But think. If I did that, everyone would assume that a telepathic did it. That would make things worse for us."

Hutchins thought something that made the young woman frown with distaste. Then she picked up a notepad and jotted down numbers. "Damn right I'll burn this when I'm done," she muttered. She crossed the room and sat down at Grant's computer.

"Let's go into the living room while Miss England works," Grant said, and led Hutchins out of the den. He felt relieved to be out of the witch's presence. Aside from the fact that she could read his mind, he had been overly conscious of her skin color. Hutchins had never thought of himself as racist; his sudden preoccupation with race in a telepath's presence was as embarrassing as passing gas in a crowded elevator.

"We have a lot to talk about," Grant said, as they entered the living room. "I want to convince you to leave Mr. Forrest alone. I imagine you want something else from me."

Hutchins slipped into a chair. " 'Mr. Forrest.' Are you always so formal with them?"

"It's a matter of respect. God knows they get little enough. Do you drink on duty?"

"When I can get away with it." Hutchins looked at him while Grant poured drinks. I've got you where I want you, he thought. Without his psychic watchdog to warn him, the astronomer might give away some useful information on Forrest. "Would you mind telling me something about Forrest?"

"Shoot," he said.

The phrase made Hutchins' arm throb. "I've done

some checking. You had nineteen witches at Berkeley. Why did the Redeemers pick on Forrest in particular?"

"It's simple," Grant said, handing him a drink. "You know what 'creation science' is, don't you?"

"Vaguely. Genesis was right and Darwin was wrong."

"Maybe it's not so simple," Grant reflected. "Okay, a little background. At first, the 'creationists' tried to discredit the theory of evolution and ban its teaching. Later, they tried to force the school systems to teach creationism along with human evolution. They made considerable headway, too."

"That was all in the high schools, I think." Patience, Hutchins counseled himself. He couldn't rush Grant without making him suspicious.

"It was, until the mid-nineties. Then—you remember the AIDS epidemic? How the fundamentalists said it was God's punishment for America's immorality, and so on and so forth?"

"Of course," Hutchins said. Fountain had ridden the issue to prominence.

"The whole scare collapsed in '96, when they came up with an immunization against AIDS. Suddenly, men like Fountain needed a new issue to stay in business. One thing they tried, before they settled on psi, was to revive creationism. They wanted teaching of *all* the sciences to include their beliefs. Geology teachers had to tell their students that mountains and valleys formed in Noah's Flood. Anthropologists were supposed to teach that all human customs traced their roots back to the Garden of Eden." He grimaced. "And they wanted astronomers to teach that the universe had been created, complete, overnight."

Hutchins recalled a fact from Forrest's dossier. "Didn't Forrest specialize in stellar evolution? That must have pissed him off."

Grant nodded. "It did. The whole thing burned everyone. At UC Berkeley, alleged adults showed up at faculty meetings and demanded 'equal time for God.' Campus ministries arranged rallies and demonstrations. Devout students disrupted science classes.

"Mr. Forrest didn't do anything about it until after he tried to kill himself—you know about that? Okay. It changed him." Grant took a swallow of his drink. "It . . . turned the key that made him into a fighter."

"A fighter against what?" Hutchins paused and tasted his brandy. Not bad, but he couldn't risk drinking too much here. "Most suicides have stopped fighting against life."

"Julian Forrest started fighting *for* it," Grant said. "He started fighting against stupidity and ignorance— the willful, arrogant kind that lets people ignore any fact that displeases them. That mental blindness pushed him into trying suicide once. He fights it now to keep from sliding into despair again."

Grant finished his drink. "You should have seen him at Berkeley. He was magnificent. Every time some bible-thumper got up on his hind legs, in a classroom or at a rally, he was there to argue them down. More than that, he'd try to persuade everyone in earshot to use their brains and think things through."

"I'll be damned," Hutchins said. "That must make him the first Berkeley radical to come out in favor of rationality."

Grant laughed richly. "By God, I never thought of that, but it's true."

"And he was effective, wasn't he? That's why the Redeemers targeted him, isn't it?"

"Yes, in part," Grant said. He got up and poured himself another drink. "I watched him debate once. A Redeemer came to my introductory astronomy class and tried to shout me down, saying that God had created the universe to *appear* billions of years old. We didn't really understand what we saw in our telescopes. All we had were theories, not divinely revealed facts—things like that.

"That was when Julian Forrest came in. He started tearing apart everything the man said, giving facts and showing the flaws in the fellow's arguments. He was brilliant, and he was right, and pretty soon he had the Redeemer contradicting himself, with everyone in the class laughing at the poor dumb schmuck."

"That sounds like a victory," Hutchins said. For the first time he felt admiration for his quarry. That was dangerous, he knew. His job was to catch Forrest, not sympathize with him. And yet . . . "I doubt any of those students became Redeemers after that."

"More than that, Hutchins, some of them got interested in rationalism." Hutchins thought he heard enthusiasm creeping into Grant's voice. "It's a very subtle thing, rationalism, and a very demanding thing. You have to learn to think all the time, to face facts you don't like, to accept conclusions you hate."

"It doesn't sound like the sort of thing that'd be too popular," Hutchins said.

"We're *Homo sapiens,*" Grant said. " 'Thinking man.' Rationality is our birthright. Why shouldn't it be popular?"

Hutchins was caught short. "What has this got to do with Forrest?" he asked in annoyance.

"Everything. Think about this: the U.S. of A. is the most anti-intellectual country in history. Do you realize that today one third of our adults are illiterate or semilliterate—and hardly anyone cares? We're willing to treat nonsense like creation science and astrology seriously. And—tell me, does the President have a college education?"

Hutchins hesitated; he didn't know. "Well . . . "

"He does. So why doesn't this savvy man ever mention it? Hell, why do so many politicians try to come across like good ol' boys instead of responsible adults? No, I know the answer—the voters want it. In this country, we make ignorance a virtue."

Hutchins remained silent. Grant was obviously stalling, but the CTO chief couldn't complain. The man was making some mildly seditious statements; link them to his association with the witches, and Hutchins would have a solid hold on Grant—with his watchband recording as evidence.

"So imagine how certain people feel about this—the eggheads. Cybernerds, pointy-headed bookworms, ivory-tower intellectuals. Neurowimps and poindexters. Those are the slang terms, right? Society depends on them for new ideas and inventions, but it despises them for using their brains. It's demoralizing.

"Then along comes someone like Julian Forrest. He sets an example for other people by standing up to the forces of unreason. You can't imagine the effect that has on people—no, you can, but it's been a long time since this country has had a leader who can inspire people that much."

"That has a nice, grandiose sound," Hutchins said scornfully. He put his glass aside. "I can finish the picture. Forrest tells people how to think—his way, naturally. Some people like his style, so they agree with him. He doesn't have anything new, or important—just a bunch of rationalizations that some people find comfortable."

" 'The greatest menace to rationalism is rationalization.' That's what Lyn Clancy said in *Sense and Nonsense*. Did you ever read her book?"

"No, of course not."

"You should. She discussed the dangers of accepting only ideas you find comfortable, and ways to avoid that trap." Grant put his glass down and crossed the room. He took a computer memory cartridge from a bookshelf and tossed it to Hutchins. "You'd have to read it anyway, Hutchins. Just between you and me and your Dick Tracy wristwatch, that's the only way you'll catch Mr. Forrest."

Hutchins stiffened. "You—that witch told you. How could I be so stupid? What sort of a game are you playing?"

"This game," Grant said. "Julian Forrest is one of that book's greatest adherents. The best way to understand him, which you have to do to catch him, is to understand that book. We're gambling that once you do that, you'll give up this hunt." Grant smiled thinly. "I'm trying to subvert you, Mr. CTO Director."

Hutchins gave the cartridge a distasteful look. "You think you can do that?"

"*Sense and Non-sense* is a very powerful book—that's

why so many people want to burn it. Religious cranks, fascists, Marxists, bigots, ideologues of any stripe—if there's one thing they can't tolerate, it's having people think for themselves."

"Are you claiming that people hunt witches because . . . because—"

"People are scared for lots of reasons," Grant said, pouring himself another glass of brandy. "Some of them believe psi is black magic. Some of them imagine that telepathics aren't trustworthy, because they wouldn't trust themselves with psi. Maybe some of them think that telepathics make the rest of us as obsolete as dinosaurs. But men like Fountain, or Savoy, or those fellows who ran Sere—"

"They're just exploiting the fear," Hutchins said.

"Imagine where they'd be if they didn't have any fear to exploit," Grant said. "I'm sure *they've* imagined it. Imagine where they'd be if people started questioning everything they said. That's the sort of thing Lyn Clancy taught in her book, and they can't risk having anyone learn *that*. So they call it evil and urge people to burn it . . . and they persecute telepathics because they know Miss Clancy was *typical* of them."

"I'm flattered." The witch came out of the den, carrying a roll of stat sheets. She gave the printouts to Hutchins. "Mission accomplished. Dekalb is as poor as a churchmouse. Here's where I moved everything." She turned to Grant. "Do you have the bolt cutters in here, Doctor?"

"Uh-huh." He went to a teak cabinet and took a tool from a drawer. Hutchins watched as he cut the bracelet from the witch's wrist. "That's a felony," Hutchins said.

"I know," Grant said, putting the tool aside, "and the bracelet is a death warrant now. Can I give you a ride to the Amrail station, Miss England?"

She looked embarrassed. "You've been drinking, Doctor. I can take the bus—no, it's safe." The witch laughed nervously. "Everyone knows only white folks have telepathy."

"So I've heard." Grant hugged her, then watched her

leave. He sat down heavily in his chair, and finished his brandy at a gulp. "She was the last of them."

"Meaning what?" Hutchins put the papers and cartridge on the end table by his chair.

"Thanks to the Iron Guard, the Redeemers, and the viggies, all of our telepathics are playing freaks 'n' sneaks now, to stay alive. Things are too hot here. It's such a damned waste, all of it. And that kid just turned eighteen last month." Grant fixed his eyes on Hutchins. "Oliver Seligman wasn't much older."

"Who?"

"He saved your life, remember? When those assassins tried to kill you on campus." Grant poured himself more brandy. "I'm only cooperating because *they* asked me to. Personally, I'd rather deal with the Devil." Grant eyed the CTO director. "Tell you what, Hutchins. Answer my questions and I'll answer yours."

"Ask," Hutchins said curtly, "but no double-talk."

Grant shrugged. "People have been terrorizing psis for years. Where has your CTO been? What good is it?"

"We preserve the stability of the nation," Hutchins answered. "We keep the system running, we defend the Constitution, so people can use it to handle their problems. That may not sound adequate to you, but it's important. If the government breaks down, no one will be safe. Things will never get better for your witches."

"I agree. Your question."

"Would you say that Forrest is fond of his family?" Hutchins held up a hand. "I'm not planning on using them. I don't work that way. I just need to know about the man."

"He always sounded fond of them when he talked about them." After a moment he added, "I met his family once. They're obviously close."

"I thought so." Would he see a substitute for them in Holstein and the boy? That could be a decisive factor, as Hartnell and Farrier had suggested. "Your turn, Doctor."

"How would you convince Julian Forrest that you're any better than Savoy? Bear in mind you can't fool

him." Grant waved a hand negligently. "The answer
you give yourself is more important than the one you'd
give me. Your turn again."

"Does ESP have a range limit?"

"It's around one thousand feet, although there are
exceptions. It's a lot like having a walkie-talkie built
into your head. Or so I'm told. Miss Clancy wrote an
entire chapter on the workings and limitations of psi."
Grant poured the last of the brandy into his glass. "That
was a freebie. I'll let you ask another."

"If you'll stay sober long enough to answer it," Hutchins said. Grant held his liquor well, but the effects were
beginning to show. "Do witches think they're superior
to normal people?"

Grant almost choked on a mouthful of brandy. "Please!
They think they *are* normal people."

"They're obviously not."

"They're obviously different. That's a point they understand; they can't help but know that *everyone* is
different." Grant hiccupped. "I could argue that they're
superior, though."

"Because they have above-normal intelligence?"

"Exactly." Grant finished his drink and set the glass
down with an overly precise movement. "That isn't a
result of the neural mutation, though. Y'see, they're
continually exposed to thought. They tap all kinds of
patterns of thought, brilliant and stupid alike. That
gives 'em an enormous opportunity to learn *how* to
think—and how *not* to think. We're lucky they want to
share that expertise. My turn again. Know how Perti
England learned about Dekalb and the RF money?"

The turn didn't surprise Hutchins, who was growing
used to Grant's twists. "Grant, I'd have to say it was
through ESP. She must've read my mind."

"No, she read the papers. She an' a lot of other
people—not all of them psychic—noticed Dekalb is
acting funny, and that no one is castin' aspersions on his
slimy character. Also noticed that column, 'Pork-barrel
People,' that linked the RF and Savoy. Realized that
anyone who wants to be president needs big bucks.

Logic, Hutchins. That's the only mental power anyone used. Impressive, isn't it?"

He's telling the truth, Hutchins thought, and that shocked him. Even if the witch had read his mind, she couldn't possibly have told Grant about Hutchins' analysis of the situation.

"Think about that," Grant said idly. "The news has everyone else jumping at shadows. But here are people who hear it, keep their heads, and figure out what's going on. Just by looking at the facts 'nd *thinking*, they see that Dekalb is a pious fraud and Savoy is a cold-blooded killer. More'n that, Perti England volunteered to stick around because everyone knew we'd need a top computer hacker—and she's the best."

"I hope that's true." Hutchins picked up the papers and the cartridge. He turned the thick plastic card over in his hand, as if looking for a trick. "You sound like you have a lot of confidence in this book."

"Not as much as the telepathics. I guess they have a higher opinion of people than I do." Grant sighed, then hiccupped. "The book doesn't do diddly-squat for a closed mind. Fountain used to misquote it left and right. I know those idiots at Berkeley read it and didn't understand it."

"Are these the people who had you tossed out?" Hutchins asked, standing. He felt he'd gotten all he could from Grant, but he was curious about that point.

"They kept me from getting tenure, which is the same thing. The idea that T-P is genetic was too much for them. They thought it meant some folks are inherently superior to others, 'ncluding them. They couldn't kick out the psis, so they got their faculty advisor 'nstead. You can get too extreme about anything, even egalitarianism." Grant stopped and cursed without imagination. "If I can say that, I'm too sober."

Well, Hutchins conceded, he has good reason to get stewed. "It's time for me to leave."

"One last question," Grant said, standing up.

"I don't know where you keep the rest of your liquor."

"Not that. I can still find it on my own. Hutchins, Savoy is now dirt-scrabble poor. No way can he run for President now." Grant blinked owlishly. "What's he going to do when he finds out?"

CHAPTER 24

MONDAY, 26 JUNE 2000

Telepathy has its price. There is no 'off' switch; the thoughts of others are always there, even in your dreams—and nightmares. You discover new kinds of pain every day. Other people can push you into despair and insanity. Forget about privacy; even if you want to avoid other telepathics, you can't feel alone with all those thoughts intruding into your skull.

Sometimes the price is subtle. I'm from Arizona, and I've always loved the deserts—the sunsets, the weird lunar landscapes, the unique lifeforms, everything. Appreciating the deserts is an art.

It's one I had to give up. I can't endure the solitude anymore. It isn't just that I'm used to tapping thoughts all the time. Doing without any contact is a form of sensory deprivation, far worse than spending time in complete darkness or total silence. It should be noted that sensory deprivation has been judged an exquisite form of torture in some circles. I've always thought of it as the telepathic equivalent of celibacy. It is not for me.

I've never had any trouble explaining this point to non-telepathics. Loneliness is a hurt everyone understands.

—from Sense and Non-sense, *by Lyn Amanda Clancy*

Birche watched the bright orange helicopter flutter

into the camp. Director Hutchins dropped out of it,
looked around, and walked over to her and Julian. "Mr.
Forrest, we need your help."

"Sure," Julian said. "What's the problem?"

"The damned Saucer People are acting up," Hutchins
said. "They plan to invade tomorrow morning, right
after breakfast. We can't stop them; they're immune to
normal weapons."

"So what can we do?" Birche asked.

"We've found a way to use telepathy as a weapon.
They can't resist it. We need you people to save Earth."
Hutchins' voice turned pleading. "Help us! We'll dis-
band the MHB and outlaw the Redeemers. We'll make
you Emperor and Empress of the world. You can have
Witchita for your capital city. Greenwitch Village for a
playground. Witch hazel will become the national flower.
Just stop the Saucer People!"

Birche felt peeved. "As nightmares go, this one is
infantile. And those puns are too obvious."

"No, I kind of like them," Julian said, smiling easily.
"They have *panache*. Well, it's an interesting offer,
Hutchins, and we'll get back to you. Right now we have
guests."

The sky peeled back and a XXor stepped into the
scene. *"I bear greetings from the Galactic League,"* she
thought. *"Now that Earth has evolved telepathy, you
are advanced enough to join our wise and benevolent
civilization. Welcome, welcome, welcome!"*

"Fuck off," Birche snarled. She woke up and looked
at Giles, who sat in his corner of the tent. *"Not bad,"*
he said. *"That was funny."*

*"A real barrel of laughs. Where are my nightmares
when I need them?"* It had seemed like such a good
idea yesterday, Birche thought. Before meeting Julian,
she had always had a bad time with her night terrors;
last night she had used autohypnosis to induce them.
She had reasoned that Julian might pull out of his
fantasy world if she became upset enough.

The effort had failed. She'd had a night of pleasant
dreams, something she would have welcomed once—

but not now. Her subconscious and its fears had failed her, and there had been nothing to stir Julian into action. *"Where is he now?"* Birche asked Giles.

"Taking a walk, downstream." He reached under his sleeping bag and got out one of the cookies he'd hidden there. Giles had a habit of squirreling away food; after starving for as long as he could remember, he was insecure about his meals, and much else as well.

"Okay." Birche dressed and pulled on her boots. They were heavy things, more suitable for wear in the mountains than her old sneakers, and they came from a military surplus store. Face it, kid, Birche thought, your mother wears Army shoes.

Giles turned angry. *"You're not my goddamned mother!"*

Birche felt a moment of anger herself, followed by shame. Giles knew that his mother had abandoned him years ago, and he had struck out in pain. She hadn't meant any harm, but her joke had hurt.

"It's all right," the boy said. *"I'm sorry I got mad."*

"And I'm sorry I said something stupid, Giles." She stood up. *"I'm going to look for Julian. I want to try something."*

Birche stepped out of the tent, idly aware of a discussion going on among the camp's inhabitants. They were playing with the idea that Shakespeare's Hamlet had not been an indecisive milquetoast, but a civilized man more concerned with justice than petty revenge. She'd studied Hamlet in an English lit class, and she could contribute some ideas to the frolic—no. She wasn't ready to plunge into that sort of thing.

Birche became aware of the odd, itchy stiffness of her flannel shirt. Dried sweat and dirt, she thought. The time is ripe to do the laundry. Birche took the path downhill to the water and followed the shore to the dam. She undressed there and washed her clothes, kneading them under the water and then wringing them out. She lay the garments to dry on the dam's flat concrete surface.

The thea was right, she reflected. I'm scared to get

close to Julian. She couldn't talk to him about how much she needed him, or even make a halfway decent effort to help him. The absurd dreams she'd had last night made her wonder if, deep down, she really wanted to help Julian.

Birche felt a sudden, bitter resentment of Giles. Battered as he was, the boy was doing a better job of helping Julian than she had done. He was the one who'd seen how to help him, and who hadn't hesitated to act. He even enjoyed the continual presence of other telepaths. Damn him, what *right* did he have to be so—so *normal?*

No, that wasn't fair, resenting Giles because she couldn't handle her own problems. She was the one keeping Julian in his fugue, endangering him. Some day soon people would come here, from the MHB or from the Iron Guard, and he would die. It would be her fault.

Driven by a sense of isolation, Julian had elected to walk into town. The other campers were okay, but his talks with them left him feeling unfulfilled. Things might be different in the town—funny. He'd driven through town on the way to camp, but he didn't recall much about the place . . . or the trip out of—where?

Lately he'd been plagued by confusing snippets of memories, floating out of nowhere. The most glaring of them centered on his scars. The messes on his back and chest might have come from accidents, but the parallel scars on his left wrist must have come from a suicide attempt. He could recall doing that, but the reason for it eluded him.

He was halfway to the mountain road when he realized he hadn't told his plans to his wife. That had been thoughtless; Birche would worry if he vanished. Julian turned around.

Birche sat on the dam, naked, her clothes drying in the sun. The sight of her full, gentle curves and creamy skin should have taken his breath away . . . no, not this time. Even at this distance he could see that she was crying. Something had made her unhappy, and her misery was oddly infectious. The sensation intensified as Julian got closer to her, until he felt as though he was wading into quicksand.

As he got near her she wrapped her arms around her legs and pressed her face against her knees, hiding her tears. "What's wrong?" Julian asked, squatting down next to her. He watched her shake her head, and knew that she wanted to tell him—something. "You can talk to me."

"Can't . . . can't . . ."

The pain in her voice filled him with desperation. "If it's anything I've done, anything I can fix—"

"It's me . . ." Her voice sounded thin and cracked. "I can't handle it. It's too much for me."

"Nothing's too much for you." Julian's voice faltered as a surge of memories dizzied him, flashing through his mind too rapidly for full comprehension. He struggled against his confusion, clinging to the thought that Birche needed him. "I want to help."

Birche looked at him, her face puffy and wet with tears. "*I know.*" She reached out and touched his face. "*I need you.*"

Julian felt weak. Suddenly there was so much to grasp, as memories and pains presented themselves in concise, logical order. The one certain factor was Birche's presence in his mind, steadying him in spite of her own anguish. For a long while he drank in the sensations of tapping her thoughts, seeing how she had thrown herself into a black depression to draw him out of his own private hell. "*You brought me back.*"

"*I had to,*" she said. "*Julian, I try to get along but I can't. I don't know what to do.*"

"*You knew what to do to help me.*"

"*Giles thought of it. He tried it first.*"

"*That attack he had—*"

"*He brought it on deliberately.*" Birche looked Julian in the eyes. "*Everything I tried was useless. I—*"

He put a finger over her lips, a gesture that made her

laugh suddenly. *"You try and you learn. That's enough. Why are you so hard on yourself, beautiful?"*

"I don't know . . . but it worked. I knew it would." Birche put her arms around him and pulled him close to her. *"God, I missed you! You've been like someone else."*

"I know. I'm all right now." Even as he thought that, he wondered how true it was. His swing through madness might have changed him, but how could he know?

"Now that's the old Julian, thought for thought." Birche slipped into the water and smiled up at him. Julian looked down at the unclothed figure in the clear, still lake, and watched Birche take a few agile strokes away from the dam. *"Race you across the lake,"* she said.

"What, me race an Olympic contender?"

"This is one race we'll both win," she promised, slowly paddling away on her back. She laughed as he fumbled to get undressed. That was the old Julian, too.

"This isn't going to last forever," Birche said, as they walked uphill to the camp. *"The MHB had some people up here Saturday, and the CTO put both of us on their 'wanted' list. We have to make plans."*

"I know, Birche-beautiful." He bumped against her playfully. *"But I want to get my bearings first. I remember most of the last week, but it's all hazy, like a dream. What's been happening?"*

"Plenty. The Iron Guard has been raising a storm, especially over telepaths. The MHB has started cracking down on us—strictly for our own good, they say. The Monday Night Massacre—"

"The what?" He looked blank.

"You haven't let yourself hear any bad news," she said. *"An hour or so after you broke down, the IG orchestrated a wave of assassinations—although the papers that sympathize with the Guard say the killings were the work of some nebulous 'conspiracy.' Either way, everyone's scared and no one knows what to expect. You could ask Giles for details. He's read every-*

thing he can get his hands on, and he remembers—and understands—all of it."

"Giles. Is he really doing as well as he seems?"

"For a six-year-old telepath who's been raised like an animal, yes, I think so. He's something else we have to plan for."

"Nag, nag, nag. We may as well be married." He stopped walking and put his hands on her shoulders. He looked into her wide brown eyes. "That's something to plan for, too."

"Yes!" She kissed him. Then her quick excitement chopped off suddenly. "But—"

"I know, I know. Even if we could stop playing freaks 'n' sneaks, the Compton Act won't let us sign a marriage contract. But the minute this is over, I'm dragging you to the altar." Julian hesitated, recalling something from his delusions. Yes, he had fantasized that this woman was his wife. Was this proposal an echo of that?

"You're not getting off the hook, mister," Birche said. "I've waited for years for the chance to get rid of my maiden name."

"What's wrong with your name?" he asked.

"A Holstein is a breed of cow," she explained, "and a woman who weighs as much as I do—"

"Oh. Well, people tell me I'm full of bull, so we're a matched set." Julian looked around as they came into the camp. He remembered all the details, yet it was as if he was seeing it for the first time. A number of improvements suggested themselves, all simple things he'd learned in high school science classes. A water pump, to replace the buckets that carried water from the lake to the camp. Something to purify the water. More efficient fireplaces. And, yes, better huts for the next winter.

"If we stay here that long," Birche said.

"We just might. Running around is no sort of life for anyone. Hello . . ."

The people in camp began to greet Julian, properly this time, identifying themselves as they tapped his mind. He exchanged greetings with them eagerly, exulting in the experience. He felt whole again, surrounded by friends. For her part, Birche sensed how the others admired her for helping Julian. While gratifying, she found it somewhat embarrassing. After all, it was what she was supposed to have done.

"That's something to admire," Julian told her as they entered their tent. *"Your attitude. You never settle for less than the best in yourself. Hello, Giles."*

"Hello." The boy looked up from his newspaper and nodded. The paper was too large for him to hold; he had laid it flat on the tent's canvas floor. *"You all right now?"*

"I think so."

"Good. Will you stop calling me Gil now?"

"Of course, Giles." Julian and Birche sat down on a foam pad, arms around one another. Giles's mind had a unique harshness, Julian noted; not caustic or surly, but rigorous, austere. Julian's recovery left him more satisfied than pleased.

The boy shrugged. *"I knew you'd come out of it sometime. You serious about marrying her?"*

"Yes, very serious."

"What for?"

"I love her, I need her. I want to be with her forever."

"Going to do that anyway, aren't you?" he asked. *"So why d'you think it's so important?"*

Julian felt Birche nestle against him. *"For a lot of reasons,"* she said. *"It tells the world we're making it permanent. It makes it* feel *more permanent to us, too. But the important thing is that it adds something to what we have."*

"It does," Julian said. *"Marriage is to a man and woman what a thea is to a group of telepathics. It makes us more than we are alone."* Julian paused. Something more than ignorance was troubling Giles. Resentment, that was it. After a week without it, Julian found his psi sense almost painfully acute. Giles resented Birche.

"I don't!" he said. His mind became wary with fear. Without moving he seemed to back away from them.

"*It's all right,*" Birche said soothingly. "*I'm not going to come between you and Julian.*"

"*I know.*"

"*That isn't what's wrong,*" Julian said, studying the boy's anxiety. Giles was afraid of being abandoned, of losing Julian again. "*Again?*" Julian wondered.

"*Again,*" Birche said. Giles himself didn't understand what troubled him, but she could put together the pieces she tapped in his thoughts. "*In a way, he lost you when you broke down. If I hadn't turned my back on you then, you might have been all right.*"

"*He would have, but you helped the fucker that killed Cliff instead,*" Giles said accusingly. He trembled, afraid of her anger.

"*Say whatever you have to say,*" Birche said. "*I promise I won't ever do anything to hurt you.*"

"*You helped that guy. Julian would have been all right if you hadn't.*"

"*Maybe not,*" Julian said. Struggling with his memory, he vaguely recalled Birche dragging the injured vigilante out of an alley. "*I think I would have cracked up sooner or later no matter what, but he might have died there if Birche hadn't moved him. Now come here, son. Come on, it's all right.*"

Giles crawled onto Julian's lap. "*I don't understand. That guy was worthless. Maybe he would've killed you.*"

"*Cliff was like that once,*" Julian said, "*but he changed. Maybe that vigilante could change, too.*"

"*What's so important about that?*" Giles asked. "*A guy like him would kill again.*"

"*But he'd never have a chance to change if he died,*" Julian said. Even as he spoke he felt dissatisfied with what he told the boy. Cliff was dead, and his killer would go unpunished, possibly would never even regret his crime. And yet—and yet—"*I can't even explain it to myself, Giles,*" Julian confessed, "*but I'm glad she did what she did. You would have done the same thing.*"

"*No. Not me. Not for him.*" The boy was sullenly defiant, but also, Birche thought, afraid that he was disappointing Julian with his attitude. "*You're trying to* grow up too fast," she said. *"Don't worry, Giles. You'll understand when you're older."*

He answered with a smoldering look. *"Don't tell me that! I seen peoples who were seventy, eighty years old. They didn't know nothing! They came to ask me for answers."*

"You're right," Birche said, sighing. She'd forgotten what Giles could not: that he was not a normal, or at least average, child, and could never be one. Raising him was an ongoing experiment, with few guidelines and no certainty as to the results.

"It's that way for everyone," Julian said. There was small comfort in that, though. In rescuing Giles he had assumed responsibility for raising him, a task more difficult than mere survival. The hazards were appalling; the wrong decision could destroy his life. It hardly seemed fair to the boy, putting his future in the hands of two people with no real qualifications—

—and Giles was tapping both of them with an intensity that bordered on mania, in an effort to learn why they were so concerned with his well-being. He approved of it, but it was an enigma. What was in it for them?

"I don't know how to answer that yet," Julian said. He knew that his parents would have answered with a bit of philosophy—something Buddhist or Biblical, perhaps, or a few of Lennon's lyrics about love—but that wouldn't do for Giles. His needs differed—

Julian heard the distant popping of gunfire, and the sound of bullets striking in the campground. *"Quick, get down,"* he said. He and Birche lay on the canvas floor, putting Giles between them, while he searched for the minds of the gunners. He found nothing.

"They're on the west slope," Ruth said, *"across the stream."*

"Can anyone tap them?" Birche asked.

The thea appeared in the tent. *"They're too far away for me to get much . . . but there are two of them, on the Plate Rock."*

"Almost a mile away," Ruth said. Then: *"Hurry up, everyone into the huts."*

"Including us," Julian said. The gunfire sounded like .22 caliber shots, so at a range of one mile, the fire wouldn't be too accurate. Even so . . . *"Move fast and dodge,"* he told Birche. *"Where's the nearest hut?"*

"Skip and Maribeth's place is thataway." Birche gestured. *"Logs and dirt—it should be bulletproof."*

"That's plenty against .22s." Birche picked up Giles and crawled out of the tent. Julian tried to place himself between them and the Plate Rock area—a shelf of stone on the west slope, easily visible in the late morning light. He saw two figures there, plinking away at the camp with their rifles. Bullets raised splatters of dust as they ran to the hut. The door popped open and Birche and Giles tumbled inside. Julian slammed the door shut on them and bolted away from the hut.

"Julian, get in here!" Birche demanded. *"You can't do anything!"*

"I can. I know what to do." He hurried downhill, to a point where the stream was broad and shallow. The firing continued, although none of the bullets fell near him. They're not trying to hit anyone, Julian realized. The snipers were simply pumping rounds into the camp. Terrorism, he thought, pure and simple, for whatever motive they had.

The woods on the west slope were not thick, and Julian could see the gunmen as he climbed the mountainside. Now he was close enough to tap their thoughts and see that they were teenagers, probably still in high school. They wore button earphones that pumped shock-rock music into their heads—*Nuke him 'til he glows, then shoot him in the dark, as you watch his death throes, it seems like such a lark!*—and they laughed as they loaded and fired. Yeah, *this* would teach the freaks to cheat them out of their reward money.

Reward money? Julian had a vague recollection of something Birche had thought, something about townies trying to report the camp to the MHB. Yes, that was right, that deputy had intervened and protected the camp. The MHB had kept its money, and for no logical reason, the youths blamed events on the refugees. The attack was a temper tantrum.

"Hey, look!" They spotted Julian and shifted their fire. He heard bullets crack into the trees around him, and watched bark chips go flying as he ran for cover.

I could die here, he thought, pressing his back against an inadequate trunk. I could die and lose Birche and Giles.

They had recognized Julian; at least, one was positive that he'd seen his picture on the tube. They got up from their beer and pretzel picnic on the rock shelf and came after him, the camp instantly forgotten. They had a mission. Now they were the lone-wolf heroes of their favorite movies, stalking the bad guy who would soon die, messily and comically.

Julian started running down the valley, toward the road. He couldn't afford to get too far ahead of the snipers, he realized. They might lose interest in him and go back to shooting up the camp—or worse. The goal was draw them away from the camp, any hope that something happened to quench their blood-lust. Julian knew there was no hope of reasoning with them, or of finding words that would shame them into submission—not when they'd grown up to see murder as an artistic expression.

He ran as fast as he could on the soft mountain dirt. The footing was bad, and several times he stumbled, half-sliding downslope until he regained his balance. Twice he dropped and let himself roll as they shot at him. Their rifles were semi-automatic weapons, capable of firing away a dozen rounds in a few seconds, and they made use of that, reloading while they sprinted after Julian, spraying bullets in his direction.

They were bad shots, a factor that did little to help him. Julian could tell where they were about to fire, and when they thought they had him pinned in their sights, but that was scant help. He had no idea of when a rifle was actually aimed at him. Death was likely to come at random, unannounced.

Julian tripped over a root and turned his ankle as he went sprawling in the dirt. He got up, took a step, and fell painfully as his ankle gave out. He started pulling himself along the ground, knowing that he had no hope of outdistancing them. Have to think of something else, he thought.

"Let's get outta here!" one of them shouted. The other stopped, turned, and fired shots toward the lake. Then he broke and ran after his friend, going uphill as quickly as he could.

Julian rolled over and looked. He could see the people in the camp coming toward him. What was going on? he wondered. At this distance he couldn't tap their thoughts. The other telepaths were barely discernible as people, wading across the shallow stretch of the stream.

The two snipers had vanished in the woods. With a shock Julian realized that there were no minds nearby for him to tap. The eerie mental silence turned the forest into a place of desolate shadows. Am I still alive? Julian wondered. A ghost might feel this way—no. If he'd been shot, it would hurt as much as his ankle. He lived, although the forest was as lonely as a grave.

Driven by the loneliness, he tried to stand and walk. He took a few faltering steps toward the camp, then toppled over again. He would have to wait for someone to find him. Until then, he had much to think about.

"He's over here," Giles said, homing in on Julian. He could sense his location readily enough, which was a great help. All the trees looked alike to him, and he couldn't tell one corner of the woods from another. He did notice that Julian had left tracks in the dirt, and he supposed that he could have followed them to Julian if he'd been in the mood to play games.

He found Julian sitting with his back against a tree. *"You okay, Julian?"*

"I did something to my leg," Julian told him. *"Was anyone hurt?"*

"Just scared. Birche thought you were going to do something dumb, like try to argue with those guys."

"No, that wouldn't have worked," Julian said. "They couldn't have understood anything I might have said. They wouldn't want to understand, anyway. They weren't like you."

Giles sighed and sat down next to him. "You got something you want to say."

"I promised I'd explain why Birche and I want to take care of you . . . and a lot of other things. Why I think it was right for Birche to save that vigilante." Julian hesitated. "It's an emotional thing. I . . . want to do the things I feel are right. I want to know what's right and what isn't, so I won't hurt someone by accident."

"Only you can't explain how you got like that." The boy felt disappointed, but not surprised.

"No, I can't," Julian said, "no matter how hard I try. The funny thing is that you can understand it, if you try hard enough. It might take a long time, though. Maybe the rest of your life."

"I've got the time," Giles said. He picked up a pebble, looked it over, and tossed it downhill. "Still wish you could just tell me."

"So do I."

"That's all right." He sent another rock skipping down the mountainside, to bounce off a tree trunk. "I used to tell people things for Fatso. Never could figure out why they needed me to tell them things, when they could make better answers for themselves. So why should I be any different?"

Julian nodded dumbly. Suddenly the idea of him raising Giles struck him as conceited. It should be the other way around.

"There you are," Birche said, as if they were a pair of children, yet she was clearly relieved to see Julian alive and reasonably well.

"What happened?" Julian asked. He watched her as she bent over him, winced as she removed his shoe and examined his ankle.

"*I got fed up with running,*" Birche said, as she decided that his ankle wasn't broken. She helped him to his feet and put his arm around her neck. "*I got tired of being scared of everything. I'm still scared, but I just had enough. I got out of the hut and started walking toward the snipers.*" She laughed a little, an uncertain rumbling. "*Maybe the MHB didn't make a mistake when they certified me.*"

"She wasn't the only one," Giles said. "She got everyone to start walking at them. Toward them? The bastards got scared."

"*You took a hell of a chance,*" Julian said. He held on to her shoulders as they staggered downhill.

"*It saved your pretty ass,*" Birche said, "*and look who's talking about chances. Didn't Granger run when you stood up to him?*"

"*Granger at least had enough sense to be scared of the unknown! But these kids were so damned ignorant—*"

"*Which made them more afraid,*" Birche said. "*It was all a game to them, until we moved out. Then they didn't know what they were facing, and that was too much for them.*" Birche hefted him over a fallen branch. "*Admit it, handsome, you're proud of me.*"

"*Only because I'm a fool for a pretty face.*" Julian chuckled suddenly, and tapped around for the attackers' minds. He found nothing. "*I wonder if they're still running?*"

They were not running. In a while they would return to the town, frightened but still after revenge. Their reprisal would take the form of a second call to the MHB. They made the call anonymously, knowing that no one would believe them a second time. They called from the village's malt shop, and while they knew they'd never get their reward money, the thought of giving the freaks the trouble they deserved cheered their afternoon.

In the Federal Building, an operator wrote down their information and sent it to the MHB offices. There, a clerk came close to tossing it into a wastebasket. The last call from that area had been a hoax . . . but this report had been written on an official form, and copies were already on file. He passed the memo into the Federal Building's paper stream.

One copy made its way to the CTO. Another, while being fed into the computer system, activated a stealthed program that relayed the information out of the Federal Building. The program was activated by the mention of Julian Forrest.

CHAPTER 25

TUESDAY, 27 JUNE 2000

Delanty: Are you making any progress on these freaks?

Hutchins: Yes, sir, I'm learning a lot. I have a definite, uh, handle on the situation.

Delanty: That's good.

Hutchins: In fact, sir, I think I can use them against the Iron Guard. I'm working on a plan—

Delanty: I'm not interested in the (expletive) IG. Stay on the, you know, the witches. That's where the votes are.

Hutchins: Of course, sir, but the IG is also part of my job. Don't be upset if you hear some odd reports concerning them, the CTO and the witches.

Delanty: I don't care about details. Right now, uh, I understand the CTO has some files on a couple of Clark's aides.

Hutchins: I don't know, sir. We have so many files—

Delanty: Well, check. It looks like the other side is going to nominate Clark. I beat him in '96 and I can wax his tail again, but I want a leg up on him. The word is that a couple of his staffers were in the Klan. If you've got the ball, toss it to me.

Hutchins: You want me to send these files to you, sir?

Delanty: No, you (expletive). If you have anything damaging, just, you know, leak it to the press, maybe cook it a bit first.

Hutchins: I don't think I follow you, sir.

Delanty: I think you do, Monty. Or will I have to get me a new quarterback?

—transcript, telephone conversation, 27 June 2000, 0912 PDT

The message from Blaine proved that the witch had been true to her word. The Mental Health Bureau's computers and databases had gone unmolested, and when Blaine sent his note, it was only to inform Hutchins that some teenagers in a mountain village claimed to have seen Forrest. While the MHB coordinator didn't believe the report—there'd already been one false alarm from the same area—it was standard procedure to relay all such reports as requested.

Something about the report rang true, Hutchins thought. That intuition was a slim thing to pin any hopes on, but he saw how the report could prove useful. If it reached Savoy at the proper time, and if events convinced Savoy it was true—yes, it dovetailed nicely with Hutchins' plans.

His other plans were bearing fruit already. News stories reported extreme and inexplicable irregularities in the Redemptive Faith's finances. The confused accounts suggested either massive computer errors or embezzlement. The IRS and several other government agencies had taken an interest, which meant it would take months to straighten out the situation. By then, Savoy's presidential campaign would have died for want of cash, even if nothing else happened to the IG.

Even so, Hutchins took the news with a feeling of ambivalence. Grant had been correct on one point; Savoy was bound to lash out when he found his plans collapsing. Hutchins had spent much of the night trying to guess Savoy's next move.

And then Delanty had called. That call troubled him

as much as anything Grant had said or Clancy had written. It wasn't the first such request Delanty had made—or Clark before him, for that matter—but this was the first time he'd felt any qualms. *Why am I going through this,* he wondered? *Why am I asking my men to risk their lives, if all we're doing is protecting one politician's job?* That was pressing on his mind when Farrier entered his office.

"Springbock and the others have confessed," Farrier told Hutchins. He sat down on the front edge of Hutchins' desk and pushed some of the papers aside. "We've got enough evidence right now to hang Savoy. Literally."

"Good," Hutchins said. "Exactly what did we get?"

"Red Ted Springbock has confessed to killing two FBI men in Eugene, Oregon, as well as to making that attack on the freaks. Kyle, Carmichael, and Wendell have also made full confessions. Best of all, Springbock admits discussing assassinations with Savoy. They've waived immunity and agreed to testify in court—"

Hutchins' eyes bulged. "They *what?* How'd that happen?"

The Bear smiled. "We ran a medical interrogation on Xavier. He didn't know much—he was fairly new to the IG—but there wasn't much left of his mind when we finished. He resisted interrogation and, well . . . " Farrier shrugged indifferently. "But before the MHB took him into custody, we made sure that the others got a good hard look at their pal. Then we asked who wanted to go next."

"And they chose to talk," Hutchins said. It had worked, but it chilled him. The four men had seen something that made trial and the death penalty look acceptable indeed.

"They talked," Farrier agreed. "And they gave us more than we could have extracted with drugs and neurostimulators. The legal staff has checked their statements. Even if the bastards recant, we still have an ironclad case against Savoy."

"Then it's time to shut him down." Hutchins picked up his desk phone. "Hartnell, I want to see you and the tactical staff in fifteen minutes. We're moving against the IG. I'll want as clean a sweep as possible." He hung up.

"You plan to arrest Savoy," Farrier said disapprovingly.

"If possible." Hutchins studied the man. "We've discussed this before, Lou. We're not judge, jury, and executioner."

"I'm not saying we should be," Farrier said, "but look at Savoy's record. Is there any question of his guilt? More than that, do you have any doubt that he's a menace to America?"

"There's no mistaking what he is, Lou, but once he's been put down, he'll stay down."

"Will he? Chief, other revolutionaries have gone to prison—then come out even more dangerous than before. Napoleon. Lenin. Castro. Hell, Hitler wrote *Mein Kampf* in prison!"

Hutchins made an angry slashing gesture with his hand. "No assassinations, Farrier! I want him alive and on trial—"

"—a trial that Savoy will turn into a public forum. What's the point in stopping him now if he becomes President in four or eight years?" Farrier demanded. "If you're scared of making him into a martyr—"

"I'm not."

"Then what are you afraid of?"

Hutchins sighed. He wasn't sure himself, and damn Grant for raising doubts. "I couldn't say, Lou."

"I can. You've been acting strange ever since you saw Grant, and it's because of this." He picked up a memory cartridge and read the label to Hutchins. "*Sense and Non-sense*. It's a damned conceited title—"

"It's a pun. It means the psi sense as well as common sense."

"And it's full of soft-headed mush," the Bear said.

"You've read it?" Hutchins asked.

"Hell, no. *I'm* not the one who's hunting witches. What do I need to know about them—"

The phone rang. "Chief," Hartnell said, his voice tight, "Savoy has given us the slip. About an hour ago he got away from the press."

"I can't claim I'm surprised." So much for making a nice, clean arrest, Hutchins thought. There'd been little enough hope of taking Savoy quietly; he was a man mesmerized by the grand gesture. Perhaps it was better this way, Hutchins decided.

"Did anyone try to follow him?" Farrier said.

"Not with four heavily armed goons blocking the road. Our agents couldn't do anything."

"No, not without starting a slaughter," Hutchins agreed. "Don't worry. I know how to find Savoy. I'll discuss it at the conference."

"Finding Savoy won't be easy," Farrier said, as Hutchins hung up. "He's mobile as hell, and he knows how to lie low. He's also got a lot of people on his side."

"So we're going to make him come to us," Hutchins said. He picked up a slip of paper, handed it to Farrier, and leaned back in his seat. "This came in an hour ago. Interesting, isn't it?"

Farrier put the paper down. "Locating Forrest isn't the same as catching him. And this report was phoned in last night."

"Yes. However—" Hutchins dug out a map and unfolded it on the desk. "According to the MHB's informants, he's *here*, outside Snowbank."

"The ski resort? It's in some damned rugged terrain."

Hutchins nodded. "A while ago I sent men out to establish checkpoints here, here, and here—" he pointed, "—to keep an eye on all traffic. We know exactly who comes out and who goes in."

"I see."

Hutchins nodded at the professional admiration in Farrier's voice. He approves, Hutchins noted, which means what I'm doing fits into his own plans. "That's why we have to catch Forrest, of course. Savoy needs to kill him."

"You're certain?"

"The IG is bankrupt, Lou." He handed Farrier the report on the Redemptive Faith's insolvency. "He can't buy the publicity a Presidential candidate requires, so he'll have to get it through the news media. That means action, and the IG has promised to kill Forrest. We'll dangle the witch in front of him, starting now." Hutchins reached for the phone and used the secure line to call the *Post*. Bureaucratic protocol ate up several minutes as his secretary worked her way through the paper's hierarchy. Telepaths would never have this problem, Hutchins thought suddenly. Communication was an open, direct act for them.

"I'd like to make a deal," Hutchins said, when Mrs. Daniels answered her phone. "If you've got a reporter who can rough it for a day or two, you can get a firsthand account of Savoy's arrest."

"I'm interested," she said, "but there must be more to the deal."

"There is. I need to leak some information, to manipulate the IG—"

"That's out of the question," the editor said. "We're not in the business of spreading disinformation."

Hutchins and Farrier exchanged wry looks. "Oddly enough, I'm leaking the truth. The CTO is cooperating with telepaths to fight the IG. They've helped us to identify several members of the Guard and to uncover their strategy. One of them was killed saving my life at Cal Tech."

A flat hum came through the scrambler: Mrs. Daniels whistling in amazement. "If that's true—"

"It is," Hutchins snapped. "I'll send you a letter with my signature, if you like. Right now I'm only asking two things. Until we nail Savoy, say that the information comes from a highly placed source who wishes to remain anonymous—which I do—and that the CTO has no official comment on the matter—which we don't, for now."

"Is there a point to all this?"

"I need to flush Savoy into the open."

"I see. All right, it's a deal. I'll send someone to you as soon as I have your letter. Good day."

Farrier slid off the edge of the desk and stood. "I can't say I appreciate her attitude. I don't see the point in pandering to her wants, either."

"I see a point," Hutchins said, "and I'll see you in the conference room."

Hutchins closed his eyes as Farrier left. So much depends on publicity, he thought, on impressing the man in the street. Savoy needed to kill Forrest because it would keep him in the public eye. Delanty wanted the freak detained because it would show the voters he was on top of this situation. Hutchins had to capture Forrest because he was a key to defeating the Iron Guard.

So we find Forrest, he told himself, and build a strong defense around him. Then we leak his location, and wait for Savoy to come to him. A lot would depend on the freak's cooperation, but one way or another, he *would* cooperate.

At least I've arranged things to make the witches look like they're helping us, Hutchins thought. That might do something to soften the public's anti-witch sentiments. As a sop to his conscience, he found that far from adequate.

"Word is out now, Chief," Hartnell said, sitting down beside Hutchins in the passenger bay. "Most of the news services are carrying rumors that we're using the witches. Some of them sound wild."

"Good." Hutchins' arm throbbed. The helicopter was two miles up, and the drop in air pressure aggravated the wound. The heavy bullet-proof overalls only added to his discomfort. "Any word on Savoy?"

"No, sir, nothing."

"Blast and damn. He's at his most dangerous when he's lying low. I wonder what he's plotting?"

"If everything's on schedule, Chief, he's licking his wounds. The arrests should have started by now. I'll check on that."

Hutchins watched Hartnell return to the copter's cockpit. For the first time, he noticed that Hartnell was the same shade of chocolate brown as Perti England. So telepathy is an equal opportunity mutation, he thought, and wondered why that was on his mind. He thought he'd exorcised the demons of racism years ago.

"Coming up on Snowbank," the pilot called out. He sounded cheerful, Hutchins thought, no doubt because he was no longer flying target-patrol over the Los Angeles area. The CTO pilots had painted their helmets orange as a sardonic comment on their new duty, but it was an uneasy humor. On the bright side, a half-dozen of the missing rockets had been wasted on them, fortunately to no effect.

Hutchins looked out a porthole. The terrain was rugged down there, and the trees provided natural camouflage. If he had to search for Forrest and his hideaway, he could be here for days or weeks. The best hope was to go into town and find someone who knew where to look. Then, move swiftly, surround the witches before they could scatter, capture a few, and use them as bargaining chips. That would bring Forrest to him.

Without snow, Snowbank looked like an ugly patch on the San Bernardino Mountains. Several mountainsides had been defoliated and developed into ski runs, accompanied by lodges and parking lots that lay dormant in the off season. It looked like a typical resort town to Hutchins. Chic skiers would crowd it during the winter, but when they and their money melted away with the snow, the town became as depressed as the rest of the country.

The CTO helicopters settled onto one of the parking lots and their passengers climbed out. The three dozen men were heavily armed and armored, but Hutchins had qualms about their readiness. He had pulled them out of training a week ahead of schedule, before they could develop any real combat proficiency.

So we go with what we have, he thought, as he watched a man from one of the other aircraft jog over to him. He looked clumsy in his heavy bullet-proof overalls. "Al Moorpark," he said, shaking hands with Hutchins, "*L.A. Post.* Sorry I didn't catch you sooner, Mr. Hutchins. Mind telling me your next move?"

"We have to locate Mr. Forrest now," Hutchins said. "He's in a camp around here, but we don't have its exact location."

"No? I thought you were cooperating with the witches."

"We are, but they're in a difficult situation. Over fifty telepathics have been killed in the past week, you realize." The essence of changing the subject, he thought suddenly, is to bring up something that the other fellow wants to discuss. "I understand you've taken over Steve Magyar's column."

Moorpark nodded. "The 'Pork-barrel People' title and logo have a solid readership identification. Mrs. Daniels wants to terminate the column once all this is over, but if I do a good job, she may let me continue with it."

Hutchins thumped him on the back, the sound muffled by the woven aluminum padding. "Stick with me and you'll get your story."

"Chief?" one of the agents called. Hutchins strode across the lot, to a parked car marked SAN BERNARDINO COUNTY SHERIFF'S DEPARTMENT. A man in a deputy's green uniform stood there, surrounded by CTO troops. "This is Deputy Martinez," Agent O'Grady said. "He's the one who saw the MHB agents Saturday."

"And I'll tell you what I told them," Martinez said. "I don't know where any telepathics are, including this Forrest character. Those reports were hoaxes. Some of the local kids got bored—"

"You're lying," Farrier said, fingering his brainwave sensor. "Martinez, obstructing justice is a felony. You'd better come clean."

"Wait a minute." Telepathics, Hutchins thought. The deputy's use of that word was a giveaway. Hutchins nodded toward the nearest copter. "Martinez, let's talk."

Hutchins waited until the hatch was sealed before speaking. "Martinez, we both know you have a colony of telepathics around here."

"If you know so much, why do you have to ask me about this?"

Hutchins settled down on a bulkhead seat. "Okay, you're protecting them. You know that's a crime, don't you?"

"Is that supposed to matter?" Martinez sighed. "It's the right thing to do. Sometimes that's more important."

Stymied again, Hutchins thought—no, wait. "Why is protecting them so important to you?"

"Protecting people is my job. Justice."

"It's mine, too. The Iron Guard wants to kill a wi— a *telepathic* named Julian Forrest. The word is that he's around here, and as soon as the IG hears that word, they'll show up. Do you think a campful of people can evade a wolf pack from the Guard?"

Martinez shook his head. "I don't imagine you'll protect them, though. I've seen your wanted posters, and the charges are bullshit. Whatever you have planned, I don't think I'd like it."

Hutchins sighed and looked out a bay window. A crowd of villagers was slowly collecting in the parking lot, drawn by the machines and the men in uniform. The CTO director switched on his radio headset for a moment, and heard Farrier asking questions about freaks.

Hutchins craned his head and spotted him, looking more bearlike than ever in his burly overalls. Who knew where the witches were? Where did the freaks have their camp? People were shaking their heads, shrugging, and walking away.

The sight jolted him. He could understand noncooperation in an ivory-tower intellectual like Grant. He could rationalize it in someone like Martinez, who talked as if he'd reached an accommodation with the witches. But *this* went beyond explanation. Those were real, normal people out there.

Hutchins looked to Martinez. "*Why* is it so important to protect them?"

"I'm an alkie," Martinez said casually. "One of them helped me get on the wagon and stay there."

"Not you." Hutchins felt the dryness in his mouth. He motioned for the deputy to look out the window. "All these people here."

Martinez looked, then sat down again. "Well, you don't turn in your friends." His voice was matter-of-fact.

"People do that every day, Martinez." Hutchins reached for his canteen and wetted his mouth. "What's going on here?"

"You know, I'm still not sure," Martinez admitted. "I know that I hardly get any domestic-violence calls anymore. The divorce rate is way down, too, and I know a lot of people are watching less TV than they did. We've got some lemons here, but most folks are living better."

"You think the witches are behind it?"

"The telepathics, yes." The deputy got out a cigarette and lit it. Watching his fingers tremble, Hutchins realized how nervous he was. Martinez expected Hutchins to arrest him. "I saw an old judo expert split a log in half, once." He looked at the grain of the wood, found the weaknesses, and gave it a little chop. "They're like that, only they look for your strengths."

"A whole town?" Hutchins asked.

"Population forty-one hundred," Martinez said. "They started something, but I think we're responsible for most of the changes. The way I figure it, most people want more out of life than fighting and watching remakes of video trash. We want to be—I don't know, civilized maybe, or more human."

Hutchins turned away from the man. I misunderstood Grant, he thought. The astronomer had been talking about something far more than an intellectual's paradise, where everyone was his own philosopher. Far more than that, and more subtle.

There was a rapping on the hatch. Hutchins opened it and looked down at his radio operator. "Sir, I'm having trouble raising checkpoint two."

"The one at Guest Ranch Road?" Hutchins drew a map from his pocket and checked it, sitting on the rim of the hatchway. "You don't get any response?"

"I get a voice that says my transmissions are garbled, but I'm not having that problem with points one and three. It isn't the mountains; we're on satellite relay."

"It could be equipment failure, Long."

The radioman shook his head. "They have back-ups, but they haven't switched them on."

"I see." Hutchins clicked on his transmitter. "Spotter one, this is Custer. Go to checkpoint two and make contact. Investigate their radio problem, stay there until it's fixed. Out." He heard turbines whine as the spotter helicopter took off.

Farrier lumbered over to him, his face a mask of white-hot fury. "This whole town is rotten," he said. "They know where the freaks are. The lice are hiding them."

"I'm aware of that."

"I can't even find the people who informed the MHB." Farrier looked at the people around the lot. "Whoever they were, they're probably too intimidated to help now. You know how these small-town types are."

I'm not sure of that any more, Hutchins thought. "Well, we can't arrest an entire town, Lou, so let's use our brains. If you were going to live in the mountains, how would you go about it?"

The Bear snorted. "First, I'd hire a good contractor. I'm strictly a city boy."

"Same here. But there are basics." He held his map so both he and Farrier could read it. "First, you need water."

"There are streams in most of these valleys."

"But not all of them. We can scratch the dry ones. Next, you need food." Hutchins looked at the landscape. Aside from a little gardening, he knew nothing about agriculture—but the little he knew counted now. "Either they have lots of farmland—"

"In this country?" Farrier scoffed.

"Exactly. The land is too steep and the soil is poor. If they get food anywhere, it's in town, at the stores. And they carry it back home. On foot, unless they live right next to a road and hitch a lot of rides—"

"So we'll find a dirt trail leading out of town."

"Or leading off one of the paved roads. It'll be well-used, too." Hutchins looked at the map, noting likely spots. The search would take hours at most.

Farrier snapped his fingers suddenly. "The Forest Service! Their rangers might know something. They have fire lookouts all over the place."

"Not since the budget cutbacks," Hutchins said. "Now they use Landsat observations to find fires and hotspots.

You're right, though, it's worth a try." He beckoned to
the radio operator.

A taut voice crackled in his earphones: "Spotter one
to all units, we are taking fire, repeat, we are taking
fire."

"Spotter one, report!" Hutchins snapped.

"Hit the backup! Hang on—" Static rustled in his
ear, then cleared. "Spotter one to Custer. Four hostiles
at checkpoint two opened fire with automatic weapons.
We are damaged but still airworthy. My observer saw
two bodies lying in a culvert by the checkpoint."

My men, Hutchins thought, and tried to remember
who he had assigned to that position. "Spotter one,
follow the road back to town. Report any, repeat any,
activity or traffic."

"Copy, Custer."

"Savoy is ahead of us again," Hutchins said. "He
already knows Forrest is around here."

"I heard," Farrier said.

"Custer, this is spotter one," the radio voice said.
"Many vehicles parked at roadside, grid coordinates
BX-12."

"How many?" Hutchins said.

"At least twenty vans and campers—uh, oh. We are
under attack, breaking off—" There was more static.

"Spotter one," Farrier said into his microphone. "Spotter one, what is your situation? Spotter one, answer!"

There was a dull boom in the distance. Spotter one,
Hutchins thought. He estimated that it had crashed
three miles from this place.

"Get everyone saddled up," Hutchins ordered Farrier. He turned to Martinez, sitting in the helicopter
cabin. "The Iron Guard is coming," he said, "and they've
already killed some of my men. They're going to hunt
down your witches. The only thing that's going to save
them is if I put my men between them. You'd better
talk while there's still time."

If there's any left, he thought.

CHAPTER 26

Some problems have no answers. Others have nothing but bad solutions. The hard part is not choosing the least objectionable answer, or deciding which choice causes the least pain. The trouble comes when you try to live with the consequences."

—from Sense and Non-sense, *by Lyn Amanda Clancy*

The helicopters dropped into place quickly, surrounding the camp. The command helicopter landed last, amid a storm of dust, and by the time Hutchins hit the ground, most of the witches had been rounded up. The advantage of mobility, Hutchins thought. For all their powers, they couldn't outrun men in helicopters. With the limited range of telepathy, they couldn't have known what was happening until it was too late.

They were a motley, frightened assortment of people, mostly young adults, with a scattering of youngsters and teens among them. Their youth was inevitable, Hutchins decided. If the telepathic mutation had appeared in the late 1960s, as Grant had said, then no true witch could be much over thirty years old.

He watched two of his men bring one forward, a short, roly-poly woman with brown hair. Birche Holstein, of course, and they'd cuffed her hands behind her back. "Where's Forrest?" Hutchins asked her.

Birche shook her head. "Julian doesn't want to see you."

"He'd better change his mind," Hutchins said. "The Iron Guard is on its way. If he'll cooperate, we can put an end to them, here and now. Then we'll leave you alone, forget we found this place."

"You want to make a deal?" she asked.

"Yes."

"I suppose you'd like to shake hands?"

"Uncuff her," Hutchins said, turning away from the restrained scorn in her voice. He'd blundered; he should have instructed the troops on how to behave here. "We can still cooperate," he said.

"You mean, we do what you say, or else?" Her look unsettled him. It seemed to say that this telepath had measured his dimensions, and found him dangerous, yet unimpressive. It was not a look that gave any comfort. "All you'll do is get Julian killed."

"That isn't what I want." Now that he could observe her firsthand, he could see how little he had learned about this woman through reports and notes. She was muscular, not fat, although oddly feminine despite her shape. Beyond that, Birche Holstein had an imposing presence, and a strength that could not be ignored. The agent who uncuffed her had a daunted, almost spooked look on his face.

"You'd sacrifice Julian to get what you want." Rubbing her wrists, Birche looked around the valley. "Well, you've got it. The Iron Guard is on its way. They've split into three groups. One will come down the west slope and cross the stream. A second will come down the east slope. The third will march up the middle of the valley. They'll converge on the camp in an hour or so. You're outnumbered and outgunned; you'd better leave."

Farrier had joined them. "And you were just going to wait here?"

She looked vexed. "D'you think we're crazy? We were getting ready to clear out."

"What about Forrest?" Hutchins asked. "Is he trying something?"

Birche looked distracted—no, not that, Hutchins realized. She was talking with someone. A thea, perhaps, the thing Clancy had described in her book. "He's going to decoy them away from us." The round face looked bleak and stern. "If he can."

"Which way did he go?" Hutchins demanded. When she remained silent, Hutchins said, "His best chance of surviving is with us."

"No. You want to shoot it out with Savoy. Julian would never survive that."

Yes, that's right, he reminded himself. Clancy had mentioned something about witches dying from shock . . . and those witches in Los Angeles had died that way. He couldn't expect cooperation.

I still have my bargaining chip, Hutchins thought: the thing that's got Forrest weighed down. It was time to improve his position. He turned to Farrier. "Get them loaded into the helicopters and get them out of here. What's that air base near here?"

"Norton Air Force Base," Farrier said.

"Take them there—no, I need you here. Pulaski!" While the witches were herded into the helicopters, Hutchins gave orders to Pulaski. "They're our guests, not prisoners. Give 'em anything they need. Keep the MHB away from them, you got that?"

"Yes, sir."

"Get moving." He saw Birche climb into a helicopter, carrying a scrawny child in one arm.

He looked around while the helicopters lifted. They flew south, up the valley, away from the approaching IG force. Good, Hutchins thought. Savoy wouldn't know how many men might be here. That could be crucial.

Everything Birche said made sense. The IG forces would make a three-pronged attack on the camp, attempting to surround it before the witches could flee. If they knew something about the mechanics of ESP, they'd stay outside the thousand-foot range until they were ready to move in. Then, the men coming down the slopes would form a perimeter outside the camp to keep the witches from fleeing. The third unit would sweep through the camp, looking for Forrest. The tactics were elementary.

"A hammer and anvil maneuver," Farrier said, when Hutchins outlined his thoughts. "And you can bet Savoy will be in the third unit. It's safest there, with both flanks covered."

"Yes." Safe from an enemy who couldn't fight, he thought. Was that why Savoy picked witches as his enemy? Because they couldn't fight back? Somehow the idea that the man was merely paranoid seemed too glib, too pat.

Hutchins stepped on top of a stump. "Listen up," he said loudly, as the helicopters droned in the distance. "We've got a group of Iron Guard killers coming this way, and they've probably guessed we're here. They outnumber us and they're heavily armed. They've killed four of our men today—" he waited for the angry murmur to die down. "They won't surrender; they're in too deep for that. They think they're going to overthrow the government; that's the only way they can avoid a date with the executioner. So they have to fight."

Hutchins looked at the men. What he said sobered them. "But we're going to win. We have something to fight for—our country. They don't have that, and they never will." He hopped down from the stump. "Lou, deploy the men. Maybe we can catch Savoy off guard. Hartnell, Carruthers, Owens, I want you to come with me."

"You're going after Forrest?" Farrier said. "What for?"

"Find him, find Savoy. It's that simple. I want everyone to maintain radio silence until we get back; they may be monitoring our frequencies."

Moorpark appeared. "I'm coming with you," the reporter said.

"You're staying here; it's safer." His tone carried enough force to make the reporter turn away in disappointment. Hutchins looked back to Farrier. He recalled something then: the old Navy dictum for winning battles. "Lou, shoot first. Shoot enough. Hartnell, let's go."

They left the camp and fanned out, searching for tracks. A trail ran along the water, but that was too obvious. If Forrest is going to lure the IG away, Hutchins thought, then the witch will have to let Savoy see him, yet manage to stay away from him while eluding the flanking force. That narrowed the search area, and after a moment Hutchins found footprints. Nodding to himself, he motioned for the other three men to rejoin him.

It was slow going. The heavy bullet-proof overalls made their feet drag, and several times they had to stop and drink from their canteens. No wonder the Army rejected these things, Hutchins thought. They were fine for quick SWAT operations, but not for extended wear, especially not for a man his age.

Hutchins looked at Hartnell, who held his assault rifle at the ready, safety off and finger on the trigger. Hutchins himself was armed with a light recoilless pistol; his arm still hurt too much for him to use a heavier weapon. "Nervous?" Hutchins kept his voice low, afraid that an IG man might be in earshot.

"Hell, yes," Hartnell whispered. He looked at Hutchins. "Why *are* we after Forrest now?"

"If the IG gets him first, they may pull out without fighting us. I want to decide the issue here and now." Hutchins looked around warily. He found conversation difficult now; he was too edgy. "But if we run into the IG first, we're running back to the camp. The IG may think there're only the four of us out here. We could lead them into an ambush."

"Good enough." He shook his head. "That woman was damned cold, Chief."

"She doesn't have much reason to trust us."

"I don't mean that. She didn't act too upset about her man running off."

"No," he said shortly. He's mistaking control for something else, Hutchins thought. Letting Forrest do the necessary thing must have cost her more than he could imagine.

"Hey, over there." Carruthers gestured with the muzzle of his rifle. Someone was sitting under a tree—a man in faded denim pants and a war-surplus jacket.

Julian Forrest looked up as they approached him. "I wondered who would find me first," he said.

"You're lucky it was us," Hutchins said.

"Am I?" He looked up at Hutchins, pity on his face. " 'Weighed down.' You've got a strange way of looking at life."

"Someone else said that," Hutchins said. He looked around, convinced that he heard movement in the woods.

"They're all around us," Julian said. Then: "No, I can't walk. I turned my ankle Saturday. It gave out on me a few minutes ago. Anyway, I'm not going anywhere with you."

"You want to get your ass shot off?" Hartnell asked.

"I just don't like people who use Birche for bait," he said. "The IG did the same thing with her."

"We're different," Hutchins said. Using his good arm, he pulled Julian to his feet. He was surprised at how small he was; the witch was short, and so light he might have carried him with just the one arm. "We evacuated the camp. Holstein and that boy—Giles, isn't it?—are safe from that paranoid SOB."

"You mean Savoy?" Julian asked. He limped along, holding on to Hutchins for support. His tone was disturbingly casual. "He isn't paranoid."

"Then what is he?" Hartnell whispered.

"Evil. He wants power at any cost. He understands our weaknesses perfectly, and he has the skill to exploit them. He calculates equations of hate and fear. It's genius of a sort. You can't put him in a neat pigeonhole."

My God, Hutchins thought in alarm, Savoy's close enough for him to read his mind! "Where is he?"

"Behind us, fifty yards or so. I told you, they're all around—uh oh."

Two men appeared in front of them, and Hutchins heard the clacking of rifle bolts and shotgun slides all around him. The men were grinning with excitement. One of them raised a walkie-talkie. "We have them, Commander."

"Forrest," Hutchins whispered, "can you tell—"

"Some of them have those teflon-coated bullets," the witch said. "Your armor is no good."

There were heavy footsteps, and Hutchins turned to

see Savoy approaching, a rifle cradled in his arm. "Well, Director Hutchins. Fancy meeting you here, arm-in-arm with your favorite witch."

"You're under arrest," Hutchins said formally. "You and all your men. Give up now and most of you will beat the death penalty."

"Nice try." There was immense satisfaction in Savoy's voice. "But everything is out of your hands."

"You can't win," Hutchins said. "All you've done is to bring the entire government against you. Give up while you're still alive."

"The government is helpless," Savoy said, raising his voice. Speaking to the troops, Hutchins decided. Some of his men must have misgivings about open war against the government. "It's not even worth quarreling with."

"He's afraid to fight you." Julian spoke quietly, pitching his voice for Hutchins alone. "He knows what it means. Once he's got me, he'll leave. Then—"

All in an instant, one of the Guard killers raised his shotgun and fired. Hutchins saw the bright flash deep in the barrel, and felt rather than heard the explosion. The impact of the buckshot slammed Julian against Hutchins' chest and stomach, knocking him over. As he fell to the ground, Hutchins felt Julian's body slide away from him, saw the hole ripped in his body. The air was thick with the smell of his blood.

There was a rippling sound of gunfire, and he heard bullets hissing above him. "No, you idiots, you damned idiots!" Hutchins barely recognized the distorted, frustrated voice as Savoy's. He looked at the ugly hole gaping in Julian's chest, saw splintered ribs and shredded organ tissue. Dead beyond question. Hutchins drew his pistol, saw a target, and fired. There was recoil, he found, and the jolting pain in his arm made him grit his teeth.

"Chief! Pull back!" He heard Hartnell's voice in his earphone. "We're covering you."

Hutchins scrambled away. "Anyone hit?" he said.

"Carruthers is dead. I got two of the bastards. They dove for cover as soon as I opened up."

"Okay." Real gutsy fighters, Hutchins thought. This must have been the first time one of their targets had shot back. He looked around, spotted Hartnell and Owens. "Leapfrog back to camp."

The retreat to camp was a slow-motion nightmare. The CTO men fell back slowly, covering one another as they withdrew. Hutchins estimated that there were at least forty men with Savoy, although none of them seemed eager to close in on the government men. Hutchins would stand behind a tree, brace himself and aim when a target presented itself. Using both hands, he found his aim was fairly good, and he hit at least two of the rebels. Running was the hard part; his armor weighed him down, and with each step, he expected a bullet to slice through the armor and kill him.

The trees thinned out, and Hutchins jogged into the camp, sweating and out of breath. He dropped behind a heap of large rocks, then covered Hartnell and Owens as they joined him. He heard Savoy's hoarse shout: "Take them alive! We have to make it look like an *accident!*"

He knows he's lost control of things, Hutchins thought, hearing the despair in his voice. His men had dragged him into open warfare with the government, laying waste to his plans.

"Hold your fire," Hutchins said over the radio. Looking around, he realized how exposed he was here. He could see rebels coming down the east slope, and even more men—at least another forty—wading into the stream. Hutchins slipped a fresh clip into his pistol and made himself wait until the rebels were halfway across, in waist-deep water. "Open fire."

The camp stuttered with gunfire. He saw men dropping in the water, caught with no cover. Some of them pressed on, while the others broke and turned back. "Let them run," Farrier said over the radio. "Stay on the attackers."

Fire poured into the camp, churning the dirt. Hutchins heard screams from wounded men, his men, and saw a tent that seemed to flap in the wind as buckshot chopped through it. The CTO troops fired back methodically, picking their targets with businesslike precision. Farrier had dispersed the men behind such cover as he could find. They were taking casualties, but still holding on.

Hutchins spotted the radio operator, crouching behind a woodpile with his unit. He had erected the horn antenna, pointing it at an unseen satellite. The man was clearly in touch with someone before he jerked and collapsed over his unit. Moorpark crawled out of a hut then, took the man by the heels, and dragged him inside, leaving a bloody trail on the ground.

A bullet pinged off the rocks and Hutchins ducked. "They're in that clump of bushes," Owens said.

"Good," Hartnell said. "Chief, can you handle a rifle?"

"If I have to."

"Great." He gave Hutchins his rifle and reached into an overall pocket. He pulled out a pair of grenades and grinned. "Cover the bushes, Chief," Hartnell said. "Waste 'em when they jump." His arm swung once, twice.

Hutchins heard shrieks, and three men tumbled out of the bushes. He braced the rifle butt against his shoulder and fired, wincing at the pain in his arm. He saw the IG men die, hurled backward by the heavy rounds that hit them.

The grenades failed to explode. "Duds," Hutchins said.

"Practice grenades," Hartnell said with a grin. "Dummies. Only I didn't expect them to wait and see—"

"—or try something brave," Owens finished. He aimed his rifle and fired into a tree. A sniper dropped from the pine branches, falling next to his weapon.

Hutchins gave the rifle back to Hartnell, and keyed in his radio's command circuit. "Reno, this is Custer—" he hesitated; the fanciful Seventh Cavalry code names sounded obscene now.

"Wait one, Custer," Farrier said. "Group B-for-Bravo. Odd numbers, move to the east slope now. Even numbers stay in position. Reno to Custer, we held them at the river."

"Understood." Hutchins saw some movement on the east slope. Although the distance was extreme, he started to aim his pistol, then paused. Three of the rebels came into the open, their hands held high. They took a few steps forward, then fell as bullets stitched them from behind.

Hutchins peered over the boulders. The firing was dropping off a bit. He could hear shouted orders from the woods, terse and desperate. "Custer to all hands. Has anyone spotted Savoy?"

There was a chorus of negatives. "Maybe we got him," Owens suggested.

"I doubt it," Hutchins said. "Reno, Custer. Jesse James may be heading back to his ranch."

"Understood, Custer. Wait one."

Can't use gas here, Hutchins thought, not in these woods. There was little enough brush and grass—he suspected the witches had cleared it out, for safety—but even so, there was too much danger of fire.

Farrier sprinted across the campground with an agility that surprised Hutchins. He dropped behind the rocks with him and clicked off his radio. "Chief, don't worry about Savoy getting away. The posse has Jesse James cut off at the pass."

"What posse?"

"I had spotters two and three, and transport four, loop back to the mouth of the valley. That's six men in their crew—seven, if that half-assed deputy is worth anything. By now they've disabled all of the IG's cars and set up another ambush. Any stragglers can either surrender or get shot, depending on their mood."

"They may have more business than they can handle," Hutchins said.

"Maybe not." Farrier handed Hutchins his binoculars and pointed. "See?"

Ignoring the now-sporadic gunfire, Hutchins focused the glasses on the stream. The water had a red tinge now, and bodies floated half-submerged as the current drifted to the dam and its spillway. On the shore Hutchins saw a wounded man drag himself toward cover.

Abandoned rifles and ammunition boxes lay everywhere, glittering in the strong sunlight.

"It happens in every battle," the Bear said in satisfaction. "A man loses his nerve. He runs. Suddenly he realizes his gun and kit weigh a lot, so he tosses them away. He can run a lot faster. Of course, he can't do much when he stops running. Well, I'd say we have this wrapped up." He stood, activated his headset, and fingered the mike. "All units, all units, this is Reno. Even numbers advance and take prisoners. Odd numbers see to the wounded. Posse, report status."

"Getting a few rustlers, Reno," a man at the road answered, "and we're rounding them up."

"Posse, this is Custer," Hutchins called. "Have you got Savoy?"

"Negative, Custer."

"I want him alive. Out." Hutchins stood up, opened his armor, and shrugged it off. As he stepped out of it he saw the blood caking its front. "Forrest is dead," he said, to no one in particular.

"Those are the breaks," Farrier said, stripping off his own overalls. He picked up his weapons belt and clipped it around his ample waist. "Follow me," he called, and stepped forward with his rifle.

Hutchins forced himself to walk briskly. The shooting had stopped. He heard his men all around, shouting forceful obscenities and orders as they rounded up the Iron Guard fighters. Abandoned weapons and distorted footprints told of men who had run. The dead lay where they had fallen. Merchants and shopkeepers, Hutchins thought, seeing their clothes. None of the rebels wore uniforms. So strange, to think that they had all once been ordinary, law-abiding citizens.

"Up ahead," Farrier said, pointing to a tangle of fallen logs and branches. Several rebels crouched in there. At a gesture from Hutchins his own men dispersed and covered them. "Lou, what's your opinion?"

Farrier raised his voice, enough to reach the rebels. "I think they either come out of there now, or we blow their shit away."

"Don't shoot!" Hoarse as it was, Hutchins recognized Savoy's voice. "I'm coming out first! I want to make sure you don't shoot my men!"

"They're covering him," Farrier said in contempt, as Savoy climbed into the open, hands held high. "He just wants to make sure we don't shoot *him*."

Hutchins nodded agreement. It would be convenient for everyone if Savoy died suddenly. He might be shot while trying to escape, later, after his men gave up—

Hutchins walked forward, covering Savoy with his pistol. As they drew closer, Hutchins saw the smile of smug confidence on Savoy's face. "You're under arrest," Hutchins told him.

"For the moment," he said. "But nothing is forever in politics."

"You've gone beyond politics, Savoy. You can't trick your way out of murder, not this time."

"It's still politics," the man said easily, as if discussing a baseball game. "I won't go on trial until next year, after the elections—and you'll hear the winning candidates echoing me, Hutchins. No judge or jury will find me guilty then, not when they see how things stand. This will all blow over."

"You don't understand," Hutchins said. "Maybe you can convince a court that this battle was some political 'incident,' but that's not the only charge against you. You're going on trial for the murder of Julian Forrest."

He smiled in appreciation. "That will make things easier for me. Much easier!"

Forrest was right, Hutchins thought. He's not insane. Even in defeat, Savoy remained calculating, weighing every factor, sizing up his chances of converting defeat into victory. "You're not going to beat this, Savoy."

"No, I will," he said. "You see, Hutchins, you're the one who doesn't understand. This country's soul is hollow. Empty. Watch the TV and movies, listen to the music, read the books and papers. Look at politics; your Delanty is hunting witches because of me, not because he sees the danger in them. America is wandering around with its eyes closed. No, I'll come back."

Hutchins felt his hand tighten on his pistol. "You think so?"

"I know so. There are always things to scare people, Hutchins. Witches, apocalypses, depressions, blacks, Jews, foreigners—I know what to look for. I know where to find the tools, like Adler and Fountain—"

"Or your hired guns," Hutchins said. "You miscalculated there, Savoy. Killers can't keep from killing."

He acknowledged that with a cocky smile. "I know. I won't make that mistake next time. And there *will* be a next time; I'll come back better and stronger. Give up, Hutchins. The future is mine."

Hutchins glanced at the rebels behind Savoy, waiting to see what would happen. The Bear might be right, Hutchins thought. Killing Savoy might be the only rational thing to do—

"No," Hutchins said to himself. He holstered his pistol and got out his handcuffs. "You'll go on trial and have your say," he said, locking Savoy's hands behind his back. "And once people hear you out, they'll say, no, that's not what we want."

"We'll see."

Hutchins pushed him between the shoulder blades, forcing him to walk. Savoy stumbled forward, one more prisoner in the straggling parade toward the road. On an impulse, Hutchins guided Savoy through the spot where the battle had erupted. The sight of a dead rebel drew no reaction from Savoy, but Julian Forrest's twisted body plainly gratified him.

At the end of the valley Hutchins guided him up an embankment and onto the road. Hutchins looked around while Savoy was herded in with the other captives. Spotter one had crashed and burned in the middle of the road. Its rotors sagged over the hulk like the tendrils of a dead monster. Trucks and vans lined both sides of the road, resting on flat tires. "We slashed them right away," Agent O'Grady said. "There was no problem, but we would've been in trouble if they'd left even one or two guards. I can't imagine why they didn't do that."

"I can. None of them wanted to miss the fun." Which is one more reason behind our victory, he thought. Savoy had picked killers to do his fighting, mistaking their blood lust for courage, overlooking their lack of discipline. Another miscalculation, that.

Hutchins looked at the crowd of prisoners, their hands pinned behind them with shrink-plastic loops. Seeing them, it disturbed Hutchins to realize that they were ordinary men, that it had taken very little for Savoy to bring out the worst in them.

"It's still not too late to kill him," Farrier said quietly, coming up from behind Hutchins.

"No, Lou," Hutchins said. The idea no longer tempted him. "We can never get rid of his kind that way. The country itself has to reject him. A trial is an important part of that process."

"And what if it doesn't reject him?" Farrier demanded.

Hutchins shut his eyes for a moment. He might have spared the life of the next Hitler. That was the danger, and he realized it would gnaw on him for a long time.

He opened his eyes again. "We'll reject him," Hutchins said, looking at the man in the crowd of hostages. Surrounded by his supporters, Savoy looked arrogantly confident. Let him feel that way, Hutchins thought. Let him fight as hard as he could; it would add to the finality of his defeat. There would be plenty of time for Savoy to show remorse later, when he sat in Leavenworth and waited to hang.

"At any rate, Lou," Hutchins continued, looking at the Bear, "he's not your problem anymore. I'm retiring in a few days; I'm going to ask Delanty to appoint you as my successor."

"You are?" Farrier said.

Hutchins nodded. "I'm too old for this anymore . . . and let's face it, Savoy was ahead of me right up to the end. No, you can do a better job than I have."

The Bear looked pleased as he walked away. Good, Hutchins thought. He doesn't suspect I'm up to something. That was important. Hutchins had plans, and there was no room for interference.

He watched the CTO agents as they searched their prisoners for weapons and ID. *Our whole fight against terrorism has been a sideshow,* he thought, *a bloody circus. If we're going to stop the violence once and for all, we need something more than force or even an end to the Depression.* A different solution was called for, and Hutchins was certain that the witches held the answer.

CHAPTER 27

FRIDAY, 30 JUNE 2000

Whistler: In New York, the reconstituted National Committee of the Republican Party announced that the party's convention will be held on schedule in August, with the addition of a memorial service for victims of the Monday Night Massacre. In Washington, the CTO announced the arrests of more Iron Guard collaborators, including Chesney Dekalb. The special prosecutor has stated that he will request the death penalty for all defendants convicted in the case. Meanwhile, President Delanty announced the end of the so-called "June Days," and will receive a special briefing from Director Hutchins today. And in Omaha, the Association of American Brewers has announced plans to test-market beer in biodegradable squeeze-bulbs. Environmentalists hail this move as the greatest thing since canned beer. And those are the headlines this morning.

Robespierre: Thank you, Tim. Next up: Think it's easy being a child star? We visit Penny Katella on the set of 'The Beaver's Grandkids,' and discuss her plans

*for a bold new spin-off show. We'll be back after these
few words.*
        —transcript, America's Morning Show, 0715 EDT 30
                                            June 2000

That morning Hutchins found himself in a private
room in the White House, waiting for his chance to see
Delanty. The Secret Service agents had scanned him,
scoped him, and taken his gun, and then told him that
Delanty would be late. A photo opportunity had been
scheduled after the meeting, to allow Delanty to be
seen in the company of a certifiable hero, and it took
time to groom the President. His appearance had to be
perfect.

Hutchins had accepted that news calmly. It had helped
to cure his cold feet. He found himself thinking of
Thomas Jefferson, the third President, who had sometimes greeted important visitors in his bathrobe. No,
Delanty was not in his league.

At a gesture from one of the agents Hutchins got up
and followed him into the Oval Office. He shook hands
with Delanty over the desk, then seated himself at a
gesture. He wondered if there were any recorders running here. Perhaps, but his pocket scrambler would
take care of that. This was not the sort of meeting to be
recorded for posterity, or for investigating committees.
He would have to count on the two Secret Service
guards to remain silent. They had faded into the background, leaving Hutchins to confront Delanty on his own.

"You've done a fine job with the Iron Guard," Delanty
said. "A fine job. I take it we'll have an airtight case
against them?"

"Yes, sir. We've collected quite a few documents
from their headquarters, along with a number of confessions. Assuming a fair trial, Savoy and some others will
hang."

"That won't hurt a bit in November," the President
said happily. "Well, I've been over your report, Monty,
and I like what you say. You're certain that terrorism is
on the decrease?"

"Definitely, sir. I attribute it to the destruction of Sere and the Iron Guard. Two decisive victories, coming so rapidly, and with such intense media coverage—I'm convinced that other terrorists see that political violence is no longer effective. Sir, did you read the recommendations in my report?"

"I've reviewed them, Monty." The President extracted a cigar from his desk humidor and lit up. "Interesting, interesting. You really want to restrict the CTO's authority?"

"Yes, sir." Hutchins nodded, and turned down a proffered cigar. "Some of the things we do violate the spirit of the Constitution, if not the letter. The country could tolerate them, barely, as emergency measures, but it's time to rein in our horses."

"I've already given that some consideration, Monty," Delanty said, so sincerely that Hutchins almost believed him. Facing him now, Hutchins sensed an odd hollowness to the man. He wasn't like Forrest or Holstein, who gave the impression of an enormous strength behind them. The President continued: "I've always been reluctant to give any government body too much power. You know what they say about absolute power corrupting absolutely. Now that terrorism is on the wane, I think it's a wise move to cut back here and there."

"My report outlines the things that can go, sir, such as the medically augmented interrogations. The CTO can still do an effective job with limited powers." Poor Lou, Hutchins thought. Farrier was about to lead a weakened army in a war that was sputtering out. With reduced powers and prestige, the Bear would have to learn diplomacy—and Delanty would be forced to keep a tight grip on the dangerously ambitious Farrier.

Delanty puffed happily on his cigar. "You, know, Monty, it isn't every day that one of my department heads comes in here and tells me he wants a smaller staff and less power. I think this will go over big with the voters."

"Yes, sir." Hutchins waited to see if Delanty would

add anything. After a moment of silence he continued. "Sir, I made other suggestions in my report."

"I'm aware of that. I've taken them under consideration." Delanty started to rise from his seat. "Well, the photographers are waiting to admire you, Monty."

Hutchins remained seated. "Sir, I'm afraid my suggestions require immediate action. We need a positive answer before noon tomorrow."

Delanty looked mildly impatient. "Monty, I realize you've been under a strain, but you have to understand that your President can't—"

"I've checked the legal aspects, sir." Hutchins held on to the arms of his chair as if bracing himself. No, this wasn't easy. Whatever else he was, Delanty remained the President. "You can begin by giving the Medal of Freedom to the telepathics named in my report; they've earned it. But getting the Mental Health Bureau off their backs is more urgent. You can order a change in MHB policy this moment."

"Impossible. The public won't take that." The President stubbed out his cigar. "We'd better clear the air before we go outside, Monty. I'm sure you're motivated by a generous impulse, and I'll admit we may owe a few witches a favor, but what you want is impossible."

It's time to play my trump card, Hutchins decided. "I'm sorry to hear that, sir," he said, taking an envelope from his coat pocket. He pushed it across the polished desk to Delanty. "It means we're going to jail."

Delanty unsealed the envelope and glanced through the papers. He looked confused. "What—this—"

"Transcripts, Mr. President, and copies of memos, detailing the way you've used the CTO for political ends. The original tapes and papers, plus copies, are in other hands. If you don't carry out all of the suggestions in my report before noon tomorrow, those copies will go to the media."

"Blackmail," Delanty croaked. His lips trembled as he dropped the papers on the desk. "Hutchins, where's your loyalty?"

"With the Constitution, where it should have been

all along." He nodded toward the Secret Service agents, standing unobtrusively by the door and window. "You lost my loyalty when I came in. I don't appreciate being searched."

"Security—"

"I've been with the government since 1967, and if you think *I'm* a potential assassin . . ." He shrugged eloquently, dismissing the point. "Well, sir, I'd suggest you put the best possible face on all this. Properly handled, I think you can turn this to your advantage."

"As if I had a choice!" The President let a measured amount of anger slip into his voice and face. "Damn it, Hutchins—*why?*"

"Guilt," he said. "People have died—my agents, telepathics, ordinary citizens—because I played politics with you when I should have stuck to my job. I took a woman hostage. I tried to intimidate people. I saw a townful of normal people refuse to help me, because *they* could see that the CTO had turned into something evil." Hutchins hesitated, then made himself continue. "And a man got killed because I used him as a tool. I want to make amends."

"I don't understand."

"I didn't think you would," Hutchins said. "That's why I stooped to blackmail. But guilt aside, I have the good of the country in mind."

"Because you, all by yourself, decided that the MHB and CTO are dangerous?" The wrinkles in Delanty's forehead emphasized his scorn.

"We both know that's true—and so did Savoy. The Iron Guard had plans to use both agencies to control the country—but they're only symptomatic of what's wrong with America."

Delanty bristled with political indignation. "There is no problem that this Administration can't correct, given another four years."

There's part of the problem right there, Hutchins thought, hearing the President answer with a campaign slogan. "I'm not sure you see the problem, sir. I've been up against its most extreme form, and I just barely recognize it myself."

Delanty stroked his chin as he looked at Hutchins. "I thought you said terrorism is on the decline?"

"It is, but I'm not talking about that now." He leaned forward in his seat, over the edge of the desk. "Sir, there's the MHB, a product of liberal policies, but it can deprive any citizen of his civil rights. And the CTO supplies all the law and order any conservative could ask for, but it can destroy the freedom we want. No one thought about the consequences. And look at me, taking orders and carrying them out, letting the ends justify everything, just like one of Savoy's henchmen."

Delanty's eyes narrowed to hostile slits. "If you're comparing my orders to Savoy's—"

"No, sir, I'm not. I'm trying to point out how easy it is to avoid thinking—and how dangerous it is. Adler never thought about the dangers of using Savoy. Neither did Fountain, or Magyar. On another level, the people who joined the Iron Guard, or Sere, or the Redeemers, or any group like them—"

"They're all different," the President said queruously.

"Only on the surface. But inside—one of the things they all offered was *certainty*. Fountain could give you the word of God, on prime-time television. Sere had Marxist theories and environmental romanticism. The Iron Guard had its all-knowing leader and his doctrines. They were able to supply the answer to every conceivable question, and that attracted people."

"Mister, everyone offers solutions," Delanty said.

"No, sir, they offer pat answers, and we've got a society of people who look for them. It's no wonder Savoy felt such incredible contempt for everyone; no con artist respects his victims." Hutchins shook his head. "We almost dismissed the man as a paranoid, but he was the one who understood our minds. He was like the witches—saner than we'd admit."

Delanty's head cocked to the side. Anger aside, he was interested now. "Is that why he hated the witches? Because they could see through him?"

"Partly, Mr. President, but he feared something else. They're rationalists, and they incite other people to rationalism. Savoy may be a master manipulator, but he can't stand against that. If he can't work on the emotional level, he's sunk."

"So that's why you're so intent on giving these witches recognition," Delanty mused. "If enough people adopted this rationalism, you think the country would be secure from takeover by the likes of Savoy."

"I do," Hutchins said, "and we'd both better get used to calling them 'telepathics.'"

Delanty smiled like a good loser as they rose from their seats. It was a false smile, Hutchins realized, the same smile he showed to the press whenever Congress overrode his veto.

The falseness didn't matter, Hutchins thought, as he stood in the Rose Garden and half-listened to Delanty string together the proper clichés. Patriotic efforts of special citizens . . . the repugnant, quasi-racist dogmas of men like Savoy and Fountain . . . against fearful odds . . . great debt owed them, time to reveal the full story, make amends . . .

It's more than just rationalism, Hutchins thought. Savoy had been as intelligent as any witch, yet he had lacked the morality Hutchins had found in Clancy's book. Without that sense of right and wrong, there was nothing to prevent anyone from making the cold, logical decision that a man like Savoy— who did, after all, have talent and genius—was a fit leader.

I ought to do something about getting Clancy's book back in circulation, Hutchins decided as he left the Rose Garden. It would help to counteract the empty cynicism that filled everything from songs to politics as it tore society apart. People might read it out of morbid curiosity, or because witches were a topical subject, but the book would transform some of them.

He wondered how long it would take for society to change. Years or decades, no doubt. Visions of swift, apocalyptic overturns were best left to men like Savoy and Fountain. A lot could go wrong in that time . . .

but if given half a chance, the change *would* come. Savoy had recognized that, and it had led him to fight the witches with all his strength, even to see Julian Forrest's murder as a triumph amid his defeat.

Funny thing, Hutchins thought, how one man's fear can become another's hope.

CHAPTER 28

There are never enough Lyn Clancys and Julian For-rests in this world. It's up to us to make the most of the few we have.
—from Sense and Non-sense, *by Lyn Amanda Clancy. Second edition, Universal Press, 2001; foreword by Montague Hutchins*

The Air Force base fascinated Giles. The fighter-trainers were sleek shapes that made elegant dances in the sky, and the crews were always happy to introduce a curious child to the mysteries of avionics, mechanics, and aerodynamics. Lots of complicated things happened here, and the people in the uniforms did everything without a thea to coordinate them. When they said "people," they meant witches as well as their own kind, and they included Giles. He could scrounge food in the cafeteria whenever he liked.

He should have been happy.

Birche spent most of her time in the room they'd been given, mourning for Julian. She'd discovered a new drawback to telepathy, a new pain. In the short time she'd had with Julian, she'd come to feel that she had spent a lifetime with him. Now he was gone.

Nothing helped her. Depressed as they were, the other witches (no, "people," he reminded himself; got to get used to that now) had tried to help her. Birche had accepted their help without fear, but it did her little good. The thea had told Giles that it took time to get over such a loss, but she would be all right eventually.

"Eventually" wasn't good enough for Giles. He couldn't understand what Birche was going through, but he wanted to see it end. Julian wouldn't have liked it.

He wandered through the housing area, avoiding a group of kids who would have asked him to play. They weren't scared of telepathy, and they'd thought up some games that used it, but right now Giles wasn't in the mood. He noticed that a lot of the adults were in front of their TVs, watching a special news bulletin. Delanty was making a speech, and he had Hutchins with him.

Giles had avoided Hutchins when the man showed up the day before. He had asked to see Birche, and she had listened silently while he gave her a sealed strongbox and outlined his plans. Giles had tapped Hutchins; the man's need for forgiveness hadn't surprised him— he'd seen plenty of guilt-ridden people at seances—but his desire to earn it was something new. Somehow that made it impossible to hate him as much as he deserved.

For her part, Birche had only had one question: "Did Julian say anything for me or Giles?" He'd shook his head, wishing he could say something to give meaning to a meaningless death, and left. Birche had felt embarrassed for turning to Hutchins for comfort.

Giles entered their room, and found Birche sitting on the sofa, staring blankly at the TV screen. A commentator was delivering an instant analysis of Delanty's speech, letting everyone know what they had just heard. *"What's it all mean?"* Giles asked.

"The Compton Act doesn't apply to us anymore. We can get our property back, vote, drive cars, work—" She shook her head at the sudden unreality. *"It means people can't shoot at us anymore."*

"Oh. Good." That was something he could grasp. *"So what do we do now?"*

"*I'm not sure. This is just a change in one law, not in the way people feel about telepathics*—" Birche stopped, overcome by a sense of futility. "*I don't know. Julian and I talked about adopting you, so we wouldn't ever lose you. I could still do that, even though I'm single.*"

"*I'd like that,*" Giles told her.

"*So would I. I'll have to call my lawyer. Then go back to Los Angeles, get my bookstore back, find an apartment . . .*" She stopped and looked at the TV. We now resume our regularly scheduled programming, the announcer said, and instantly two soap-opera mavens filled the screen. An addlepated witch had conveniently revealed the secrets of a neighbor's sex life to them, giving them something to discuss over their wine coolers.

"*Everything is going back to normal,*" Birche thought in growing anger. "*As if none of this ever happened. Julian is dead, and they're trying to pretend that nothing has changed. Well, I won't let them!*"

"*I know you won't.*" There was a growing determination in her— but the anger was growing even faster. Julian wouldn't like her this way, Giles thought, turning off the TV. Maybe now he could do the thing for her that he hadn't been able to do for Julian. "*I didn't get to know him,*" he said, sitting down next to Birche. "*Not really.*"

"*You knew him.*"

"*Not the way you did. I didn't know all those things you know, the . . .*" He fumbled for words. "*The ways to get close. Tell me what he was like.*"

After a while she told him, taking the rest of the day and the following night. She was still teaching him when the sun came up.